Also by Ana Huang

KINGS OF SIN SERIES
A SERIES OF INTERCONNECTED STANDALONES
King of Wrath

King of Pride

King of Greed

King of Sloth

TWISTED SERIES
A SERIES OF INTERCONNECTED STANDALONES
Twisted Love

Twisted Games

Twisted Hate

Twisted Lies

IF LOVE SERIES
If We Ever Meet Again (DUET BOOK 1)

If the Sun Never Sets (DUET BOOK 2)

If We Were Perfect (STANDALONE)

if love had a price

ANA HUANG

Bloom books

Copyright © 2020, 2024 by Ana Huang
Cover and internal design © 2024 by Sourcebooks
Cover design by Emily Wittig
Cover images © mirabellart/Depositphotos, Eclectic Anthology/
Creative Market, photoquest7/Depositphotos

Sourcebooks, Bloom Books, and the colophon are registered trademarks of Sourcebooks.

All rights reserved. No part of this book may be reproduced in any form or by
any electronic or mechanical means including information storage and retrieval
systems—except in the case of brief quotations embodied in critical articles or
reviews—without permission in writing from its publisher, Sourcebooks.

The characters and events portrayed in this book are fictitious or
are used fictitiously. Any similarity to real persons, living or dead,
is purely coincidental and not intended by the author.

All brand names and product names used in this book are trademarks,
registered trademarks, or trade names of their respective holders. Sourcebooks
is not associated with any product or vendor in this book.

Published by Bloom Books, an imprint of Sourcebooks
P.O. Box 4410, Naperville, Illinois 60567-4410
(630) 961-3900
sourcebooks.com

Originally self-published in 2020 by Ana Huang.

Cataloging-in-Publication Data is on file with the Library of Congress.

Printed and bound in the United States of America.
WOZ 10 9 8 7 6 5 4 3 2 1

Playlist

"Price Tag"—Jessie J featuring B.o.B.
"California Gurls"—Katy Perry
"Billionaire"—Travie McCoy featuring Bruno Mars
"Heart Attack"—Demi Lovato
"California Love"—2Pac featuring Dr. Dre
"All I Know"—DaniLeigh featuring Kes
"West Coast"—Lana Del Rey
"Beautiful, Dirty, Rich"—Lady Gaga
"Summer Love"—Justin Timberlake
"Money Honey"—Lady Gaga
"Love Don't Cost a Thing"—Jennifer Lopez
"Bleeding Love"—Leona Lewis

CHAPTER 1

"I'LL PAY YOU TEN THOUSAND DOLLARS TO FUCK MY stepmother."

Kris's mouth curled into a smirk when the green-eyed Adonis stopped walking and turned, his handsome face a curious mask of boredom and disbelief.

He'd ignored her for the better part of the summer, which she didn't appreciate.

No one ignored Kris Carrera.

But he was perfect for her plan, so she was willing to play nice. And by nice, she meant not ripping his balls off and tossing them to the cougars that stalked Rodeo Drive in a pack of bad Botox and tacky Versace.

Oh, and her $10,000 offer was pretty sweet too. But for the daughter of one of the richest men in America, ten grand was a drop in the bucket.

"You're mistaking me for someone else." Adonis's whiskey drawl slipped over her skin, as smooth and dark as onyx. Polished at first glance but rough beneath the surface. "I'm not a prostitute."

Kris's smirk sharpened. She closed the distance between them until she could count every sun-kissed strand of his wavy brown hair and see the veiled fury glittering in his green eyes.

The fury was interesting. She supposed most people wouldn't enjoy being pegged as a prostitute, but the tense set of his jaw told her there was a deeper reason behind his anger.

If Kris cared, she'd have ruminated on the reason.

She didn't.

All Kris cared about was throwing her gold-digging, fake-titted stepmother-to-be onto the streets, and Adonis here was going to help make that happen.

He was exactly Gloria's—aka the Stepmonster's—type: tan, ripped, and so gorgeous he looked Photoshopped. Bonus points for the ability to string two words together in a coherent sentence without using the term *dude*.

He was every straight female's type, really, and he was the perfect candidate for the job. All she had to do was convince him.

"I should've been more clear," Kris purred. "I'll pay you $10,000 to *pretend* to fuck my stepmother. Whether you actually stick your dick inside her is none of my concern."

Adonis barked out a laugh—a low, husky sound that caused her stomach to flip in the strangest way.

It better not be that sandwich I ate earlier, she thought.

If Kris got food poisoning, she'd sue the café they'd just left to kingdom come, which would be a damn shame because she liked the place. Located between her family's Beverly Hills mansion and her summer job as an assistant to top Hollywood publicist Bobbi Rayden, Alchemy Café was an airy haven of perfectly crafted lattes and eye candy—including the chiseled hunk standing before her.

She didn't know his actual name, so she'd secretly dubbed him "Adonis" after the beautiful Greek god. He was a waiter at

Alchemy, though she'd bet her last dollar he was also an aspiring actor or rock star.

This was LA, after all.

"Lady, you must be on drugs. I'm not going near your step-mother, if you even have one." Adonis narrowed his eyes. "If this is for a prank show, you're wasting my time. I don't do reality TV—especially shows I didn't consent to."

Kris bristled, both at his mocking use of the word *lady* and the fact that he was wasting *her* time by being so stubborn.

His immunity to her charms also irritated her. Kris rarely engaged in flirting or romantic affairs, but she expected a certain level of drool when she turned on the heat. Big brown eyes, full lips, and a petite, curvy figure—including a natural set of 36Cs—usually caught a guy's attention.

But no, Adonis here looked about as interested as a card-board eunuch.

Wisps of irritation curled through her.

"This is not for a prank show." As if Kris would touch something as tacky as reality TV. "My time is precious, and I won't spend it arguing with you, so here's the deal in a nut-shell: my father is getting married to his gold-digging fiancée this fall and refuses to listen to reason, so I'm going to *force* him to see reason, a.k.a., toss her out with nothing but the cheap clothes she wore when she seduced him at that bar she was working at."

"And you're going to do that by hiring someone to fuck—sorry, *pretend* to fuck"—the sarcasm was evident—"your future stepmother."

"And take photos of her doing it." Kris shrugged. "She'd cheat on my dad in a heartbeat after she becomes Mrs. Carrera. I'm saving him from future heartbreak."

Kris cared about her dad, even if he was so busy she only saw him a few weeks a year. She *knew* he could do better than that redheaded pile of trash, Gloria.

Not to mention, Kris still hadn't forgiven the Stepmonster for convincing her father to cut her off *over Christmas break*.

Luckily, Roger Carrera soon caved to his only daughter's silent treatment and reinstated Kris's credit card privileges—albeit with a monthly limit—but Kris never forgot a slight.

She would make Gloria pay.

"How are you so sure she'll cheat?" The fury had bled out of Adonis's eyes, replaced by derisive amusement.

Kris ticked the reasons off on her fingers. "One, she's half his age and looks like Jessica Rabbit, while my dad, bless his heart, is no George Clooney. Two, she has zero morals. Three, judging by the way she eye-fucks other guys when she thinks no one is looking, she has a thing for young, muscly, pretty-boy types." She ran her eyes over Adonis's sculpted lips, sharp jawline, and broad shoulders. "Someone like you."

Although she wasn't sure Adonis qualified as a pretty boy. He was beautiful, but he exuded a raw, intense masculinity that eluded most of the plastic-perfect Ken dolls living in LA.

Kris grimaced the second the thought crossed her mind.

She'd clearly been in the so-called City of Angels for too long because her inner dialogue was starting to resemble that of a bad rom-com character.

"I'm flattered." The sarcasm returned. A breeze swept by, ruffling Adonis's floppy hair. "But it's still a no."

Kris sputtered in disbelief. "Are you kidding? It's ten thousand dollars. You don't even have to kiss her. Just make it look like you're fucking her. You're an actor, aren't you?"

Adonis's brows snapped together. "How did you know that?"

"Please. This is LA. If you're a good-looking waiter, there's an eighty-five percent chance you're an aspiring actor."

"Fair enough." He rubbed his jaw. "Why me? There are plenty of actors in LA who'd jump at the opportunity."

"I told you, you're the Stepmonster's type." Although Kris would never admit it, Adonis also intrigued her. She'd been a regular customer at Alchemy since she landed in LA three weeks ago, and he was the only male staff member who'd never spared her a glance except to ask if she'd like a refill. That, plus the fact he just turned down $10,000—money he needed if the beat-up, old car he'd been about to get into before she stopped him was anything to go by—made him a smidge more interesting than his Y-chromosome compatriots.

Kris averted her eyes from the beat-up car in question. Just looking at its scratched paint and dented driver's door made her skin itch with discomfort; the sad, old thing was like the visual equivalent of polyester.

"And I told you, I'm no whore," Adonis said softly.

The air between them crackled with tension, and the hairs on the back of Kris's neck prickled with unease. Her senses had never been more alert, picking up everything from the way Adonis's muscled chest rose and fell to the faint, not-at-all-unpleasant scent of coffee and leather that wafted from his clothing.

"We're going around in circles." Kris struggled to maintain her cool demeanor. "Like I said, you don't actually have to sleep with her. This is an acting job. You'll be *acting* as her lover. Seduce her, get her into a compromising position where my PI can snap a few quick pics, and you'll be ten grand richer. It's the easiest job you could ask for."

Adonis leaned against his car and crossed his arms over his chest. With his hard glare and insouciant slouch, he resembled a modern-day James Dean with a dash of Liam Hemsworth thrown in.

"Make it fifteen thousand dollars, and I'll think about it."

Disbelief swirled in Kris's veins. "You're fucking kidding. You're *negotiating* with me?" Who the hell did he think he was?

"Ten grand was already a lot for a minimum amount of work. I could hire any wannabe actor in this town for that price."

"Then hire them." A mocking smile flirted at the edges of Adonis's mouth at her subsequent silence. "If it was that easy, you wouldn't be arguing with a waiter in a parking lot." Somehow, he made the word *waiter* sound like an insult toward Kris, even though he was the server. "What'll it be, princess?"

She ground her teeth. "Fifteen K and you'll do it?"

"I'll think about doing it."

Kris was this close to punching him in his perfect face. She should've worn her Dior cocktail ring today—then her punch would've *really* hurt.

"Fine." Her agreement surprised herself. "Give me your phone."

Adonis did so without a word—another surprise. Kris had expected him to deny her request, given how hell-bent he seemed on making things difficult for her.

She added her number to his contacts and texted herself from his phone. "What's your name?"

"Nate."

Nate. It suited him somehow.

"I'm Kris, with a *K*." She returned his phone, her tone crisp and efficient. "You have forty-eight hours to decide. If I don't hear from you by Monday at five p.m., the offer goes to someone else—someone who wouldn't be foolish enough to let the deal of a lifetime slip through their fingers."

"Princess, you'd have to offer me a lot more than Fifteen K for this to be the best deal of my life." Nate's gaze dipped to her lips, the tiny movement charging his words with a sexual innuendo that sent an unexpected blast of heat through Kris's body. His mocking smile reappeared. "Talk to you in forty-eight hours. Or not."

He climbed into his car and drove away, leaving a fuming, strangely turned-on Kris in the parking lot.

CHAPTER 2

NATE REYNOLDS'S GOOD MOOD EVAPORATED THE second he stepped inside his house. The booze-drenched air clogged his nostrils, and the familiar sight of his father passed out on the living room couch with a half-empty bottle of Jack Daniel's clutched in his hand chased away any lingering amusement Nate had felt after his conversation with the beautiful brunette from the parking lot earlier.

Kris.

She'd been a favorite of Alchemy's male staff since she'd first shown up at the café a few weeks ago. She was a regular now, but her perfect hair and designer clothes screamed "spoiled princess," which was why Nate had steered clear of anything resembling flirting. His coworkers could drool over her sultry looks and aloof haughtiness all they wanted, but uppity rich girls weren't his type.

However, she'd turned out to be more intriguing than he'd expected—fiery and sharp-tongued, instead of dull and vapid like the few heiresses he'd hooked up with in the past. Kris's extravagant five-figure offer didn't hurt either. Nate may not like spoiled rich girls, but he had no problem taking their money, and God knew his family needed the green. However, the idea of selling his body for cash—even if he was only pretending to do so—caused his stomach to churn with nausea.

Nate had forty-eight hours to decide whether his values were worth the roof over his head.

I'll deal with it later.

He had more pressing issues at hand—namely, getting his father up to his room and airing out the sickly smell of whiskey before Skylar returned home.

Michael Reynolds grunted and shifted in his sleep. He'd been a handsome man once, with the same sharp bone structure and olive complexion as his son, but age, grief, and alcohol had transformed him into a shell of the person he used to be.

A familiar cocktail of resentment, resignation, and weariness bubbled in Nate's veins as he opened all the windows and spritzed the air with a lemony-smelling spray Skylar had bought on their last Walmart run. He tidied up the things Michael had knocked over—the umbrella stand in the tiny entry hall, the framed picture of a ten-year-old Nate and four-year-old Skylar on the side table—before attempting to pry good ol' Jack from his father's hands.

Michael stirred. Nothing kicked his ass into gear like the threat of being separated from his precious alcohol.

"Nate?" His bleary, bloodshot eyes blinked up at his son. "Whaddaya doing here?"

"I live here," Nate said, voice clipped. "Is this what you've been doing all day?"

Michael was supposed to be job hunting. He'd gotten laid off from his construction gig for showing up to work late and drunk, and he'd said he would find another job soon.

That had been two months ago.

"I sent out a few résumés," Michael mumbled. "Don't know what happened after that. Must've fallen asleep."

Nate exhaled a controlled breath. His patience with his father had run out a long time ago. He understood Michael's heartbreak—he and Skylar battled the same grief. No matter how many years passed, the sadness lingered in their household like a dark fog that wouldn't go away.

But life didn't stop moving because you were sad, and Michael had two children to take care of. Since he'd traded in his responsibilities for the oblivion only found in a bottle, Nate had taken over as de facto head of the household.

He was twenty-three, but he acted more like a father to Michael than Michael did to him.

"Shower and get dressed. Skylar will be home soon," Nate ordered.

He knew when to pick his battles. There was no use pushing Michael on the job hunt when he was like this—he'd just stare at Nate with that empty look in his eyes, like he'd lost the will to live.

He basically had five years ago, when Joanna Reynolds got on a plane home from visiting her best friend in Chicago. She'd never arrived. Her plane had suffered a mechanical failure and crashed in the Rockies, leaving behind no survivors and dozens of devastated families, including Nate's own.

Michael struggled to sit up. "Didya get any new roles this week?" he asked.

It was both his and Nate's dream for Nate to become a successful actor, only they had wildly different motivations. Nate had dreamed of taking over the big screen since he was a child; Michael just wanted Nate to earn enough money to keep him flush with alcohol.

Yeah, no.

Once Nate had the cash, he would ship his father off to the best rehab he could find. Maybe then, he could glue the pieces of his family back together.

"I had a modeling gig," Nate said, sidestepping the question as he looped an arm under Michael's and pulled the older man to his feet.

Nate took the occasional odd job to supplement his salary from the café—modeling, catering, bartending. It didn't matter as long as they paid him. Every dollar counted.

The Reynoldses weren't destitute. There were families in far worse straits than theirs, but between Michael's unemployment and alcohol addiction, Skylar's expenses as an incoming high school senior, and Nate's acting aspirations, they were stretched paper-thin. Thin enough that rent day sent spirals of anxiety tunneling through Nate's body every month.

If Nate were selfless, he'd cut back ruthlessly on their spending and give up his dreams of Hollywood stardom. The pursuit of an on-screen career wasn't cheap—headshots, acting classes, an inordinate amount of gas spent driving all over LA for auditions and networking events. It added up. He'd dropped the acting classes when Michael lost his job, but it wasn't enough.

However, Nate wasn't a financial genius or a saint. He was a twenty-three-year-old with a dream. Call him selfish, but he'd be damned if he was going to let his hopes slip through his fingers as easily as his youth.

He'd shouldered the responsibilities of an adult twice his age since he was eighteen. Now all he needed was a big break in his career.

Just one. That's all I need.

A car door slammed outside.

Nate stiffened and quickened his pace until he reached his father's room and laid Michael awkwardly on the bed. By the time he yanked the elder Reynolds's shoes off, tucked him beneath the comforter, and drew the curtains closed, Michael had passed out again.

"Dad? You home?" Skylar's voice floated up the stairs.

Nate shut the door to his father's room behind him and met his sister in the living room. She wore a blue and white jersey and matching shorts with a soccer ball tucked beneath her arm. Her grinning face was flushed, and her hair was slicked back into a ponytail. She'd inherited their mom's hazel eyes and golden locks, and sometimes, Nate's heart splintered at the resemblance.

Skylar's face lit up when she saw him.

"Nate! You're home early." She tackled him with a sweaty hug and laughed when he faux grimaced.

She was a big hugger, no matter the time or situation.

"Get away from me. You stink." His teasing lilt tempered his words.

"Duh. I just came from soccer." Skylar rolled her eyes, then wrinkled her nose. "Actually, this entire room stinks. Ew."

"Blame your BO."

"Shut up. I do *not* have BO." She gnawed on her lip. "Dad's been drinking again, hasn't he?"

"No, he hasn't," he lied.

"Bullshit. It reeks of whiskey." Skylar's eyes landed on something behind Nate. He followed her gaze and cursed silently when he saw the bottle of Jack Daniel's on the coffee table. He'd forgotten to stash it before dragging their father upstairs.

Skylar knew about their father's drinking, but Nate tried to shield her from the worst of it as much as he could. She still held on to the romantic notion that Michael would snap out of his stupor and transform into a doting father again, even though it'd been five years, and Nate didn't have the heart to shatter her fantasy.

"Language," he warned, zeroing in on her use of *bullshit* instead of the half-empty whiskey five feet away.

Skylar rolled her eyes again. "Whatever. I've heard you say worse things."

"How was camp?" Nate switched topics. He and Skylar could bicker for hours, but he was exhausted after a busy day at the café. He also needed time to mull over Kris's offer.

"It was great!" Skylar's ponytail swished with excitement. Nothing animated her more than soccer, except maybe a new issue of *Scientific American*. Nate didn't know where she got her love of science from—their mother had been an English teacher, and their father wasn't exactly Bill Nye either. "I scored two goals, and Coach said if I keep up my performance, she'll write me a recommendation for Stanford at the end of the summer."

"That's awesome." A genuine grin stretched across Nate's face. He'd dropped out of college to work after their mom died and their dad spiraled; while his school grades had been average at best, he missed the college experiences of crazy roommates and new friendships, of parties and girls and all-night adventures, of being young and wild and free.

He hadn't had the pleasure of living life the way an eighteen-year-old should've lived it, but he'd do everything in his power to ensure the same opportunity didn't slip by Skylar. She was smart and spirited, a straight-A student with dreams of studying biology at Stanford. It was an expensive dream—even more so than Nate's—and getting a full-ride scholarship was their only hope of affording it if she got in.

To get a scholarship, Skylar needed an edge over the other applicants. Luckily, she was as talented at soccer as she was at academics, which was why Nate hadn't given a second thought to forking over an ungodly sum of money for a prestigious summer soccer camp that boasted Olympians and World Cup athletes as alumni.

He'd worked his ass off for weeks to make up for the drain in their bank account, but it was worth it. *Hopefully.*

"By the way." Skylar tugged on her ponytail, her tone so

casual it immediately raised Nate's suspicions. "Can you drive me to the movies tomorrow night? I'm going with a new friend from camp."

His shoulders relaxed at the mundane request. Thank God she wasn't going on a date or anything like that. Nate had enough to worry about without having to beat hormone-driven teenage boys away from his sister. "Sure."

"Thanks!" Skylar gave him another hug before bounding up the stairs. "I'm going to take a shower while you order pizza."

"Who says I'm ordering pizza?" Nate yelled after her.

She answered with a knowing laugh.

Takeout was a luxury these days, but Saturday night pizza had been a family tradition since they were children. Sometimes they missed it if there was an event or something else going on, but they stuck to it as much as possible. It was the one nonessential item Nate made sure he budgeted for every month.

Silence descended in Skylar's wake.

Nate placed the pizza order and leaned against the wall, scrolling aimlessly through his phone until he stopped on Kris's name.

Memories of her huge dark eyes and lush curves sent twin thrills of arousal and challenge through his veins. She was bad news. The princess types always were.

But $15,000...that was enough money to pay several months' rent. Nate would have peace of mind and time to focus on auditions. Who knows? Maybe one of the auditions would lead to his big break.

Plus, he wouldn't mind seeing Kris again.

For payment purposes, of course.

Nate's jaw clenched as the logical side of his brain battled with his resistance to selling his body for money. There was also the moral dilemma of seducing someone to break up a relationship.

Perhaps he was being hypocritical—modeling and acting were, in their own ways, selling bodies, and Nate was no saint. But he had his values, and the idea of faking interest in a woman for cold hard cash sat like greasy pizza in the pit of his stomach.

After another ten minutes of waffling back and forth, he shoved his phone into his pocket and walked upstairs. Skylar had already exited the bathroom, and his mind swirled with indecision as he scrubbed away the day's headaches with a long, hot shower.

He didn't need to decide now.

Kris had given him forty-eight hours.

He had forty-five left.

CHAPTER 3

KRIS'S IRRITATION AND INEXPLICABLE AROUSAL FROM her encounter with Nate lingered throughout her retail therapy session on Rodeo Drive. By the time she arrived home, the sun had dipped beneath the horizon, but she still trembled with uncharacteristic agitation.

Forty-eight hours. She'd never waited that long for anything in her life, and the fact she'd offered Nate that much leeway when she could get any empty-headed pretty boy to take his place baffled her.

It was a job. She was an employer hiring an employee—a temporary one, at that. Why did Kris care who it was as long as they got the job done?

Her foul mood ratcheted up another notch when she saw the Stepmonster's red Ferrari Spider parked in the ten-car garage. The Ferrari, along with Kris's silver Mercedes convertible, was one of three cars Roger kept in LA for when he was in town.

The Carreras' mansion in Beverly Hills was, like all their other properties, huge, and Kris had avoided the Stepmonster nine times out of ten so far. Even so, knowing the redhead roamed the estate at the same time as her put Kris's teeth on edge.

She slammed her car door shut and entered the main building, bypassing the dome-ceilinged foyer, massive sunken living room, and gourmet kitchen on her way to her suite. Shopping bags from dozens of designer boutiques hung from her arms, but Kris was too consumed with thoughts of emerald eyes and whiskey drawls to take comfort in the weight of thousands of dollars' worth of clothing and accessories.

She tried to shake the image of Nate out of her mind, but it clung to her consciousness like Saran Wrap.

Dammit.

Kris made it to the bottom of the staircase right as Gloria's sickeningly sweet voice seeped into the air.

"How was work, darlin'?"

The exaggerated Southern accent caused the hairs on the back of Kris's neck to prickle.

She straightened her shoulders, turned, and leveled the Stepmonster with a disinterested gaze.

Gloria wasn't her stepmother yet, thank God, but Stepmonster-to-be didn't roll off the tongue quite as smoothly.

Her father's twenty-seven-year-old fiancée wore a green floral bikini top that showcased the best double Ds money could buy and a sheer sarong that stopped midthigh. With her flame-colored hair, hourglass figure, and fluttering lashes, she resembled Jessica Rabbit, only she was even faker than the cartoon.

"I feel so bad for you, havin' to *work* all day." Gloria's glossy lips pushed out into a pout. "Must be so…tedious. But you know what your father said. You need to learn the value of money and hard work, darlin'. Can't go fritterin' away the family fortune on designer handbags and shoes." She raised an eyebrow at Kris's proliferation of shopping bags.

Fury simmered in Kris's veins. Gloria was one to talk, given her addiction to Hermès and Louis Vuitton. She'd been a cocktail waitress scraping by on tips from lecherous men at a high-end bar before she'd landed her big fish: Roger Carrera, aka Kris's dad. In the eighteen months since she and Roger met, she'd transformed from an unsophisticated nobody who considered Target high-end to a designer snob who racked up monthly bills equivalent to the average American's annual salary.

Still, Kris maintained her composure. She and Gloria were locked in a cold war, not a hot one. They fought their battles in the shadows, through subtle poisonous barbs and behind-the-scenes machinations. Whoever lost their cool first put themselves at a serious disadvantage.

"Thank you for your concern. I'm sure you've had enough experience with...hard work for both of us. But there's no need to worry about me 'fritterin'' away the family fortune. I plan to protect the Carerras' money from anyone and anything that may threaten it."

The real meaning behind her words hung in the air, clear as day.

Gloria was the threat, and Kris would annihilate her before the Stepmonster ever stepped foot in the wedding aisle.

Part of it was pure vindictiveness on Kris's part. Her father had insisted she get a "real" job this summer and learn the value of money because Gloria had planted the idea in his head. Roger had been happy to provide Kris with as much money and freedom as she wanted—until the Stepmonster entered the picture.

Instead of arguing, Kris had agreed and convinced her father to land her a job as a summer assistant for Bobbi Rayden. She knew when to pick her battles, and if she was going to work like a plebeian, she might as well work at a glamorous job in LA, where she could take advantage of the beaches and boutiques in her spare time, instead of pushing papers at her father's company's Seattle headquarters.

To her surprise and dismay, Gloria had offered to join her in California, framing it as an opportunity to bond with her future stepdaughter before the November nuptials. Roger, who was blind to Gloria and Kris's mutual loathing and eager for them to get along, had jumped at the idea. Never mind the fact that Kris and Gloria wanted to bond as much as Kris wanted to drown in a sea of itchy polyester sweaters.

No, the Stepmonster had merely seized the opportunity to spend a summer in sunny SoCal instead of gloomy Seattle while Roger closed a major business deal in Manila. The deal had sucked up all of his attention the past few months, and he'd decided to stay in the Philippines until it was done, instead of flying back and forth between Washington and Asia every few weeks.

"Oh, sweet darlin'. How naive you are," Gloria said softly. "To think you could protect anything from anyone. You grew up with a silver spoon in your mouth. You have no idea what it's like havin' to fight for survival."

Kris bared her teeth in a semblance of a smile. "Care to wager on that?"

"Oh, I don't do wagers. Silly little things." Gloria waved a dismissive hand in the air. Her massive ten-carat Cartier engagement ring flashed in the light, and a cold gleam of satisfaction entered her eyes when she saw Kris's eye twitch with anger at the sight. "Besides," she drawled, "you won't have enough to wager with."

The Stepmonster spun on her heels and strutted toward the pool, her hips swaying like a pendulum.

You won't have enough to wager with.

What the hell was that supposed to mean? Gloria had convinced her father to cut her off after Kris spent an extravagant sum of money on her friend Courtney Taylor's birthday weekend during study abroad, but a guilt-ridden Roger had reinstated

Kris's credit card privileges soon after. She doubted Gloria would try that trick again.

Besides, Kris's checking and savings accounts were flush with cash, and once she turned twenty-three, she'd come into a trust fund large enough to ensure she'd never have to work a day in her life.

She decided Gloria was merely fucking with her and ascended the rest of the stairs to her room. Once Nate accepted Kris's offer—and he *would* accept—Gloria would be out of her life forever. Kris had faith in his ability to seduce the Stepmonster.

Despite her giggly facade and damsel-in-distress routine, Gloria was no dummy. But she also hadn't seen her fiancé in over a month, and Nate was beautiful enough to bring even a nun to her knees. A lusty, bored housewife-in-training would be a piece of cake.

Kris kicked off her Jimmy Choos and flexed her feet against the plush carpet. Her stomach tangled again when she pictured Nate's broad, strong shoulders and exquisitely sculpted face. She wondered what poor bastards were wandering around with warts and sagging jowls so Nate could enjoy his surplus of beauty. God had to have poured at least three males' worth of handsomeness into him; his gorgeousness made little sense otherwise.

Kris attempted to push him out of her mind by unpacking her purchases, but she was so distracted, she couldn't even appreciate her new Rag & Bone booties.

Her eyes strayed to the clock on her nightstand.

"Ticktock, Nate," she whispered. "I don't like to be kept waiting."

———

Kris spent the next morning at Alchemy, knee-deep in research. She was sure Nate would accept her offer, but *just in case* he didn't, she needed a backup.

By the time noon rolled around, she'd scrolled through so many actor headshots, her eyes swam. Six-pack abs, strong jawlines, perfect tans. *Blah, blah, boring.*

Nate had all those things too, but he imbued them with a confidence and swagger that captivated at first sight. The guys Kris found online were the opposite of captivating.

To be fair, it was only their pictures.. Maybe they were more charming in person. But Kris needed a break before she banged her head against the table out of frustration.

"Vanilla oat latte, double shot of espresso." The blue-haired barista/waiter with a wicked-looking nose ring slid the drink in front of her.

"Thanks." Kris flicked her eyes at the rest of the staff. No Nate. He usually worked the morning shift on Sundays—not that she was keeping track or anything.

He'd caught her eye the second she saw him, but she'd never thought about engaging with him until she came up with her brilliant plan to get rid of Gloria a week ago.

A strange wisp of disappointment curled through Kris at his absence.

"Looks like a full house today," she said casually. "I'm surprised there are only three people on staff."

The café was a tranquil coffee shop during the week, but on the weekends, it buzzed with trendy brunch-goers. Kris had arrived early enough to claim a corner table, and she'd justified hogging her spot for hours with a steady diet of coffee, pastries, and an order of delicious french toast.

"It's okay. No more or less busy than other weekends." Blue Hair looked startled by Kris's sudden chattiness. She'd never initiated a conversation before beyond the usual *hi, thanks, bye.* "Another waiter was supposed to come in this morning, but he had a last-minute emergency and switched to the afternoon shift."

Kris sipped her latte. "Everything is all right, I hope."

"Yeah, he's fine." A group of drunk blonds demanding more mimosas snagged Blue Hair's attention. He flashed Kris a rueful grin. "Let me know if you need anything else."

After a few minutes of scrolling through more headshots without actually seeing them, Kris slammed her laptop shut and caught the eye of an older woman sitting at the next table over. The woman was beautiful, with high cheekbones and tan skin. She was also a regular at Alchemy.

Kris couldn't shake the feeling that she'd seen this woman before they both stumbled into the same coffee shop in LA. Maybe she was a small-time actress?

The woman smiled; Kris didn't return the overture. Just because they were familiar with each other's faces, didn't mean they were friends or acquaintances. For all Kris knew, the woman was a stalker.

Kris slid her laptop into her bag, tossed a twenty on the table, and glided out of the café. She was done with work today. Her next appointment wasn't until six, which left her plenty of time to…do what?

Shop? She did that yesterday.

Go to the spa? Also did that yesterday.

Go to the beach? Too hot and crowded. Kris preferred private stretches of sand owned by five-star hotels in the Mediterranean.

Ugh.

"I'm a goddamn cliché," she muttered, climbing into her Mercedes.

Poor little rich girl with nothing to do.

Boo-fucking-hoo.

Kris wished her friend Farrah, whom she met in Shanghai during study abroad, were here so they could hang out. Farrah lived in LA, but she was interning in New York this summer along with their other study abroad friends, Olivia Tang and Sammy Yu.

Kris knew a handful of other people in L.A., mostly celebrity offspring who frequented the same jet-set resorts as the Carreras, but she didn't feel like hitting any of them up. Teague was the only one she could stand, and he always spent his summers surfing it up in Hawaii or the South Pacific.

After a moment of deliberation, she drove east toward La Brea. Less than half an hour later, she arrived at a two-story office building that housed a dentist's office, Chase Bank, and Allstate Insurance branch, among other businesses. It was so bland and suburban it depressed the hell out of her.

Kris killed the engine and got out of the car. It was only when she tried to open the locked building door that she realized it was Sunday, which meant no one was working.

She groaned. "I'm an idiot."

"Don't be so harsh on yourself."

Kris spun around, ready to pepper-spray the shit out of whoever was behind her, but relaxed when she saw Susan's twinkling eyes and warm smile.

"What are you doing here?" Kris demanded. "It's Sunday."

Susan arched an eyebrow. She wore a pair of old jeans and a yellow T-shirt that had seen better days, and she carried a large cardboard box of what looked like craft supplies. "I could ask you the same thing."

If Kris were the blushing type, she'd have been beet red. "I mixed the days up. I thought it was Monday."

"I see." Susan was too nice to call her out, but her knowing glance showed she saw through Kris's blatant lie. For one, Kris usually showed up in the early evenings since she had to work during the day, and it was barely past lunchtime. "While you're here, would you be a dear and open the door for me?"

She pointed her chin toward the key card dangling from her fingertips.

Kris took the card, waved it in front of the building's electronic pad, and held the door once it buzzed open. She followed Susan to MentHer's office in the back, feeling somewhat like a daughter tagging along with her mother to work.

Not that Kris would know what that felt like. Her mother had abandoned her and her dad when Kris was two.

Perhaps that was why Kris had been drawn to the MentHer flyer she saw at Alchemy two weeks ago. MentHer was a nonprofit for girls who'd lost their moms, and it offered events, mentorship, and virtual programming for girls up to the age of twenty-two.

At twenty-one, Kris was too young to be a mentor—not that she would've signed up for the role even if she met the age requirements. She preferred her charitable contributions in the form of checks, thank you very much. She also had zero desire to be mentored herself. Kris had done just fine growing up without a mom. She'd figured out the whole period thing, never had her heart broken, and possessed kick-ass makeup and styling skills.

However, some weird part of her had compelled her to take one of the flyers and show up at MentHer the day after, offering her volunteer services—help with events, office work, that sort of thing. It made no fucking sense. Kris *hated* office work. She had to deal with enough of that bull in her day job. Contrary to what she'd thought, working for Bobbi Rayden was less red-carpet parties and more tracking media mentions of Bobbi's high-profile clients. It was a total snooze fest.

Susan flipped on the lights, illuminating the empty front desk and threadbare navy carpet. They bypassed the reception area and beelined to the back, where motivational posters and pictures of mentors and mentees at various outings papered the orange walls.

"So." Susan set the cardboard box on a table and surveyed Kris with intelligent eyes. "Do you want to help me sort the supplies for next week's group activity, or do you want to share why you're really here on a Sunday afternoon?"

Kris scowled. She liked Susan, who'd quit her job in movie production and taken up her new calling as the founder of MentHer four years ago, but she didn't like her *that* much. Plus, Kris wasn't sure why, exactly, she was here on a Sunday when she could be flirting with cute guys at Chateau Marmont.

"Sort supplies." Kris pushed a thick lock of hair out of her eyes. She'd dyed her naturally black locks an overall dark brown and layered them with multidimensional chocolate and caramel balayage highlights. Thank God she'd found a stylist in LA who could do her Seattle hairdresser's work justice.

Susan's lips curved into a wry smile. "All right, then."

They worked in silence for the next few hours. It didn't take long to sort the supplies, but Susan also needed help planning MentHer's annual summer gala in August. Kris gladly pitched in—she enjoyed event planning and had helped her father organize dozens of charity events in the past. MentHer's budget wasn't exactly on the same level as the charity balls that charged $5,000 per plate, but a little creativity went a long way.

"Why are you doing this on a weekend?" Kris scribbled a list of theme ideas for the gala on a yellow legal pad: *Disney. Secret garden. Nautical.* Nothing exciting, but they accommodated the mentees' wide age range. "I thought event planning was Melinda's job."

"I don't mind. When you love something, it doesn't feel like work." Susan's eyes crinkled into a smile. "I appreciate you staying, though, when you could be off breaking some poor boy's heart instead."

Kris brushed off the other woman's teasing. "Please. Boys are more trouble than they're worth."

Nate's image flashed through her mind *again*, like an annoying gnat that wouldn't go away, and she shoved it aside with no small amount of irritation.

"Most are," Susan agreed. "But wait till you find the one you're willing to go through hell and back for."

"I don't like waiting." Kris was over this topic. "Are the movies still happening tonight?"

"Yes. Thanks for the reminder." Susan checked her watch. "We should leave now if we want to make it in time. You know LA traffic."

If there was one thing in life Kris hated more than designer knockoffs, it was Los Angeles traffic. She should've hired a private helicopter for the summer instead of taking the Mercedes. She would've gotten hours of her life back.

They made it to the movie theater ten minutes past the agreed-upon meeting time. Luckily, Melinda, MentHer's program director, had been there to receive the girls and their mentors.

Her face broke out into a relieved smile when she saw Susan and Kris. It probably wasn't easy, wrangling two dozen people on your own.

While Susan and Melinda conferred over business, Kris took in the mentor-mentee pairings with cool detachment. Most of the girls didn't annoy her, which was saying a lot, but a few could use a makeover. Hadn't these people ever heard of deep conditioner?

"Kris!" A bubbly blond in jean shorts and a white T-shirt with a pastel rainbow splashed across the front bounded over. "I'm so happy you're here!"

Kris's face softened a smidge. "Wouldn't have missed it for the world."

Skylar, who'd joined MentHer around the same time Kris started volunteering, was the one mentee she'd taken a liking to. Kris's predisposition toward the girl baffled her, considering her tolerance for perkiness hovered near zero on a one-to-ten scale. Until now, Courtney was the only person whose bubbliness didn't make Kris want to gouge her eyes out.

"Your brother still doesn't know you're coming to these meetings?" Kris followed the rest of the group inside. Susan had bought their tickets online, so they bypassed the long lines and headed straight for the bored-looking attendants to the left.

"No. He thinks I'm here with a friend from soccer camp." Pink bloomed across Skylar's cheeks. "It's stupid. He probably wouldn't mind, but I don't want to hurt him, you know? He's done so much for me since our mom died, and I never want him to feel like he's not good enough. But there are some things…"

"That you need to talk to a female about," Kris finished.

Skylar flashed a grateful smile. "Yeah."

For a seventeen-year-old who'd grown up in LA, the land of backstabbing vipers and fake smiles, she was startlingly innocent and well-adjusted. Not naive, per se, but she possessed a fresh, optimistic outlook on life that Kris couldn't fathom. Maybe that was why she liked the girl so much. Skylar was an oddity, a rare gem amongst a sea of hard-hewn pebbles.

Plus, Kris sometimes glimpsed deep, abiding loneliness behind Skylar's sunny smile. And that, she could relate to. The feeling of being all alone in the world, even when you were surrounded by people, could be a real bitch.

"I'd feel less bad if he had a girlfriend," Skylar said as they settled into their seats. "Someone to take his mind off family and work. He's wound so tight, I'm afraid he'll have a cardiac arrest before he hits thirty." She cocked her head and narrowed her eyes at Kris. "You guys are around the same age…"

"Don't even think about it." Kris's tone brooked no opposition. "I don't do romance, and I'm only here for the summer."

Skylar's brother sounded like a stand-up guy. He also sounded boring as shit.

Family and work.

Kris was halfway to Snoozeville already.

"But summer romances are fun!" Skylar insisted.

Kris arched a perfectly shaped eyebrow. "Have you ever had one?"

"No. But—"

"Shh. The movie's starting."

Sure enough, the lights dimmed, and the rest of the theater settled into quiet anticipation.

Since some mentees were as young as eleven, Susan had chosen a sweet PG-rated movie. By the time they reached the forty-five-minute mark, Kris wanted to shoot the screenwriter, the voice actors, the director, and whoever invented the concept of animation.

There were only so many rainbows and unicorns she could take.

It didn't help that Skylar snuck glances at her throughout the entire thing with a mischievous gleam in her eyes that Kris didn't like. At all.

After ninety minutes, the movie blessedly ended. Susan and Melinda stayed with the girls who were waiting for their family members to pick them up, but Kris had had enough group fun for the night. She said her goodbyes to the MentHer staff and Skylar—ignoring the girl's last-ditch attempts to talk her brother up to Kris—and drove home.

She was halfway to Beverly Hills when her phone rang. It was connected to the car, so she could see the caller's name flashing on the radio screen.

Nate.

Kris's heart did a silly little skip, and her fingers tightened on the steering wheel.

"You're cutting it close," she said, dispensing with the usual greetings.

"Last I checked, I still have twenty-one hours left." Nate's smoky drawl filled the car, so deep and velvety Kris could almost feel it.

Her nipples puckered beneath her $300 silk bra, and heat oozed between her thighs until she bit back a surprised gasp.

Kris didn't succumb to irrational lust. Ever.

Yes, she'd been aroused after her encounter with Nate in the parking lot yesterday, but this was on another level.

She was soaking wet after one sentence from a guy she wasn't even sure she liked.

What the hell was wrong with her?

You and I need to talk later about appropriate responses, she told her traitor body, which only heated further in response.

"Did you call to debate the timing, or have you made a decision?"

Kris congratulated herself on her aloof tone. No one could tell from her voice that she was trembling like a leaf in the wind.

Nate chuckled, and dammit, the rough rumble of amusement turned her on even more.

He could make a killing as a phone sex operator.

"Yes. I'll do it." A brief pause. "With conditions."

Conditions? *Conditions?*

Anger tempered Kris's arousal. She'd already caved on his $5,000 upsell. $15,000 was a helluva lot of money for what he had to do, which was basically nothing except look pretty and toss a few compliments Gloria's way.

"You must be smoking crack if you think—"

"I'll do it for $15,000—"

They spoke at the same time, but Nate wasn't finished, and his next words stunned Kris so much she couldn't find her voice for a long time after he spoke.

"—and a kiss. From you. At any time I choose."

CHAPTER 4

SHE WAS PISSED.

Nate's mouth tipped into a grin when he saw Kris standing in Hilltop Park, her eyes sparking with fury as she watched him approach. With her white dress, dark hair streaming in the wind, and deep scowl, she resembled an avenging angel on the verge of smiting the poor mortal who'd dared cross her.

Except Nate was no mere mortal. She needed him. If she didn't, she wouldn't have called for an in-person meeting a week after she'd listed a few creative places where he could shove his counteroffer and hung up on him.

Nate had taken a huge risk with the counteroffer, but if there was one thing he'd learned about life and business, it was this: always negotiate. The opening offer was rarely the best one, which was why he'd tested the waters and upped the price to $15,000. An extra five grand may not mean a lot to Kris, but it meant a shit ton to the Reynoldses.

As for the kiss part of the deal…well, it'd surprised Nate as much as it had Kris when the words fell out of his mouth, but the more he thought about it, the more he wouldn't mind confirming whether her full lips tasted as sweet as they looked.

He hadn't been able to stop thinking about her since they met, and it was driving him insane. Nate wasn't the type of guy who worked himself into a tizzy over a girl. Normally, he barely had to lift a finger before members of the opposite sex threw themselves at him, promising everything from BJs to threesomes to the kinky shit you only found on porn sites.

Then again, nothing about this situation was normal.

"You're late," Kris said flatly.

Nate hitched his shoulder up in a shrug. "Sorry. My audition ran over, and Long Beach is a long way from Hollywood, especially during rush hour."

The audition had been for a minor role in an upcoming crime thriller, and he was sure he'd nailed it. The role comprised only a few lines, but it involved direct interaction with Oscar Bravo, the biggest action star in the world.

Nate thrilled at the thought. Oscar was one of his idols.

Kris huffed. "First your ridiculous counteroffer, now tardiness. You're pushing your luck."

"If it's so ridiculous, why are we here?" Nate leaned against one of the stone columns bracketing the low concrete wall.

True to its name, Hilltop Park sat perched on a hill overlooking Long Beach, Rancho Palos Verdes, and downtown LA in the distance. It wasn't huge—just a round space dotted with benches and surrounded by a rolling carpet of lush grass. The only other people there were a high school couple too busy making out on a bench to pay attention to Kris and Nate.

"None of the other actors I hired could get the job done," Kris grumbled.

Nate's eyebrows shot up. "It's been a week. How many did you hire?"

"Three. And no, I didn't pay them all $10,000, just a hundred each to flirt with Gloria and see if they could catch her interest." A frown creased her smooth brow. "No dice."

Thank God.

Nate had been consumed with dread and guilt all week, thinking he'd thrown away ten or fifteen grand by being too bold in his negotiations, but now, his usual confidence made a comeback.

"You think I'll be different?"

Nate knew he would; he just wanted to hear her say it. He wasn't the boasting type, but he also wasn't going to fake humility over his looks. He was aware of his effect on women—including Kris. The heat in her eyes wasn't entirely due to anger.

Nate hadn't had sex in a public space since he banged Sheri Cummings at the beach when he was sixteen and learned the hard way that beach sex was not, in fact, that sexy. It'd taken him days to get all the sand out of areas he didn't even know he had.

But there was no sand around now, and Kris was so small, he could lift her with one arm and use his other hand to—

"You better be, given your terms." Kris's cold words snapped Nate out of his X-rated fantasy. Instead of dampening his arousal, they only turned him on more. He loved a good challenge, and he couldn't remember the last time he'd had to do more than smile to get a girl into his bed—or car, or bathroom, or whichever surface was nearby.

Nate didn't drink. Didn't gamble. Didn't do drugs. Sex was the one thing he indulged in regularly, though it had been a good two weeks since he'd seen action from anything besides his right hand. He'd been too busy.

"...plan, which is going to guarantee her interest in you," Kris finished.

Shit. He'd missed the first part of what she said.

"What makes you so sure it'll work?" Nate asked, hoping to draw more details out of her. He didn't want to let on that he hadn't been paying attention, not when their deal wasn't set in stone yet.

"It'll work. Gloria's a vindictive, envious bitch who wants everything I have." Kris pulled a manila envelope out of her giant purse and shoved it at Nate. "I'll discuss the plan in more detail after you sign the contract and NDA."

His disbelieving laugh filled the air. "You're joking."

"I don't joke."

"You're seriously making me sign an NDA?"

"I have a fifty percent deposit waiting for you—in cash—after you sign."

Five minutes later, Nate handed over the signed contract and NDA in exchange for $7,500 worth of green. He split up the hundred-dollar bills, tucking some in his wallet, the inside of his jacket, and even his socks.

Instead of weighing him down, the money buoyed him. How many shifts would he have had to take at the café to earn that kind of money? Too many. And now, he'd gotten it without having to do anything except scribble his signature on a few documents.

He'd looked the contract and NDA over—they were straightforward enough. It wasn't like Nate was planning to tell anyone about his and Kris's agreement, anyway.

After a night of agonizing over whether to accept her offer, he'd concluded that he would be an idiot to pass up the opportunity. Black-and-white morals were a luxury when you had a family to feed and a roof to keep over their heads.

Besides, Nate could get Kris her incriminating pictures without having sex with her father's fiancée. The right angle captured at the right moment could work magic on a person's imagination.

As for breaking up someone else's relationship...

Nate felt a stab of guilt. He was no home-wrecker. But if he had to choose between his family and someone else's, he'd choose his. Every time.

"Paranoid, aren't you?" Kris watched him stuff the last of the cash in his left sock.

"You can never be too careful." He smiled a slow smile. "I'm missing one part of my payment, though."

"I told you, I'll pay you the rest—oh."

Kris had agreed to Nate's One Kiss stipulation—not verbally, but in the contract. It had been one line, buried in the middle of legal mumbo jumbo, but it had been there.

"Fine. Get your kiss." Kris lifted her chin.

Nate stepped closer until they were mere centimeters apart. She smelled like warm amber and lush florals—rich, sensual, and so damn sexy he wanted to bury his face in her hair and fill his entire being with her scent.

He grazed his knuckle over her cheek and along her jaw. Her skin was softer than velvet, and he'd have bet his last dollar that having all that softness wrapped around him while he pounded into her would feel like heaven.

Kris had concealed the earlier heat in her eyes with a concrete wall. Those big dark irises betrayed no emotion, but there was no mistaking the faint pink tint on her skin or the quick, shallow rise and fall of her chest.

She wanted him to kiss her.

Nate curled his hand around her back of her neck and leaned in until their lips almost touched, and Kris's eyes fluttered closed.

He wanted to devour her. To throw her on the ground, shove her dress up, and take her right then and there, witnesses be damned.

Who knows, maybe the teenyboppers over there would learn something.

Instead, he moved his mouth to her ear and nipped her lobe.

Quick. Gentle. A promise of future pleasures to come.

"Not yet," he whispered. "I'll kiss you when you're begging for it."

A wicked grin slid across his face when Kris's eyes flew open and she shoved him away.

Anger and a hint of frustration touched her features before she shut it down. "That'll be never." She tossed her thick dark hair over her shoulder. "Not that I care. You're the one who insisted on a kiss. If you don't want to claim it, that's your problem."

"Oh, I'm going to claim it." Nate slouched against the stone column, confidence oozing from every pore. "And when I do, you're going to remember it for the rest of your life."

CHAPTER 5

KRIS WAS OUT OF HER MIND. DELIRIOUS FROM TOO much sun, boredom, and frustration after a month of living and working in LA.

That was the only reason she could come up with for not only allowing Nate to live after the stunt he'd pulled in the park but also agreeing to dinner with him.

We can nail down the details of the plan without starving, he'd said.

Bullshit. After his arrogant proclamations—*I'll kiss you when you're begging for it...and when I do, you're going to remember it for the rest of your life*—Kris was sure he was trying to seduce her.

If so, he'd chosen the wrong target. She was immune to seduction, and she'd hired him to ensnare the Stepmonster, not anyone else.

She killed the engine and exited her car at the same time Nate eased out of his with panther-like grace.

Kris leveled him with a glare, which he ignored.

"This place better be good," she warned. Her stomach

cramped, reminding her she hadn't eaten in over eight hours. She'd gotten into a huge argument with Gloria earlier that day over redecorating the pool house, Kris's favorite part of the estate, and had relied on her irritation for sustenance until she met up with Nate.

"It is." Nate opened the door with a flourish. "After you, milady."

She narrowed her eyes, sure he was mocking her, but she was too hungry to put up a fight.

The restaurant was in a strip mall, squeezed between a Western Union and a discount shoe store. The interior resembled that of any cheap, casual café—light brown tile floors, rickety four-top tables crowded with uncomfortable-looking wooden chairs, and a counter in the back for ordering. Miscellaneous announcements and posters papered the green and orange walls, and a string of Christmas lights fluttered in the breeze coming from the ceiling fans, even though it was June and the holidays were long over.

"Thursday nights are the chandeliers' and linen tablecloths' nights off," Nate drawled when he noticed her inspection.

"I eat at non-five-star restaurants all the time." Yes, Kris preferred chandeliers and linen tablecloths, but some of the best restaurants were holes-in-the-wall. Her year abroad in Shanghai had cemented that belief. The soup dumplings in that dingy little hole by campus? To die for. Never mind the fact that the first time Olivia dragged her to that place, Kris had thought she *would* die of some terrible disease by letting her skin touch the gross chairs.

"If you say so." Nate's long legs ate up the distance between the door and the order counter, where he picked up a laminated menu and tossed it at her. "You'll love the food here. Promise. Best Filipino in town."

"So you keep saying."

Despite her disbelieving sniff, Kris's mouth watered at the

sight of the food on the nearby tables, and a wave of nostalgia crashed over her at the familiar delicious smells. Even though Kris was a third-generation Filipino-American, her family didn't eat Filipino food often—not since their old cook and housekeeper, Rosa, passed away when Kris was thirteen. Rosa had been with the Carreras for decades. She'd helped raise Kris from birth and had been the closest thing to a mother figure in Kris's life.

Rosa's death had devastated Kris. None of the chefs and housekeepers her father had hired since compared, and none of them could whip up a home-cooked Filipino meal like Rosa could. In fact, their current chef in Seattle, a whip-thin blond named Charity—yes, that was her real name—delighted in making meals more suitable for rabbits than humans.

After consulting their menus, Kris and Nate placed their orders and snagged a table by the window. Nate insisted on paying, and Kris let him. It was his money; he could do with it what he liked. Plus, according to the handwritten sign taped to the front of the cash register, the restaurant didn't accept Amex.

Nevertheless, Kris felt compelled to set the record straight. "This isn't a date. You didn't have to pay."

"It was the gentlemanly thing to do."

"You're no gentleman." She wavered between setting her crocodile Saint Laurent bag on the sticky wooden table or the cracked vinyl seat cushion next to her; both options caused her to shudder. She finally hung the bag delicately from the back of the neighboring chair. "You're far too arrogant."

Nate, who'd watched her debate the best resting place for her handbag in silence, looked like he was trying not to laugh, and Kris didn't know why. What was so funny about taking care of her Saint Laurent?

"Those things have nothing to do with the other," he said.

"Gentlemen don't need to broadcast the fact they're gentlemen," Kris pointed out haughtily.

"Perhaps not." A mischievous gleam lit up his eyes. "But you don't look like the type of girl who'd want a gentleman, so I'm not too bothered."

A lazy curl of heat stretched and yawned in her stomach, filling her insides with warmth. "Save your flirting for Gloria. It won't work on me."

Nate smirked.

Luckily, the waiter brought out their food before he could contradict her, which she was sure he would do because he seemed to enjoy contradicting everything she said.

Fortunately, the food was so good, they both lapsed into silence as they devoured their feast: tender pork adobo, lechon kawali (crispy deep-fried pork belly), kare kare stew, and sinangag (garlic fried rice).

The quiet gave Kris time to regroup. She hated that Nate rattled her so much.

Normally, she had little use for the opposite sex other than, well, sex. Men were untrustworthy, boring, or indifferent—too caught up in their work to pay attention to the women in their lives, like her father—and Kris would rather be alone with her freedom than suffer through a relationship with someone she didn't like.

She'd quickly tired of the few boyfriends she'd had in the past and had settled for casual flings and one-night stands when the need arose. Luckily, Kris had remarkable control over her libido, and she could satisfy her sexual urges herself most of the time.

However, Nate stirred a lust inside her she hadn't thought possible. The way his throat flexed when he swallowed his food…

Kris reached for her glass of water. Was it just her, or was it hot in here?

"How did you find out about this place?" she asked. "Long Beach is, as you mentioned, a long way from Hollywood."

Kris wasn't one for idle conversations with strangers—and Nate was, at the end of the day, a stranger, considering she knew next to nothing about him—but the warmth and food had lulled her into an odd complacency. She wanted to know what lay beneath Nate's chiseled good looks, and her conviction that he actually possessed depth surprised her almost as much as her interest in his background did.

"My mom. She loved exploring new neighborhoods and trying new things, especially food. Oddly, she wasn't great in the kitchen except for baking cookies"—Nate's mouth curled with amusement—"but she could sniff out a good restaurant like no other. This was one of her favorites."

Kris examined the far-off look in his eyes and the smile lurking at the corners of his lips, the kind people only got when they were lost in the wells of memory. "*Was*, as in past tense?"

The smile fell. Pain clouded Nate's face before he covered it up with a blank expression. "She died five years ago. Plane crash."

Something welled in Kris's throat. The emotion was so unfamiliar, it took her a few beats to identify it as sympathy. "It sounds like she lived a good life before she passed."

That was the only response Kris could think of. She hated platitudes like *I'm sorry* in the wake of tragedy. Such sentiments were so common and expected, they'd lost all meaning. Plus, what the hell was someone supposed to say to *I'm sorry*? *Thank you*? *It's okay*?

"She did." Nate's mouth softened. He appeared grateful that Kris hadn't showered him with pity the way most people would have. "Sometimes I bring my sister here for old times' sake but not as often as I'd like. She's coming up on her senior year of high school and is swamped with activities and college prep, and I have work and auditions all the time." He stabbed at a piece of pork. "It's the first time I've been here in months."

The knowledge Nate had brought her to this specific restaurant, one that meant a lot to him and his family, stirred a part of Kris she hadn't known existed.

"My mother's gone too." She wanted to snatch her confession back the instant it left her mouth. She never talked about her mother. Ever. Not with her father, not with her best friends, and certainly not with beautiful men who made her heart pound for the first time in God knew how long.

But it was too late. She'd already said them, and Kris wasn't one to back down from her words.

"She didn't die," she added. "She left. When I was two."

She pushed the rice around on her plate. Her parents had been a love match. That was what her father told her, but if that were true, how could her mother just walk away like that from the man she loved? From her *daughter*?

To this day, Kris hadn't received an explanation as to why her mother left. Roger Carrera shut down any discussion of his ex-wife and had removed all traces of her from the house. No pictures, no trinkets, no heirlooms.

Other than hazy memories of dark hair and tanned skin, Kris barely remembered what her mother looked like. She supposed she could have fought her father harder on the subject, but Kris was too proud to dwell on anyone who abandoned her.

Even if that person had brought her into this world.

"Her loss," Nate said.

Kris's gaze snapped up to meet his. The tiniest of smiles touched her lips. "Yes, it is."

She was glad she wasn't the only one who hated platitudes.

Kris and Nate lingered over dinner, discussing any topic that came to mind—food, movies, music—and exchanging random facts related to their respective areas of expertise long after they'd cleared their plates of food. Nate made an impassioned argument for why the Lakers were the best basketball team in the country— like he wasn't biased as an LA resident—while Kris explained the difference between St. Moritz and Aspen for ski aficionados.

"St. Moritz has more glamour and five-star hotels, but celebrities love Aspen," she said. "It's where the beautiful people go."

Personally, Kris preferred St. Moritz, especially after a dreadful Christmas vacation in Aspen with her father and Gloria this past winter. She would never forgive Gloria for convincing her father to spend winter break in Colorado instead of St. Barts like the Carreras always did.

A white Christmas. Who would want such a thing? The whole point of a winter getaway was to get away to somewhere *warm*.

"Good to know," Nate said dryly. "I don't intend to visit either place, since I hate flying."

Kris's water glass paused halfway to her lips. "You want to be an actor. That involves a fair amount of flying. Even if you only shoot movies in LA, you still have to go on press tours."

He shrugged. "I'll do it if I have to, but I don't fly for fun."

She assessed his unease with a sharp eye. "Is this a lifelong fear, or did it pop up five years ago?"

Nate glared at her, and Kris met his gaze straight on, unflinching.

"It doesn't matter."

"If you say so."

He made an impatient noise. "We've stayed too late. The restaurant is about to close."

Sure enough, the waiters were stacking chairs on the tables in a not-so-subtle hint for Nate and Kris to leave. It was as clear an end to their conversation as Nate's abrupt subject change.

Kris glanced at the clock and was shocked to see they'd been here for hours. Normally, that much time in one person's company would've compelled her to stab herself out of boredom, but she'd actually enjoyed herself.

She had enough cash for a tip, which she insisted on covering since Nate had paid for the food, and they exited the restaurant with full bellies and a strange charge in the air.

"No signs of food poisoning yet, so you're in the clear—for now," Kris said, but her voice lacked its usual bite.

Nate smirked. "Lucky me."

The lights from a passing car swept across his face, illuminating his finely carved features. A thick lock of golden-brown hair fell over his forehead and partially obscured one eye.

The urge to brush the wayward hair back seized Kris, who crossed her arms over her chest to prevent any foolish actions on her part.

Electricity danced in the air between them, so thick and strong, her skin buzzed. Was it just her, or had Nate's eyes changed color? They were no longer emeralds but dark lustful pools of sin that sucked her in until she couldn't breathe.

She suddenly realized he had a mole near his upper lip. It was so tiny, it would've escaped most people's notice. Far from an imperfection, the mole only drew more notice to the firm, sensual curve of his lips.

Kris's heart pounded against her chest. They were so close. All she had to do was take one step forward and—

Nate drew back, and a shutter fell over his face. "Saturday at noon, then?" The crisp, detached rumble of his voice chased away any remaining electricity.

Kris blinked, caught off guard by the sudden change in the atmosphere before she remembered what they were doing here.

They weren't lovers parting ways after a date. She'd *hired* him, for chrissakes. Their relationship was as romantic as that of a chauffeur and passenger, or plumber and client. Not to mention, a kiss would've been so unpleasant.

Hello, they'd just eaten garlic rice.

At least, that was what she told herself.

"Yes. See you then." Saturday at noon was the only time Kris could guarantee Gloria would be at the house. That was when she had her weekly sessions with her yogi/personal trainer/spiritual teacher—or whatever the fuck he was—in the mansion's Planet Fitness–sized gym.

Kris flashed Nate a brittle smile and speed-walked to her car, furious with herself for the momentary lapse of control.

Nate Reynolds was a means to an end. Nothing more.

CHAPTER 6

"WHY DO YOU LOOK SO SPIFFY?" SKYLAR'S EYES NAR-
rowed with suspicion.

"You used the word *spiffy*. Are you sure you're seventeen?"
Nate eyed her with equal suspicion.

"Don't change the subject." His sister leaned against the
doorframe of their kitchen and sipped her orange juice with a
speculative expression. "Are you going on a date?"

Excitement shimmered in her eyes at the prospect.

"Sorry to crush your hopes but no."

Not in the usual sense, he added silently.

Nate straightened his collar, feeling itchy and uncomfortable
in his pale blue button-down. He preferred the comfort of his old
T-shirts, but Kris had mentioned Gloria was fond of the preppy
look, so he'd dutifully dressed for the part.

He'd also put more effort into taming his tousled hair and
applied cologne, even though he despised cologne almost as much
as he did button-downs.

Skylar persisted. "Why not? You could totally get a date if
you wanted to. My friends all have huge crushes on you."

Nate suppressed a flinch. "Your friends are in high school. Are you trying to land me in jail?"

"I'm not saying date one of *them*. Ew, gross much? I'm just pointing out the fact that you are not without appeal."

"Thanks," he said wryly.

"I'm serious." Skylar finished her juice, set it on a nearby table, and walked over to Nate. She circled him with a critical eye. "Hmm. I think she'd like you."

Tension bunched in Nate's shoulders. "No."

He knew Skylar well enough to know what she had in mind, and he was *not* on board. He'd rather have his fingernails pulled off one by one than get set up on a date. By his baby sis, no less.

Someone get the pliers.

Skylar pouted. "You don't know who I'm talking about."

"No."

"You're around the same age, and she is *so* pretty."

"No."

A huff of exasperation. "Do you *want* to die old and alone?"

"I don't need you matchmaking for me. I do just fine with women, thank you very much." Nate wasn't being arrogant; it was the truth. It took him less time to pick up a girl than it did for him to check out groceries at the supermarket. That was the way it'd been all his life.

Except for Kris, but she was a special case.

His heart rate kicked up at the prospect of seeing her in less than an hour, and he ran a hand through his hair until it—

Wait. What the hell was he doing? Racing heart and fidgeting with his hair? He was acting like a damn schoolboy with a crush.

Nate lowered his arm with a frown.

"Yeah, but you haven't had a girlfriend since high school, and she only lasted six weeks," Skylar pointed out. "Don't you think it's time to—"

"No."

Her face crumpled into a scowl. "You need to expand your vocabulary."

"You need to stop being so nosy about my love life," he countered. "As much as I'm loving this conversation"—*not*—"I have to go. Lunch is in the fridge. Do *not* order takeout, especially not from that sketchy place down the street. Remember what happened last time?"

They both grimaced, remembering the deceivingly delicious tacos that had sent them running to the bathroom all night long. Talk about Montezuma's revenge.

"I won't. Even though reheated chicken tastes like ass," Skylar grumbled.

"Language."

"Whatever, Steve Rogers."

"Nice Captain America reference."

Nate ruffled his sister's hair on his way out, which earned him another scowl. She hated when he did that.

That was what she got for bugging him about getting a girlfriend. You'd think Skylar would be busy enough with school, soccer, and her own social life, but she'd been nosing around his love life for years. He needed to find his "lobster," she said, proving she watched way too many *Friends* reruns.

Nate input Kris's address into Google Maps and turned on the radio, flipping through several screechy pop hits, a maudlin eighties ballad, and a head-splitting metal scream disguised as a song before he settled on a tolerable indie-rock jam.

He'd canceled his Spotify subscription to save money, which meant he was always at the mercy of the radio gods, but sometimes the DJ powers that be threw him a bone.

Half an hour later, he arrived in Beverly Hills—the land of the rich, famous, and obscenely wealthy. Multimillion-dollar mansions, expensive cars, and tall skinny palm trees flashed by as Nate maneuvered his old Honda Civic through the perfectly manicured streets. He loved his car, but he'd never been more conscious of how out of place it looked than now, amongst all the Ferraris and Lamborghinis.

Still, nothing prepared him for the sight of Kris's house. He'd known she was rich but *holy shit*.

Nate passed through the security gates, parked in the circular driveway, and stared at the enormous modern structure looming before him. It was all glass, gray stone, and white concrete, and it looked less like a home and more like a hotel. Two ultra-wide flights of stone stairs flanked the mansion, leading to the back of the property. The first level, nestled between the stairs, was a white marble rectangle framing a wall of windows and a set of intimidating double doors that looked like they could withstand a nuclear blast and wouldn't be out of place in a spy movie. The upper levels were less neat—there were so many layers of roofs, jutting angles, and outdoor staircases, he couldn't discern how many floors the house had.

Nate's phone buzzed with a new text as he tried to figure out whether that was an infinity pool on the second (third?) floor terrace.

Kris: Stop dawdling in your car. Hondas are not that nice, and you have a job to do.

His head snapped up. He scanned the house for a sign of her in the windows, but he couldn't see shit through all that tinted glass.

His thumbs flew over his keyboard.

Nate: Is that any way to speak to your boyfriend?

He sent the message flying through cyberspace with a smirk. Kris's plan to ensure Gloria's interest in him was devious and all too fitting for Hollywood. A role within a role. Very meta, and he was going to enjoy the hell out of it.

Kris's reply came just as swiftly.

Kris: If you're not out of the car in thirty seconds, I will force you to wear salmon shorts and Sperrys on our next "date," BOYFRIEND.

Ten seconds later, Nate was out of the car and ringing the doorbell.

He'd expected a maid or butler to open the door—this seemed like the type of joint that would have a butler—so when he found himself face-to-face with Kris herself, he chalked his speechlessness up to surprise.

Except he was more surprised by her appearance than he was by her greeting him.

Instead of designer clothes and heels, Kris wore a soft-looking white T-shirt that slipped off one shoulder and a pair of tiny green shorts that bared miles of smooth, tanned leg. She had no makeup on—or if she did, Nate couldn't tell—and she'd twisted her hair into a loose, messy bun that begged him to unravel it and run his fingers through those thick, luxurious locks.

No longer an untouchable ice princess but a girl. A ridiculously touchable, beautiful one.

Kris crossed her arms over her chest. "My eyes are up here."

It was only then that he realized he'd been laser-focused on the lacy bra strap her shirt revealed.

Get it together.

He lifted his gaze and relaxed into his confident playboy

persona the way he slipped on his favorite T-shirt—smooth, comfortable, and so easy it was like breathing.

"Yes, I know. I'm well acquainted with the female anatomy," Nate drawled. "Every last inch."

Kris stared at him a beat too long before she spun on her heels and marched through her foyer. "Good. You brought your A game. Save it for Gloria."

Nate shut the door behind him and followed her through the marble corridors and enormous rooms. She gave him a brief description of the spaces they passed—the indoor theater, the game room, the two-story living room—before they stopped in the kitchen, which was larger than the restaurant where they'd eaten dinner the other day.

He ran his hand over the smooth marble of the center island. "So where is the glorious Gloria?"

A soft chuckle escaped his throat when Kris's nose wrinkled at his cheesy play on words.

"She's with her trainer. She'll be done in a half hour, and she always comes to the kitchen afterward for one of her disgusting hemp smoothies." Kris examined him from head to toe. "Good call on the shirt. She loves the Brooks Brothers look."

"I always dress for the part." Nate gave her his own once-over. "Speaking of which, should I be offended or flattered that you didn't feel the need to dress up for our official debut as boyfriend and girlfriend?"

"Neither, because this debut is as about as real as the Stepmonster's breasts." Kris hitched her shirt up on her shoulder, covering her bra strap, much to his disappointment. "And FYI, this is my yoga outfit. I didn't have time to change before you arrived."

"Yoga, huh?" His mind conjured up some *very* interesting images of Kris in the downward dog position.

She rolled her eyes as if she knew exactly what he was thinking. "Do you remember everything I told you?"

"Of course. I'm a pro." Nate grabbed an apple from the fruit basket on the island and bit into it. He chewed and swallowed before he asked, "Where's your staff? I'd expected to see maids, butlers, footmen…"

Another eye roll. "You've watched too much *Downton Abbey*. This isn't our full-time house, so we don't have a full staff. Risa, the housekeeper, maintains everything for us. She has the weekends off."

If this was her family's secondary home, Nate couldn't imagine what their actual home looked like. "Why do you need two houses in the same city?"

"What are you talking about? Our main house is in Seattle." Realization washed over Kris's face, and her eyes widened. "You didn't know that."

Shit.

"No."

"It's something you would know if we were actually dating."

"Yes."

They stared at each other. Their dinner conversation the other night had been more topical than personal, save for their brief bonding moment over losing their moms, and they'd been so focused on getting the physical part of their plan right that they hadn't stopped to think about the fact that they should know basic things about each other—like where Kris was from.

Nate felt a pang in his stomach that he attributed to the apple, not the fact that Kris was from Seattle and might leave soon.

"She's not going to grill you about me." Kris recovered, though a troubled look remained in her eyes. "We just have to act the part."

"She might if everything goes according to plan."

"We'll worry about that later. For now, focus on getting her attention."

Nate finished his apple and tossed it into the state-of-the-art stainless-steel trash can. "That won't be a problem."

"Good. Because she's coming."

Sure enough, the sound of footsteps approached.

That was their cue.

Nate snapped into acting mode and leaned against the island, widening his stance while Kris pulled her bun loose and stepped between his legs. She looped her arms around his neck, and he rested his hands on her hips, resisting the urge to fist her hair in his hand and crush his lips to hers. That would make this scene believable for sure, but he didn't want their first kiss to be fake.

Like he said the other day, he wanted her to want it. Beg for it.

Chalk it up to Nate's innate competitiveness—nothing got his blood pumping like a good challenge, and he couldn't think of a better challenge than melting the ice princess in his arms.

But work came first.

The footsteps got louder, and Nate's pulse kicked up another notch.

Showtime.

CHAPTER 7

NATE WAS SO CLOSE, KRIS COULD SEE THE GOLD flecks in his eyes. His hands gripped her hips, firm and strong, and heat radiated from him in lazy, sensual waves.

It was an act, but she'd never been more aware of every breath, every movement, every second ticking by.

"You smell good." His soft drawl scraped against her skin, so rough and textured Kris could *feel* it.

Her thighs clenched, and her nipples tightened in response.

"Custom-made perfume," she managed. "From Paris."

"I like it." Nate lifted one hand from her hip and trailed it over the curves of her waist and breast, the slope of her shoulder, and the slender column of her throat before he curled his fingers around the nape of her neck. He wrapped his other arm around her and yanked her close until they were flush against each other.

Kris's pulse pounded in her ears. Frantic. Wanting. "What are you doing?"

"Practicing." Nate rubbed his thumb over the soft skin of her neck, and she bit back a moan. How could one simple motion feel so good? "Since we have to rely on our physical chemistry to make this believable."

"That doesn't mean you can grope me at will."

Amusement crinkled the corners of his eyes. "You're free to leave anytime."

"It's my house!"

"I meant leave my arms." Nate's amusement deepened. "Do you want me to stop, princess?" He lowered his head and pressed his lips on the curve between her neck and shoulder.

Kris tried to control her breathing. What was wrong with her? She wasn't the type of girl who turned to putty in a guy's hands. Yet here she was, trembling like a virgin when he hadn't done more than hold her and kiss her neck.

But she wasn't the only one affected—Nate's arousal pressed against her stomach like a steel pipe. It sent another bolt of lust through her, which she shoved aside so she could focus on the task at hand.

Two can play this game.

"No. Why would I? This is all part of our act..." She lowered her voice so the last word was barely audible. She arched her back and pressed her hips against his, performing a small slow grind that created delicious friction. Nate's entire body turned rigid, and she smiled. "Right?"

"Careful, princess," he growled. "You're playing with fire."

"Am I?" Another grind. "I thought I was playing with something else."

A hiss escaped his lips, but he didn't let go. Instead, he tugged on her hair hard enough for it to hurt and bit the curve of her neck in punishment.

Pain and pleasure bloomed in equal measure. Kris sucked in a breath, unsure whether to slap him or kiss him senseless.

She realized they might have to kiss as part of their act, and she wondered whether those kisses counted toward the one in their contract.

Oops, didn't think that one through.

Though the idea of kissing Nate no longer seemed as onerous—

A delicate cough interrupted Kris's musing.

Kris turned her head to see Gloria standing in the doorway, looking like Workout Barbie in a sports bra and leggings so tight they might as well be painted on. Her thick red ponytail swung around her bare shoulders, and her eyebrows arched in surprise at the scene before her.

"Kris, darlin', I didn't realize we had a guest," the Stepmonster drawled. "You should've told me. I would've whipped somethin' up. It's bad manners not to offer a guest something to eat and drink."

Right. Kris would rather eat the poisoned apple from *Snow White* than anything the Stepmonster cooked.

"It's all right," Nate said easily. He'd lifted his head to face Gloria, though his arms remained wrapped around Kris. "I have all I need right here."

Damn, he was good.

"Hmm." Gloria swept her gaze over Nate. Her face remained neutral, but Kris spotted the spark of interest in the Stepmonster's eyes as she took in Nate's lean, powerful frame and fallen angel face.

The guys Kris had sent the Stepmonster's way last week hadn't turned her head, despite their good looks, but as Kris had suspected, there was something about Nate that set him apart from your typical LA pretty boy.

"I don't believe we've met." Gloria walked over and extended one pale, perfectly manicured hand like she expected Nate to kiss it. "I'm Gloria."

No mention of her marital status or her relationship to Kris, Kris noticed.

"Nate." His hand dwarfed Gloria's as he shook it. The handshake lingered—not so long that it was overtly inappropriate, but long enough that the spark of interest in Gloria's eyes escalated to a flare.

Correction: he was *very* good.

Kris should've been pleased because wasn't this what she was paying him for? But an irrational part of her wanted to yank their hands apart and hiss at Gloria like a territorial cat.

"I'm Kris's boyfriend," he added, just like he and Kris had rehearsed.

Kris watched the Stepmonster's reaction closely. The "news" shouldn't have come as a surprise, given the position Gloria had found them in, but Gloria needed to think Nate was more than a random hookup.

The redhead may be engaged to Kris's father, but she wasn't home free yet. They had another five months before the wedding, but Gloria was ambitious and cunning enough not to do anything that might jeopardize her future fortunes. She'd certainly been cunning enough to get Kris's father to scrap a prenup, which meant she was entitled to half of Roger's earnings and assets gained during their marriage should they ever divorce.

However, there was one thing that overrode Gloria's greed: her envy. She seemed hell-bent on obtaining everything Kris had, whether that be a pair of Rag & Bone jeans or a new Porsche. Hell, she'd even hijacked Kris's summer in LA.

Gloria's obsession was downright disturbing, but it was also a godsend because it made her predictable.

She wouldn't be able to resist making for a play for Nate, especially since he was the first guy Kris shown an interest in since the stepmonster entered her life. Kris had planted the seeds all week by letting Gloria "catch" her in a lovey-dovey phone conversation or coming home with flowers.

Sure enough, Kris spotted the tightening of Stepmonster's features—which told her Gloria was irritated Kris had snagged such a fine male specimen—followed by a calculating gleam, which meant she was devising ways she could snatch said male away from Kris.

She couldn't be overt about it, but Kris was willing to bet Gloria would be more than satisfied with tempting Nate into an "affair" and dropping subtle hints about him cheating around Kris.

Hubris and predictability had been the downfall of many a schemer.

Kris hid a smile. She had her PI all lined up, waiting in the wings. Once Nate got Gloria alone and her PI did his job, it was *Game Over, Sayonara, Don't Let the Door Hit Your Ass on Your Way Out* for Stepmother dearest.

"I didn't realize you were dating someone." Gloria tightened her ponytail in a way that highlighted her generous breasts.

Kris was gratified to see that Nate's gaze remained firmly on the redhead's face.

"We've only been in LA for a few weeks. Seems soon for you to get a boyfriend," the Stepmonster added with the barest hint of suspicion.

"Nate and I met the day after I arrived," Kris lied smoothly. "I had some car trouble. He spotted me on the side of the road and offered to help. Such a gentleman."

Nate's mouth twitched. No doubt he remembered what she'd said to him at dinner the other night—*You're no gentleman. You're far too arrogant.*

"What can I say?" He smiled down at her, his face so open and genuine, Kris almost believed they were in an actual relationship, even though she knew he was acting. "I can't resist helping a beautiful woman."

"How sweet," Gloria said sourly.

"Did you come in here for something other than idle chit-chat?" Kris arched an eyebrow.

"I'm makin' a smoothie. I just finished my trainin' session." Gloria's ponytail swished as she walked toward the fridge with an exaggerated sway of her hips. For Nate's benefit, no doubt. "He's not takin' any more clients, but I can put in a good word for you if you'd like, darlin'. You could benefit from some extra time in the gym."

Oh please. Kris wasn't stick thin—she had boobs and curves and a butt—but she was healthy and fit, and Gloria could shove her extra gym time up her ass.

"Thanks, but no thanks," she replied with an equal amount of saccharine. "Nate works me out just fine."

Nate let out a wheeze that he quickly covered up with a cough.

The fridge door slammed shut. Gloria set a carton of almond milk on the counter and pursed her lips. "How nice to hear."

Translation: *Die, bitch.*

"Speaking of which, Nate and I have to work out now," Kris drawled. "Hope you enjoy your...smoothie."

"It was nice meeting you," Nate added after he recovered from Kris's unexpected double entendre. "I'm sure I'll see you again."

Gloria's red lips curved up into a slow smile. "Yes. You can count on it."

CHAPTER 8

SEDUCING GLORIA WAS THE EASIEST AND HARDEST job Nate had ever had.

Easy because Gloria fell for his and Kris's ruse hook, line, and sinker.

Hard because Nate had to pretend to be Kris's boyfriend—a shitty one who flirted with her future stepmother behind her back at that—while not touching her the way he wanted to.

Yes, they cuddled and hugged when Gloria was around, but that wasn't the same. Nate wanted Kris alone for real. No acting. He wanted her beneath him, screaming his name while he drove into her. He wanted her mouth around his cock and his fingers bringing her over the edge, and—

"Dude, careful!" Elijah's voice jerked Nate out of his fantasies.

Nate cursed as coffee spilled over the edge of the mug and scalded his fingers. He quickly set the drink on the counter and washed his hands with ice-cold water before cleaning up his mess.

It'd only been two weeks since he and Kris started their boyfriend-girlfriend act, and he was already in over his head.

That was what happened when you spent time with someone almost every day.

For their plan to succeed, he had to be around Gloria, which meant regular trips to Kris's house. Not that Nate was complaining. The mansion boasted everything a guy could want, and he enjoyed hanging out with Kris. She was spoiled, yeah, but he supposed it was hard not to be when you had that many zeros in your bank account. Plus, she was funny and incisive and hot as hell. No bullshit, which he appreciated, and she smelled amazing—

Nate stifled a groan. Two weeks in and he was already blurring the lines between business and pleasure. What had started as a challenge (melt Kris's icy exterior) and side hustle (the whole seduce-Gloria scheme) had turned into something else entirely—and he and Kris hadn't even had a proper kiss yet.

Fuck.

"What's with you lately? You've been distracted as hell." Elijah crossed his arms over his chest. With his spiky blue hair, nose ring, and penchant for black, he would have been more at home in a hipster Brooklyn dive bar than a trendy all-white LA café named Alchemy. Then again, his father was the café's owner, so he didn't have much choice when it came to where he worked.

"Lot on my mind." Nate made a new latte. This time, he stopped the machine right as the coffee hit the brim.

He couldn't afford any mess-ups. Elijah was an old friend from high school and had done Nate a solid getting him this job. Decent salary, nice coworkers, clean environment, and flexible enough when Nate had to adjust his shifts for auditions or family emergencies. He didn't want to fuck it up by giving Elijah's dad—a notorious hard-ass—any reason to fire him. Luckily, Elijah's father was rarely around, and Liza, the manager who ran daily operations, loved Nate.

Still, better safe than sorry.

"I can see that. At the risk of sounding like a clingy girlfriend, we haven't hung out in weeks." Elijah popped an eyebrow. "Wait. Do you have a new girl? That why you've been so MIA lately?"

"Not really," Nate said with a twinge of guilt. He spent most of his time with Kris these days, to the detriment of his other relationships. "Sorry, man. Let's hang soon. I'll kick your ass at *Call of Duty*."

Elijah snorted, all ire gone. That was the great thing about him—he never held a grudge. "You couldn't kick my ass if I glued it to your foot."

Nate finished the latte art and smirked at his friend. "Wanna bet? Twenty bucks says I can."

"Since when do you bet money?"

Never. Nate never bet with money. But he had $7,500 sitting pretty in his bank account, twenty bucks wasn't that much money, and he was in a good mood—he'd gotten a callback for the crime thriller role.

"It's a good day."

Nate rounded the counter and walked over to the dark-haired woman who'd ordered the coffee. She smiled her thanks. She was a regular who kept to herself most of the time, but she was nice and tipped well, which was more than he could say for most customers.

"Can I get you anything else?" he asked.

"No, thanks." The woman's gaze strayed to the entrance like she was waiting for someone. She did that a lot, except Nate had never seen her here with another person. "I'm okay for now."

"If you change your mind, you know where to find me."

Nate flashed a charming grin and returned to his spot behind the counter. Elijah was on his phone, playing some stupid game, and Nate was refilling the pastry case when the chimes over the door rang.

He saw Elijah straighten out of the corner of his eye.

"Dude, that's her," his friend hissed.

"Who?" Nate slid a croissant onto the shelf, not really caring about the answer. Elijah had more crushes than a middle-school girl.

"The hot chick with the attitude. The one who's always here on the weekends, though she hasn't been around in a while."

Nate stilled. He looked over the counter, and sure enough, there was Kris, sitting at her usual table by the window.

"You think she'll go out with me?" Elijah sounded dreamy. He'd gone on and on about Kris since he first laid eyes on her at the beginning of the summer. It had been annoying then, but it was downright irritating now.

A muscle ticked in Nate's jaw. "Doubt it."

He resisted the urge to yell, *That's my girlfriend!* Because that wasn't accurate, was it? He and Kris put on an act around Gloria, but in their free time, they were free to do whatever—and whoever—they wanted.

The thought incited alarmingly murderous thoughts in Nate's head.

"Ye of little faith." Elijah's eyes remained on Kris while he swiped his tongue over his lip ring. Nate wanted to yank the damn thing out. "I may not be a pretty boy like you, but I know how to get a girl all hot and bothered."

"Not if you keep saying things like *hot and bothered*."

"Watch and learn." Elijah ignored Nate's barb and sidled off to take Kris's order, even though she was sitting in Nate's section.

Nate watched, pastries forgotten, as Elijah said something that made Kris smile.

There was no way Elijah was her type. He couldn't imagine a princess like her going for someone with blue hair and facial piercings.

But what did he know about her, really? He knew she was from Seattle and had a summer job working for top Hollywood publicist Bobbi Rayden—not of her own volition. He knew she was Filipino-American and that her father earned his first fortune in the video game world before he branched off into other sectors like e-commerce and technology. He knew little things like her favorite color (green), astrological sign (Scorpio), and the way her nose scrunched when she saw something she didn't like. He knew she was beautiful and sarcastic and that he wanted her more than he'd ever wanted anyone in his life.

But he didn't know *her*. What made her tick. What made her afraid. What type of guy she liked.

Nate assumed Kris went for the douchey trust-fund types. The ones with college degrees who summered in exclusive European resorts and bought girls diamonds on the third date because they could.

That wasn't Nate. But that wasn't Elijah either.

Elijah took out his phone and handed it to Kris.

Nate stifled a snort. There was no way Kris would—

What the fuck?

His jaw unhinged when Kris input what had to be her number and handed it back to Elijah with a smile. Who was this girl? She *never* smiled that much. Scowls? Yeah. Eye rolls? All the time. But smiles? Those were few and far in between.

Now she was smiling at Elijah like he was Harry Styles and she was a tween fangirl.

Nate's eye twitched as Elijah bounced over with a huge grin on his face.

"I got her number," his friend said, sounding giddy. "Told ya. I'm irresistible."

"Congrats." Nate remembered the pastries and shoved the remaining croissants into the pastry case with more force than necessary. "Good for you."

He hadn't told Elijah or anyone else about his arrangement with Kris. As far as his friend knew, Kris was just another
customer—one who'd given him her number.

Nate's eye twitched again.

"She's nicer than I thought," Elijah mused. "I talked to her
once or twice before, but in passing. I thought she'd be one of
those stuck-up types, but she's not so bad. A bit prickly, but she's
hot, so I don't mind."

"Did she place an order?" Nate abruptly changed the subject.
The last thing he wanted was to listen to Elijah ramble on about
how hot Kris was. He had eyes, thank you very much.

"Oh, yeah. Vanilla oat latte with a double shot of espresso
and a blueberry scone."

"I'll make it." Nate started the order before Elijah could
argue. "There's another customer."

While his friend took care of the overly bleached blond in a
pink tracksuit, Nate put the order together and stalked over to
Kris. He couldn't slam the drink on the table unless he wanted
another spill situation, but the plate with the scone hit the wooden
surface with an angry *thud*.

She didn't flinch. "Someone woke up on the wrong side of
bed today."

Wrong. He'd been having a great day until she came in and
got all cozy with his best friend.

"I don't know what you think you're doing, but you need to
stop," he said.

Kris raised one perfect dark brow and sipped her latte. "I'm
enjoying a drink at a café—the one you work at. I don't think your
boss would be happy with you shooing away paying customers."

"That's not what I meant," Nate said through gritted teeth.
"I'm talking about you and Elijah."

"Who?"

"The guy you just gave your number to," he spit out.

"Oh. Blue Hair." Kris's expression cleared. She cocked her head and stared at him with a teasing smile. "Nate Reynolds. Are you...jealous?"

He almost laughed out loud. "Uh, no. I don't get jealous."

Not over girls, anyway. Yes, Nate wanted Kris, but that didn't mean he was *jealous*. He was just...protective of his friend. He was convinced Elijah wasn't her type, and who knew what nefarious plans Kris had up her sleeve? Her Gloria scheme proved she was capable of anything.

At least, that was what he told himself.

"Hmm." Kris broke eye contact and ripped off a piece of her scone. "Then why are you so concerned about who I give my number to?"

"I don't want you to hurt him," Nate said after a pause.

That caught her attention. "What makes you think I would be the one doing the hurting?" She sounded offended.

"Because you're not the type of girl who would ever let your guard down enough to get hurt."

The words spilled out before Nate could stop them.

Damn. He hadn't planned to say that. He didn't even know where the sentiment came from. But it was too late—both he and Kris froze, like they were afraid any movement on their part would bring the words crashing down until they splintered into a million pieces at their feet.

"You don't know the first thing about me." Kris broke the silence first. The ice princess shield was back, so thick and cold, it froze the blood in Nate's veins. "How dare you act as if you do."

That wasn't true. They weren't best friends, but they'd gotten to know each other a helluva lot better these past few weeks.

Not that Nate was going to tell her that. He was pissed and

confused as to *why* he was so pissed, so he simply turned and left without another word.

He spent the rest of his shift avoiding Kris, but as luck would have it, she left at the same time he clocked out.

They walked to their respective cars in silence.

They'd have to make up eventually, thanks to the Gloria Plan, but for now, Nate welcomed the animosity. It was better than wanting her and not being able to have her.

He could tease her, flirt with her. Hell, he could even kiss her—he had one unclaimed kiss on his docket, and for all their cuddling in front of Gloria, their lips had yet to touch. But he could never *have* her because they weren't just from different cities—they were from different worlds, and the princess-and-pauper stories only ever ended well in fiction.

Irritated, Nate flipped on the radio, hoping the music would silence his thoughts. He was glad he'd agreed to meet Skylar at the Santa Monica Pier tonight; he needed the distraction.

He glanced in his rearview mirror and realized Kris's silver Mercedes was right behind him, even though they were going the opposite direction of Beverly Hills.

He made a left. She made a left. He made a right. She made a right.

Was she following him?

Excitement and curiosity warred in his stomach. The thought of a stalker shouldn't have excited him, but it did—*if* the stalker was Kris.

"I have issues," he said out loud. The song on the radio dropped its bass like it agreed with him.

Jerk.

Great. Now I'm angry at a song.

Nate parked at a metered spot near the pier, and wouldn't you know it; Kris pulled into the space two cars behind him.

Nate texted his sister to let her know he was here before he got out of the car and glared at Kris, who glared right back.

"Are you following me?" Kris demanded.

He laughed in disbelief. "You were driving behind me the entire time. Hard to follow you when I was first."

"Maybe you sensed which way I was going."

Nate couldn't believe his ears. "That's insane."

"But not impossible."

"You think too highly of yourself. I have better things to do with my evenings than follow you around." His phone chimed with a new text.

Skylar: I'm by the carousel. See you soon!

"And *I* have better things to do than argue with you." Kris tossed her hair over her shoulder and marched by him. Even in her crazy heels, she barely reached his shoulder.

"Whatever." Nate pocketed his phone and headed toward the pier.

Their silence was awkward as hell, considering they were walking next to each other toward the same destination. Nate didn't even remember why they were mad at each other, but he'd be damned if he caved first.

After a couple of minutes, the Santa Monica Pier came into view. It was one of the most iconic spots in LA, and while it was nice at any time of day, it shined brightest at sunset. The jungle of neon lights and brightly colored rides battled for attention against the fiery oranges and deep purples streaking the skies, and the famous Ferris wheel spun lazily in the background—a comforting anchor to the chaos.

Nate and Kris both turned toward the carousel.

"Don't say it," Kris said without looking at him. "I'm meeting someone at the carousel."

"Me too." Nate paused. "Who are you meeting?"

Was it a date? The possibility set his teeth on edge.

"None of your business." Kris crinkled her nose at a passing group of tourists wearing fanny packs.

Fine. Whatever. He'd find out soon enough anyway.

As they approached the carousel, Nate kept his eye out for Kris's date. The douche in the Ray-Bans and salmon shorts was a possibility—he screamed, *Look at me, I have money,* and begged for a punch in the face—but a girl appeared and wrapped her arms around his waist right as the thought crossed Nate's mind.

Before he could continue scouting, he heard Skylar call his name.

"Nate! Over here!" She waved. One of Skylar's soccer camp friends had dropped her off, and in her pink tank top and jean shorts, she looked younger than her seventeen years.

Nate's face softened into a smile. He was looking forward to a night of cotton candy and silly rides with his sister. It'd take his mind off—

"Kris!" Skylar waved again. "Oh my God, you guys came at the same time. What a coincidence."

Nate's smile dropped.

What. The. Fuck.

How did his sister know Kris? What the *hell* was going on?

"Hi!" Skylar hugged Kris and gestured at Nate. "This is Nate, my brother. Nate, this is my friend Kris. I met her at, um, the movies. I thought it'd be fun if we had a group hang tonight. The more the merrier, right?" She beamed, ignoring the daggers flying from Nate's eyes. "Plus, you guys are around the same age. I thought you'd get along. Make new friends and all that."

Oh God. The pieces clicked into place.

I think she'd like you.

You're around the same age, and she is so pretty.

The girl Skylar had been talking about a few weeks ago—the one she'd wanted to set him up with—was Kris.

One look at Kris and Nate saw she'd deduced what was going on as well because her expression matched his—pure horror.

There was no doubt about it: they were on a matchmaking date.

CHAPTER 9

MURDER IS A CRIME, KRIS REMINDED HERSELF FOR THE umpteenth time as she, Skylar, and Nate waited in line for the Ferris wheel. *You cannot murder a seventeen-year-old girl.*

She liked Skylar. But after tonight, the girl would be lucky if Kris didn't throttle her.

She couldn't believe Skylar had set her up on a date with her brother—or that her brother was Nate, of all people.

What were the fucking chances?

At least Nate seemed as shocked as she was. He'd been silent the entire time and let Skylar gab away to her heart's content.

"Did I tell you Nate's an actor?" The blond's eyes gleamed with mischief. If she sensed the hostility in the air, she didn't show it. "He's been in a few TV shows and movies. You should watch *Four Kings*. It's his latest movie—came out last year—and he played one of the mobster's henchmen."

"Kris doesn't like mobster movies," Nate said, handing the Ferris wheel operator their tickets.

Kris bristled at the assumption. She *didn't* like mobster

movies. But once again, Nate was pretending he knew her—what she liked, what she didn't like—and it pissed her off.

"How do you know?" she and Skylar asked at the same time, though Kris's voice was far sharper.

Skylar had no clue Kris and Nate already knew each other. Kris doubted Nate had told his sister he was seducing an older woman for money—not that Gloria was much older than him. She was twenty-seven, and he was twenty-three. A four-year difference.

"Just a guess." Nate stepped inside the gate.

Kris followed him, her blood heating at the certainty in his tone. "Well, you're a shitty guesser."

"You're saying you *do* like mobster movies?" Nate's smirk made her want to punch him in the face.

"I do."

"What's your favorite one?"

Crap. She scrounged her memory for a mob movie, any mob movie. "*The Godfather.*"

"A classic." Nate nodded. "I especially loved the scene where they put the severed dog's head in Johnny's bed."

Kris's stomach churned at the mental image. "Me too."

She wasn't a big dog fan—she preferred cats, who were independent, aloof, and far less yappy—but who the fuck would be sick enough to cut off a dog's head? Even if it was fiction.

Nate burst into laughter.

Her brows snapped into a frown. "What's so funny?"

"You're so full of shit." Nate grinned a genuine grin, and the sight hit her in her heart and lower belly at the same time. Flutters and heat. A one-two punch. "It was a horse's head, not a dog's head. And they put it in Jack Woltz's bed, not Johnny's."

Double crap.

"I forgot," Kris said with as much dignity as she could muster. "I watched the movie a long time ago."

"It's one of the most iconic scenes in the film and probably Hollywood history. Trust me. If you've ever watched *The Godfather*—even if it wasn't your favorite—you'd remember it."

Dammit.

"You tricked me." She couldn't bring herself to be that upset. Maybe it was Nate's smile or the electric energy in the air. Whatever it was, it smoothed the jagged edges of her earlier ire until they melted into a warm pool at the pit of her stomach.

Nate's eyes crinkled into a wider smile, and the warmth intensified. "Sorry," he said, not sounding sorry at all.

"Hey, you gotta get in a pod," the operator interrupted, looking annoyed. "Everyone's waiting on you."

"You and Skylar go together," Nate said. "I'll—" He frowned. "Sky?"

He and Kris swiveled their heads toward the other side of the now-closed gate, where Skylar clutched her stomach with a faux pained look on her face. Kris knew it was fake because she could see the smile threatening to break out on the girl's face.

"I'm not feeling well," the blond announced. "Must be the cotton candy. You guys stay and have fun. I'm going home."

"The hell you are," Nate growled. "Get over here, Sky."

"Nope." His sister shook her head. "I'm going to vomit."

The operator paled. "You're not getting on this ride if you feel sick," he said.

"Nate. Keys, please." Skylar let out a dramatic moan. "I need to lie down."

After much cursing and scowling from both Nate and the operator—who complained that they were holding everyone up—Nate handed his keys to Skylar and told her where he'd parked.

"How am I supposed to get home?" he demanded.

"Kris can drive you," Skylar said, innocent as a doe. "You wouldn't mind, would you, Kris?"

Kris's urge to throttle the other girl resurfaced with a vengeance. "No," she grumbled.

"Great. See you two later! Have fun!" Skylar rushed off, leaving Nate and Kris alone with the irate operator, who shooed them into a pod with a dark glare.

"Your sister isn't very subtle." Kris stared over the edge of their pod as the wheel creaked to life and they rose into the air. The people on the ground grew smaller and smaller until they were nothing more than specks amidst all the lights. Farther out, the dark, white-tipped waves of the Pacific crashed against the beach in a hopeless embrace—always chasing, never catching. Doomed to arrive onshore only to get sucked back into the vastness of the sea. Proving that you couldn't ever escape who you were.

"No, she isn't." Nate drummed his fingers on his thigh. "I'm going to kill her."

"Not if I kill her first." Kris tore her gaze away from the view and focused on the man sitting across from her.

His mouth kicked up into a smile. "How'd you two meet? Don't say the movies because no one talks at the movies, much less make new friends." He paused. "You're not some psycho stalker trying to get to me through my family, are you?"

"You have an overinflated opinion of my interest in you." Kris didn't mention the lust licking her skin at the sight of him slouched in his seat, wearing an old blue T-shirt that stretched across his shoulders and muscular biceps. A crazy urge to run her hand over the front of his shirt gripped her. Just to check if the tee was as soft as it looked, of course. "We're working together. I don't need to get to you through your family."

"Fine, but you didn't answer my question. How did you and Sky really meet?"

As mad as she was at Skylar, Kris didn't want to give up

the girl's secret. Skylar didn't want Nate to know she'd joined MentHer, and Kris was no snitch. "Ask your sister."

"You're seriously not going to tell me?"

"Ask your sister," she repeated.

Nate let out a long, exasperated sigh. "Women."

"Speaking of women, how are things going with Gloria?" Kris switched the subject to safer territory.

He side-eyed her but didn't comment on the change in conversation. "Good. She's gotten bolder. She all but offered me a blow job in front of the downstairs bathroom the other day."

Kris grimaced. She should be happy—their plan was right on track—but the thought of Nate getting physically involved with Gloria irritated her beyond measure.

"I'm going to pull the trigger soon," Nate said. "Ask her to meet me at a hotel. You can get your PI in place."

"Great." Kris twirled her gold bangle around her wrist. She'd been focused on getting rid of Gloria for so long that she expected to feel more excited about the Stepmonster's imminent departure from her life, but she found it hard to muster up her previous enthusiasm.

The past few weeks, she'd been wrapped up in her fake relationship with Nate, only it didn't feel fake. The chemistry was real. The laughter was real. The way her heart leapt when she saw him was real.

Fuck.

The Ferris wheel ground to a halt. Kris thought the ride had ended, but when she looked up, she realized they were sitting at the top of the ride.

"Is it supposed to stop like this?" Kris hadn't been on a Ferris wheel in forever. She didn't like amusement parks, but the experience had been tolerable so far.

"No." Nate peered over the edge. "Seems like we're stuck."

"*What?*"

"They'll fix it soon," he assured her. "Don't worry."

A few seconds later, they heard an announcement confirming that they were indeed stuck because of a mechanical issue and that engineers were working on getting them down as soon as possible.

Kris's heart pounded against her chest. "If I die on a fucking Ferris wheel, I'm going to haunt you for eternity."

Nate looked unfazed. "I didn't force you to get on."

"Technicalities."

"Are you scared of heights?"

"No." But that didn't mean she enjoyed getting stuck in a giant metal contraption eighty-five feet above the ground.

"We might be stuck for a while," Nate mused. "Could be hours."

Hours?

Kris groaned. She *knew* she should've said no when Skylar asked her for a girls' night at the pier. This was what she got for trying to be nice.

"Why do you sound so unconcerned?"

Something squeaked, and Kris forced herself not to jump at the sound. She'd meant what she said about haunting him—and everyone who had anything to do with this Ferris wheel—if she died here.

Vengeance would make the afterlife so much more interesting.

"There's nothing we can do about it." Nate shrugged. "At least we're not in a life-or-death situation. We just have to wait it out. In the meantime, there's a beautiful view, beautiful girl..."

Kris snorted. By now, she knew how he operated. Nate was flirty and charming by nature, so his words didn't mean anything. At all.

They fell into a comfortable silence, during which she stared out at the admittedly beautiful view while Nate leaned back and closed his eyes like he was taking a nap.

After ten minutes of no sound other than the waves, wind, and distant laughter of people on the ground, Nate spoke up. "You're not really going to go out with Elijah, are you?"

His eyes remained closed, but his body was tense and coiled, like a cobra waiting to strike. He resembled a beautiful statue in repose.

"Who?"

He made an impatient sound. *"Blue Hair."*

Right. Blue Hair's real name was Elijah. Nate had said so at the café—and Elijah had told her too, probably. Kris hadn't paid much attention. She only gave him her number because he'd mentioned he played in a band, and she'd promised Susan she would help look for entertainment options for MentHer's summer gala. They had a limited budget, but Elijah said he'd check with the band and let her know if they were up for a charity gig. If so, Kris would have to screen them first and make sure they weren't totally shit-tastic before she booked them.

"Because you're supposed to be dating me," Nate continued. "Don't want to mess things up with the Gloria Plan until it's finished."

"I thought you were worried about me hurting your friend."

You're not the type of girl who would ever let your guard down enough to get hurt.

It hadn't been an insult, per se, and Kris shouldn't have gotten as worked up as she had, but Nate's words had hit a little too close to home. Her last boyfriend had been Colin, whom she'd dated for a few months her freshman year of college. She'd met him at a charity event, and they'd hit it off. He was a few years older than her, but she'd liked how mature he was compared to the frat bros on campus.

Colin had been nice. Cute. Successful. But Kris had never let him into her private thoughts and life, and when he'd pushed her on it—always wanting to know more than she was willing to reveal—she'd broken things off.

Displaying vulnerability was not her thing. Yet sometimes, she wished it were. It'd be nice to talk to someone about the fears and insecurities that plagued her in the middle of the night. Not a therapist, but someone who actually cared about her and who could relate to how she felt.

But you couldn't get everything you wished for. Not even if your name was Kris Carrera.

Nate shrugged, the movement drawing Kris out of her thoughts. "There are multiple reasons why you guys are a bad match."

She brushed a stray strand of hair out of her eyes. "You seem awfully invested in my love life."

"Maybe I am."

The air shifted. It happened so fast it was like someone flipped a switch, and the change did something to Kris's insides—to her heart, which suddenly pounded; to her stomach, which suddenly twisted; to her throat, which suddenly dried. For once in her life, she didn't have a sarcastic comeback or a witty insult.

Nate hadn't moved an inch, but his chest rose and fell harder than it had a minute ago. His eyes flickered with heat, and the tendrils of warmth traveled the space between them and wrapped themselves around Kris. Silk ribbons against sensitive flesh.

"Do you remember our contract?" His voice was all gravel.

Kris nodded.

"You promised me a kiss."

She'd thought he'd forgotten. He hadn't mentioned it since the day they signed their contract, and he hadn't tried to kiss her once. All he did was nuzzle her neck and put his arm around her when they were in front of Gloria.

Kris didn't like it when people strong-armed her, and that'd been what Nate did when he made their deal contingent on a kiss.

But in this moment, on this Ferris wheel, the girl who thought she had everything wanted nothing more than for the boy sitting across from her to kiss her.

"You said you wouldn't kiss me until I begged for it." She struggled to keep her voice even. "Newsflash: Still. Not. Happening."

Kris might be dying to feel his lips beneath hers, but she had her pride, and it was the only thing keeping her from launching herself at Nate like a lust-crazed heathen.

Nate erased the distance between them and settled in the seat next to hers. "That's where you're wrong," he drawled, his eyes dark with intent.

"I'm never wrong."

"There's a first time for everything."

A breeze swept by, blowing a few stray hairs into her eyes again. Nate brushed them out of the way before capturing a thicker lock between his fingers.

"Like silk," he murmured, rubbing the smooth dark strands. "Tell me. Have you ever been kissed on a Ferris wheel?"

Thump. Thump. THUMP.

"No," Kris managed, ordering her heart to shut up. It didn't listen. "It's horribly cliché."

Nate looked thoughtful, as if he was mulling her words over and searching for any signs of untruth. "Perhaps, but that doesn't mean it's not enjoyable. I think we should test it out."

"Nate Reynolds, are you trying to seduce me?"

That's not what I'm paying you for, she should've added. Except she didn't.

His dangerous grin did wonderful, horrible things to her suddenly shaky knees. Thank God she was sitting down. A face-plant would've been humiliating and, judging by the state of the floor, unhygienic.

"No. If I were trying to seduce you, I'd do this." Nate pressed his mouth to the hollow of her throat, his coffee-and-leather scent enveloping her. "And this." He made his way to her ear, which he nibbled. "And this." His hand drifted to her bare thigh, which he caressed with slow, lazy sweeps of his palm.

Kris shivered, the warmth of his touch contrasting with the chill in the air now that the sun had set. Goose bumps blossomed on her arms and legs while something inside her melted and pooled in her belly and between her thighs.

"You're cheating." Her voice sounded far more breathless than she would've liked.

"Am I?" Another lazy sweep of his palms, this time inching closer to her heated core. "How so?"

"You know how."

"I want you to say it." Nate's lips whispered over the delicate skin of her throat. His thumb rubbed a circle on the inside of her thigh, and Kris gripped the edge of her seat with one hand, her breath turning shallow.

"No."

He tsked in disappointment. "Perhaps you want me to stop instead."

Silence.

A soft laugh. "That's what I thought."

"You are insufferable," Kris ground out, even as her skin throbbed with frustration and arousal. Nate wasn't right for her in so many ways. He wasn't even a good candidate for a casual fling, given how tied up he was in her Gloria scheme.

But she wanted him all the same.

"Not the worst thing I've been called." Nate lifted his head and captured her gaze with his. "All you have to do is ask, and we could do something a helluva lot more fun than talking."

"You mean kissing."

"Sure. Kissing." His eyes shone with laughter.

Hmph. If he thought he could get past first base with her on a freakin' *Ferris wheel*, he had another think coming.

Never mind the fact that she was already halfway to orgasm.

"I don't beg."

"So you said." Nate's voice deepened into a soft growl. "But if you don't stop looking at me like that, I might kiss you anyway—and not on your lips. Or your neck."

Kris's thighs clenched as another wave of heat consumed her. She should've slapped him for how forward he was being, but all she could think about was his hands pinning her hips down and his head buried between her legs. She wasn't big on public sex, but the thought that someone could catch them sent a thrill through her body.

Why am I even thinking about this?

It wasn't like she was *actually* going to let him go down on her here. Or anywhere.

Her eyes dropped to his mouth, taking in the sculpted curve of his lips.

Another growl emitted from his throat. "Kris—"

A loud whine sliced through the air, and she jerked back in surprise.

Another quieter whine, a short stutter, and then the wheel started moving again.

They were no longer stuck.

Kris scooted to the other end of the bench until she was as far away from Nate as possible. The wheel's slow descent shook her out of her fog and straight into *what the hell were you thinking?* territory.

Nate didn't speak or attempt to close the distance between them again. Instead, he watched her quietly with those mesmerizing eyes, all emotion wiped from his face.

When they hit the ground level and the operator opened the gate to their pod, she all but flew out of her seat.

Damn you, Skylar, Kris thought, her heartbeat a loud snare drum that overrode the rest of her senses. She should be at home, FaceTiming Courtney or watching Netflix, not getting messed up in the head about a guy she'd known for, what, a month?

She and Nate walked down the main drag of the pier in silence for a few minutes before she felt compelled to clear the air. "Listen, this isn't a good idea."

"What, walking?" Nate drawled.

She released an exasperated sigh. "No. This." She gestured between them. "What happened back there wasn't—we're not really dating."

"Never said we were."

"We shouldn't get involved in any way, except for the Gloria thing."

"Agreed."

Kris frowned, a little irritated by Nate's quick, casual reply. "Okay." She cleared her throat again. "Okay."

Damn. She'd already said that, hadn't she?

More walking. More silence.

She supposed she could leave now that Skylar was gone, but she was strangely reluctant to do so.

I could use more fresh air, Kris told herself. And the pier was nice at night if you overlooked the hordes of badly dressed tourists.

"I never figured you for the punk-rock type," Nate said.

Her brow knitted in confusion. "Excuse me?"

"Elijah." Still with that casual tone of his. "Didn't think you'd be into the blue hair and facial piercings."

Dear God, not this again. She was too tired to get into another argument.

"I'm not." Kris had nothing against unnatural hair colors or piercings per se, but she wasn't attracted to Blue Hair—er, Elijah—in the least.

"You gave him your number."

"Not that it's any of your business, but I wanted his help with an event I'm planning," she said coolly. "He said his band might be up for a free gig."

If she weren't so annoyed, she would've laughed at the stunned look on Nate's face.

"Oh." He coughed. "That's... He didn't tell me that."

"That's on him." Kris wasn't an idiot—she could tell Elijah was attracted to her, but it wasn't like the guy was in love or anything. He probably hit on every decent-looking female who walked into Alchemy. "But like I said, it's none of your business. We're not actually dating."

She was tired of saying that, but she hoped repeating it would drill the sentiment into Nate's—and her own—head.

"Right." This time, Nate was the one who frowned. "My bank account isn't big enough for that."

Kris wasn't sure she'd heard him correctly. "Excuse me?"

"I imagine you only go for the Richie Riches." His jaw flexed. "Which I get. Parity in net worths and all that."

For the umpteenth time that day, her temper flared. "Is that what you think of me? That I would date someone based on how much money they had?"

He cut a glance in her direction. "I don't know, you tell me. How many of your exes came from a non-upper-class background?"

Kris opened her mouth, but no rebuttal came forth.

Shit. He was right. She didn't date much, but all her ex-boyfriends—hell, all her ex-hookups—belonged in the trust-fund category.

It was funny. She had no problem being a snob about clothes and cars, but distilling a person down to their net worth felt gross.

"My exes and I ran in the same social circles," she said, sounding defensive to her own ears. "I didn't date them *because* they're rich. It just...happened that way."

"Sure."

Kris's lips thinned. "Look, I don't know what hang-ups you have about money—"

"I don't have hang-ups about money—"

"But you need to slow it with the accusations—"

"I don't know why we're—"

The loud chime of an incoming call interrupted their argument. Nate glanced at his phone. "I have to take this," he muttered.

Kris turned her head and stared at the Ferris wheel glowing against the night sky. It had been less than half an hour since they'd gotten off the ride, but it felt like a lifetime ago. The pier's energy electrified the air, bouncing off the people and buildings until it swirled around Kris in a maelstrom of anticipation.

Nate's voice was low as he spoke into his phone. "Hey, this isn't a good—wait, what?"

Her gaze snapped back to Nate. He'd gone pale, and panic tinged with fear bled into his voice.

"Hold on," he said. "I'll be right there. Don't worry, everything will be fine."

"What's wrong?" Kris asked when he hung up. Concern eroded her earlier irritation.

Nate raked a hand through his hair, his eyes glassy. "It's my dad. He's in the hospital."

CHAPTER 10

THEY MADE IT TO THE HOSPITAL IN RECORD TIME, probably breaking a few laws along the way.

Kris hadn't asked questions. Hadn't given Nate the sad pity eyes he hated—the kind he couldn't escape after his mom died. Instead, she'd marched them straight to her car after his announcement and driven like the devil to Los Angeles County hospital.

All the tension from their stupid argument had disappeared, replaced by fraught worry.

They found Skylar in the waiting room, shaken but holding it together, all things considered. Based on what she'd told Nate when she called, she'd gone straight home from the pier and discovered their father passed out at the bottom of the stairs. At first, she'd thought he was unconscious after drinking too much—a common occurrence—until she'd noticed his blue-tinged skin and weak, irregular breathing. That was when she'd freaked out and called 911 and Nate.

A quick check-in with the doctor revealed Michael contracted alcohol poisoning after, yep, drinking too much. It was a new low, and Nate was torn between fury and panic over his father's situation. Luckily, Skylar had found Michael in time—if she'd come home even an hour later, the elder Reynolds might've already choked to death on his vomit.

Michael was in stable condition after the doctor gave him intravenous fluids with vitamin and glucose to stop the dehydration and increase his blood sugar, but the hospital was keeping him overnight for monitoring and evaluation.

Kris drove Skylar home while Nate filled out paperwork, much to Skylar's consternation. She'd wanted to stay, but Nate had insisted she get some rest since she had soccer camp tomorrow. Their dad was fine—he was asleep, and the nurses would take care of him.

Nate sat in front of his father's room after he finished the paperwork, too exhausted to move. He was pissed at his old man for putting himself in danger like that—for drinking so much he'd planted himself at death's door. But Michael was still his father. He was still the man who'd taught Nate how to swim and let him win at arm wrestling. Seven-year-old Nate had thought he was the strongest kid in the world because he'd beaten his dad—his superhero dad—at arm wrestling.

What Nate wouldn't give to get those days and his dad back.

He leaned his head against the wall and closed his eyes, tempted to pass out right there in the hospital hallway.

Maybe he did pass out; he didn't know. But after an indeterminate amount of time, a whiff of amber and florals edged out the omnipresent antiseptic in the air and caused him to crack open his eyes.

He raised his head and blinked once. Twice.

"What are you doing here?" His voice came out scratchy and tired.

"I brought you food." Kris handed him a soda and an In-N-Out bag. "You need to eat."

"I'm not hungry."

"*Eat.*" Her tone brooked no opposition, and Nate was too exhausted to argue.

The minute he opened the bag, the smell of a burger and fries slammed into his nostrils and woke the monster. His stomach had been asleep all this time, playing second fiddle to his nerves and overworked brain, but now it roared to life, demanding attention.

Five minutes later, he'd demolished all the food.

Nate finished the last fry and looked up to find Kris staring at him with wide eyes.

"Sorry." Guilt crawled into his now-satiated stomach. "I should've offered you some before I went all Conan the Barbarian on the food."

"No, I already ate with Skylar." Kris's mouth twitched. "You eat like a starved bear."

A laugh rumbled in Nate's chest, catching him by surprise. It felt damn good, though. "Guess I was hungry after all." He crumpled the bag into a ball and tossed it into a nearby trash can. "You didn't have to come back. You could've—should've—gone home after dropping Skylar off."

Kris lifted her shoulder. "It's not like I had anything else to do. Besides, I wanted to make sure..." She hesitated. "Skylar's fine, by the way. She passed out right after she got home."

She'd known what Nate was going to ask before he asked it.

"Thanks for driving her," he said softly. "And for staying."

He hadn't expected her to be so...nice, especially not after he'd been such a dick to her at the pier. He hadn't meant to go so hard on her, but he'd been all wound up from their Ferris-wheel ride—the sexiest, most frustrating Ferris-wheel ride of his life— and the way she'd repeated *We're not actually dating.* like she'd never dream of being with someone like him.

Fuck. It had driven him crazy and straight into Assholeville.

Yet here she was, keeping him company in front of his alcoholic father's hospital room after driving him here, driving his sister home, and feeding him.

Gratitude, regret, and embarrassment sloshed in his stomach.

"About earlier, at the pier." Nate grimaced. "I was a dick. I shouldn't have said those things to you. I don't think you're that..."

"Snobby? Vapid? Stuck-up?" Kris shrugged. Her dress was wrinkled from sitting too long, and her normally perfect hair fell in messy waves around her face. She'd never looked more beautiful. "It's water under the bridge. Besides, I *am* snobby and stuck-up, though I'd like to think I'm not that vapid. And I don't choose who I hang out with based on the size of their bank accounts."

"You're not stuck-up," he said automatically.

A ghost of a smile touched her lips. "But I am snobby?"

"Shit, no. I mean—"

"It's fine." She laughed. "I appreciate the apology, and I know what you meant. It's been a long day." Kris's gaze drifted toward Michael's room. "How's your dad doing?"

"He's fine. Stable." Nate rubbed a hand over his face. "You really don't have to stay. You've done more than enough."

"I don't have to, but I want to."

Something reached inside Nate's chest and squeezed. Hard.

He let out a sharp exhale and averted his gaze. "You wanna get out of here?" He couldn't bear to look at the white walls and listen to the faint, incessant beeping of monitors any longer. "There's a place I wanna show you—if you're not too tired."

Kris hesitated, and he suppressed a flinch at his idiotic question.

Of course she's tired, asshole. It's past midnight.

"Let's do it," she said.

Relief and a strange warm feeling he couldn't identify fizzled through him. Nate cast one last look at his father's room before leaving.

They entered the elevator and rode it to the garage in silence.

Shit, he couldn't believe Kris had witnessed all the drama with his father. He never let anyone outside his family in on how bad things were, not even Elijah. It was none of their business, and the last thing Nate wanted was anyone feeling sorry for him.

Fortunately, Kris hadn't thrown him a pity party. She was sympathetic, but she didn't look at him like he was some sad-sack charity case whom she wanted to "help."

Nate was more grateful for that than anything else she'd done that night.

Their footsteps echoed in the garage on their way to her Mercedes. Once they reached the gleaming silver convertible, Kris unlocked the car and tossed him the keys. "You drive."

His eyebrows shot up. "You're kidding."

"I don't kid." She slid into the passenger seat, and Nate had no choice but to take the driver's seat.

His heart rate kicked up as he surveyed the shiny high-tech dashboard and sleek black leather interior. This was hands down the most expensive car he'd ever been in, and as much as he loved his loyal Honda Civic, it would be nice to drive something that didn't have a fifty-fifty chance of dying on him in the middle of the freeway.

Let's test this baby out—niiiiice.

A Mercedes wasn't a Mustang or a Corvette, but the smooth, powerful purr of the engine was still music to his ears.

"Buckle up," Nate said with a grin. "Warning: you might regret giving me the keys when this is all over."

He was careful getting out of the garage and on the side streets, but once they were on the freeway? He put the top down and let it rip.

Holy. Shit.

If Nate weren't so dedicated to acting, he would've seriously considered a career in racing or something similar. The wind on his skin, the ability to control all that speed and power with a tap of his foot and a turn of the wheel...this must be what freedom felt like.

During the ride, he checked on Kris to make sure she was doing okay. He shouldn't have worried—her cheeks were flushed, and her eyes sparkled like she was enjoying their wild ride through LA as much as he was. She'd even put her hair up in a bun—so it wouldn't get messed up by the wind, he assumed.

He found that oddly charming.

By the time they arrived at their destination, Nate's heart pumped with adrenaline and exhilaration sang through his veins. When he cut the engine, the pounding in his ears intensified, prolonging his rush.

"So?" He draped an arm over his headrest and twisted his body to face Kris. "You regret giving me the keys or what?"

"Hardly." Kris smiled, smug as a cat that got the cream. "I enjoy being chauffeured."

Nate's laugh rang loud and clear in the still night air. "You're something else, princess."

"I know." She smoothed her hands primly over her dress. "Good thing you didn't nick the car or I would've had to kill you."

"You could've tried."

Her smile turned feral. "There are ways to kill a man that don't involve brute strength."

Nate narrowed his eyes, examining her words and expression the way a detective might. "Remind me never to get on your bad side."

Another smug expression before she swept her gaze over their surroundings. "This view is amazing."

They'd parked on a hill overlooking the city, and the view was pretty damn spectacular. Not many people knew about the spot, though—it wasn't clearly marked, hence why they were the only ones here. Nate had stumbled upon it by accident one day when he'd gotten lost after a disastrous audition. He'd been so in his head about what he could've, should've done at casting that he'd taken a wrong turn, and *boom*, Lostville.

He had figured it out in the end—*thank you, Google Maps*, even though it liked to glitch and fuck with him sometimes—and snagged himself a secret hideout in the process.

Not bad for what had been a shitty day.

Today was also a shitty day, but he was with Kris, so it wasn't all bad. Her presence...soothed him.

She was the only other person he'd brought here. This was his getaway—the place he went when he needed to escape other people and think. But it felt right, having her beside him as they gazed out over the glittering sprawl of the city.

"A lot of people hate LA," Kris said, propping her elbow on the top of the car door and resting her chin in her hand. "They say it's fake and plastic. Materialistic. Coincidentally, they say that about me too."

She didn't sound too bothered by that fact.

Nate ran his gaze over Kris's profile. The stubborn tilt of her jaw, the sensual curve of her mouth. Illuminated by nothing other than moonlight, she resembled an ethereal goddess come to earth. "That's not true. You're the realest person I've ever met."

He meant it.

Kris was prickly and a little spoiled, but she never pretended to be someone she wasn't. That was more than Nate could say for most people in this town—including himself.

Her lips twisted into a wry smile. "But I'm materialistic."

"We all are in our own ways." Nate ran his hand over the

polished wood of the dashboard. "Money can't buy happiness, but it can buy comfort. Peace of mind. Freedom from the stress of worrying about whether you can pay next month's rent."

The people who said money didn't matter were probably rich hippies who didn't have to worry about it. Money might not be everything, but it meant a helluva lot to those who were struggling to keep their heads above water.

Nate knew that better than anyone.

"You forgot one thing," Kris said.

He cocked a questioning eyebrow.

"Money buys…" She paused, as if searching for the right word. "Loyalty, I guess, in its most fucked-up form. If you buy something, it's yours, and people who are there for money will stay for the money. They're predictable that way, and it's less fickle than relying on love or innate decency. I guess that's why I like LA, because it's all so predictable. No offense," she added.

"None taken. It's true." Nate chuckled. "God, we're cynical."

"But realistic."

"Yeah." Nate sometimes wished he could be as optimistic as Skylar—it seemed like a happier way to live life—but optimism didn't pay the bills. Which reminded him, he needed to check whether their health insurance covered the total cost of Michael's hospital stay and treatment. If not…

I have the money from my arrangement with Kris. That should cover it.

Nate exhaled. He'd wanted to save the money for rent and a small emergency fund, but he supposed unexpected medical expenses fell under "emergency."

"Speaking of realistic…"

"Yeah?"

"Be honest," Kris said. "Is this a make-out spot?"

The question was so unexpected, it took a few seconds for it to sink in. Once it did, Nate barked out a laugh, grateful for the spark of levity.

Plus, the dark hilltop did resemble one of those make-out spots you saw in teen movies.

He flashed Kris a roguish smile. "It could be."

He had no qualms about turning his hideout into a make-out spot. His father's trip to the hospital had killed the lingering arousal from the Ferris-wheel ride, but now that he knew his family was safe, and he was alone with Kris...well, let's just say, Nate Jr. was up and about again. Literally.

"All you have to do is ask," he added.

He wasn't kidding about making her beg. He'd kind of been joking at first, but the more he thought about it, the more he liked the idea of Kris coming to him. He wanted her to kiss him because she wanted to—not because she had to.

Though judging by her reaction on the Ferris wheel, she already wanted to. She just wouldn't admit it.

"Is that so?"

Kris appeared to be thinking it over, which surprised the hell out of him. He'd expected her to put up another fight.

His cock was on board, though. Life vest on, head poking over the railing, all ready to go on this particular version of *The Love Boat*. It was so eager, you'd think she'd offered him a BJ instead of contemplating a simple lip-to-lip. Though there would be nothing "simple" about it once they reached that point.

Chaste pecks were for visiting your great-aunt, not for beautiful girls with a body made for sin and a mouth made for—

"Kiss me," Kris said.

Nate narrowed his eyes, sure he'd heard wrong.

"Kiss me," she repeated. "Right now."

Cool. Detached. Not what he'd had in mind when he said *beg*.

"Just like that?" Suspicion bled into his voice.

"Sure." Kris hitched a shoulder. "Look, it's part of our contract and it's just a kiss. I've kissed plenty of guys before."

Nate's lip curled up into an involuntary snarl.

"You said all I have to do is ask, and I'm asking," she continued. *Damn.* He should've been more specific in his language. "So let's get this over with."

Oh, hell no. She was not going to get away with treating this like a doctor's appointment or a chore on her to-do list.

Just like that, his plans changed.

Kris shifted like she sensed the change in the atmosphere—or spotted the sinister gleam in his eyes.

"Since you asked so nicely"—Nate's teeth flashed white in the darkness—"who am I to say no?"

He leaned forward, enjoying the small hitch in her breath as he got closer...closer...

And then his lips were on hers, and *fuck*, she tasted like rich wine and honey and heaven. Nate hadn't touched alcohol in years, but he was getting drunk off the taste of her. His head swam, his cock and his heart pounding in unison as he devoured her.

Kris was stiff at first, like she didn't quite trust what was happening, but after he nudged her lips open with his tongue and deepened the kiss, she melted into him.

Pure male satisfaction swirled inside him at her unspoken surrender.

Mine.

Nate angled Kris's head back so he could explore her mouth, his fingers gripping her hair so tight she gasped. She didn't flinch at his punishing hold—in fact, her hands clawed his shoulders and her breath came out in shallow, needy pants. She swiped her tongue across his bottom lip, and he growled, tugging her hair harder while his free hand caressed all that smooth, soft skin on her thigh.

But the damn center console kept getting in the way, and he couldn't press his body against hers like he wanted to.

Impatient and aroused beyond belief, Nate broke the kiss, lifted Kris out of her seat, and planted her on his lap so she straddled him. It took some creative maneuvering, but the convertible's open top helped.

"What—" Kris's question or whatever she'd been about to say broke off into a soft moan when he scraped his teeth down the delicate length of her throat.

He had to hand it to her, though—she bounced back quick.

"This is a second kiss." Another moan when he licked the hollow of her throat and gripped her hips, thrusting his throbbing erection against her core. He'd never hated jeans or underwear— the only barriers separating them—more than in that moment. "That wasn't...in the..."

She trailed off, her eyes fluttering closed when Nate swept a hand beneath her dress.

"Technically, we're not kissing," he said in a reasonable, if husky, tone. "We're...getting to know each other."

Kris's eyes opened at that, and her soft laugh shot straight to his cock, which didn't need any additional encouragement. "Is that what this is?"

"Yep." Nate's hand edged toward her core while he kept his eyes on her face, searching for any sign that she wanted him to stop.

Nope. She was all in.

Her nipples were so hard, he could see them poking through the thin material of her bra and dress, and her skin was flushed and hot beneath his.

She was the sexiest thing he'd ever seen.

Nate clenched his jaw, running through baseball rosters and the fucking food pyramid in his mind to keep from coming.

Bread, pasta, fruit—oh, who the hell cares?

"How well do you think we should get to know each other?" he murmured.

Silence—except for their heavy breathing, that was.

"Should we call it a night?" Nate maneuvered her backward, so she no longer sat directly on him. He brushed his fingers over her core, unsurprised but still pleased to discover she was soaking wet. "It's getting late."

Kris's eyes flared with both arousal and warning. "I hadn't noticed," she said through gritted teeth.

"No?" He increased the pressure and smiled at her small whimper. She was getting close—he could tell by the way her breathing changed and the way she ground against his hand. She clutched his arms, her pants growing heavier by the second.

Almost there...just a bit more...

Right before Kris tumbled over the edge, Nate pulled his hand away.

Her eyes flew open again, and he would've laughed at her stunned indignation if his balls hadn't been bluer than a Smurf.

"Long day. I'm tired." Nate feigned a yawn. "Think we *should* call it a night, but thank you for the kiss." The yawn morphed into a mischievous smile. "It was nice getting to know you better."

This time he did laugh as Kris scrambled back in fury—but since she was still straddling him, she hit the car horn, which blared through the still night air at the same time as her curse.

"You *bastard*!"

Nate's smile widened. *"Let's get this over with,"* huh? *Try forgetting our first kiss now*, he thought smugly.

CHAPTER 11

IN HINDSIGHT, PROVOKING KRIS MIGHT NOT HAVE BEEN the best idea. She could hold a *grudge*.

"Don't tell me you're still pissed," Nate said as he trailed her through the Carreras' vast foyer. "It's been..." He paused, calculating the time. "Three days!"

Okay, so it hadn't been that long since he gave her the female version of blue balls, but Kris's cold shoulder treatment turned out to be surprisingly effective at filling him with regret. She hadn't talked to him since Saturday night except for a text this morning telling him to come over after work, since Gloria was going to be home for a Skype meeting with her wedding planner.

Kris slid open the glass door leading to the backyard, where the perfectly landscaped grounds boasted everything from clay tennis courts to an Olympic-size swimming pool to gardens worthy of a royal villa.

"Gloria likes to come out here in the evening to gossip with her friends," she said, ignoring Nate's statement. "So this is where we'll be." She headed toward the giant cabana by the pool, where an older woman with a gray-streaked bun was setting out glasses of lemonade. "Thank you, Risa."

"Of course." The woman inclined her head and smiled at Nate before disappearing into the house.

He sank into the deep green cushions and sighed. Fine. Kris *was* still pissed at him—and so was his cock for interrupting its fun. Nate's right hand had been wholly unsatisfactory all weekend, and he seriously regretted his oh-so-bright idea to leave Kris wanting the other night.

Men are, indeed, idiots.

"Tonight's the night," Kris said, crossing her legs.

Nate choked on a mouthful of lemonade. "Wha...?"

"Make your move on Gloria. It's already mid-July." Kris grimaced. "I saw the bridesmaids' dresses this morning—and before you ask, yes, my dad forced me to be a bridesmaid. The dresses are monstrosities that should be burned before they breed and multiply. There is no way in hell I am wearing one this November, so let's get this shit done."

Right. She was talking about Gloria. He'd thought—

Nate shook his head. "Don't you think it's too soon?"

"It's been weeks." Kris arched an eyebrow. "I thought you were good."

"I *am* good," he growled. He could've gotten Gloria into a compromising position a while ago, but he found himself strangely reluctant to pull the trigger.

Once he finished the job and Kris got her pictures, that was it. No reason for them to see each other anymore, except for her visits to the café.

The thought didn't sit well with him. At all.

But Kris was right—the clock was ticking, and if Nate wanted the rest of the contract money, he'd have to man up. No more pussyfooting around. His family's financial security meant more—*should* mean more—than a girl he barely knew. Kris didn't even live in LA, for God's sake. She was leaving at the end of the summer.

He released a long, low sigh. "Okay. Tonight. You got it."

"Good." Kris didn't look all too pleased either. Then again, she never looked pleased, except for when she was writhing and moaning beneath his mouth—

Aaaaannnnd cut. Nate didn't need to spring a boner before work.

He cleared his throat. "Listen, about the other night—"

"How's your dad?" she interrupted. "Is he out of the hospital yet?"

He paused, recalibrating in light of the abrupt subject change. "Yeah. He's...fine. Doing well, all things considered."

The hospital had released Michael Sunday evening. He'd tried to talk to Nate a few times since he returned home, but Nate had had to run off to work or pick up Skylar each time. He already knew what his father was going to say: *I'm sorry, won't do it again, blah blah blah.* Then days or a week later, if they were lucky, Michael would reunite with his friends Jack Daniel's and Jose Cuervo and the cycle would start all over again.

Been there, done that, bought the T-shirt.

"And Sky? How is she?"

"Good, now that our dad is up and moving again. She's like Teflon."

Thank freakin' God. While Sky had her typical teenage melodramatic moments, she was overall a good kid and way too mature for her age. Nate wasn't sure if he would've been able to handle a moody, misbehaving teenager on top of everything else in his life.

"You're still not going to tell me how you guys met, huh?" Nate finished his lemonade and set the glass on the table.

Kris shrugged. "Like I said, ask—"

"My sister. Yeah, yeah." Part of him was suspicious over all the secrecy—if it'd been an innocent meeting, why was Kris so close-lipped about it? But he doubted Kris was dealing drugs to his baby sis or involved in anything dangerous. That would be out of character for both of them. Maybe they met at a nightclub? Skylar was underage, but fake IDs abounded in LA.

That wouldn't be the end of the world, though Nate blanched at the thought of his sister drinking and partying it up with the Hollywood crowd. He trusted her; he didn't trust the mother-fuckers in this town.

He made a mental note to grill Skylar about it the next time he saw her.

Kris reached over and grabbed his hand, a soft, sweet expression taking over her face. "Are you sure you won't be able to make it? Think of how romantic a weekend getaway would be."

What?

Confusion flitted through Nate at her sudden about-face and nonsensical words...until he smelled the heavy flowery scent drifting on the breeze.

Gloria was here.

Without turning his head, Nate smiled and squeezed Kris's hand. "I wish I could, babe, but I have to work. I'll make it up to you after you get back, I promise."

He had no clue what she had cooked up, but based on her lie, she was leaving him wide open to schedule a "tryst" with Gloria this weekend without him having to make up an excuse about why he wasn't with Kris.

Smart.

"Where are you goin', darlin'?" Gloria's syrupy drawl invaded the cabana and stuck to Nate's skin like a thick gooey film.

Nate supposed some guys went for that sweet Southern sexpot thing, but Gloria overdid it to the point of cringe.

"I was goin' to have you try on your bridesmaid dress." The redhead came into view, wearing a white crochet halter top and tiny shorts. "I think magenta is *just* your color."

"Of course you do," Kris said, equally sweet. "Your taste always *did* run toward the questionable end of the spectrum. As much as I would love to try on my dress—which showcases your aptitude for style *so* well—I'm afraid I've already booked a spa weekend in Ojai."

"Really?" Gloria pushed her sunglasses on top of her head. "Which spa?"

"Seven Oaks," Kris replied without missing a beat.

The other woman's eyes narrowed. "Seven Oaks is booked out for the next year."

Kris smiled. "The Carrera name opens a lot of doors. But you wouldn't know that, so don't feel too bad."

Her dig at Gloria's engaged-but-still-not-Mrs.-Carrera-yet status hit its mark. The redhead's cheeks flushed, and her body vibrated with anger.

"Oops." Kris glanced at her phone. "Friend emergency calling—or texting, in this case. Seems like one of my sorority sisters is having major boy problems. I'm going to call her before she does anything crazy. She's a bit melodramatic." She stood and kissed Nate on the cheek. "I'll be right back."

She left without another glance at Gloria, who took Kris's seat and eyed Nate the way one would eye a prime slab of meat at the butcher's.

"So," she purred. "Did I hear wrong, or will you not be accompanyin' our dear Kris to Ojai this weekend?"

Nate slouched against the cushions and draped his arms over the back of the couch in a way that he knew exuded casual confidence, sex appeal, and a nonchalant detachment that drove women crazy.

"You heard right." His drawl matched hers. "I have work, and spas aren't my thing."

Gloria leaned forward, giving him an all-access view of her generous cleavage.

"What is your thing?" The sexual innuendo dripped like honey.

Objectively, Gloria was banging. The red hair, green eyes, and *insane* body all added up to one firecracker-hot package. Nate should've been all over it, but his current tastes were stuck in the petite, dark-haired, sharp-tongued category, and he was as attracted to Gloria as he was the half-empty pitcher of lemonade on the table.

Maybe less because that lemonade was amazing.

Still, he had a job to do, and he was going to do it damn well.

"How can I choose one?" Nate hitched a shoulder up. "The Lakers, Ferraris, *Die Hard*...redheads."

Not his most subtle moment, but screw subtle. The clock was ticking.

Besides, judging by the smile on Gloria's face and the gleam in her eyes, it worked.

"Kris isn't a redhead," she murmured.

"Kris is great." A purposeful, perfectly timed pause. "But no, she's not."

A stab of guilt pierced Nate's stomach at the flirty banter. He and Kris weren't dating for real, but it still felt like a betrayal.

"And she's out of town this week..." Gloria allowed the suggestion to linger, unspoken, in the air.

"Yes, she is." Nate allowed his eyes to go heavy-lidded. "I'll need a way to pass the time. Any suggestions?"

Slimy. As. Fuck. But a guy's gotta do what a guy's gotta do, especially when he was paid to do it.

Gloria examined him in silence, like she was debating whether to take this next step. She'd flirted shamelessly with Nate in the past few weeks and had even offered him a BJ once—which he got out of thanks to a perfectly timed interruption by Kris—but this was the first time he'd reciprocated in such an obvious manner.

Come on, Nate thought. *You know you want to. Just say it...*

Based on what Kris told him, Gloria hadn't seen her fiancé—Kris's father—in months. Assuming she wasn't already banging someone on the side, she had to be crawling out of her skin with sexual frustration. Women who looked like her were used to getting some on a regular basis, and self-pleasure only went so far, as Nate knew firsthand (pun not intended).

Besides, Kris's dad had to be, what, in his forties? Fifties? Probably not stud material, unless he was George Clooney 2.0. Nate no longer had any qualms about shutting their engagement down either, since it was clear Gloria "loved" her soon-to-be husband the way she loved her fancy car—i.e., it was a useful status symbol that kept her comfortable and brought her places she wouldn't have been able to reach otherwise (in Kris's father's case, it was social and financial rather than a physical destination). No heartfelt, for-better-or-worse shit. Otherwise, Gloria wouldn't be on the verge of fucking her future stepdaughter's fake-but-she-didn't-know-that boyfriend.

To prod her along, Nate stretched his arms over his head, his shirt lifting to reveal a flash of his tanned tight six-pack.

Gloria's eyes dropped to take in the view—and stayed there.

"I hear the restaurant at the Del Mar Hotel is good," she said. "I was plannin' to make dinner reservations there myself...but I don't mind bringin' a plus one if you're up for it."

"Count me in," Nate said easily. "Nothing gets me going like a good feast."

The redhead smirked at his double entendre. "Good to know.

There won't be any Ferraris there…" Her voice dropped to a low purr. "But I'm sure we can find something else for you to ride."

Nate's grin widened.

Gotcha.

"Kris, dear, can you file this for me?" Bobbi Rayden breezed into the office, polished and sophisticated in a sleek white suit and bun. A large black Chanel bag hung on one bony shoulder, and she carried a folder in one hand and a large Starbucks coffee in the other.

Grande iced sugar-free vanilla latte with soy milk, natch. She ordered the same thing every day.

Bobbi tossed the folder on Kris's desk, and a few press clippings slid out.

Kris pressed her lips together and forced herself not to lose her shit. Bobbi was a family friend and had done her father a favor by granting Kris a coveted summer assistant position, but Kris did not appreciate being treated like a paper jockey.

Assisting a famous Hollywood publicist *sounded* exciting, but her day-to-day was a whole lot of media monitoring and epic boredom. Scouring the internet for YouTube drama videos and snarky blog posts of Bobbi's worst-behaving clients was not her idea of a good time. Who cared about pop-star train-wreck Riley K.'s latest boyfriend? Kris had met Riley—the girl was as interesting as dish soap, and her slacker boyfriends were worse.

"Sure," Kris said through gritted teeth.

Bobbi's phone rang—no doubt another crisis, like one of her clients taking a swing at the paparazzi—and she was off and running without a second glance in Kris's direction.

Kris took the press clippings into the copy room and started the tedious task of scanning each article before she organized them in Bobbi's extensive digital collection.

The whir of the machine filled the air. Kris tapped her fingers on the table, bored beyond belief. She'd much rather plan MentHer's summer gala than sit in an overly air-conditioned office, pretending she gave a shit about coddling celebrities.

Kris had nothing against celebrities—she just didn't want to work for them. She was Kris Carrera, for chrissakes. When she turned twenty-three, she was going to inherit a trust fund that would make most of these stars' net worths look like pennies.

She slipped another press clipping onto the glass. Two more hours until she could leave and work on the MentHer gala. She enjoyed event planning, and she liked the mentees a helluva lot more than she liked the newest teen idol.

Kris's phone buzzed with an incoming text.

Nate: What are you doing tonight?

Her heart flipped. It was so sudden and unexpected, she actually stumbled and nearly twisted her ankle in her Louboutins.

What the hell?

She hoped she wasn't having a heart attack. She was too young and beautiful to die.

Kris stared at Nate's message. No more flips, but the stupid organ in her chest pounded like she'd just finished a marathon.

She liked it better when she was pissed at him, like she'd been... Wow, had that only been four days ago? The Ferris wheel, the hospital, their kiss—it all felt like a lifetime ago. And yet, her skin flushed and her blood pounded at the memory of his lips and hands on her like they were making out right now on top of the copier.

Get it together.

Kris sucked in a deep breath and, after a minute of deliberation, typed a terse reply.

Kris: Party planning.
Nate: Victory party?

She assumed he meant victory over Gloria. She couldn't believe he'd closed a hotel date with the Stepmonster. Well, she could, but she'd been planning it for so long, it seemed surreal.

It had gone a long way toward dousing her anger over his dick move on Saturday.

Kris: No…but I like the way you think.

Kris mentally added *plan victory celebration* to her to-do list.

Nate: Any chance you're free for another victory party tonight?
Nate: I got a new role. For Oscar Bravo's latest movie. It's a small part, but it's with Oscar freaking Bravo. Figured that's worthy of dinner.

A grin spread across Kris's face as pride fizzled in her chest. When was the last time she'd been this excited over someone else's accomplishments? Probably never.

Kris: Are you asking me on a date?
Nate: Do you want it to be a date?

The fluorescent lights hummed overhead, and Kris's heart did another flip. She'd always imagined she would die in her bed, dressed in her most glamorous Oscar de la Renta gown and smelling of Chanel perfume. Now, she was sure she was going to die in this tiny beige room, surrounded by reams of printer paper and finicky office equipment.

She had no other explanation for why her heart was acting up.

But until death claimed her, Kris had to respond to Nate's question.

Did she want to go on a date with him? Logic said she shouldn't. She'd hired him to seduce her father's fiancée, and they were from two different worlds. Mars and Venus. Saturn and Jupiter. Mercury and Pluto (she didn't care what anyone said—Pluto was a planet).

Kris: I can spare a few hours.
Kris: Since you're starring opposite Oscar freaking Bravo and all.

Question evaded. It was the coward's way out, but she'd never claimed to be a brave hero.

There was a long pause, longer than the one Kris had taken to answer, before Nate replied.

Nate: "Starring" might be an overstatement, but I'll take it. Meet me at Marina del Rey, 7pm?
Kris: Sounds good.

She stared at the screen for a while longer before pocketing her phone. Her stomach was all twisted up in knots. If she didn't know better, she'd say she was nervous.

It's not a date. It's a celebratory dinner.

"Kris!" Bobbi's voice cut across the office and scratched against the walls like nails on chalkboard. "Are you finished with the filing? I want to see all press mentions of Riley K. in the past twenty-four hours. ASAP."

Shit. Kris had forgotten about the press clippings.

"Almost done!" She injected her voice with enough sugar to

give everyone in a fifty-foot radius cavities. Kris picked out the Riley K. articles and scanned them first, cursing Bobbi, her father, and Gloria under her breath.

She should've chosen a more exciting summer job—like scraping gum off the sidewalk. At least then, she could've worked on her tan.

Kris glanced at the clock. An hour and a half until the end of the workday. A lot of other assistants stayed late, but she wasn't trying to climb up the company ranks or impress Bobbi. She had zero compunction about leaving at 5:00 p.m. sharp.

It was bullshit anyway, this whole stay-after-hours-to-prove-your-commitment work ethic. If management wanted people to stay later, they should adjust salaries and working hours accordingly. Don't even get Kris started on the unpaid internships, though thankfully, she'd never had to take one. Like hello, people should be paid for their work? Not to mention, they had lives outside of the office.

If anyone tried to shaft her out of her dues, she'd shove a Jimmy Choo up their stingy ass.

Kris fed the last article into the scanner.

Ninety minutes.

The only thing that got her through the rest of the day was the prospect of dinner with Nate.

CHAPTER 12

"WHAT IS THIS?" KRIS STARED AT THE STRUCTURE IN front of her.

Nate grinned at her from the deck, looking ridiculously handsome with his windswept brown hair and green T-shirt that matched the color of his eyes. He was a yacht club ad come to life. "It's a boat."

"Thank you, Captain Obvious."

"Hey, you asked."

"It was a rhetorical question and you know it." Kris pushed a lock of hair out of her face. It was windy as hell by the water, and her carefully coiffed waves were unraveling faster than the seams of a cheap sweater. "I thought we were getting dinner."

"We are. On here." Nate held out his hand. "C'mon, princess. Don't tell me you've never been on a boat before."

"Of course I have," Kris sniffed. She took Nate's hand, the sensation of his rough, warm skin on hers sending a pleasant shock through her system. "Is it yours?"

"I wish. Nah, it belongs to an old sailing buddy of mine. He let me borrow it for the night."

Kris stepped onto the boat. It swayed gently beneath her, and she was glad she wore her Roger Vivier suede flats tonight instead of heels. "I didn't know you sailed."

"I used to. There's nothing like the peace and freedom you feel on the water..." Nate's voice trailed off before he cleared his throat. "I don't have time for it anymore but figured tonight is a special occasion, so why the hell not?"

He took Kris on a quick tour of the boat. There wasn't much to see beyond the deck and a tiny cabin with a V-berth bed, bathroom, kitchenette, two stripe-cushioned benches, and an adjustable table. It was the smallest boat she'd ever seen.

"It's nice," she said, following Nate back up to the deck.

His laughter rumbled in the salty sea air. "You say *nice* the way a vegan would say a steak is *nice*."

Kris's mouth twitched. "I'm serious. It's not a yacht, but it's cozy."

"You prefer this to a yacht?" Nate sounded skeptical as he steered the boat out of its slip.

"*Prefer* is too strong a word, but I don't hate it. The boat, I mean."

He flashed a quick smile. "High compliment, coming from you."

"It is," she said solemnly.

Nate laughed again, and this time Kris joined him.

She couldn't keep up with her feelings toward him. They flipped constantly from lust to irritation to...whatever. She wasn't going to think about it. It didn't matter. It wasn't like she was going to see Nate again after this weekend. Once his job was done, it was done.

A sudden bout of nausea hit her, and she wasn't entirely sure it was from the rocking motion of the waves.

"Also, I didn't mention this earlier, but..." Nate tapped his fingers on the steering wheel. "I also wanted to apologize for Saturday. For..."

"Leaving me high and dry on the verge of orgasm like a total asshole?"

He broke into a coughing fit, his face so red it could've doubled as a stop sign. "Uh, yeah."

"No worries." Kris smiled sweetly. "Too bad you stopped before I could live out the fantasies I had while I got myself off later that night. Your loss."

Another coughing fit, accompanied by a far more interesting development below Nate's belt. Either he had a gun in his pocket, or he was doing some fantasizing of his own.

Payback's a bitch.

Kris conveniently left out the fact that Nate had starred in every one of her fantasies and that she'd come harder to mental images of him than she had during any of her actual sexual encounters.

"Don't suppose you can share some of those fantasies with me? Or better yet, reenact the whole shebang." Nate paused. "Get it? *She-bang.*"

She burst into laughter. "Thank God you're not a stand-up comedian."

"Is that a yes?"

"Focus on the boat," she said serenely. "Last thing we need is to get lost in the middle of the Pacific."

"We're not going *that* far out," Nate grumbled, but he did as she said and refocused on steering the boat.

They settled into a companionable silence as he navigated them farther into the open waters. The sea breeze brushed over them like a lover's caress, soft and full of promise. Kris watched as the lights of the marina grew smaller and smaller until they were nothing more than diamond pinpricks in the distance. Meanwhile, the sun descended beneath the horizon to an explosion of cotton-candy pinks and soft purples whose hues deepened with each passing minute.

Kris could see other boats bobbing in the water, but they were so far away, they might as well be in another world.

It was just her, Nate, the sky, and the sea.

They stopped at some point between land and infinity. The motor fell silent and gave way to the gentle whoosh of the waves lapping against the sides of the boat.

"I'll be right back." Nate disappeared into the cabin and returned with a woven picnic basket. "Dinner," he explained. He opened the basket and took out two cans of ginger ale, a bottle of wine, cheese and crackers, grapes, and roast beef sandwiches. "It's not anything fancy, but this is more comfortable than dressing up for some stuffy restaurant."

"You don't have to justify it. It's your big day. You can celebrate however you want." Kris inhaled a lungful of fresh sea air. "Besides, this is nice. I love being by the water. It calms me, helps me think and...process, I guess."

After a minute or so, she felt a prickling heat on her face, and she turned to see Nate staring at her with a strange smile.

"What? Do I have something on my face?"

"I like you like this." Nate laid on his side and propped himself up on his forearm, looking for all the world like a movie star lounging on a yacht.

Kris arched a questioning eyebrow.

"Relaxed," he clarified. "Yourself. Without the armor."

"I don't have armor." She sat next to him and unwrapped a sandwich.

"The Chanel and Prada and whatnot. That's armor."

"No, that's clothing. High-quality, expensive clothing."

He appeared undeterred by her sharp tone. "You're rich. We both know that. But who are you without the money?"

"Still me, only poor." Kris took a small bite of bread, roast beef, cheese, and condiment. *Oh, wow.* Who knew a simple sandwich could taste so good? "Can we talk about something else? This is the most depressing celebratory dinner I've ever been to."

"You said I could celebrate however I want. Maybe I want to get to know you better." Nate's mouth quirked up. "By talking. Not...by what we did a few days ago."

Kris zeroed in on his straining erection. "Sure, Jan."

"Don't worry about Nate Jr. He'll behave."

She almost spit out her food, which was so not attractive. Red stained her cheeks as she wiped her mouth with a paper napkin. "You are something else. You know that?"

"Yep." Nate stretched lazily before popping open one of the ginger ales. "This is one of our last nights together. Figured we should, you know, make the most of it."

Emotion swelled in Kris's throat, and her sandwich suddenly tasted like cardboard. Was she *sad* about her contract with Nate ending? She didn't even like the guy.

Well, fine, she liked the way he looked. He made her laugh. He was smart and talented and hardworking. Plus, he was an amazing kisser and her heart went all wonky around him...

Double fuck.

"I don't know," Kris blurted, more out of a desire to take her mind off her dangerous thoughts than to answer Nate's question about who she was beneath the gloss and glamour. "I am who I am. An heiress. It's shaped my childhood, my *life*. Every relationship and experience I've had has been colored by money. To ask who I am without it would be me asking you who you are without..."

"My incredible good looks and charm?" he suggested.

"Don't forget your modesty."

"I was going to include that too, but I don't like to brag."

Nate's mouth tilted up at her laugh. "You want to know what I think?"

"No."

He ignored her and continued. "I think, beneath all the designer clothes and spoiled princess routine, you're a good person. You care about people—maybe not everyone but the ones you allow close to you. You could snap at strangers all you want, but the people you love? They know you'll burn the fucking city down for them. Skylar thinks the world of you, and for a seventeen-year-old, she's an excellent judge of character. I've noticed it too, even in the way you're handling this whole Gloria thing. I mean, the plan is kinda twisted, and it's obvious you two can't stand each other, but at the end of the day, you're doing this for your dad, even though you only see him a few weeks out of the year. If Gloria truly loved him and wasn't using him for his money?" Nate shrugged. "You would've gone through the wedding, ugly dresses and all."

Kris's heartbeat was a deafening staccato in her ears. A burning sensation blossomed behind her eyes, tightening her skin, and she couldn't seem to draw enough oxygen into her lungs despite all the fresh air around them.

"Admit it," Nate murmured. "You're a good person, but you don't want anyone to know. You hide behind your armor because you're afraid of getting hurt—"

"Stop it," Kris said roughly. "I didn't sign up for a therapy session. And why the *hell* are we on a boat in the middle of nowhere? I want to go back to the marina. Now."

"No."

Her jaw dropped. "Excuse me? This is kidnapping. You're holding me here against my will."

Silence. Nate merely stared at her with those piercing green eyes of his, and dammit, there went that burning sensation behind her eyes again.

Kris was not one for sharing feelings. All that touchy-feely, mushy-gushy stuff gave her hives. But out here, in the middle of the ocean with only Nate and the moon as witnesses, she felt stripped. Laid bare.

Maybe it was the deafening silence or the fact that she wouldn't see Nate again after this week. Or maybe it was because he lost his mother too, albeit in a different way, and she'd already seen him broken down and vulnerable after his father's hospitalization last week. They might be from different worlds, but they were kindred spirits in a way.

Whatever it was, Kris spoke up—and she didn't stop speaking until she'd gotten everything that had weighed on her for over two decades off her chest.

"I told you my mom left when I was two," she said, uncorking the wine and pouring herself a glass so she had something to do with her hands. "I still had my dad, technically, but he was never around. He bought me everything I wanted, but we never spent much time together. He was always busy at the office or traveling for business. There were tons of hired staff, but I was just a job to them. The person who came closest to being my family was our old housekeeper, Rosa. She basically raised me, cooked the most amazing meals, was there to soothe me when I was upset. Then she died of a heart attack when I was thirteen and I was on my own." Kris paused, gathering her thoughts. "The only thing I had was money. And look, don't get me wrong. I love money. I love nice cars and fancy restaurants and designer clothes. So I'm not saying I hate those things and use them to cover up…anything. But they've become an intrinsic part of who I am because they're the only things I've ever had that were mine. Once I bought them, they stayed. They're a lot more loyal than people in that way.

"But the way I grew up, having my mom abandon me like that…" Damn, there went a tear. Kris brushed it away angrily.

"I don't like letting people get too close. Even my closest friends who know me best don't *know* me. When I was a baby, I couldn't help attaching to my mom. It was biological. And her walking away? It's something that'll stay with me forever. But now that I'm older, I can control who I let in, and I will never, ever let anyone come close enough to hurt me when they walk away again."

"Not everyone walks away," Nate said softly.

"Don't be ridiculous. Everyone walks away eventually."

Before she could brush away yet another tear, Nate did it for her, his thumb burning her skin as he caressed her damp cheeks. "I wouldn't."

Kris wasn't sure if the dizzying sensation came from the waves or the tumult that erupted in her head at those two words. "What are you talking about?"

Nate paused, like he wanted each word to be perfect before he spoke them. "If all things go according to plan, our contract is up Saturday, but that doesn't mean we have to stop seeing each other. I know." He held up a hand when she opened her mouth to protest. "You're leaving LA at the end of the summer. That's in a little over a month. Until then...why can't we enjoy each other's company? I know you're attracted to me. I'm sure as hell attracted to you. We have fun together, and neither of us will be the one walking away because we have a set deadline. It'll be a mutual thing. Clean, easy. No hard feelings."

Kris pressed a finger to her temple, trying to sort through her jumbled thoughts. "You're saying you want to be friends with benefits?"

"I'm saying I don't want this week to be the last week I see or speak to you."

She released a pent-up breath. Her emotions were all over the place tonight, ping-ponging from amusement to sadness and hurt to whatever the hell she was feeling right now. Excitement? Worry? Panic?

Nate's proposal sounded good on paper, but he'd already torn down more barriers around her heart in a few weeks than people she'd known for years had. Kris was terrified of what would happen once their so-called deadline came to pass. Long-distance relationships didn't work—everyone knew that—and... God, what was she doing, thinking about a relationship? More proof she should shut down Nate's suggestion and never speak of it again.

On the other hand, she agreed with him. She didn't want their quasi-friendship or whatever they had to end once their contract was over either. Another month of Nate Reynolds sounded pretty fantastic.

And, well, Kris had always been a selfish, short-term kind of gal. "Okay."

Nate's eyebrows popped up. "Okay?"

"Okay, let's continue seeing each other and...do whatever after the Gloria thing is over, with two rules: it ends the day I leave LA and we don't put a label on it. We just...go with the flow."

A slow, sexy grin spread across his face. "I can work with that."

"Great." Kris held out her hand. "It's a deal."

"No handshake." Nate closed the distance between them, the moonlight casting a soft glow on the chiseled planes of his face. "We seal the deal the old-fashioned way."

Her heart rate picked up. "How's that?"

He responded with a kiss. A soft brush of his lips that held all sorts of promises and sent tingles racing down her spine.

"Done," he whispered, so close his lips brushed hers when he spoke. "Now it's a deal."

Kris stared at Nate, so beautiful and perfect beneath the stars, he seemed unreal, and she was suddenly aware that every second ticking by brought them closer to their deadline.

When was the last time she'd met a man she connected with so much on every level? She wasn't in love with him, but she liked him. A lot. Considering she despised or at least disdained most of the people she came across, that was no small deal.

"Not yet," she said. "Remember how you apologized earlier for being a dick last week?"

Wariness took over his features. "Yeah..."

"How about you make it up to me—and really seal the deal—by finishing what you started?"

The wariness melted into wicked delight, and before she knew it, he'd pinned her beneath his powerful body and her mouth had gone Sahara-dry. The thick blanket he'd laid down for their boat picnic cushioned her from the hard wood of the deck floor, but that was nothing compared to the steel-like erection pressing against her thigh.

She swallowed hard, and Nate's eyes tracked the movement of her throat with fascination.

"You never told me what your fantasies were earlier," he said, his voice low and dark with lust. "So we're gonna start with mine. First." Kris gasped when he reached underneath her dress and caressed her through her soaking wet panties. "I'm going to fuck your pussy with my tongue until you come all over my face. Then I'm going to flip you onto all fours and pound you until people in the fucking marina can hear you scream. And after that? You're going to take the reins, princess, and ride me until you can't come anymore."

Kris had never been big on dirty talk, but hearing those words come out of Nate's mouth? Orgasm incoming. She was going to fall apart in a minute, maybe less.

"Please," she whimpered, arching her hips while Nate pushed her dress up around her waist. "Do it. *Now*."

He chuckled, sliding her panties down her legs in an agonizingly slow fashion. "Which 'it' are you talking about? The tongue fucking, pounding, or riding?"

"Any. All. I don't care." She rolled her hips again, desperate for friction. "Just do—oh God!"

Kris's not-exactly-holy missive to the Lord blended with a shout/moan/whatever as Nate placed his mouth on her sex and did things with his tongue that had her seeing stars, both literal—they were still on the boat deck, bared to the open air—and figurative. As he promised, she came hard after...seconds? Minutes? An eternity?

It didn't matter. All that mattered were the blinding waves of pleasure crashing over her, so intense she might have levitated out of her body.

Kris was still on the fringes of her high when Nate flipped her over on all fours and prowled up, covering her body with his.

"Comfortable?" he murmured, reaching around to pinch one of her nipples. Between her arousal and the soft chill of the sea air, they were rock-hard and sensitive to the touch.

She gasped and bucked back against him. "Not...the word... I'd use," she managed, her mind hazy from one of the best orgasms of her life.

Nate chuckled. "I meant the deck. We can move this downstairs if the blanket isn't enough of a cushion."

Um, no. Kris would scream if she had to wait another second for round two. Besides, even though there were no other boats around, there was something so erotic about having sex out in the open like this. The salty breeze was another caress, and the gentle rocking of the boat? Better than a waterbed.

"What happened to pounding me until people in the marina can hear me scream?" she taunted.

She knew the challenge would get Nate's blood roaring, and he'd take her the way they both wanted him to—hard, wild, no-holds-barred.

She smiled when a low growl emitted from his throat. He moved back, and she heard the unmistakable zip of his jeans being undone.

Kris couldn't resist—she twisted her head around and watched with hooded eyes as he shed his clothes, revealing a body sculpted with glorious muscles. Broad shoulders, powerful thighs, and washboard abs that narrowed into a V pointing directly at a long thick erection that had her mouth watering like she hadn't eaten in days.

As he sheathed himself in a condom from his wallet, she faced forward again and arched her back, eager for round two to start.

A minute passed. Two.

When nothing happened, she frowned and turned again. Nate remained in the same position he'd been in when he'd undressed, his eyes soaking her in with enough heat to turn the surrounding air into a furnace.

"What are you doing?"

His lips curved into a small smile. "Enjoying the view. You look so beautiful on your hands and knees, waiting for me to fuck you."

A shiver of delight rolled down Kris's spine. She was starting to *love* dirty talk.

"And how long are you going to keep me waiting?" she breathed, her voice husky with need.

Nate cupped the curve of her bare ass with his palm, his thumb rubbing circles on her heated flesh. "This is how you want me to take you for the first time?" he growled. "There aren't any rose petals and champagne around, princess."

"If I wanted rose petals and champagne, we wouldn't be in this position." A pause. "Literally."

He chuckled and finally moved closer. He gathered her hair in his fist and moved it to the side so he could nip at her neck while his other hand played with her nipples. His stubble rasped against her skin, and she shivered from the delicious sensation.

Kris felt like prey being toyed with by a predator before the kill, and another rush of moisture spiraled down to her core. She was so rarely helpless and hated being vulnerable. But being at another's mercy during sex? Huge fucking turn-on.

"You had your chance," Nate said.

Before she could say anything else or even take another breath, he slammed into her with such force, her body slid forward along the deck, dragging the blanket with her. All the breath whooshed out of her lungs and every thought emptied from her mind. The only thing Kris could focus on was the pleasure consuming her as reality blurred into a series of blissful climaxes. Nate kept one fist in her hair and one hand around her throat while he fucked her with deep, forceful strokes. She realized dimly that the cries filling the air were her own, and yeah, people back at the marina probably *could* hear her.

She couldn't care less.

After what seemed like both the blink of an eye and forever, Nate found his own release and came with a roar, his hips continuing to pump until he was completely spent.

Kris collapsed on the blanket, her skin slick with sweat and her nerves buzzing with the aftershocks from her lost-track-of-how-many orgasms.

Nate released her and sank onto the ground next to her, his breath ragged.

"Fuck," they said at the same time.

They eyed each other and dissolved into simultaneous laughter.

"That was..." Kris blanked, most of her brain functions still offline after the sex they'd just had.

"Yep." Nate wasn't winning any awards for articulation tonight either.

They lay there in silence until their breathing returned to normal and Kris's head cleared. She stared up at the sky, tracking the blinking light of an airplane as it transported its passengers to some far-off location. It reminded her of what Nate said about not liking to fly.

"Do you ever think about leaving LA?" she asked. "Moving somewhere else? Or just, I don't know, taking some time to travel?"

A long, long silence. So long Kris thought he'd fallen asleep and hadn't heard her.

But no, Nate's eyes were wide-open and fixed on the heavens as hers had been.

"Nah," he finally said. "Not moving. LA has its ups and downs, and shit, sometimes there are a helluva lotta downs. But it's my city. My home. I love it, no matter how fucked up it is. Plus, there's no better place for a wannabe actor to crash and burn." His tone was self-deprecating.

"Hardly crash and burn. You got the Oscar Bravo movie role," she pointed out. "Speaking of which, congratulations." She glanced at their largely untouched dinner. "Though we kind of skipped the meal portion of the evening."

Nate flashed a wolfish grin. "I didn't."

Her cheeks stained pink at the memory of his head buried between her legs, and his grin widened.

Great. Now she was blushing like a schoolgirl. Then again, considering the orgasms he'd given her, she couldn't be all that upset.

"I thought about studying abroad in college," he said after a while. "But then my mom died, I dropped out, and yeah, the rest is history. As for traveling...not really in the cards, given where my family's at."

Of course. Kris felt foolish for asking. She hoped the money from their deal could help Nate's family. Not because she considered them a charity case, but because they were good people—at least, she knew Nate and Skylar were—and deserved a break. Plus, it wasn't like she'd given Nate the money as a handout; he'd earned it. He was a talented actor, and he'd spent weeks on the Gloria scheme when he could've used that time to hang out with his friends or audition.

Speaking of Gloria...

"What are your plans for Saturday?" she asked casually. She didn't actually have a spa weekend in Ojai planned; she was just going to stay at the Beverly Hills Hotel and gorge on room service while Nate did his thing.

The only question was what that "thing" entailed.

Nate shot her quizzical look.

"With Gloria. Are you...?" She trailed off, already regretting bringing the subject up.

"Am I actually going to sleep with her?"

Her muscles tightened, erasing the last vestiges of her postcoital contentment. "Yeah."

"Hell no."

Just like that, Kris relaxed again, and she cursed herself for allowing a freakin' guy to control her emotions like that. That had never been her. She'd never gone gaga over a member of the opposite sex, certainly not to the point where what they said and did affected her state of mind.

But Nate was in his own category, and not just when it came to sex.

"I'm not attracted to her like that," he said. "I mean, yeah, she's hot—"

Kris frowned.

"—but she's not my type. This is a job." Nate cleared his

throat. "And I know how much it means to you. So I'm going to do what I need to do for your PI to snap some good pics, and that's it. What happened between us just now?" He gestured between Kris and himself. "Not gonna happen with her."

"Right." Relief blossomed in Kris's stomach, the reason for which she studiously ignored. "Okay."

"Jealous?" Nate drawled.

"You wish."

"Maybe."

She turned her head so fast, she almost got whiplash. Nate wore a sneaky grin, but his eyes were dead serious.

"You know," Kris said slowly, "we never finished sealing the deal. I believe there was a third part to it?"

You're going to take the reins, princess, and ride me until you can't come anymore.

Heat flared in Nate's eyes, and it didn't take long before Kris was straddling him and taking them to the heights of ecstasy once more. *Now* she understood all the hubbub about sex. Her past encounters had been fine, but she'd never had the toe-curling, explosive orgasms you always heard about in romance novels or movies.

But with Nate? Holy shit.

By the time they returned to the marina, it was close to midnight and Kris was walking around in a daze. She was so relaxed, she didn't even snap at the two frat-tastic bros who wolf-whistled at her on her way to the parking lot. Nate's snarl, however, put them in place, and Dumb and Dumber held up placating hands before returning to their Natty Lights or whatever they were drinking.

Nate wrapped a possessive arm around Kris's waist and shielded her with his body until they reached her car.

"Let's reconvene Friday," she said, trying to refocus on the looming milestone ahead. *Just a few more days until Gloria's out of our lives forever.* "Go over final details."

"Sounds good," Nate said lazily. "Drive safe. Text me when you're home."

He kissed her on the cheek good night, and Kris was off, speeding toward Beverly Hills while a part of her remained in the marina, reliving the past few hours over and over again.

When she arrived home, she was surprised to see the lights blazing. Gloria was usually asleep by now.

Kris parked in the garage and entered the foyer, blinking rapidly until her eyes adjusted to the bright lights. Her muscles ached from all the...exertion earlier that night, and she looked forward to a few hours of deep sleep before she had to go into work.

She stretched and walked across the cool tiled marble, already envisioning herself in her silk—

"Kris!" a deep, familiar voice boomed through the entrance hall, followed by the quick strides of a dark-haired man in a custom-tailored Hugo Boss suit.

Kris stopped dead in her tracks. Her jaw unhinged, and shock unfurled in her stomach.

No. *It can't be.*

He shouldn't be here. He *couldn't* be here. Not yet.

But he was.

"Daddy?"

CHAPTER 13

NATE HAD MANAGED TO AVOID HIS FATHER FOR A week, but things came to a head the night after his boat date with Kris. Skylar was out with friends, and Nate had stayed home to run lines for both the Oscar Bravo film and a few upcoming auditions.

He was reheating a leftover casserole in the microwave when Michael shuffled into the kitchen, wearing plaid pajama pants and a white NACHO AVERAGE DAD T-shirt that Skylar had gifted him as a joke for Father's Day (in addition to treating him to dinner at his favorite Mexican restaurant).

Nate stiffened. "I thought you were sleeping."

"I woke up." Michael shrugged, his voice raspier than usual. He'd kept to himself since his trip to the hospital, only venturing out of his room for food, but his eyes were sharp and intelligent as he surveyed his son.

Was he *sober*?

Nate hadn't seen his father hit the bottle in, what, five, six days? But that didn't mean shit. It was only a matter of time before alcoholics backslid, and he'd never been able to convince his father to quit and join AA. Hell, Michael wouldn't even admit he had a problem, much less spill his guts to Alcoholics Anonymous.

"Great." The microwave beeped, the sound loud and jarring in the tiny kitchen. Nate didn't bother waiting before he yanked open the door and pulled out the steaming-hot casserole. He winced when the plate burned his fingertips.

Fuck. He quickly dropped it onto the counter and ran his hand under a stream of cold water, eager for something to do other than stare at his father and wonder how the vibrant, doting dad from his childhood had ended up like this.

He understood Michael was hurting from his wife's death. Of course he did. Michael's wife was also Nate's *mom*, and Nate felt her absence in every inch of his soul. But if he, an eighteen-year-old at the time she passed, could pull his shit together, why hadn't his father? Michael was older and supposed to be wiser. He should've stepped up and pulled his family through the darkest time of their lives.

Instead, he'd abdicated all responsibility and left his teenage son to pick up the pieces.

"Nate." Michael shifted awkwardly from foot to foot. "We should talk."

"About what?" Nate couldn't wait to get to his room, where he could lose himself in his scripts and count down the days until he saw Kris again. He wasn't sure where their relationship stood exactly, but he'd much rather figure that out than talk to his father, even if he and Kris had agreed not to put a label on things.

"About, ah, last week."

"You'll have to be more specific." Nate wiped his hands on a dish towel and faced the elder Reynolds, his jaw flexing. "By last week, do you mean when I had to cut one of my shifts at the café short so I could run home and let the AC repair guy in because that was the only time he could come and you were too out of it to hear the doorbell ring? Or do you mean missing another job interview because you didn't know what day it was? Or perhaps you meant when you drank so much you almost *died* and your teenage daughter was the one who had to call 911, wondering if she was going to lose the only parent she's got left? Not that you've done much parenting over the past five years."

Michael's face turned the color of old crumbling chalk.

"I'm trying," he said, his voice trembling. "I know I messed up. I never ever wanted Sky or you to see me like that. I haven't touched a drink since—"

"Don't." Nate's chest was so tight, it was hard to breathe. "Don't tell me you've quit until you join AA or rehab or stay sober for more than a month. Hell, I'd settle for two weeks. You've gotten our hopes up in the past, but I'm not falling for it again."

"I mean it this time." Michael looked like he'd aged ten years in ten minutes. "When I was lying there in the hospital, I kept thinking of your mother and what she would say if she could see me now. And I know I haven't been the best—"

"I can't do this." Nate shook his head. "You expect me to believe that after five years, you're only now realizing Mom would've been horrified by what's happened to you after she died? That's BS. You've always known. But you've become too addicted to the bottle to care."

Michael blanched, and a pinprick of guilt stabbed at Nate's stomach. Okay, that had been beyond harsh, but it needed to be said. He'd held on to his resentment for so long that he was afraid it had become an inextricable part of himself, and it felt damn good to get some of it off his chest.

Plus, Michael needed the reality check. God knew Skylar wasn't going to give it to him—and she shouldn't, considering how young she was—and Nate had been enabling him for too long. But that trip to the hospital? That had opened his eyes.

If Michael didn't start taking better care of himself, and soon, Nate and Skylar were going to end up orphans.

Then again, that wouldn't be a huge change from the way things were. Michael was there physically, but he'd checked out mentally and emotionally a long time ago.

Nate yanked a paper towel from the roll above the sink and used it to cushion his plate as he stalked past his father and up the stairs.

Michael didn't stop him.

There wasn't much left to say.

If this was God's idea of a joke, he had a shitty sense of humor.

Kris shifted in her seat and tried not to scream as Risa slid a plate of rosemary and garlic lamb roast and mashed potatoes in front of her. It smelled amazing, but her appetite was in milk carton territory, aka lost and not yet found.

She glared across the dining table at Gloria, who was cooing at Kris's father and asking him about his business in Manila.

She had to hand it to the Stepmonster—she was good at making a guy feel like he was the only person in the room. Maybe that was how she'd snared a savvy businessman like Roger Carrera.

Given his net worth, Kris's father had had no shortage of women throwing themselves at him since Mariana Carrera up and abandoned him all those years ago, and while he wasn't handsome by conventional standards, he exuded power and authority. He'd dated on and off over the years, but none of the relationships lasted. He'd certainly never *proposed* to anyone. Then along came Gloria, with her over-the-top Southern accent and double Ds, and he was a goner.

Roger was too smart to fall for just a pretty face and a great rack. However, Gloria was a master manipulator and no dumb bunny. For all her shallowness and vindictiveness, she knew exactly how to flatter Roger's ego and make herself seem interested in whatever he was interested in.

"...with Bobbi?"

It took Kris a minute to notice both her father and the Stepmonster were staring at her—her father with raised eyebrows, the Stepmonster with a tiny smirk.

"Sorry, what did you say?" She reached for her water and took a quick sip, if only so she didn't throw her lamb in the redhead's perfectly made-up face.

"How are things going with Bobbi?" Roger repeated.

"Fine. I've been learning a lot." *About how stupid celebrities can be once they get a little alcohol in their systems*, Kris finished silently.

"Good." Her father dabbed at his mouth with his napkin. "It's good that you're learning the value of honest work this summer. Perhaps I've been too lenient with your finances in the past, but I want to make sure you understand the value of money. Your spending has been out of control recently, especially with the bill for Courtney's birthday last year." His thick brows pulled low.

Kris's lips thinned. He'd never had an issue with her spending until Gloria came onto the scene and "gently" advised him to curb Kris's shopping habits. Like Gloria didn't throw away money left and right herself. Case in point: the tacky crystal-studded dress she'd bought the other day for $2,000. She'd flaunted it in front of Kris like it was something to be proud of instead of a migraine-inducing nightmare.

At least Kris swiped her plastic for *nice* items and gifts for friends.

Besides, she'd take her father's claims about teaching her the "value of money" more seriously if Roger hadn't reinstated her credit cards and access to her flush checking account. Sure, she had a monthly card limit now instead of a black Amex, but there were enough zeroes in the bank to make up the difference. That was how she could afford to pay Nate.

Technically, her checking account was for emergencies only, but saving her father from a greedy gold digger counted as an emergency, right?

"You're coming into your trust fund in a few years," Roger continued. "I want to make sure you're ready to handle it responsibly once the time comes."

"Yes, Daddy." Kris poked at her lamb, annoyed. She'd heard the same speech in multiple forms since she returned from Shanghai, and she was over it. "How long are you going to be in LA?" she asked, switching the subject before she blew her fuse.

Her father's sudden appearance two nights ago had been an utter shock for both her and, apparently, Gloria. It'd also thrown Kris and Nate's plan awry. She was supposed to be ironing out final details with Nate right now—and perhaps enjoying another series of mind-bending orgasms—instead of eating dinner and getting lectured at the massive fifteen-person dining table.

"I'm here until the end of summer." Roger adjusted his tie, because he was the type of man who wore ties even to a family dinner. "The Manila deal is all but closed, and I can wrap up the loose ends remotely. Given the wedding is in only a few months, I want to make sure I spend some quality time with my girls before the big day."

Kris almost choked on her lamb.

He had to be joking. Until now, Roger had spent a cumulative of two or three weeks a year with Kris, and he chose *now* to get all *we are family* on her?

Not that she didn't want to spend quality time with her father, but he had the worst timing on the planet. If he'd waited another week, the Gloria Plan would've been done-zo. But now that he was here to stay, at least until late August, there was *no chance* Gloria would be stupid enough to follow through on her tryst with Nate. Nate had already texted Kris, informing her Gloria had postponed their previously scheduled hotel date tomorrow night.

Fuck.

All that time and energy they'd spent on the plan, wasted. And unless Kris managed to throw another scheme together in the next few months, she was going to be walking down the aisle in her hideous bridesmaid dress and watching Gloria become Mrs. Carrera Number Two, in which case the Stepmonster would be entitled to half of the family fortune.

Kris wanted to hurl.

"That's *incredible* news, sweetheart," Gloria oozed, playing the role of excited, lovestruck fiancée perfectly. "I'm so happy you'll be here. There are so many things we need to go over for the wedding…"

Kris tuned her out as she discreetly texted Nate beneath the table.

Kris: Dad's here to stay. It's a no go.
Nate: Shit.
Nate: How are you? Anything I can do to help?

Kris's heart melted a little. He was so—

"Who are you texting?"

Once again, Roger's voice yanked her out of her thoughts.

"What?"

"Who's so important that you have to text them during a

family dinner?" Roger repeated, sounding more curious than upset.

"No one," Kris lied. He may not be an attentive father, but Roger was quite particular when it came to the boys she dated. Only upper-class, Ivy League types need apply.

Not that she was dating Nate. They were just...hanging out.

"Perhaps it's her new boyfriend," Gloria said primly. "They've been spending a *lot* of time together."

Kris's gaze snapped toward the Stepmonster. The redheaded troll stared back with unnerving composure, considering she'd been ready to ride said "boyfriend" like a bronco before her fiancé showed up. What the hell was she doing, bringing Nate up?

Something dark and insidious stabbed at Kris's stomach.

"Really?" Roger's frown reappeared. "A boyfriend this soon? It's not one of those British boy band singers, is it?"

"God no." Kris grimaced. "It's he's s not—" *Shit*. She didn't want to endure her father's inevitable interrogation, but she couldn't say Nate *wasn't* her boyfriend. Not when she'd been all over him in front of Gloria and had all but professed her love for him to bait the other woman into making a move. The Stepmonster was a jealous, vindictive bitch like that. "He's an actor."

"Hmm." Roger didn't seem impressed. "What's his name?"

"Nate."

He shot her a look.

Kris sighed. "Nate Reynolds."

"I've never heard of him. What movies has he starred in?"

What she wouldn't give for a glass of wine right now. "He has a role in an upcoming Oscar Bravo film."

A tiny role, but Nate would be the star during those two minutes. That counted, right?

"What about his past films? Any Academy Awards?"

Kris's skin itched the way it did whenever she touched polyester. Except she was wearing silk, and her discomfort had everything to do with her father's questions and nothing to do with cheap fabrics. "He's done mostly TV work."

"Oh, darlin'." Gloria's laugh grated against Kris's nerves. "Don't lead your father on. Nate isn't a *full-time* actor."

"Then what the hell is he?" Roger demanded.

"He's a waiter, aspiring to be an actor." Gloria's mouth was a triumphant slash of red against her face. "It's quite romantic, really, the heiress falling for the help."

Kris clenched her hands into fists beneath the table. Her Chanel camellia cocktail ring dug into her palm with a sharp bite. Yes, Nate was a waiter, but she hated the way Gloria said it. *The help.* Like it was a disease and Gloria herself hadn't been in his position a few years ago. It wasn't like Nate's socioeconomic status had stopped the Stepmonster from offering him a blow job—and more—out of either lust for him and/or spite toward Kris.

"If shacking up with *the help* is good enough for my father, it is for me," Kris said coolly, even as her blood simmered with anger. "At least Nate has higher ambitions than spending someone else's money and going to the spa every week."

Gloria tsked. "You would know, wouldn't you, sugar? Like your father said, your spendin' has been out of control." She paused delicately. "I'm sorry. I forgot about your job this summer. Are you sure everythin' is goin' okay with Bobbi? I saw her at Fred Segal the other day. She mentioned you seemed...distracted at work. Somethin' about press clippings and not pullin' your weight? I hope Nate isn't distractin' you."

Bobbi, you bitch.

Kris's mouth curled into a snarl. "Speaking of Nate, why don't you tell us what you—"

"Enough!" Her father slammed his hands on the table. The silverware rattled with alarm, and Gloria and Kris both fell silent.

"This is not how I envisioned dinner," Roger ground out. "You two were supposed to get to know each other better this summer. Kris, you're my daughter, and Gloria, you're going to be my wife. I expect you to have a *harmonious* relationship. Understand? You don't need to be best friends, but I will not tolerate you squabbling like this every night."

"It's not like you're around often enough to hear us argue." Kris regretted the words the minute they left their mouth.

Gloria smirked, and Roger glared at her with an intensity that made Kris's toes curl in her suede Prada boots.

"Perhaps I haven't been around as often as I would've liked," Roger acknowledged. "But I *will* be here this summer. I'm staying in Los Angeles until your job with Bobbi Rayden is over and we return to Seattle—together." He took a deep breath and smoothed a hand over the front of his shirt. "Meanwhile, you and Gloria will spend time together, one-on-one, at least once a week."

Kris's jaw dropped while Gloria froze, looking like a displeased mannequin in a department store.

"But—" They spoke at the same time.

"*Once a week*," Roger repeated firmly. "I don't care if it's shopping or brunch or a damn knitting club. Clearly, living in the same house isn't enough. You *will* spend quality time together until you get along."

Kris resisted the urge to tell her father that just because you got to know someone better, it didn't mean you'd like them more. She was sure she'd like Gloria better if she *never* saw her.

But that wouldn't go over well, so Kris remained silent.

"I also want to meet your boyfriend."

She blanched. "I don't think—"

"I'm hosting a dinner party for some of my entertainment

industry friends in a few weeks," Roger said. Gloria's eyebrows shot up, betraying her surprise. Kris was equally caught off guard. Her father hated parties. He only tolerated them for networking and publicity purposes, and he avoided hosting them as much as possible. "Movie studio heads. Directors. Producers. Invite Nate. Perhaps he could make some useful connections."

Huh. Was her dad trying to *help* Nate? Roger Carrera was all business when it came to his high-powered contacts, and it was not like him to invite someone he'd never met to a hobnobbing event with some of LA's most powerful.

"Make sure he's prepared," her father continued. "If he embarrasses me, I'll make sure he won't get so much as an appearance in a dog food commercial."

That sounded more like Roger.

"Okay." Kris didn't know what else to say.

In the span of forty-eight hours, her hire-Nate-to-seduce-Gloria scheme had veered so far off the rails, she couldn't see the tracks. She could only hope she wouldn't be crushed at the end of all of this.

CHAPTER 14

"I WON! I WON!" KRIS DID A LITTLE JUMP IN AN UNCHAR-acteristic display of glee, and Nate would be damned if it wasn't the most adorable thing he'd ever seen.

A smile tugged at his mouth. "Congrats. Your speed is impressive." He closed the distance between them until they both stood on the peak of Runyon Canyon Park.

Los Angeles sprawled before them, the relatively flat buildings nearby giving way to the sleek skyscrapers of downtown in the distance. From this vantage point, they could see the distinctive Capitol Records Building—which resembled a stack of records, though contrary to popular belief, such a design had not been intentional—and the ritzy mansions in Hollywood Hills. The neighborhood of the rich and famous was a hodgepodge of architectural styles, ranging from ecofriendly abodes with solar panels to Mediterranean behemoths with sparkling turquoise pools.

Kris collapsed on a bench nearby. She'd thrown her hair up in a ponytail and wore a tank top, yoga pants, and sneakers. It was the most casual Nate had seen her outside her house, and he was feeling it.

"You didn't let me win, did you?" she asked, her earlier excitement giving way to suspicion.

"No," Nate lied.

Not really. He and Kris had spent the morning hiking Runyon Canyon, and toward the last quarter mile, they'd made a bet on who would reach the top first.

Nate supposed he *could've* picked up his pace, but the sight of Kris's round firm ass in yoga pants had distracted him. Getting distracted wasn't the same as letting her win.

He was usually a competitive person, but he wasn't even mad. The view had been worth it.

God bless whoever invented yoga pants.

"Good." Kris looked satisfied. "Cough up the prize, pretty boy."

Nate laughed and took the seat next to her. "Fine." He racked his brain for a good one. "So I was manscaping for a role..."

"Oh no." Kris covered her eyes with her hand. "Any story that begins with 'I was manscaping' doesn't end well."

His mouth twitched. "Shh. Let me finish. So I was manscaping for a role, and like an idiot, I decided to do it myself. I was in the bathroom, doing my thing with the trimmers—"

She shook her head, the horror evident in her eyes.

"—and it was going fine until Sky, who was watching some horror movie in the living room, screamed and startled me. I slipped and...well, let's just say that was the most embarrassing trip to the ER I've ever taken. People say doctors don't judge, but they totally judge. You should've seen the look mine gave me. I swear she shook the entire time from trying not to laugh. Not good, considering she was working on a very delicate area of my anatomy."

Kris burst into laughter. "I don't blame her. It's pretty funny."

"You would say that; you're not a man. You don't understand

the pain of stabbing yourself in the nut sack on what should've been a normal Friday night." Nate released an exaggerated shudder. "Now you tell me." He draped his arm over the back of the bench. His fingertips grazed Kris's shoulder, and a tiny electric shock sizzled through his veins. "What's your most embarrassing moment?"

"I don't have to tell you. I won." Her eyes shone with amusement. "The whole point of winning was so I *wouldn't* have to share my most embarrassing moment."

"If you were a good friend, you'd share it anyway."

She tilted her head. "Is that what we are? Friends?"

Nate paused, unsure how to answer that question. If he had the choice, they'd be more than friends. Their night on the boat would forever have a starring role in his fantasies, though they hadn't discussed whether their unlabeled relationship was casual, serious, or something in between. But it was more than lust. He *liked* Kris. When he first met her, he'd thought she was cold, spoiled, and superficial—and sometimes, she could be. But she was also passionate, funny, and sarcastic. She'd stayed with him the night his father was hospitalized, and Skylar adored her. No matter how hard she tried to hide it, Kris did care about people—or at least, those she deemed worthy of her trust and attention.

Nate desperately wanted to be one of those people.

"Sure," he said. "If you want to be. We'd make great friends. With benefits."

He might've imagined it, but he thought he saw a flicker of disappointment in her eyes at his response.

Kris turned her head and tugged on her ponytail. Her diamond studs glinted beneath the bright summer sun. "Right. Well, you're in luck because I have one spot left on my friend roster," she said briskly. "I suppose you could fill it."

"I wasn't aware you had a friend quota."

"Of course I do. Friendships are exhausting. They require so much energy and emotional labor. If I don't didn't limit my friend circle, I'd go insane." Kris shrugged, and her skin brushed his fingertips again. Nate swallowed hard. "Luckily, I dislike most people, so it's never been an issue."

"I'm flattered," he said wryly, trying not to focus on his suddenly-too-tight shorts. If a brush of her skin could elicit such a powerful reaction from the man downstairs, he was in deep shit. Nate shifted his weight and removed his arm from the back of the bench. Thank God he'd worn loose shorts for jogging so Kris couldn't see how much she affected him. "Speaking of people you dislike, how goes it with Gloria?"

She'd filled him in on her father's ultimatum. Nate had been equal parts bummed and relieved that they wouldn't be able to carry out the rest of Kris's plan. He was out $7,500, which sucked, but he was secretly glad he didn't have to do anything more with Gloria. That woman put him on edge; she was the human equivalent of a viper hiding in the sand.

"It's fine. For our mandatory one-on-one time"—Kris rolled her eyes—"we go to that spa she's always raving about. It's perfect because we get our treatments done alone and don't have to talk to each other. My father will never know. He's too busy with work to get into the specifics. All he cares about is that we go somewhere together once a week."

"Maybe you *should* try to get to know her better," Nate ventured. "She's going to be your stepmother, so a truce would be useful."

Kris's glare could have put a zombie back into the ground.

"Or not," he said.

"I don't want to talk about her. Even hearing her name raises my blood pressure." Kris fiddled with her earring. "Actually, I have a favor to ask of you."

Nate clutched his chest. "Kris Carrera, asking a favor of little ol' me? I never thought I'd see the day."

"Shut up," she grumbled, but she was smiling. "Anyway, Gloria spilled the beans about our 'relationship' to my father and now he, uh, wants to meet you."

Nate's grin disappeared. Meet the parents? He wasn't ready for that. He liked Kris a lot, but they weren't really dating, and he'd bet his last dollar that her father was scary as hell.

Fathers didn't like Nate. They took one look at him and—correctly—assumed he would corrupt their daughters' precious virtue. Never mind the fact that their daughters wanted to be corrupted and it was their choice what they did with their bodies.

Plus, Nate couldn't see a multimillionaire businessman like Roger Carrera being all that thrilled about his only daughter dating a broke college dropout.

"I would've told him we broke up," Kris added, "but we put on such a show for Gloria that it'd seem suspicious if we ended it just like that. It's also not a one-on-one meeting. He's hosting a dinner party and there'll be some big Hollywood people there. It could be useful networking for you. I would've asked you earlier, but I wasn't sure whether he was going to go through with the dinner. He sent the official invites out this morning, so I guess he is."

He'd never seen Kris look so nervous.

She was right. It would be good networking, but Nate dreaded the thought of meeting her father in some fancy-schmancy environment even more than he dreaded meeting the man one-on-one. What if Nate wore the wrong clothes or used the wrong fork? He wasn't schooled in rich-people etiquette.

There was no way he could say no, though. Not with Kris looking at him like that, all big brown eyes and soft skin.

"Okay." He forced a smile. "Sure."

"Great." Relief flooded her expression. "Oh, and I'll pay you the rest of your money tomorrow. Do you want cash, or would you prefer I wired it to you? It's been so crazy at work that I didn't get a chance to withdraw—"

"What money?"

"The seventy-five hundred dollars. For the remainder of your contract."

Tension crawled its way down his spine and lodged itself in the pit of his stomach. "I didn't see the contract through. There's no reason to pay me the rest of the money."

"Technically, no," Kris allowed. "But it's not your fault my dad showed up all of a sudden. Plus, you put in the time and effort, and you're pretending to be my boyfriend at the dinner. You deserve it."

A muscle ticked in Nate's jaw. "You don't have to pay me seventy-five hundred dollars to attend a dinner party."

Kris looked taken aback by his harsh tone. "*Why* are you being so stubborn about this?" She threw her hands in the air. "It's just money. Take it! seventy-five hundred dollars is not a lot to me, but it—" She stopped.

Something dangerous pulsed behind Nate's temple. "But it is to me. Is that what you were going to say?" His voice was quiet. Deadly.

Kris looked away. "I'm trying to help. I know things have been difficult with your dad, and Skylar's senior year is coming up. She's going to have homecoming, prom, college application fees. It's expensive."

Twin tornadoes of fury and humiliation blazed through Nate's chest. "It's *my* family. *My* dad. *My* sister. We don't need your handouts. We're not some charity case that you can throw money at to make yourself feel better."

His family may not have been perfect, and he and his dad

still weren't speaking after their blowup—well, after Nate's blow-up—in the kitchen last week, but they were still his family, and he wouldn't have anyone looking down on them.

"That's not it," Kris said hotly. "I don't think you're a charity case—"

"Then stop treating me like one!"

The wind rustled in consternation. Nate suddenly realized how quiet it was—too quiet. A glance around confirmed that the other hikers in the vicinity had stopped what they were doing to watch his and Kris's drama unfold with wide eyes. He was pretty sure one of them was the star of the latest hit Netflix show.

The humiliation deepened.

"I'm going back to the car." Nate stood, forcing himself to unclench his fists. *Huh*. He hadn't realized he'd clenched them. "I'll wait ten minutes. If I don't see you, I'll assume you're walking home."

It was an asshole thing to say, but Nate didn't feel particularly gentlemanly as he stormed off. Unlike during the hike up, he didn't slow his stride to keep pace with Kris. By the time he made it to his car, a portion of his anger had burned away, but the humiliation remained. It tasted sharp and bitter in his throat.

Nate was a lot of things, but he was no charity case. His family may not have much money, but the money they did have, they'd earned. He refused to live off other people's pity.

He ran a hand through his hair and glared at his phone. He'd been sitting here for seven minutes. Three more minutes and he was outta here. Kris could find her own damn way home.

Another minute passed. Then another. And another.

Nate turned on the engine and glanced down the road. Runyon Canyon didn't have a parking lot, so he'd parked on a street by the main entrance. Other than a woman walking her dog, there was no one else in sight.

Where is she?

"I'm leaving," Nate said, like Kris could somehow hear him. Nothing.

"Five more minutes, *then* I'm leaving." He sounded like a crazy person, talking to himself in his car.

It shouldn't have taken Kris that long to get to the car. Was she lost? Hurt?

His heart banged against his chest at the thought.

After a vicious inner war, Nate composed a quick text to make sure she was okay. He was still pissed at her, but he wasn't a monster. He refused to have her death on his conscience.

That's the only reason I haven't left yet, he assured himself.

In an uncanny coincidence, his phone pinged with a message from Kris right before he hit send.

Kris: You've probably left by now, but just FYI, I ran into a friend and he's driving me home.

What. The. Fuck.

Nate stared at Kris's text in disbelief. His earlier anger rushed back, a hundred times fiercer than before. Was she messing with him? What were the odds of her running into a friend in the past hour? Who was this *he* she was talking about?

His molars ground together.

Nate: Fine.

That was the only reply he could muster without blowing up.

Nate maneuvered out of his parking spot and gunned it toward his house, furious for reasons beyond his comprehension.

This was turning out to be the shittiest day ever.

Nate's temper didn't improve when he arrived home to a barrage of questions from Skylar.

"How was your hike with Kris?" she chirped from her position on the couch, where she was watching old Tom and Jerry cartoons over a bowl of Cinnamon Toast Crunch.

"Fine." That seemed to be the only word he was capable of since he'd left Kris sitting at the top of a hill.

Guilt wormed its way into its stomach, but he grabbed it by its neck and shoved the fucker aside. He didn't have time for guilt. He was too busy being mad—at Kris, at the asshole who supposedly drove her home, and at himself.

Nate exhaled a long sigh at Skylar's raised eyebrows. "You shouldn't eat cereal for lunch," he said in a gentler tone. "There's leftover lasagna in the fridge."

"I ate that for breakfast." Skylar grinned at her brother's exasperated expression. "Come on. No one ever died from eating lasagna in the morning and cereal in the afternoon."

"No, but you'll be the death of me," Nate muttered. He sank into the armchair next to the couch.

"So cranky. I thought you'd be flying high after your date with Kris."

"It wasn't a date."

"Maybe it didn't go as well as you'd hoped." Skylar ignored his denial and examined him with shrewd eyes. "What did you do?"

"Why do you assume *I* did something?"

"Did you?"

"No." *Yes.* "You still haven't told me how you and Kris know each other." It was an obvious ploy to change the topic, and it worked.

Skylar became fascinated by the few remaining pieces of

soggy cereal floating in her bowl. "I told you, we met at the movies."

"I don't know which is more insulting: you not coming up with a more believable story or you thinking I'm stupid enough to fall for your excuse. No one talks to strangers at the movies." Nate's eyes narrowed. "You didn't meet her at a nightclub, did you? Because if you have a fake ID—"

"Ugh, no!" Skylar wrinkled her nose. "I don't like clubs."

"How would you know unless you've been to one?"

She shot him a dark look. "Leave me alone and take a shower. You stink."

Nate didn't budge. "Where do girls meet random new friends?" He frowned, his mind flipping through the possibilities. "Beach? Mall? But if so, you wouldn't be so reluctant to—"

"I met her at MentHer, okay?"

His frown deepened. "Is that a store?" If so, it had a stupid name.

"No." Skylar avoided his gaze and swirled her spoon in the milk. "It's an organization. For girls."

"What kind of organization?" Suspicion seeped into his voice.

She mumbled something under her breath.

"I'm sure your cereal finds your answer fascinating," Nate said dryly. "But if you want a two-way conversation, you'll have to speak up."

Skylar heaved a sigh that sounded annoyed, guilty, and exasperated at the same time. "It's an organization for girls who lost their mothers."

Nate greeted the revelation with a blank stare.

"Every girl is assigned a mentor," Skylar rushed. "An older female who can help her with, like, girl stuff. And they have events and activities and things like movie outings and arts-and-crafts day. I found out about it through one of the girls at soccer camp. I only joined in June—around the same time Kris started volunteering there—and they haven't matched me with a mentor yet, which is fine, because Kris has been acting as my de facto mentor and she's great and I—"

"Wait. Stop." Nate held up one hand and pinched his temple with the other. "You and Kris met through a nonprofit. For girls. Who've lost their moms."

"Yes?" Skylar said meekly.

"*That's* the secret you've been keeping from me?" He was incredulous. "Why?"

"I didn't want you to be mad or, like, feel bad." Skylar gave up on her cereal and set the bowl on the coffee table. Her brow pinched with guilt. "You've done so much since…well, you know. Since mom died. Taking care of Dad and me and everything. I didn't want you to feel like you weren't *enough*. But sometimes…" She picked at her shorts. "I dunno, I want another female to talk to."

Nate's heart squeezed. "You don't have to feel guilty about that. I know I'm not—" He waved his hand in the air. "I know there are certain things you wouldn't feel comfortable talking to your brother about."

Skylar nodded. "Like the Great Tampon Fiasco."

"Jesus, Sky. We promised we would never bring that up again."

Skylar had gotten her period for the first time three months after their mom died. Their dad had already been deep in the bottle by that point, so Nate had run out to buy her tampons. That had gone well enough. The humiliating part came after, when he'd tried to explain to his then-twelve-year-old sister how to use said tampons.

Nate had no clue how those things worked. He'd Googled it and ended up delivering a stilted presentation that involved cranberry juice, flower analogies, and one traumatized tampon before a horrified Skylar cut him off and said she already knew how to use one. She'd taken sex ed, thank you very much.

The presentation remained one of the most cringe-inducing experiences of Nate's life, second to his, er, nutty visit to the ER.

"Sorry." Skylar giggled before the wariness returned to her eyes. "So you're not upset?"

"Of course not. You can come to me about anything *if you want to*. But I'm not equipped to handle all the inner workings of the teenage female psyche." In truth, Nate was relieved that Skylar had someone else to talk to. He tried his best, but some things were meant for female ears only. "But if there's anything big going on—any reason you joined this organization *now*—let me know. You don't have to tell me the details, but we're family and we got each other's backs, right?"

Skylar's lower lip trembled. She nodded once before she flew across the space between them and tackled Nate in a blur.

He grunted at the sudden impact. *Oof.*

Nevertheless, he hugged her back, a mess of emotion clogging his throat. The last time they'd hugged like this had been on the one-year anniversary of their mom's death, and that had been a sad, we-have-to-hold-each-other-up-or-we'll-fall-apart hug. This was a decidedly happier embrace.

"There's nothing out of the ordinary. I joined now because I didn't even know MentHer existed before. Promise." After a minute, Skylar seemed to realize she was a teenage girl and it was uncool of her to hug her brother. She unwrapped herself and wrinkled her nose. "You're all gross and sweaty. Like I said, you need a shower, Stinky."

She squealed when Nate grabbed her in a playful headlock and tried to make her smell his armpits. "Who are you calling Stinky?"

"Ew, stop!" she scream-laughed. "My *nose*!"

They tussled for a few minutes before they called a truce. By then, they were both winded and Nate's sides hurt from laughing.

Man, that felt good after a crap-tastic morning.

"You're a good brother," Skylar said. "Even if you sweat like a pig."

He bumped her shin with the toe of his shoe. "Seventeen-year-olds. Queens of the backhanded compliments."

"Don't you forget it," she sassed before switching topics. "So, you didn't answer my question earlier. What did you do to Kris?"

Nate's smile faded when he remembered how he'd left Kris in Runyon Canyon. Sort of. He'd technically waited for her, and she'd left with some other guy—unless she'd been lying. But she had no reason to lie.

Guilt and jealousy churned in his stomach.

"I was an asshole to her," he admitted.

"Language." Skylar giggled when Nate bopped her with a throw pillow for turning his own words against him.

"Apologize," she said. "Kris is great. I wish she could be my official mentor, but she's too young. The MentHer staff is only letting it slide for now because they've been so busy and there's a shortage of volunteers." Skylar sighed. "She taught me how to do a smoky eye and gave me boy advice."

Nate flinched. "You're dating?" That was one area of Skylar's life he didn't want to dwell on. Just thinking about her prom night gave him an ulcer, especially when he remembered how he'd spent his own prom night—in a hotel room with the head cheerleader, doing things that would make a porn star blush.

He'd been a teenage boy himself not too long ago, and he knew exactly what went through teenage boys' minds.

"Not yet." Skylar grinned. "Don't worry. Kris gives *great* advice."

"Oh yeah?" Nate narrowed his eyes. "Like what?"

"Apologize to her and maybe she'll give you the advice herself." Skylar's grin widened at his sour expression.

"Way to take sides," he muttered, even though he knew she was right.

He owed Kris an apology, and soon.

CHAPTER 15

"THANKS FOR COMING WITH ME TONIGHT." KRIS smoothed a hand over her skirt. "And for driving me home earlier."

"Anytime," Teague said easily. "It was good catching up, and the band wasn't bad."

No, it wasn't. It was actually *good*. The revelation had surprised and relieved Kris, who'd attended Blue Hair, aka Elijah's, band practice out of desperation. She'd promised Susan she would find musical performers for MentHer's summer gala, and the task had proven more difficult than she'd anticipated. Given the event's entertainment budget—as in, there was none—she'd had to scour LA for decent singers who would be up for a gig that offered zero money *or* exposure to music bigwigs.

Needless to say, the search was a freaking trial, and Susan refused to let Kris pay for a performer out of pocket—not even if she billed it as a donation. Something about ethics and legal complications.

Kris remembered she'd gotten Blue Hair's number as a backup when she found out he played in a band and, lo and behold, the

Prophecy Kings—medieval name notwithstanding—were decent. They did both cover and original songs, and they were up for a free gig. That last point made them the best damn band on the West Coast in Kris's opinion.

"I'd invite you in, but I don't want my dad to get the wrong idea." Kris rolled her eyes. "He's in love with you."

Teague grinned. "Nah, he's in love with the family business. You know my dad created the animations for your dad's first video games."

"Maybe."

Teague's family, the Collinses, owned one of the largest animation studios in the country. They'd started out doing small-time stuff for little-known games and videos but were now one of the go-tos for visual effects in Hollywood.

Kris and Teague saw each other every Christmas in St. Barts. Well, except for this past Christmas, when Gloria had convinced Roger to go to Aspen instead. Teague was a good-looking guy—blond hair, hazel eyes, lean muscles—and Kris had made out with him once a few years ago after too many mai tais. It had been a one-time thing. He was too clean-cut for Kris, and Kris was too barb-tongued for him. Teague liked the sweet, bubbly type.

Plus, Kris didn't do long-distance relationships. Emotional taxation with no physical satisfaction? No thanks.

That didn't stop her dad from dreaming about an alliance between the Carreras and Collinses, though. Everything was a business transaction to him, even his daughter's love life.

"Call me if you want to hang out or need another mountain-top rescue," Teague said. "I'll be here for the summer."

Kris snorted. "You drove me home from Runyon Canyon. You didn't rescue me from Mount Everest."

Her stomach twisted when she remembered her argument with Nate earlier. She'd been debating whether to let him drive her home or call an Uber when she'd run into Teague on her way down. It had been a random, shocking coincidence. She knew Teague lived in the city, but he always spent his summers surfing in the South Pacific. She hadn't thought to hit him up because she hadn't expected him to be in town.

Turned out, he'd delayed his surfing adventures to help his dad out on a project for a big upcoming movie.

It had been good to see him, especially since she'd been smarting from Nate's accusations, and she'd invited Teague to the Prophecy Kings' band practice at the last minute. Watching a local band play in a garage by herself would've been just sad.

Teague clutched his chest. "I'm hurt."

"Please. Your ego's like Teflon."

"True. I also know that tone—you're seconds away from throwing me out of my own car, so before I can suffer the indignity, I'll take my cue." Teague kissed her on the cheek. "See ya later."

"See you."

Kris got out of the car and waved as she watched the lights of Teague's Tesla disappear down her driveway. Once they were out of sight, she walked toward the front door and dug for her keys. The one downside of large purses was that it took forever to find small items.

Her fingers had just closed around the metal when a voice growled from the dark.

"Who the hell was that?"

She screamed and instinctively raised her bag over her head, brandishing it as a weapon. The Gucci tote contained her hair products, wallet, makeup, and a change of shoes—more than heavy enough to inflict serious damage.

"Whoa." The owner of the voice stepped out of the shadows and held up his hands. "Put that thing away before you hurt somebody."

"That's the plan." Kris's breathing slowed enough for her to note the familiar mess of sun-kissed brown hair, green eyes, and tanned skin. "Nate? What the hell are you doing here? How did you get in?"

"The guard recognized me and let me in." His expression turned sheepish. "I came to apologize for being a dick earlier today and for leaving you at the top of a hill."

Kris lowered her bag, her heart rate slowly returning to normal. "You *were* a dick, but you didn't leave me. I left you. I caught a ride with a friend. And Jesus, don't scare a girl like that outside her own house. You're lucky I didn't have pepper spray on me."

Note to self: buy pepper spray.

"Friend," Nate echoed, scowling. "Same guy who kissed you just now?"

Kris brushed past him on her way to the door. "As a matter of fact, yes."

"Only douches drive Teslas."

She didn't dignify that with a response.

Kris unlocked the door and glanced over her shoulder. "Are you coming in or not?"

She should've been pissed that Nate blew up at her and stormed off that morning, but it was exhausting, fighting battles on multiple fronts. She already had her hands full with the Gloria situation, and Nate was the only person she could talk to about it. Plus, she had to admit she hadn't phrased her words in the most tactful manner at Runyon. Nate had his pride, and yeah, she kinda did make it sound like she viewed him as a charity case.

Nate glanced inside. "Is your dad here?"

"No. He and Gloria are having a date night. They won't be back till late." Kris almost gagged on the words.

Nate's shoulders relaxed. Reassured, he followed her through the mansion's cavernous rooms until they reached the kitchen. She didn't trust herself enough to bring Nate up to her bedroom.

"Who was the guy?" Nate propped his forearms on the marble-tiled island. His tanned, muscular biceps strained against the soft confines of his green T-shirt, and his brows were still set in a deep frown, emphasizing his dark stare and the hard set of his perfect mouth.

Even angry, he was so mouthwateringly sexy, Kris wanted to lick him from head to toe. Hell, maybe she was so turned on right now *because* he was angry. She wanted someone who wouldn't be cowed by her, and the guys she'd been involved with in the past had all been different shades of Gentle, Polite, and Boring as Fuck.

That was what she got for dating within the confines of the "well-bred" upper class like her dad wanted her to.

"He's an old friend."

"Looked like more than a friend." Nate's grumpiness intensified. He swept his eyes over her dress. "Were you on a date?"

"Did you come to apologize or grill me about Teague?" Kris pulled a carton of Ben & Jerry's Phish Food from the fridge and a spoon from the drawer.

Nate's lips curled. "Teague? Even his name is douchey."

She glared at him, and he blew out a sigh. There was a long pause before he spoke again.

"Okay, you're right. I came to apologize. I shouldn't have blown up at you like that. I just don't do well with pity." Nate's throat flexed with a hard swallow. "That's all anyone sees when they look at Sky and me. The kids with the dead mom and alcoholic father. Me, the college dropout who has to wait tables to keep the roof over our heads. Sky, the smart, talented athlete who might get stuck in the same dead-end life as me because we can't afford college. In the first year, people tried to give us clothes and make us dinner or whatever, and I know they meant well, but it was too fucking much. Even now, when we run into someone we know, they give us these sad poor-you eyes and I want to scream." He shook his head. "We lost so much. We can't lose our pride too."

Kris's heart ached for the beautiful, strong, resilient man standing in front of her—the one who carried the weight of the world on his shoulders, even though he hadn't asked for or prepared for the job.

"I'm sorry if I made you feel like a charity case," she said. She couldn't remember the last time she apologized, and the words tasted unfamiliar on her lips. "I don't think you're a charity case at all. I *know* you can take care of your family—you've been doing it for years. And judging by how Skylar turned out, you did a great job. I just wanted to help, and the only way I knew how was to give you money." She chewed on her bottom lip. "That's my dad's solution to everything, and I picked it up from him. I get why you were upset. I really do."

Nate's face softened, and somehow that made Kris's chest hurt more. He rounded the counter and pulled her into his arms, shocking her, but she quickly got over her surprise and buried her face in his chest. His T-shirt was soft against her skin, and he smelled like coffee and warm, sensual masculinity.

"Thank you," he whispered. "I know you had good intentions. I was just being an insecure ass."

"And I was being a presumptuous ass," she admitted. She pulled back and examined Nate's face. His eyes shone with sincerity and a deeper emotion she couldn't pinpoint. "Now that we both agree we were in the wrong, let's put the argument behind us."

"Good idea." A small grin teased his lips. "Does this mean we can kiss and make up now?"

She swatted his arm while he laughed. "Seriously?"

"It was worth a shot." Nate shrugged before he grew serious again. "But that guy earlier. Was he your date?"

"Sort of," she hedged.

He shot her a dark look. "What do you mean, *sort of?*"

"It was a nondate date. It wasn't romantic or anything." This time, Kris was the one who shrugged. "I ran into him in Runyon Canyon and invited him to this music thing because I didn't want to go alone."

"I would've gone with you."

"Uh, hello? We weren't speaking to each other."

"I still would've gone with you. Tesla Teague could've stayed the fuck home. And hopefully home is far, far away."

"He lives fifteen minutes away," Kris informed him, suppressing a laugh. "It's cute that you're jealous, but we're not dating. You don't have a say in who I see. You don't have a say even if *were* dating. I do what I want."

Nate's eye twitched. "If we were dating, no other man would dare touch you."

Okay, the possessiveness was strangely hot, but they were going around in circles. "But we're not."

"We should."

Everything went silent except for the quiet hum of the refrigerator in the background. Condensation dripped onto Kris's hand, and she realized she was still holding her pint of ice cream. Phish Food had probably become Phish Puddle by now.

"You can't be serious," she said, a swarm of butterflies taking nervous flight in her stomach.

"I am serious." Nate leaned against the counter. "Everyone thinks we're dating already."

"Not *everyone*. Only my dad and Gloria." Kris wrinkled her

nose. "If this is your romantic idea of how to ask a girl to be your girlfriend, you need more help than I thought."

"You're right. I'm sorry," Nate solemnly. "How about this instead?"

Before she knew it, her ice cream was on the counter, Nate had pushed her up against the fridge door, and he was kissing her in a way that made her toes curl and stomach clench. He tasted like mint and coffee, and every hard ridge of his body molded against hers like they were made for each other. Two pieces in a puzzle.

She didn't know how long the kiss lasted. A minute? An hour? A century? All she knew was that it ended too soon.

Nate drew his head back and smiled down at her with smug male satisfaction. "How about that? Kris Carrera, will you be my girlfriend?"

"That's not fair." Kris resisted the urge to yank his mouth back to hers. "You cheated."

"Never said I wouldn't. I'm a complete scoundrel."

She fought back a laugh. "We said we wouldn't put a label on things."

"We can change our minds." Nate searched her face for the answer to a question she didn't know. "Look, I know we haven't known each other for that long, but I know that you have a good heart, and it's made better by the fact you don't flaunt it. You're beautiful and smart and funny. We have fantastic sex. *And—*" He paused dramatically. "You have great taste in clothes."

Oh, he was *good*.

"You're correct. I'm all of those things, and I do have excellent taste," Kris affirmed. She was wearing a next-season Valentino, wasn't she? "But FYI, tell anyone about the 'good heart' part and the 'fantastic sex' part goes away. The acceptable explanation is that I have split personalities. Sometimes the good twin sneaks out and I have to lock her in her room again."

A laugh broke out of Nate's throat. "Got it."

"Good." Kris listened to the hum of the fridge, wondering if she was doing the right thing or setting herself up for heartbreak down the road. Not that it mattered. She couldn't walk away from Nate now if she tried. "So we're doing this, huh?"

"Yeah." The smile lingered in Nate's eyes as he curled a palm around her cheek. "I'm game if you are."

"How would it work? We date until I leave for Seattle?" The thought of not seeing him again sent a sharp jolt of pain through her chest. "Full disclosure, I don't do long-distance relationships. They never work."

"I agree. Neither do I. But let's cross that bridge when we get there." Nate stepped closer, his scent filling her senses as he caressed her cheek. "For now, let's enjoy the time we do have together."

Yep, she was definitely setting herself up for heartbreak down the road.

"Okay," Kris said softly.

His smile could've lit up all of Los Angeles.

"So, now that we're officially dating..." He lowered his head. "I have a few ideas for how we could spend our first night as boyfriend and girlfriend."

CHAPTER 16

SKYLAR COULDN'T HAVE BEEN MORE EXCITED ABOUT Kris and Nate's relationship than if she'd gotten into Stanford *and* met Shawn Mendes on the same day.

When Nate broke the news, Skylar contained herself for all of thirty seconds before she blurted, "I *told* you, you guys would be perfect together!" and demanded bridesmaid privileges at their wedding. She'd then rushed off and returned an hour later with a list of romantic date ideas because she would "not let Nate mess this up."

The entire ordeal had been disconcerting. Nate supposed his sister had been right about him and Kris up to this point, but they weren't getting married. For one, he doubted Kris's father would approve. For two, they'd both agreed they wouldn't do the long-distance thing. He'd seen the toll such relationships took on other couples—the missed calls and texts, the frustration over not being able to see the other person when they wanted, the resentment over being tied to someone thousands of miles away. That was only the beginning. After that came jealousy, suspicion, irrational fights, and finally, a resigned, inevitable breakup. Days and weeks and hours wasted clinging on to something that never had a chance.

Nate didn't want that to be them. He'd rather they end things at the height of their heat and passion, untainted by broken promises and faded dreams—even if the thought of not seeing Kris again twisted his insides into suffocating knots.

"You okay?" She peered at him beneath thick dark lashes. "You have a weird look on your face."

"Yeah." Nate stroked her shoulder, savoring the soft warmth of her skin. "I was just thinking about the shoot."

Screw it. If they were on borrowed time, he would enjoy every second while it lasted. So far, dating Kris had been a blast. They bantered and bickered like normal, only now there were a lot more make-out sessions and date nights involved. They both drew the line at hand-holding, though—too juvenile and cheesy, they'd agreed.

Plus, Nate hadn't entirely been lying when he said he'd been thinking about the shoot. His appearance in *Six Doors Down*, the Oscar Bravo thriller, had him on edge. Shooting started soon, and while the role wasn't Tom Cruise in *Risky Business* or Brad Pitt in *Thelma and Louise* big—Nate only had a few lines—he could parlay it into something much bigger down the line if he played his cards right.

"You'll blow Oscar's socks off." Kris snuggled deeper into his side. "You're hotter than him anyway."

Nate chuckled. "Thanks, but that's not exactly a bonus." Oscar was mega-talented, but he was also notoriously vain and competitive. He couldn't stand being upstaged.

"Hey, guys. Sorry I'm late!" What had to be Tesla Teague loped toward them, looking particularly douchey in a pale blue polo shirt and khakis. "Traffic."

"No problem," Kris said. "Nate, this is Teague. Teague, this is Nate."

"Her boyfriend," Nate couldn't resist adding, baring his teeth in a semblance of a smile.

Teague looked amused, but at least he was smart enough not to offer his hand for a shake. Nate would've been liable to bite it off.

"Nice to meet you, and hey, congrats." The blond's eyes sparkled. "Not every guy has what it takes to date Kris Carrera."

"I'm taking that as a compliment," Kris said.

"It was," Teague reassured her.

Nate growled. Maybe the guy wasn't so smart after all, if he was flirting with Kris right in front of him.

His *Six Doors Down* role involved knocking a few guys around. He could punch Teague and write it off as character prep.

The blond cleared his throat and took a tiny step back. "Anyway, you guys ready? I have a sport pilot license and have taken a half dozen friends on flights before, so I know what I'm doing. Don't worry."

"I'm sure you do." Kris twisted her hair up into a bun. "Conquering the seas and now the skies? Not bad."

"You know me, always chasing the next thrill." Teague glanced at the sleek white aircraft waiting for them. "I'm going to fire *Maverick* up. You guys decide who wants to go first."

Kris arched an eyebrow. "Seriously? You named your plane *Maverick*?"

"*Top Gun*," Nate and Teague said at the same time.

She sighed. "I'll never understand men and their obsession with naming their vehicles, land-based and otherwise."

"We have deep bonds with our cars," Nate informed her while Teague walked off to ready the aircraft. "Or planes, if you're a douche."

"Nate."

"Just saying."

Kris tilted her head and examined him. "You don't have to do this, you know," she said. "Not if you don't want to."

He looked away, swallowing hard. "Yeah. I do."

When Kris had mentioned that Teague invited her on a private flight to show off his flying chops, Nate had invited himself along because he didn't trust that Tesla-driving, Kris-kissing (it had been on the cheek, but still) fucker as far as he could throw him. He soon realized it didn't matter if he was here because sport pilot rules stipulated the pilot could only bring one passenger at a time, which meant Nate would be waiting on the ground like a chump while Teague took his girlfriend on a romantic flight in the skies.

That was bad enough, but *then* he'd gotten the bright idea that this would be a good time to get over his flying phobia, which had manifested itself...yep, five years ago. Right after his mom died in a plane crash.

Imagine that.

Nate wasn't completely debilitated by the thought of being in the air, but as he'd told Kris earlier this summer, he would rather not fly if he didn't have to. Why tempt fate?

"You sure?" Kris didn't seem convinced.

He ran a hand over his face, his heart thumping with nerves as the hum of the plane's engine filled the hangar. "Not at all. But if I don't do it now, when am I going to do it?" His features tightened. "I chewed out my dad for not facing up to my mom's death and drowning his sorrows in alcohol. My method of coping has been...different, but it's been five years, and while I will always miss my mom, I need to let go of the hang-ups I have around how she died. That includes getting over my fear of flying. So no, I'm not sure this is what I want to do. In fact, I know I *don't* want to do it. But I need to."

Now that he'd gotten all of that out, he could breathe easier, but a coil of tension remained at the base of his spine. Fuck, why were plane engines so *loud*?

"I understand." Kris squeezed his hand. "I'll be here waiting for you when you land. Maybe you and Teague will become friends during your joyride in the sky," she teased.

Nate snorted. "Yeah, I think the chances of me getting my own sport pilot license *and* private plane are higher."

Teague popped open his door, looking like the preppiest pilot on the planet with his aviation headset and polo shirt. "Ready when you are!" he shouted over the engine noise. "Who's first?"

Kris glanced at Nate.

"I'll go first," he said, controlling the shake in his voice. "Rip it off like a Band-Aid, right?"

"Exactly." She kissed him, and he felt marginally better about marching toward his death. "You got this."

Nope. As Nate walked toward the plane, he most definitely did *not* have it. His palms were sweating like a motherfucker, and his heart was about to climb its way out of his chest.

But it was too late to turn back.

He settled into the passenger seat and slipped on the headset Teague gave him.

Get your shit together. You can do this.

"You okay, man?" Teague cast a concerned glance in Nate's direction as he taxied onto the runway. "You look a little green."

"I'm fine," Nate said in a clipped voice.

"All right." The other man sounded dubious, but he didn't push it.

Despite what Nate said, his mild aerophobia had ratcheted up in intensity.

Shortness of breath? Check.

Increased heart rate? Check.

Waves of nausea rolling in his stomach? Check.

Mental images of the plane crashing in a fiery ball? Check.

Fuck. Nate should've never gotten into this tiny death craft. What would happen to Skylar once he died? God knew their father couldn't take care of himself these days, much less his daughter. And Kris. He would never see Kris again. He should've kissed her harder, longer. He should've told her—

The plane ascended, and there was a strong possibility he was going to throw up.

Nate closed his eyes, trying to steady his breathing. The last—and only—time he'd been on a plane since his mother died had been two years ago, when his family had flown to North Carolina for his cousin's wedding. If Nate hadn't been a groomsman, he would've skipped the whole thing.

Fortunately, he'd taken an Ambien and been knocked out for the entire flight.

He didn't have that luxury now.

"...that view." Teague's voice came through his headset, staticky and irritating.

"What?"

"Look at that view," the blond repeated. "You seen anything like that before?"

Nate forced himself to crack his eyes open, because no way in hell would he admit his phobia to Teague.

Thump. Thump. Thumpthumpthump.

Yeah, his heart wasn't happy at all, but Teague was right about one thing—that was a helluva view. From this vantage point, LA was a canvas of green interspersed with tiny boxes that, on the ground, were massive mansions and studio sets and theaters. Dark mountains loomed in the distance, their outlines sharp against the afternoon sky.

"It's pretty cool," Nate managed.

It was the truth. There was nothing like a bird's-eye view to make even the biggest earthly concerns seem like small, trivial matters. Here, it was just Nate and the sky and...a scrap of metal kept afloat by an engine that could fail any minute—

"I'm glad you and Kris are together," Teague said.

"Is that so?" Nate's suspicion overrode his phobia for a brief second.

"Yeah. She and I, we've been friends for a long time, but I've never seen her let anyone in. She doesn't date often, much less date guys she's only known for a month or two." Teague flicked a glance at Nate. "Except for you."

Nate's smile was equal parts warning and satisfaction. "What can I say? Guess I'm special."

"Guess you are." Teague maneuvered the plane to the right. "I know what you're thinking, but Kris and I aren't like that. We kissed once—"

"*What?*"

Fuck crashing because of engine failure. Nate was about to toss the pilot out of the plane with his bare hands.

"A long time ago, and we were sloshed," Teague added quickly. "Confirmed what we both knew, which is that we're better off as friends, and—can you please stop growling?"

That was when Nate realized the low, threatening snarl reverberating through the cockpit was coming from his own throat.

He simmered down but continued glaring at the other man.

"All I'm saying is, I hope you can bring Kris out of her shell. She hasn't had the easiest time, with her mom gone and her dad not around much."

I can relate, Nate thought, his heart pinching at the thought of Kris experiencing the same dark emotions that kept him up late at night.

"Our relationship is our business," he said gruffly. "But

Kris...yeah. I'm gonna do my best. She's worth it, though she doesn't always make it easy."

Teague laughed. "No, she doesn't. That sharp tongue of hers can slice a man in half."

"Try in quarters."

Another laugh, then sudden absolute silence. As in, no engine humming.

What the...?

Nate's head jerked around. He expected to see the earth hurtling toward him in the last moments of his life, but everything was still and quiet.

Concrete. Grass. Kris waving in the distance.

Holy shit, he'd survived. Not only that, he'd been so caught up in his conversation with Teague that he hadn't noticed their descent.

Relief fizzled through Nate's body in a rush, leaving him light-headed and woozy. He took off his headset, mumbled his thanks to Teague, and clambered out of the plane. It took everything he had not to run to Kris, who watched him approach with a half-hopeful, half-wary expression.

"How was it?"

He responded by sweeping her up in his arms and kissing her senseless. God, holding her felt good. He'd been so sure he was going to die up there and never seen her again.

"I take it, it went well," Kris laughed when they broke apart. "And Teague isn't sporting a black eye or any broken bones, so that's good."

"It went okay." Nate tucked her protectively into his chest. "I'm still not a hundred percent comfortable with flying, but it's one of those things I have to ease back into, I guess."

"It's a good first step." Kris brushed her lips over his jaw. "I'm proud of you."

"Thanks." He flashed a quick smile. "Does that mean we can go now? No need for you to be alone with the dou—uh, Teague—in that tiny aircraft. He's not *that* good of a pilot."

He glared at the blond, who was waiting for Kris in the plane. "Nice try."

Nate's shoulders slumped. "Had to give it a shot." Then he remembered what Teague said and straightened up, narrowing his eyes. "Before you get on that plane...tell me: When, exactly, did you two make out? And who's the better kisser, him or me?"

Kris was still flying high (no pun intended) from her time with Nate and Teague when she and Gloria left for their Roger-mandated "bonding time" the next day. Once she'd assured a grumpy Nate that he was a superior kisser to Teague—whom she'd have to kill for telling Nate about their ill-advised make-out session all those years ago—she'd had a blast. Teague was a fantastic pilot, and after they left the private airfield, they'd all gotten dinner at a restaurant that served some of the best seafood in the city. Teague had split after that, and Kris and Nate had gone back to her house, where they'd had multiple rounds of mind-blowing sex.

As usual, Kris's father had been holed up in his study and had missed Nate's coming and going. Gloria, on the other hand, had spotted him on his way out, and now she glared at Kris in the back seat of their Uber like Kris had stolen her favorite Hermès Birkin.

Kris ignored the Stepmonster and examined her nails.

Hmmm, might need to get a touch-up at the spa...

"I'm surprised you and Nate have lasted this long." Gloria's drawl carried more bite than usual now that Roger wasn't around.

"Why is that?" Kris asked, bored.

She and Gloria hadn't been able to agree on whose car to take for their oh-so-wonderful bonding sessions and had settled on a private Uber to take them to the spa. Not a regular Uber either, but an Uber XL, so they could sit as far from each other as possible.

Usually, these car rides were filled with nothing but the sound of the driver's music of choice and the *clack-clack-clack* of Gloria's talon-like nails as she e-shopped Nordstrom on her phone, but it appeared the Stepmonster was in a chatty mood.

Lucky Kris.

"You've never been able to hold on to your men." Gloria clucked. "So disappointin', darlin'. If you'd only come to me, I could give you a few tips."

"Thanks, but I have no desire to learn how to dig for gold. I have my own." Kris let out a deliberate yawn. "Excuse me, but Nate kept me up all night, and I didn't get a lot of sleep."

Gloria's smile turned nasty. "I'd just be careful your boyfriend doesn't go straying on you. That would be a tragedy."

Her Southern accent had all but disappeared—Kris *knew* the other woman played that shit up. According to the background check she'd run on Gloria when the Stepmonster first started dating Roger, Gloria had been born in Georgia, but her family moved to Washington when she was nine. That whole Southern-belle thing was basically a fraud.

Whatever. Kris had bigger fish to fry than the Stepmonster's Dixie delusions.

Gloria was acting so smug because she thought Nate was unsatisfied with his relationship and stepping out on Kris, per his now-canceled hotel engagement with the redhead.

If you only knew...

Kris was tempted to spill the truth about Nate's "interest" in Gloria just so she could knock that triumphant smirk off the woman's overly glossed lips, but that would be a huge tactical error.

There'd been a brief period when she thought she and Gloria might get along—before she met the woman. But the moment they laid eyes on each other, it had been animosity at first sight, with Kris seeing right through the redhead's fake smile and fake boobs and fake (or at least overplayed) accent, and Gloria looking Kris over like she was her competition in a Miss Georgia pageant.

Which was *so* inappropriate, considering Gloria was marrying Kris's freakin' father. Then again, Gloria was only a few years older and a few dozen IQ points slower than Kris.

"I'm not worried," Kris said coolly. "You focus on your relationship, and I'll focus on mine. There are still a couple of months left until the wedding." A tight smile. "Wouldn't want anything to go wrong before the big day."

"Oh, nothing's going to go wrong." Gloria fiddled with her engagement ring—on purpose, no doubt. "Since we're dispensing advice, I'd caution you to be careful with your spending, darlin'. I've been talking to your father, and he's not happy. I'd hate for anything to happen to your trust fund."

Kris was over this conversation.

Gloria was getting desperate if she was trying to threaten Kris's trust fund, which was rock solid and would come into her possession in less than two years.

"Once I get my trust fund, I'll buy you a new perfume," Kris said as the Uber rolled to a stop in front of their destination. "Eau de Desperation doesn't suit you."

She thanked the driver, exited the car, and sauntered toward the spa without a backward glance.

CHAPTER 17

"KRIS, I NEED TO SPEAK WITH YOU." BOBBI'S VOICE CUT through the office bustle and interrupted Kris's distracted internet browsing for new updates about Sabrina Winters, an up-and-coming actress and the newest client on Bobbi's roster.

Kris stifled a sigh. She hated her job more and more every day. She would rather spend her time planning MentHer's summer gala, but here she was, reading about what Sabrina wore to a nightclub yesterday. The actress's style wasn't even that great—her shoes were from last season, and her dress clashed with her skin tone. She needed to fire her stylist ASAP.

Kris pushed back her chair and walked into Bobbi's office.

"Yes?" Her tone came off imperious instead of accommodating.

Oh well.

Bobbi examined Kris with sharp eyes. She was an attractive woman, with shiny blond hair and cheekbones that would make a Slavic supermodel jealous, but the tension in her brow and hard set of her mouth made her appear decades older than her thirty-four years. Managing the public images and tempers of Hollywood's biggest, brightest, and brattiest—especially in the era of social media—wasn't easy, and it showed.

Still, Bobbi was the best in the business, and Kris admired her. She just didn't want to *be* her. She may be a public relations major, but there was no way in hell she'd go the Hollywood publicity route after she graduated.

"Sabrina Winters has a photo shoot with *Mode de Vie* this weekend," Bobbi said without preamble. "For a story on rising stars in Hollywood. It's a huge deal."

"That's great." Why was Bobbi telling her this? Kris pulled press clips *after* shoots.

"I want you to go with her."

"Go where?"

Bobbi shot her an impatient look. *"To the photo shoot."*

Kris was sure she'd heard wrong. Bobbi accompanied her clients to press junkets and photo shoots and red-carpet events. No one else. *Ever.*

"You want *me* to go with Sabrina to *Mode de Vie*?" she spluttered. "Not you?"

"Believe me, I'd be there if I could." Bobbi leaned back in her chair and played with her gold Montblanc pen. "But there's been a last-minute change in my schedule. I'm picking Riley K. up from rehab—I don't trust anyone else to do it, and those bastards refuse to hold her for an extra day. Last time her agent tried to get her, she gave him the slip and ended up in Tijuana, dancing topless in a bar. The strings I had to pull to keep that out of the press… Anyway, *Mode de Vie* can't move the shoot date either. They need all twelve of the rising stars there, and it's the only day that works for everyone. Hence, I need someone to go with Sabrina while I deal with Riley."

"Why me?" The last thing Kris wanted was to babysit an actress barely older than her.

"You're strong enough to deal with any outrageous demands, and you've been around celebrities before. You're even friends with some of them." Bobbi's glossy red mouth turned up into a smirk. "I'm more concerned for Sabrina than I am for you."

"Thanks," Kris said, tone dry. She could imagine how this was going to go down with the rest of the assistants. They already hated her for landing the job through family connections. She didn't give a shit what they thought of her, but Kris had better things to do with her time than fend off passive-aggressive remarks from Bobbi wannabes.

"I'll email you the details," Bobbi said crisply. "This is an important shoot, Kris. I don't expect a crisis—the magazine knows what it's doing, and Sabrina is well-behaved. But it's critical you're there, on time and on point, in case anything does happen."

"Don't worry." Kris tried to muster up a smidge of enthusiasm. "I'll be there."

"Kris, I need to speak with you."

Déjà vu.

Kris's father summoned her with the same words Bobbi used earlier when she passed by his study that night. She'd just gotten home from MentHer, where they'd held a college application workshop for the older girls, and she was looking forward to a nice long bubble bath and a glass of champagne.

That would have to wait.

"What is it, Daddy?" Kris stepped into her father's office. Roger liked to have a designated workspace in all his properties, even his ski chalet in Switzerland and holiday villa on the Amalfi Coast, because there was no such thing as a vacation for him. She'd seen him close a business deal while toasting a European prince's engagement on a yacht in St. Barts. "Is everything okay at work?"

Her father rarely summoned her. The last time he'd done so had been when he cut her off over Christmas.

Kris's skin prickled at the memory.

"It's fine. Some issues with suppliers in Manila, but that'll be sorted soon enough." Roger gestured at the chair across the desk from him. "Sit."

She obeyed, her stomach cramping with unease.

Moonlight spilled through the large window behind her father and mingled with the soft glow from his sleek brass desk lamp. The silver streaks in his hair glinted in the dimness, and world-weariness settled deep in the lines and crags of his face.

He steepled his fingers beneath his chin and surveyed his only daughter with an unreadable expression.

"How is everything going with Gloria?"

"Fine."

His brows rushed down at her unenthusiastic response. "I hope you're putting in the effort to get along with her. It's important."

"Why do *I* have to try to get along with *her*?" Kris retorted in a rare slip of control. "Why can't she try to get along with me? She's the intruder."

"Gloria *is* trying, and we've been engaged for almost a year now. She says you spurn her attempts to get to know you better at every turn."

"Right. And there's no chance she's lying."

She was going to cheat on you! If you hadn't arrived when you did, she would've been rolling around in bed with my boy-friend! Kris wanted to yell.

Fine, Nate hadn't been her real boyfriend at the time, and Kris had concocted the setup, but Gloria had fallen for it hook, line, and sinker. If she truly loved Roger, she wouldn't have been tempted by another man, no matter how good-looking he was.

But Kris couldn't say that. She had no evidence, and her father would dismiss it as another sign that she was unjustly biased toward his bride-to-be.

Kris sucked in a deep breath and tried to think happy thoughts. *Sample sale. Limited edition. Chanel.*

"You forget I'm your father," Roger said dryly. "I know how defensive and guarded you can be. I'm not blaming you, after what your...mother did." A shadow crossed his face the way it always did when he spoke of the woman who'd abandoned him and her then-two-year-old daughter. "But you need a maternal figure in your life. Gloria can be that for you."

Fury and disbelief seized Kris's throat. Her father couldn't be serious. He thought Gloria, who was only six years older than Kris and was as cuddly as a den of vipers, could be a *maternal figure*? "She's twenty-seven," Kris said, striving for a calm, even tone. It didn't work. "She's only a few years older than me, and I'm well past the age where I need a 'maternal figure.'" She placed the last two words in air quotes.

She'd needed a mother when she'd gotten her period for the first time. She'd needed a mother when her father went away on weeks-long business trips, leaving Kris in a mansion with servants who treated her like a china doll instead of a human being. She'd needed a mother to talk to about boys and makeup and the devastation she'd felt when she found out her middle school "best friend" had only been friends with her for the free holiday trips and extravagant gifts. Roger, while inattentive, had never shied away from showering his daughter and her friends with monetary affection.

But Kris hadn't had a mother to hold her hand through childhood or guide her through her teen years. She'd figured shit out on her own when it became clear no one would be there to do it for her, and she'd turned out fine. She sure as hell didn't need a mother now, at the ripe old age of twenty-one.

Her father shot her a warning look. "Gloria may be on the younger side, but she's been through a lot. She can help guide you."

"Through what? Pilfering your bank account? I thought you were a savvy businessman." Kris's eyes flashed. "How can you be so blind to what's right in front of you? Gloria is a gold digger!"

Roger's expression darkened. "Watch your tone," he growled. "Don't forget whose roof you're living under and whose money paid for your car, your clothes, and your vacations. I've been lenient with you all these years, but I will not let you speak to me that way in my own house. Gloria is going to be your stepmother, and that's final. I suggest you come to terms with it. It will make life easier for you and everyone else in the household."

Kris's throat and nose burned with unshed tears. "That's what this is about, isn't it? You just want to make things *easier* for yourself. You never stopped to consider that maybe I need a father more than I need some woman masquerading as my 'mother.' But why should you? You're never around anyway." She stood, so angry her body trembled. "Marry Gloria if you want, but you can't make me like her. It's never going to happen."

She fled from the library before the tears could spill over. When she arrived at her room, she locked the door behind her and took huge gasping breaths.

It wasn't until her breathing evened and her mind cleared that she realized what a big mistake she'd made.

Stupid, stupid, stupid.

Losing her cool like that in front of her father was a dumb move, but the words had spilled out like water through a broken dam. Trying to hold them back would've been futile.

She pressed her knuckles to her eyes. *Sample sale. Limited edition. Chanel.*

For once, the mantra didn't soothe her.

Kris walked to her closet and yanked open the doors. It wasn't as well stocked as her five-hundred-square-foot walk-in in Seattle, but it resembled an exclusive boutique with its rows of colorful dresses, designer heels, and sparkling jewelry displayed in glass boxes on the center island.

She soaked in the sight, seeking comfort in the most luxurious items money could buy.

That didn't work either.

The ache in her heart remained, as did the hole in her stomach.

Frustrated, Kris returned to her bedroom and picked up her phone. After a slight hesitation, she dialed Nate's number.

He picked up on the second ring. "Hey," he said, his whiskey drawl easing the tension in her shoulders. "How was the workshop?"

She flopped onto her back and stared at the ceiling until the smooth white paint blurred before her eyes. "It was good. Skylar liked it."

He picked up on her unease. "What's wrong?"

Before Kris knew it, she'd divulged what had happened with her father. She wasn't used to sharing her feelings and personal life with other people, but she needed to talk to someone or she'd explode. Plus, she trusted Nate and just having him on the other end of the line made her feel better.

"I'm sorry." Sympathy softened his voice. "Do you need me to come over and knock some sense into his head?"

She choked out a small laugh. "That might not make the best first impression on your girlfriend's dad."

"Maybe not," Nate acknowledged. "Let's try another tack. How about an orgasm? Would that help?"

"Are you offering one to me or my dad?"

"I'm not that desperate to get him to like me." She could practically hear his grin over the phone. "But ask me again after the dinner party."

"Gross." Kris laughed again, louder this time. "Okay, switching subjects before I hurl. What did you do today? Take my mind off this Gloria bullshit."

"Nothing that exciting. I had a shift at the café, then came home to practice lines for *Six Doors Down* and a few upcoming auditions."

"Run the lines by me. I've never heard you in action."

"You sure? I don't want to bore you."

"Oh, yeah. Talk dirty to me, baby."

Nate's rich laughter suffused the line. He obliged, changing his voice as needed—a cold, menacing tone for his *Six Doors Down* character as a corrupt FBI agent; surfer dude slang for a slapstick beach comedy; a British accent for a romantic drama set in World War II–era London.

After Nate finished, he and Kris segued into conversations about everything and anything they could think of—Hulu versus Netflix, their number-one most-hated pizza toppings (pineapple for Nate, anchovies for Kris), whether aliens existed, what superpower they'd like to possess the most.

They talked on the phone for hours. The topics were silly and random, but they did the trick—by the time Kris hung up, her cheeks ached from smiling and she'd almost forgotten about her argument with her father. The call with Nate had been better than a bubble bath with champagne by far.

She showered, changed into silk pajamas, and climbed into bed, her eyes heavy with sleep after a long day.

Kris quickly drifted into slumber, but although her body buzzed with warmth from memories of her conversation with

Nate, a small part of her brain whispered that her father hadn't bothered to stop by her room once since she'd walked out on him.

MentHer HQ was in chaos when Kris arrived the next evening. She didn't volunteer on weeknights unless there was a mentee event, but she'd received a frantic text from Susan that morning asking if she could come in as soon as possible.

She didn't mind. Nate was having guy time with Blue Hair and a few of his other friends, and she wasn't exactly looking forward to a showdown with her father or Gloria at the mansion, part deux.

Kris raised her eyebrows when she saw the mess in the office. Other staff members usually clocked out at the end of the workday, but tonight, they were all running around like chickens with their heads cut off.

"What's going on?" Kris asked Melinda, the program director, who wore a wide-eyed, frazzled expression and a blue T-shirt that did her coloring no favors.

"Summer gala venue." Melina tugged on a loose curl, her face etched with panic and frustration. "Pipes leaked overnight and the whole place is flooded. It won't be fixed in time for the event, and they're booked for the rest of the summer, so they can't move our date. They refunded everyone who's affected and promised a discount for the next event, which doesn't help us *now*."

Shit.

The gala was two weeks away, and the chances of securing a new venue in that timeframe with MentHer's budget was slim to none.

Kris tracked down Susan while Melinda rushed off to do whatever she needed to do.

"This is quite a mess," Susan said wryly when she saw Kris.

Lines of tension bracketed the older woman's mouth, but she managed a wan smile. "Not what I needed in the middle of the grant-writing process."

"I can brainstorm new venues," Kris said. "Two weeks isn't *that* bad."

"We were thinking the YMCA. I know the director and she said she can squeeze us in this weekend. It's sooner than expected, and we'd have to scramble—let the girls' families know immediately—but it's better than nothing."

Kris blanched. "The YMCA? Like the song?"

Susan's eyes crinkled with amusement. "Technically."

"But..." Kris trailed off. The gala was supposed to be a grand event for the mentees, complete with live music and fancy food and swag bags. For one night, the girls would be pampered beyond their dreams.

She couldn't see anyone being pampered in a YMCA.

"I'm going to come up with an alternative," Kris said, determined.

Two hours later, it was clear no alternative existed. It would've, had Susan allowed her to pay for a venue as a "charitable donation," but the director kept bringing up "ethics." Kris, who'd never had much use for ethics, vacillated between intensely annoyed and grudgingly admiring of the other woman's dedication to her values until she settled on deeply frustrated.

Susan made the call to confirm the YMCA at ten minutes past eight.

It was already hella late, but Kris stayed behind to help contact the mentors and mentees' parents. Luckily, they were all understanding of the sudden change in date and venue, and most of them could still make it. A call to Blue Hair confirmed the Prophecy Kings had no issues with the date change. The caterers would have to be dealt with tomorrow, since it was after work hours, but if worse came to worst, Kris would tap into her checking account and drop the Carrera name—no matter what Susan said. The girls deserved a blowout event, and it was amazing what a couple extra thousand bucks could do for someone's motivation and work speed.

Susan kicked Kris out at half past nine.

"Go home," she ordered, her tone warm but brooking no opposition. "You've done more than enough, and you need rest. You look exhausted."

"It's my makeup," Kris said. "I'm never using this foundation again."

Susan laughed and shook her head. "I mean it, Kris. I appreciate all that you're doing, but as a volunteer, you're putting in more hours than some of my full-time employees. It's not right."

"I enjoy doing it." Kris hitched a shoulder. "No big deal. I leave in a few weeks, so it evens out."

Sadness blanketed her at the thought of her imminent departure. She had big plans for her senior year at the University of Washington, and she looked forward to seeing Courtney and her other friends again, but leaving Nate, Skylar, and MentHer...

She rubbed her chest, feeling a twinge of heartburn.

"Yes, I know. We'll miss you. You've done a lot." Susan sat in the chair opposite Kris. "I realize you're a volunteer, but if you want to participate in any of MentHer's programming as a mentee, you're welcome to do so. You're within the age range."

"Thanks, but I've already applied to college."

"Yes, of course. I was thinking more about the relationship aspect. If, for example, you want to speak to someone about topics you're not comfortable discussing with your father or anyone else in your life, we're here." Susan's eyes were unbearably kind. "I'd be happy to serve as...well, perhaps not your mentor, given how much we've worked together, but as your friend. Sounding board. Whatever you need."

A lump rose in Kris's throat. Susan knew about her whole mom-abandonment thing—Kris had told her when she first applied to be a volunteer—but this was the first time she'd alluded to it.

Kris wished she had a mom like Susan. Someone warm, down-to-earth, and, you know, *there*. But she didn't, and treating MentHer's director like she was a maternal figure or sounding board or whatever wouldn't change that.

"I appreciate the offer, but I'm okay," Kris said. "I don't need any help."

CHAPTER 18

NATE FELT LIKE A PENGUIN IN THE SAHARA: OVER-dressed, out of place, and at the mercy of brutal, sear-your-skin-off heat—only in this case, said heat came not from the sun but from the glare of his girlfriend's father.

Roger Carrera loathed him. No ifs, ands, or buts about it.

Nate sensed it in the tightness of Roger's smile, the painful grip of the other man's hand when he shook it, and, oh yeah, that unrelenting glare.

Perhaps it was the normal suspicion a father would have about his daughter's new boyfriend, but Nate sensed it ran deeper than that. Failing the Fatherly Interrogation hadn't helped either.

Nate's college degree? Nonexistent.

His upcoming movie role? An unnamed, inconsequential one in the grand scheme of things, even if it was opposite Oscar Bravo.

His side job? A waiter, with a few modeling and catering gigs thrown in if he got lucky and had the time.

His parents? Oh boy.

Luckily, the arrival of the remaining guests saved Nate from having to expound on his father's career—as in, Michael had none—or broach the morbid subject of his mother's death, which Nate had zero desire to discuss at a fancy Beverly Hills dinner party hosted by his girlfriend's father and attended by his biggest idols.

"You're doing great," Kris whispered while Roger greeted the new guests.

"You and I have different definitions of *great*." Nate adjusted his tie and winced at the reminder he was wearing black tie while the other male guests milled around in button-down shirts, dress pants, and the occasional blazer. He thought people got all dressed up for occasions like this; he was wrong. And now, he looked like an idiot. "Did you see the way your father looked at me? Like he wanted to barbecue my hide and serve me to the dogs for dinner."

"We don't have dogs, and no, he doesn't."

He slanted a glance in Kris's direction. "Come on. He nearly broke my hand when we shook."

"It has more to do with me than you." Kris, of course, looked perfect in an elegant black dress that clung to her curves and a diamond necklace that flashed beneath the lights.

Shit, Nate wished he were better at this fancy etiquette/dress code stuff. His first time meeting Kris's father and he was already embarrassing himself.

"We're still not talking to each other after our argument the other night," Kris said. "And I think he's been having issues at work. It has nothing to do with you." At Nate's arched eyebrow, she amended, "It doesn't have *everything* to do with you. He'll come around."

Yeah, except Kris was only here for a few more weeks, so Nate didn't have a lot of time to improve Roger's impression of him.

On that note, why did he care what the other man thought of him? It wasn't like Nate was asking for his daughter's hand in marriage. Per their deal, Kris and Nate's relationship was going to be over at the end of the summer, and they were going to part ways, never to see each other again.

Summer romances were just that: summer romances. As in, no extensions into other seasons.

Which was fine. It wasn't like the thought of walking away from Kris made Nate want to throw up and punch a wall or anything.

Uh-huh. Sure.

Even he didn't believe his own bullshit—but that was a problem for another time.

For now, he had to get through the night.

"Sorry I didn't clarify about the dress code," Kris said sheepishly when a producer whom Nate recognized from the latest issue of *Variety* passed by and smirked at Nate's tuxedo. "I thought... well, *smart dressy* can be interpreted in a lot of ways, and you look incredible in your tux."

He grunted, only somewhat soothed by the compliment. He'd rented the tux for tonight, and he regretted spending the money. "I look like a penguin."

"Penguins are adorable."

Well, didn't that make him feel better.

No guy past the age of eight wanted to be called "adorable," especially not by their girlfriend. Might as well throw him in the same category as puppies and babies in onesies.

"In your case, you look like a sexy, masculine penguin," Kris said, almost as if she'd read his mind. "And I can't wait to get you out of that suit later."

Okay, *that* improved Nate's mood considerably, except now he had a new problem: his pants had gotten ball-crushingly tight, and it wasn't because he'd picked up the wrong size at the rental shop earlier.

He didn't have time to fix the issue—not that he was going to rub one out in the Carreras' downstairs bathroom while

Hollywood's A-list drank their champagne and ate their pigs in blankets a few feet away, anyway—because Roger had returned with an older man in tow.

"Kris, so good to see you," the man boomed. He had steel-gray hair, a hard jaw, and a voice like thunder. Nate didn't recognize him, but if he was here, he had to be important in the Hollywood circuit. "Heard Teague showed you his new toy."

Teague? Jesus, Nate couldn't get away from that guy.

"It's great," Kris said. "I had no idea he was interested in flying, but he's an excellent pilot. He took Nate and me both on a flight."

Her father frowned at the revelation but didn't say anything.

"Ah." The man inclined his head toward Nate, who flashed a smile that masked his inner unease. Hey, he was an actor. He could put up a front with the best of them. "You're Nate, I assume?"

"Nice to meet you, sir." Nate shook the other man's hand.

"Nate's my boyfriend," Kris said. "Nate, this is Steven Collins, Teague's father. He owns one of the biggest animation studios in the country."

"It's a shame Teague couldn't come," Roger said. "He and Kris would've had such a good time."

Like Kris didn't already have a date—one who was standing right there.

Nate's jaw tensed and he bit back a scathing remark. Meanwhile, Kris shot her father a glare and slipped her hand into Nate's.

"Yes, well, apparently he has front-row tickets to a concert tonight that he couldn't miss," Steven said, sounding both indulgent and exasperated.

"What about Linda? I thought I saw her earlier." Roger glanced around the room, where the other guests mingled and laughed.

Nate spotted Gloria with an ultra A-list movie-star couple—
he'd nearly choked when he first saw them earlier, because
holy shit, they were even more intimidating and better-looking
in real life—on the other side the living room, preening like a
peacock in a dress so tight it might as well have been painted
on. The couple smiled politely, but Nate saw the man check
his watch and the woman stifle a yawn when Gloria wasn't
looking.

"She went to freshen up. She should—ah, there you are,
dear." Steven smiled at someone over Nate's shoulder.

He turned, more out of habit than actual curiosity. Then he
blinked. Once. Twice.

No. Nonononono.

The thirtysomething brunette appeared equally stunned to
see him. Her blue eyes widened, and her skin turned ash white
beneath her tan.

She joined Steven's side, avoiding Nate's eyes.

Nate thought he heard Steven introduce her as his wife, but
it was hard to be sure given the blood rushing to his head and
pounding in his ears.

Someone announced dinner was ready, and people started
moving en masse toward the dining room. Meanwhile, Nate
remained rooted to the spot, twin spirals of shock and panic tunneling through his veins.

LA was a big city, and he'd been lucky with not running into
his past clients so far, but out of all the places for his luck to run
out, it *had* to be here, tonight. Not only that, but it had to be
someone in his extended circle.

Fuck.

Nate was going to hurl. He wondered if Roger would mind
him borrowing that antique Ming vase in the corner for a little
regurgitation session.

Probably, but there were at least half a dozen of those things lying around—

"Are you okay?" Kris's voice floated through the hazy landscape of his shock-addled brain. "You look like you're about to be sick."

"Yeah. No." He grimaced and shook his head, forcing the bile back down his throat. "I'm good, just a bit dizzy. Must be this suit." He tugged on his tie. "It's hot in here."

"I'll have Risa turn the air-conditioning up." Kris's brow pinched with concern. "C'mon. Maybe the food will make you feel better."

The food did not make Nate feel better. Sure, the eight-course meal was delicious, but the pork tenderloin and stuffed mushrooms and whatnot only increased the nausea churning in his stomach.

Finally, Nate couldn't take it anymore.

"Excuse me," he said as the staff cleared their plates off the table. "I'll be right back." He placed what he hoped was a reassuring hand on Kris's arm before he pushed back his chair and beelined for the nearest bathroom.

Once he was inside the gold and cream marble space, he locked the door behind him and dry heaved into the toilet bowl. Nothing came out, though the nausea remained.

Eventually, he gave up trying to coax his dinner back out through his throat and sank onto the floor, resting his head against the cabinet doors beneath the sink as he fought to calm his breathing.

Nate wondered if Linda had been married when she came to him that summer. She was too young to be Teague's biological mom, and second, third, even fourth wives were common in this town. Not that it mattered in the grand scheme of things. He was still ashamed of what he did—what he had to do—and he was determined to take the secret to the grave with him.

But what if Kris found out? Would she ever look at him the same? Probably not. Nate doubted Linda would say anything, but he'd ghosted her—stopped answering her calls and messages, changed his number—when he couldn't do it anymore, and that had to have stung.

"Get your shit together." His voice sounded tiny and hollow in the grand bathroom.

It was going to be fine. He was freaking out over nothing. The blast from the past was unwelcome, but it wasn't the end of the world.

It'll be fine, he repeated to himself, like saying it multiple times would make it come true.

After a few more minutes, Nate pushed himself off the ground and attempted to fix his rumpled appearance before he returned to the dining room. They were probably wondering where the hell he was. Well, Kris was at least. The other guests probably didn't care.

Tonight would've been an amazing networking opportunity, but between Kris's father and Linda's unexpected appearance, Nate was not up to the task of hobnobbing with people who would've left him stuttering and starstruck on a good day.

He smoothed a hand over his hair. Straightened his shirt and tie. Splashed his face with water and dried off with one of the soft-as-a-cloud towels hanging on the gold-plated rack.

He still looked pale as fuck, but there was only so much he could do.

He took a deep breath, opened the door—and ran straight into Linda.

You gotta be kidding me.

Nate wanted to lock himself in the bathroom again and never come out, but it was too late. Linda was already talking.

"Hi." Her hand fluttered up to her stomach, throat, and hair, like she couldn't decide where to put it. "It's...a surprise to see you here."

"Likewise." He flashed a tight smile. "Listen, I have to get back—"

"Don't say anything," she rushed out. "Okay? Even if Kris has hired you for tonight, I'd appreciate it if you didn't mention our...past acquaintance. Steven and I didn't get married until last year, but we were dating and going through a rough patch when I reached out to you. I know he's good friends with the Carreras, and he can't find out what I did."

Nate recoiled.

"Don't get me wrong," Linda continued, unaware of his reaction. "You were the best sex I ever had, and I was pretty upset when you stopped answering my calls, but, you know. Steven is the type of husband I've always wanted—"

Because he's rich, Nate added silently.

"—and I don't want to mess things up between us."

Silence.

This was a hell of a reunion. Right up there with getting his balls ripped off by pliers and watching Mariah Carey's infamous *Glitter* on repeat 24/7.

Linda stared at him, her pretty face lined with tension. "Nate? Promise me you won't tell. I'll even pay you—"

"No," Nate interrupted, grinding his molars so hard they ached. It was better than slamming his fist into the wall, which was what he wanted to do.

He didn't bother correcting Linda's assumption that Kris had hired him for the night, because why would someone like her be dating someone like him, right? Never mind the fact that a woman like Kris didn't need to hire an escort. "I won't say anything."

"Great." Relief washed over Linda's features. "Listen, I have a few friends who would love—"

"No thanks. I'm not in the business anymore. Now, if you'll excuse me, I have to return to my date."

Nate left Linda in the hall without a second glance and quickened his pace. He had to get out of here before—

"Not so fast." Roger's deep voice stopped him in his tracks.

Dread coiled in Nate's stomach when he saw the older man standing in the open doorway of what looked like an office. Judging by his expression, he'd heard everything.

Nate glanced over his shoulder; Linda was nowhere to be seen—she'd probably ducked into the bathroom after he walked away. *Great.*

No buffer. Just him and his girlfriend's pissed-off father.

He closed his eyes.

Tonight was not his night.

———

The grandfather clock ticked in the corner, steady and loud as a jackhammer. The office smelled like leather and expensive cigar smoke, and unlike the rest of the Carreras' pad, it was done up Old English style—big mahogany desk, wood-paneled walls hung with landscape paintings in gold frames, a Persian carpet that probably cost more than the Reynoldses' monthly rent. The difference between this room and the mansion's other airy, modern spaces was jarring.

Nate shifted in his chair and winced when the leather let out a loud creak.

Roger stared at him, the picture of authority and intimidation behind that massive desk. He hadn't said a word since he'd asked (translation: ordered) Nate into his office ten minutes ago, and Nate was over this silent stare-down they had going on.

"I think we should head back out, sir," he said, making a conscious effort not to move so the leather chair didn't squeak its indignation again. "Kris is waiting, and your guests are probably wondering where you are."

"Dinner is over. The guests are mingling on the back patio, and last I saw, Kris was deep in conversation with Angelina." Roger tapped his fingers on his desk. "This is as good a time as any for us to chat."

So chat, Nate wanted to say.

"You and Kris. How long have you been dating?"

Nate *really* wished he hadn't worn a tux tonight. He was sweating his ass off in here. "A month and a half, but I met her soon after she arrived in LA," he replied, careful to keep up the lie they'd told Gloria.

In reality, they'd been official for a week, but he and Kris had connected long before they slapped a boyfriend-and-girlfriend label on it—not that he could tell Roger that.

"Hmm." Roger looked unimpressed. "And how do you and Linda know each other?"

Every one of Nate's muscles locked up at the same time. Damn, he thought he'd have more time before they navigated that minefield. Toss back some scotch—if there was ever a night for Nate to start drinking again, it was tonight—discuss the weather, shoot the breeze about the latest Lakers game.

But nope, Roger went straight for the kill.

It was a trick question. It didn't take a genius to figure out the subtext of Nate and Linda's conversation, and while Roger may not be Einstein, he wasn't in the double-digit-IQ club either.

"We met through a mutual friend," Nate replied.

Technically true. Brandon, a fellow aspiring actor, had been the one who suggested Nate earn cash on the side by servicing Hollywood's richest and horniest. Viagra only did so much, and there were plenty of both wealthy singles and wives whose husbands couldn't get the job done to go around.

Brandon had introduced Nate to a famous director's wife who liked the brown-haired, green-eyed type, the woman had told her friends—including Linda—and boom, Nate had been in business.

Technically, he'd been an escort, which was legal in California. Exchanging money for sexual favors was not. While Nate had strived to keep his activities in the over-the-clothes category, he'd sometimes stepped over the line for the right amount of Benjamins, as had been the case with Linda. He hadn't been proud of it, but it'd put his family back on its feet faster, and he'd been careful not to leave a paper or money trail.

"Anyone I know?" Roger asked.

"Probably not. Sir," Nate added, because manners.

The other man's nostrils flared. "Let's cut the bull, shall we? Unless I'm misinterpreting what I heard in the hall—and I don't think I am—we both know how you and Linda met. I wanted to see if you were man enough to own up to it, but apparently not." Roger settled back in his chair, his eyes harder than black steel. "Now, you're dating Kris. My only daughter. I'm not sure what you did to put her under your spell because she's not the type of girl who falls for a guy so fast, but I will give a courtesy you didn't give me: I'll be honest. By that, I mean to say, you two are not well suited. You live in different cities. You come from different… backgrounds. You are from two different worlds, and that's not taking into account the things you've done in the past." Roger grimaced. "I suggest you end things with Kris before they get more out of hand. It's for the best."

Flames of anger licked at Nate's insides, and his vision hazed over with red. He clutched the armrests of his chair, his fingers digging into the polished wood as he tried to reign in his temper.

"With all due respect, sir, Kris and I know what's best for our relationship. We may be different in some regards, but we understand each other. If she doesn't want to see me anymore, fine, but

I won't let anyone else tell me what to do. And"—Nate took a deep breath, wondering if he should go there. *Oh, why the hell not?* Roger already hated him—"I'm sorry to say that I probably know Kris better than you, considering you haven't really been there for her. You make it sound like you want what's best for her, but you barely spend any time with her. You give her money and buy her nice things, and that's about it. You have no idea what she likes and dislikes, what her dreams and goals are, what *she* wants for her life. As for my past? That's in the past. I did what I had to do to keep the roof over my family's head because not everyone is lucky enough to be rich. I work hard, and just because I don't have a trust fund or an Ivy League degree, that doesn't make me any less of a person. So again, with all due respect, sir, you can take your suggestion and shove it."

The silence following Nate's speech was louder and more pervasive than any that had preceded it.

Shock, anger, and—was that regret?—carved deep grooves into Roger's face, but they quickly hardened into a smooth, stern mask.

"Perhaps," Roger said. "You raise good points."

Nate almost fell out of his chair in surprise. Just as hope bubbled in his stomach, the other man's next words shut it down.

"That doesn't change the fact that you and Kris are doomed to fail. She leaves for Seattle in a few weeks, but am I correct in assuming you'd like to prolong the relationship even when you're in different cities?"

Of course not. We have a deadline. We promised each other we would end things once she leaves LA. Neither of us is into long-distance relationships.

That was what Nate should've said. But to his horror, he realized that was no longer true—at least, not on his end. He wasn't sure how Kris felt, but he wanted to keep something going between them after this summer. In just two short months, she'd burrowed her way inside his heart, and unless he tore the entire damn thing apart—maybe not even then—she was there to stay.

"So I'm right," Roger correctly deduced from Nate's silence. "Kris might even agree. She's infatuated with you, and I can see why. You are young, charming, good-looking. The type who holds many women in thrall, I'm sure. But where exactly do you see this ending up? She'll be in Seattle, you'll be in LA. She's accustomed to a certain lifestyle, one that you cannot provide for her, and while she has her own funds, I won't let anyone use my daughter as an ATM."

Funny Roger should say that, considering his fiancée was using *him* as an ATM.

Since Nate didn't have a death wish, he kept that thought to himself.

Roger wasn't finished. "You're an actor. Quite a good one, I might add. You've put on quite a show so far, especially with that little speech you just gave. But you and I both know the real motivator at play here, so let's cut to the chase."

He leaned across his desk, his dark gaze unflinching. "I had an investigator do a little digging after Kris told me you were dating, and it seems like your family is in quite a financial bind. So here's my offer: I will get your father his old job back, and I will pay you fifty thousand dollars. All you have to do is stay away from my daughter."

CHAPTER 19

THE MULTIPURPOSE ROOM AT THE YMCA LOOKED nothing like a multipurpose room and everything like a proper ballroom. It was the small touches that counted—floral centerpieces twinkled with tiny fairy lights, and the tables lining the walls boasted a casual, elegant spread of hors d'oeuvres and mocktails. Meanwhile, dim lighting and a perfectly curated playlist comprised of lesser-known masterpieces, throwback jams, and clean Top 40 hits (for the sake of the younger attendees) contributed to the festive atmosphere.

It wasn't the Four Seasons, but it turned out pretty dang good, considering the budget and crunched deadline.

Kris surveyed her work with a satisfied smile. It had been a crazy few days, what with yesterday's dinner party and the last-minute scramble to shift the gala up one week, but she—*they*—did it. The MentHer team and volunteers had pulled together and made the event of the season happen, and the mentees were thrilled.

The girls were currently going wild on the dance floor to a mellow rock cover of the latest Ariana Grande song, courtesy of the

Prophecy Kings. It was a multigenerational event, and a few fathers had braved the mosh pit to dance with their daughters while others stuck to the sidelines, no doubt worried about losing an eye to a stray flailing arm or getting stomped on by an errant heel.

Kris's mouth tilted up at the sight.

"Kris!" Skylar waved from the dance floor, flushed and glowing in an ice-blue dress with a tulle skirt. In that outfit, she looked like Elsa from *Frozen*. "Come dance!"

"In a bit!" The music was so loud, Kris had to yell to be heard. "I have to check in with the caterers first."

"Oh no you don't." Susan bustled into view, wearing not a dress but a black sequined jacket-and-skirt combo that suited her perfectly. "You're going to enjoy yourself. I'll handle the caterers."

"But—"

"No buts," the director said firmly. "You've done *more* than enough. Now go dance and do whatever it is you young people do at these parties."

There was no arguing with Susan when she was like this. "All right. But make sure you ask them not to take out the chocolate mousse—"

"Kris, *go*." A gentle push accompanied the command.

"I'm going, I'm going." Kris raised her hands in surrender.

She stepped away from the appetizer table, but instead of joining Skylar and the rest of the mentees on the dance floor, she ducked into the room across the hall where the staff had stashed their belongings.

Kris fished her phone out of her bag and cursed when she realized it was dead and that she'd forgotten her charger at home. A glance around told her there no were no stray chargers lying around, and she didn't want to bother the other staff members for something so small.

She was hoping for a message from Nate, who said he might come tonight. He'd acted weird when they'd parted ways yesterday, and her dad hadn't been the most welcoming host on the planet. She wanted to make sure he was okay.

The gala had only started an hour ago, though, and Nate had had a shift at the café this morning. She'd wait a bit and ask Skylar for an update if Nate didn't show up in the next hour.

Kris shoved her phone into her Prada and was on her way back to the multipurpose room/ballroom when she spotted someone coming down the hall. At first, she thought it was Nate, and her heart skipped a beat, but when the figure got closer, she realized she was slightly off the mark.

"Mr. Reynolds." She hid her surprise as she surveyed Nate's father. He had the same thick brown hair and green eyes as his son, but his skin was pale and clammy, and his hands trembled in a manner that had nothing to do with the high-blast AC. He wore a slightly rumpled gray suit, and perspiration dotted his upper lip. Still, he looked better now than he had lying unconscious in a hospital bed. "What are you doing here?"

Stupid question. There was only one reason for him to be here.

"Is this, ah, the MentHer gala?" Michael Reynolds shoved his hands in his pockets and jiggled his foot. He hadn't been awake the first time she saw him, but she'd met him briefly when she dropped by Nate's house the other day.

"Yes. It's in here." Kris gestured toward the makeshift ballroom. "Are you all right? You seem…"

Twitchy. Jumpy. Nervous.

"Yes, yes." Michael ran a hand over his face. "Sorry, I'm just—I'm having withdrawal issues, but I'll get over it. Is Skylar in there?"

Of course. The paleness, the shakiness—classic withdrawal

symptoms for alcoholics. Not great for the person suffering, obviously, but a clear sign that he was taking his newfound sobriety seriously. Nate still didn't trust his father not to fall off the wagon again, but it had been weeks since Michael's hospitalization. It was progress, and what was more, Michael had shown up for the gala. Skylar had confessed she'd invited her father but didn't expect him to show, as he'd lost all interest in social functions after his wife died.

"Yep. Go on in."

Kris watched Michael shuffle into the festivities. Look around. Wince. Then Skylar spotted him, and the girl's face lit up like a Christmas tree. She flew across the room and hugged her father, who hesitated for the briefest moment before hugging her back. Kris couldn't see the man's face, but she imagined it displayed a mixture of nerves and joy.

She swallowed the lump in her throat. She and her father still weren't on normal speaking terms, though he'd stopped her before bed last night. It seemed like he'd wanted to tell her something, but all she got was a "good night" before he disappeared into his study.

Kris shook her head and rubbed her 24K-gold and emerald necklace for lack of anything better to do. She was getting soft. Instead of dwelling on her relationship with her father, which had always been mediocre at best, she should be focusing on a new scheme to get rid of Gloria before November.

The only problem was, she had none. Nothing. Nada. Zilch.

Kris had tapped out her creativity, but if she was honest, she was also distracted by—

"Nate," she breathed.

It was definitely him this time, his long sexy strides eating up the distance between them in no time. Instead of yesterday's tux, he wore a pair of dark-wash jeans and a black blazer over a white T-shirt.

Sex personified.

"I didn't think you were going to make it," she said, inhaling that delicious leather-and-coffee scent of his as she kissed him hello.

"I got out of work a little early." Nate flashed a quick smile.

His color was better—he no longer looked green around the gills like he had yesterday—but his eyes lacked their usual warmth and his shoulders were so tight, they were almost up to his ears.

"You okay?" Kris's brows pulled together. "You seem tense."

"All good. Just nervous about the shoot on Monday." He held out his arm. "Shall we? I can already picture Sky dancing like a maniac in there."

She laughed. "You got that right. But before we go in...did you see who came in before you?"

Nate's quizzical smile told her all she needed to know.

"Your dad's here," she said softly.

Nate's shoulders jumped up another inch. "You're shitting me."

"Nope. He got here a couple of minutes ago, and he's with Sky now. I think..." She paused, thinking of the best way to phrase it. "He's going through withdrawal. I'm sure you've noticed. I know you don't trust him, and I don't blame you, but he's trying."

No response.

Pharrell Williams's "Happy" filtered through the multipurpose room's doors and walls, its upbeat tempo at odds with the strained atmosphere in the hallway.

"Nate?" she prompted.

Her boyfriend rubbed his eyes, looking so tired her heart broke. "Let's not do this right now, okay? Sky wanted him here, so I'm glad he's here. As for all the other stuff, let's shelve it. I just want to hang out with you and Sky, dance to bad music, and eat too many carbs."

"Blue Hair—uh, Elijah—would probably take offense to the 'bad music' part."

That earned Kris a small smile.

"He's tough. He'll survive."

"True. He survived all those facial piercings." Kris took Nate's arm. "Okay. No tough talk tonight, only bad music and carbs."

Skylar squealed when she saw her brother, and she dragged both him and Kris onto the dance floor. Michael, obviously not up to the task of doing the Cupid Shuffle—damn, that was a throwback—sat at a nearby table, watching his daughter with indulgence and his son with trepidation.

Except for a curt nod, Nate didn't acknowledge his father, but Kris supposed it was better than nothing.

The night flew by far too fast for her liking, and not just because she'd spent countless hours perfecting the details just for the gala to end in the blink of an eye. She may be a cold bitch sometimes, but even she was not immune to the joy and smiling faces around her.

The mentees were having the time of their lives with their dads and mentors, and that was enough. Tonight, there was no melancholy over the people they'd lost, no worries about money or school or family issues. It was all about pure, unbridled fun.

Kris didn't even mind when a mentee spilled soda on her new Alexander Wang dress. The girl apologized profusely, but Kris waved it off. You couldn't see the stain on the black fabric unless you looked closely, and they invented dry cleaners for a reason.

As the party wound down, the music segued from upbeat pop into slower jams.

"I hope everyone's having a good time," Blue Hair said into the mic, grinning when the crowd responded with cheers and whistles. "We're coming to the end of the night." A chorus of boos. "*But I* think we should wrap this up in an appropriate fashion. Dads, this is your time to shine. It's father-daughter dance time."

More cheers, as well as a few groans from embarrassed teenagers.

Nevertheless, they shuffled onto the floor along with everyone else, their faces bright with smiles as the Prophecy Kings launched into a slow cover of Stevie Wonder's "Isn't She Lovely."

"What do you say? You up for a dance?" Nate held out his hand. "I hope this isn't creepy, since it's a father-daughter dance, but I don't think couples are the theme of the night."

Kris laughed. "We'll make it work."

They wrapped their arms around each other and swayed to the music. Kris spotted Skylar and Michael dancing a few feet away and smiled. She hoped things worked out with Nate and Skylar's father. She really did.

"How are things with your dad?" Nate's palm glided up and down her spine, and she snuggled closer to him, feeling warm and content.

"Same old, same old. We haven't discussed our argument over Gloria, but it'll blow over like every other argument we've had." Kris didn't want to talk about her fucked-up household situation, but there was something she had to get off her chest. She lifted her head so she could look at Nate. "I'm sorry about how he treated you yesterday. He may not be around much, but he's overprotective when it comes to my dating life."

"That's understandable." Nate's eyes were unreadable, though he continued to rub her back with long soothing strokes. "Don't worry about it. You are his only daughter, and even if he isn't around much, I think he genuinely wants what's best for you."

"I guess," she said, surprised by how reasonable Nate was being.

Not that he *wasn't* a reasonable person by nature, but she'd just expected a little more...fire. Indignation. Instead, he was as cool and calm as if they were discussing the weather.

Wait, no, that wasn't it. He wasn't cool and calm. He was remote, distant in a way that he hadn't been since...ever. Even when they'd bickered and snipped at each other in the past, he'd always been present and full of crackling passion.

That wasn't the case now.

A thread of unease unraveled down Kris's spine and wrapped around her stomach, squeezing until she was short of breath.

Before she could bring up Nate's strange behavior, he spoke again. "Can I ask you something? Be honest. This isn't a trick question."

The unease intensified. "Okay."

"Have your views changed on long-distance relationships?"

It was a good thing he was holding her; otherwise, Kris would've fallen over in surprise. Of all the things she'd expected him to ask, that had not been in her top ten—or even top fifty.

But, of course, she thought, a measure of relief easing her tension. Nate was thinking about their looming deadline and what would happen after Kris left LA.

In truth, her views on long-distance relationships in general hadn't changed. But a long-distance relationship with Nate? That was another matter. She didn't want these next few weeks to be the last time they spoke to each other, and the thought of him moving on and dating someone else made her stomach clench in protest.

In just a few short months, she'd revealed more of herself to him than she had to anyone else in her life, and she felt connected to him in a way she didn't think possible. Kris normally wasn't a fairy-tale romance, head-in-the-clouds type of girl, but nothing about her relationship with Nate was normal—and she didn't want it to be. It was uniquely theirs, and she didn't want it to end.

Not at the end of the month, not ever.

The realization slammed into Kris with the force of a tidal wave. She should've seen it coming from a mile away—her ease in sharing her deepest thoughts and darkest secrets with him, her giddiness when his name popped up on her phone, her anticipation at seeing him again, all the dang butterflies and pounding hearts—but when it hit, it hit hard.

She was in love with Nate Reynolds.

The question was, was he in love with her?

"I…" Kris hesitated, debating how to answer. Her heartbeat thudded in her ears, and her palms were slick with sweat. "I think there are merits to such relationships that I may have been blind to before."

"Hmm." No change in Nate's expression. "Like what?"

She thought carefully before answering. "Like developing greater trust in the other person and appreciating the moments you get to spend together. Like learning how to communicate better and figuring out whether it's lust or"—*love*—"something more."

"You've thought about this." There was a shadow of a smile on his lips, but the tension and remoteness remained.

Kris shrugged, hoping she looked and sounded casual. "I'm good at thinking on the fly."

Meanwhile, her mind blared with enough alarms to make a security breach at the Pentagon look like a chill day at the park.

Love! Love! I'm in love! Shit!

"Among other things." Nate kissed her then—a kiss so deep and soulful it quieted her inner freak-out. There was no tongue—hello, there were children around—but Kris melted all the same.

A delicate cough nudged them apart.

"Sorry to interrupt," Skylar said, grinning. "Everyone's wrapping up, and I wanted to say bye. Dad's driving me home."

She gestured at Michael, who nodded at Nate but didn't come any closer.

Smart move.

"I can take you," Nate said.

"Nope. I'm going with Dad. You and Kris...do your thing. See you later!" With one last grin, Skylar bounded off in a flurry of tulle and wheat-colored hair.

A visual sweep of the room revealed that the party was, indeed, over. While the band broke down their equipment—Kris hadn't realized the music had shut off—MentHer staff cleared off the tables, boxed up leftover food, and took down assorted decorations.

"I'm going to help clean up," she said. "Talk to you tomorrow? I know you've had a long day, so don't feel like you have to stay."

"It's all good. I'll say hi to Elijah and help too. I'm not tired."

She watched Nate walk toward his friend and remembered with amusement how the first thing Nate did after they agreed to date was tell Elijah. Blue Hair had been shocked and a bit crestfallen that Kris was no longer available, but he'd quickly gotten over it—he was now casually dating another of the café's customers, a cute pixie-like girl with green hair. They'd probably bonded over Manic Panic.

It took Kris, Nate, and a half dozen staff members and volunteers another hour to restore the multipurpose room to its former not-so-much-glory. The party rental company needed to pick up the tables and chairs, but otherwise, they did a damn good job of cleaning up.

After Kris thanked the band and bid the rest of MentHer good night, she and Nate stepped out into the mild evening chill.

"Do you want to grab something to eat?" she asked. "You didn't touch the food all night."

"Nah. I had a big lunch."

She fiddled with her purse, feeling uncharacteristically on edge. She wasn't crazy. Nate *was* acting weird, and she doubted it had to do with Monday's shoot.

That, combined with her big-*L* revelation, had her all out of sorts.

"Nate, why'd you ask me whether I'd changed my mind about long-distance relationships earlier?"

His silence stretched between them, turning several feet of physical distance into miles of separation.

Kris didn't like beating around the bush, and dammit, they had such limited time left. They needed to unscramble whatever mess had popped up between them—she might not know what it was, but she sensed it was there. It was not the time to play coy.

"Look," she said. "I'll be honest. When we agreed to date for the summer, I *didn't* believe in long-distance relationships. I still don't...for some people. But I think you and I..." She took a deep breath. "We could make it work. I really like you, and I'm not ready to end things yet. I'm willing to give the long-distance thing a shot if you are."

Fuck, that had been hard to get out. At least she hadn't said the *L* word out loud. She wasn't ready for that, not when she wasn't sure if Nate reciprocated her feelings.

There was only so much vulnerability a girl could throw out there in the space of one minute.

And when Nate opened his mouth after her little spiel, she was really freakin' glad she hadn't divulged her revelation of the night.

"I can't do this."

Not the three words Kris had wanted or expected to hear.

Nate stepped back, his expression more distant than it had been all evening, and that was saying something.

Her heart sputtered and lurched like a car running out of gas after going full speed on the Autobahn, confused as to what was happening but sure it couldn't be anything good.

"Can't do what?" For once, Kris couldn't control the tremble in her voice. "The long distance or the—"

"This. Us." He gestured between them. "I'm sorry. I like you a lot, but this has always been a short-term thing for me. I can't do long distance. I have too much on my plate—with my family, with work—and it's just not going to work out."

His words were so flat and monotone, they may as well have been delivered by a robot.

It was funny, how your emotions, your world, your *life* could change in the blink of an eye. Less than an hour ago, Kris had been exhausted but on top of the world, riding high on an event well done and kissing the man she loved.

Now, she was numb from head to toe—her pulse pounding and her head throbbing as her brain scrambled to make sense of the words coming out of Nate's mouth.

Kris supposed she should say something. Scream at him, maybe? But he technically hadn't done anything wrong. He'd told her from the start that this was a summer thing, nothing more.

We have fun together, and neither of us will be the one walking away because we have a set deadline. It'll be a mutual thing. Clean, easy. No hard feelings.

Nate's words from their night on the boat came back to her, drowning out the sounds in the parking lot—the beep of a car unlocking by remote, the rustling of leaves when a breeze swept by, the bass drum of her heart as it kicked at her rib cage in a tornado of fury and anger.

How could she have been so stupid? Kris had always prided herself on not letting her emotions get the best of her, but she'd allowed the attraction and connection she'd felt with Nate blind her to the truth—for him, it was only lust. He'd wanted to date her because... why? So he could have sex whenever he wanted without having to go through the effort of wooing a different girl every night? Probably. Given it had an end date, that must've seemed like a good deal.

It was only now that Kris realized they'd never discussed their deadline when they'd agreed to be boyfriend and girlfriend, and she couldn't even be upset with him because he'd told her from the beginning what to expect.

But just because she couldn't, didn't mean she wasn't.

Sample sale. Limited edition. Chanel.

Her previously soothing mantra had all the effectiveness of a surgeon using a butter knife instead of a scalpel. No fixing the massive crack in her foolish heart. Thankfully, her pride, though battered, remained intact, and it was that small mercy that kept her tears at bay.

"Okay." Her voice sounded far away, like she was listening to herself through a bad phone connection. "Fine."

Words that meant nothing, but they were all she could come up with.

Nate ran a hand over his face. For the briefest moment, his stony facade cracked and pain shone through—a blinding, devastating slash of white-hot torment that disappeared when the shutters slammed shut once more.

"I didn't want it to end this way," he said. "I meant everything I told you so far. You're amazing, but you and I, we're not the right fit. Not for the long term. It wouldn't be fair to keep this going when you're—when you're developing feelings for me. You should be with someone more like you, who can give you—"

"Don't." The word cracked through the air like a whip. "You don't want to be with me? Fine. But don't you *dare* tell me what I should do with my life or who I should be with. That's not your place."

Nate's throat bobbed with a hard swallow. "You're right. I'm sorry."

"Well, it's been fun," Kris said stiffly, willing her tears to hold the fuck on and wait until she got home because the one thing she couldn't handle more than having her heart broken was letting the heartbreaker see the destruction he'd wrought. "I guess our 'deadline' is a moot point. Things between us are over as of tonight."

Nate flinched. His skin paled beneath his tan, and his fists clenched and unclenched like he was straining to keep his emotions bottled up.

"This is for the best," he said. "We don't—"

"Spare me." Kris made a show of digging her keys out of her purse. "Now, if you'll excuse me, I'm going home. It's been a long night."

She didn't wait for his reply before she walked to her car, switched on the ignition, and drove home.

She made it only a quarter of the way before her vision blurred, at which point she calmly pulled over to the side of the road, turned off the engine, and collapsed into body-wracking sobs.

CHAPTER 20

KRIS HAD A ROCK-SOLID STRATEGY FOR MANAGING emotional pain, which she dubbed the three *s*'s: shopping, spa, and sex.

The morning after the MentHer gala and her breakup with Nate, she took her credit cards on a field trip to Rodeo Drive, where she racked up so many purchases, the plastic grew hot to the touch. Once she maxed out her monthly limit—thank God she had her checking account as a backup—she unwound with a deluge of treatments at her favorite spa: an exfoliating body scrub, an oxygen facial, a ninety-minute deep-tissue aromatherapy massage, and a mani-pedi complete with paraffin wax treatments.

Except she didn't unwind. She was tense and agitated the whole time, to the point where her massage therapist would've given up on her had Kris not paid four hundred dollars for the service.

The shopping and spa twofer had always worked in the past, yet the jagged spikes tearing up Kris's chest remained. It scraped against her tender flesh every time she breathed until blood dripped from the shattered pieces of her heart. She'd look down every few minutes, half expecting to see drops of red liquid glistening on her skin, but her exterior remained as flawless and well-groomed as ever.

It was only on the inside that she died.

Luckily—or unluckily, depending on how you looked at it—Kris had another problem that distracted her from her metaphorical death: the Bobbi Rayden Tornado and Its Aftermath.

She'd woken up Sunday morning to a deluge of furious texts, missed calls, and emails from her now ex-boss because she'd completely forgotten about Sabrina Winters's *Mode de Vie* shoot… which had been on the same day as the MentHer gala. While Sabrina posed and preened in front of the camera, Kris had been running around, perfecting the centerpieces and liaising with the band at the YMCA.

Bobbi had not been happy, and she'd fired Kris in her last all-caps text. Kris didn't particularly care, though she experienced a frisson of guilt over her lapse of memory. She didn't make promises often, but when she did, she kept them—for the most part.

The guilt had compelled Kris to call Bobbi and apologize. She managed to get the "sorry" out before the other woman hung up on her.

Bobbi told Roger about Kris's fuckup, and Roger had been livid. The fact that Kris had been volunteering for a nonprofit had tempered his anger somewhat, but he'd still laid down his ultimatum: find a job for the rest of the summer or he'd cut her off. Again.

Never mind the fact there were only three weeks left before the fall semester.

It had been an epically shitty weekend, and her group video chat with Courtney, Farrah, and Olivia Sunday night only made her feel worse. As much as she enjoyed her friends' company, they reminded her of the halcyon days of study abroad in Shanghai, when she'd been unencumbered by interest in the opposite sex. While Courtney got caught up in her drama with Leo, and Farrah and Blake turned into a total shitshow, and Olivia and Sammy became the world's most nauseatingly sweet couple—though judging by Olivia's current tone, there was trouble in paradise in New York—Kris had flown above it all, secure in the knowledge that she would never debase herself by falling for a guy.

Ha. Joke was on her.

However, she kept what happened with Nate to herself. She was so not in the mood to rehash her whirlwind romance and heartbreak. The wounds were too fresh, and she didn't trust herself not to break down over Skype. Talk about Humiliation Central.

"I hate to cut this short, but we have to go," Olivia said eighty minutes into their call. She sat next to Farrah, who was also interning in NYC, and they both wore casual-dressy black tops—standard attire for nights out in the city. "We have dinner reservations for a new pop-up restaurant in the Village that I had to practically sell my firstborn to get. But let's talk again soon? I miss you guys!"

"Miss you too." Courtney blew a kiss through the screen. "We need to have an in-person reunion. Maybe a long weekend or spring break?"

Olivia brushed a strand of silky black hair out of her eye. "Sounds good to me. I'll research and come up with a list of options."

"Kris, when are you leaving LA?" Farrah asked. "Maybe we'll overlap." The girl was still twisted up over her breakup with that asshole Blake Ryan—Kris could see it in her eyes—but she made a valiant effort to appear upbeat and cheerful.

When Kris gave her the date, Farrah's face fell. "Damn, so close. You leave the day before I get back."

"I'm sure I'll see you soon," Kris said, trying on Upbeat and Cheerful herself for size. *Nope, not happening.* Probably because she wasn't an upbeat and cheerful person even on a good day. "I have faith in Liv's scheduling skills."

Olivia dipped into a mock bow. "Why thank you."

After a few more minutes of idle chitchat and goodbyes, Kris's friends signed off, and she lay on her four-poster bed, trying and failing to find solace in her luxurious surroundings. The things that used to fill her up—the designer clothes, the fancy furniture, the knowledge that she possessed the triple privilege of being young, hot, and rich—left her cold.

Not even Harry Winston could make her feel better.

Kris owned things that most girls would kill for, but they were just that—*things*. They couldn't fill the hole in her heart, soothe her when she cried, or infuse her with a pleasure that went far deeper than the short-lived dopamine hit she got from a new handbag.

A tear slipped down her cheek, and she wiped it away angrily.

"I don't cry over guys." Her voice echoed in the silence and sounded unconvincing to her own ears.

Fuck this.

Kris refused to be one of those girls who couldn't get out of bed because she was heartbroken. It wasn't like she and Nate would've lasted anyway. He was right. They were too different, and her initial misgivings about long-distance relationships were correct. They would've broken up eventually.

At least, that was what she told herself.

It took Kris ten minutes to gather enough energy to reach for her phone. She stared at the screen for a moment before she pulled up a familiar name and sent him a quick text.

Kris: What are you doing tomorrow?

She didn't have a job anymore, so her schedule was wide-open. As for her father's ultimatum…well, she'd deal with that later.

The reply came less than a minute later.

Teague: Hanging out with you.

Excellent.

Kris: Manhattan Beach, 9 a.m. See you then.

Shopping and the spa may not have cured her of her heartbreak, but she still had one *s* left.

———————

Sex with Teague was off the table.

Not because he wasn't attractive—his lean muscles and tousled hair drew the eyes of more than a few women when he and Kris walked along the beach Monday morning, but despite his good looks, she couldn't summon an iota of sexual attraction toward him.

She would've chalked it up to their friendship, except her lack of attraction also ran toward every other guy at the beach, many of whom looked like they moonlighted as Calvin Klein underwear models.

Clearly, Kris's body was not ready for sex with someone else this soon after her breakup, no matter what her mind said. Her heart was out of commission altogether; even if it weren't, it wouldn't have had a seat at the Table of Rebounds.

"You okay?" Teague eyed her with concern. "You've been unusually quiet. You didn't even comment on my attire."

Kris cracked a half-hearted smile. Teague wore the bright

orange board shorts she'd dared him to buy in St. Barts one winter, but if anyone could pull off swimwear so glaringly bright it practically glowed, it was Teague.

"I have a lot on my mind."

"Bobbi and the new job thing?"

She'd filled him in on that part of the weekend earlier.

"No." They were close enough to the shore that a gentle wave lapped at Kris's ankles before it receded. "Nate and I broke up Saturday night. His decision."

Teague let out a low whistle. "Not a good weekend."

"Nope."

"Nate's an idiot."

"Yep."

"Honestly, I'm surprised. I only met the guy once, but I thought..." Teague trailed off. "Did he say why?"

"Some bullshit about us not being right for each other." No way was Kris telling anyone she'd wanted a long-distance relationship and Nate had shut her down. Hard. "Whatever. We wouldn't have lasted anyway. I leave in—"

"Kris!"

Kris turned her head and watched in disbelief as Skylar bounded toward her with two athletic-looking brunettes—one with a long thick braid; the other with a pixie cut that enhanced her catlike, green eyes—in tow. Kris recognized the girl with the braid as Briana, the mentee who'd introduced Skylar to MentHer. Pixie Cut was a stranger.

"Hey, Sky. Hey, Briana." Kris forced a smile. "Small world."

She'd come to view Skylar as the little sister she'd never had, but the teen reminded her too much of Nate. One look at her and the spikes in Kris's chest intensified their assault.

"Briana, Lacey, and I came here to relax. And to ogle the hot guys." Skylar wiggled her eyebrows and slid an appreciate glance toward Teague. "Soccer camp was brutal this week."

"Coach is trying to kill us," Briana confirmed.

"She just wants us in tip-top shape. We have our big exhibition game coming up, and scouts from a bunch of colleges will be there," Lacey explained to Kris and Teague.

"Sounds fun. I'm Teague," he added, and Kris realized belatedly she hadn't introduced him yet.

He didn't seem to mind. He just shot her a bemused smile, like he wasn't sure why a bunch of high school girls were so excited to see her.

MentHer, she mouthed. She'd told him about the organization when they ran into each other at Runyon Canyon.

Understanding dawned in his eyes, and he nodded.

"You guys should come to the game!" Skylar chirped. "Every player can invite up to four people. I've only invited my dad and Nate, so I have two spots left. It's perfect."

Kris's heart squeezed at the sound of Nate's name. The sun suddenly felt too hot on her skin, the sand too rough beneath her feet. "Thanks for the invite, but I don't think that's a good idea."

Skylar frowned. She tugged on her ponytail and glanced at Briana and Lacey, who took the hint and announced they were going for a dip in the water.

"I'll scout out a prime sunbathing spot for us," Teague said, also catching on. He loped off, leaving Kris and Skylar alone.

Skylar waited until he was out of earshot before she spoke. "I know what happened between you and my brother. He was in a total mood yesterday, and it took me forever to pry it out of him, but he told me." Her brows formed a sharp, angry V over the bridge of her nose. "He's being a stupid, asshole-y jerk and I'm mad at him."

A rusty laugh emerged from Kris's throat before it died a quick death. But it was her first laugh in forty-eight hours so that counted for something, right? "He's your brother."

"Which is how I know what a colossal idiot he is." Skylar

rolled her bottom lip between her teeth. "He's sad, you know. He called in sick to work yesterday, which he *never* does, and he just moped around the house in these ugly old sweatpants. He didn't even run lines for today's shoot."

Something sparked inside Kris before she crushed it with a ruthless fist. She would not get her hopes up. "Whatever he's sad about, he'll get over it."

The Oscar Bravo shoot today would revive him. Nate had a minor role, so he only needed to be on set for two days max, but he'd been looking forward to it since he got the job.

"No, he won't. He's sad over *you*."

Kris sucked in a deep breath and tried for patience. "He was the one who broke up with me."

"Maybe he regrets it." Skylar sounded hopeful. "Maybe he realizes he made a mistake and wants to get back together but hasn't found the courage to contact you yet."

Kris had to appreciate the younger girl's romantic optimism, even if she didn't share the sentiment. "I doubt it."

Skylar's jaw set in a stubborn line. "Fine. But will you come to the game? It's Wednesday night." Her eyes searched Kris's face. "It's a huge deal, and I want you there if you can make it."

Kris had manipulated enough people in the past to know when she was the one being manipulated. Her skin flushed hot and cold at the thought of seeing Nate again so soon—she wasn't ready. She wasn't sure if she'd ever be ready. But soccer meant a lot to Skylar, and this game *was* a big deal. Coaches from Division I schools all over the country would be in attendance. Skylar wasn't lying about that.

"I'll go if Teague goes." If Kris were to face her ex again after getting dumped, she needed armor. And if that armor came in the form of a six-foot-tall blond with a ripped surfer's body?

All the better.

CHAPTER 21

KRIS REGRETTED HER DECISION TO ATTEND SKYLAR'S game the second she stepped foot in the stadium Wednesday evening. The area buzzed with activity—the players warming up on the field, the friends and family laughing and shouting encouragement to their sisters and daughters and friends, the soccer camp employees huddled on the sidelines.

Despite the crowd, her eyes zeroed in on the glint of golden-brown hair in the bleachers. She didn't have to look for him— her body was so attuned to his, she could pinpoint his presence within seconds with missile accuracy.

Nate sat on the fifth row of bleachers on the far side of the stadium, devastating in a white T-shirt, olive-green camouflage jacket, and jeans. His skin stretched taut over his cheekbones, and even at a distance, Kris spotted shadows beneath his eyes that indicated he hadn't been sleeping well. His bronzed skin appeared wan beneath the field's fluorescent lights.

Despite all that, he remained the most heartbreakingly beautiful man she'd ever seen.

One. Two. Three. Kris tracked the painful thuds slamming against her rib cage with curious detachment.

"You okay?" Teague asked. Being the good friend he was, he'd agreed to accompany her tonight even though he must have had better things to do than attend a high school soccer game.

"Yes." Kris straightened and squared her shoulders. She could do this. It was just a game. She didn't have to speak to or look at Nate if she didn't want to.

She had, however, come prepared for battle. Her blowout this morning left her hair a sleek, shining waterfall of multi-toned brown down her back, while her expertly applied makeup enhanced her huge dark eyes and full lips. She wore a loose, pale blue silk blouse tucked into faded hip-hugging jeans and unbuttoned enough to reveal the white lace bralette corset underneath. A pair of strappy neutral wedges completed the perfect casual-but-sexy outfit.

The eyes of more than a few interested males followed Kris as she and Teague edged their way toward one of the few empty spots in the bleachers. The seats also happened to be directly below and to the left of where Nate sat with his father.

Kris hadn't realized the elder Reynolds was here—Nate's body had blocked Michael from her earlier vantage point—but there was no mistaking the olive skin and strong jaw. He was the spitting image of his son, only older and more beaten down by life.

Interesting. He and Nate had come together. She wondered if they'd patched things up. Michael still looked like he was in withdrawal—the shakes were a dead giveaway—but his color had improved since Saturday.

It's none of your business. You're not Nate's girlfriend anymore.

Kris purposefully avoided looking in the father and son's direction when she took her seat.

"I'm going to grab a hot dog before the game starts," Teague said. "You want anything?"

Kris's stomach growled at the promise of food. She'd been too anxious to eat anything except a small salad and smoothie all day.

"A hot dog and water would be great."

"You got it."

Teague left his jacket on his seat, and Kris had to place her hand on it to prevent it from sliding onto the floor after the person behind them kicked at the bleacher like he was trying out for a college soccer team himself.

She turned to give the baseball-cap-wearing frat boy a piece of her mind, but her gaze caught and locked onto Nate's instead.

Nate's green eyes bore into hers, dark and simmering with barely veiled fury. His handsome face appeared carved from granite.

What the hell did he have to be mad about? He was the one who broke up with her! Kris should be the pissed-off one.

Another crack split her insides open, but she lifted her chin and returned his glare, refusing to be cowed. Let him stare. Let him see what he'd lost.

All the while, she bled inside.

Thankfully, Teague returned before the stadium exploded from the intensity of Kris and Nate's silent stare-down.

When she tore her gaze away from her ex-boyfriend to focus on her friend, oxygen returned to her lungs, and it took all she had not to gulp in lungfuls of fresh air.

"If looks could kill, you'd both be eating dirt right now." A faint glimmer of amusement threaded Teague's words.

There was no need to clarify who he meant when he said "both."

"Good thing they don't. I imagine dirt tastes like shit." Kris smiled when she saw Teague had dressed her hot dog just the way she liked it—ketchup, no mustard, and a sprinkling of relish. "You remembered."

"I've been on the receiving end of too many drunk, hangry Kris tantrums *not* to remember."

That elicited a genuine laugh. Poor Teague. He was right—God help whoever was around Kris when she was drunk, hungry/angry, and craving random foods.

She glimpsed the hard set of Nate's jaw over Teague's shoulder. He was still staring at her like she'd killed his (nonexistent) dog.

Acting on pure instinct, she leaned over and kissed Teague on the cheek.

The position gave her an unobstructed view of Nate, who ignored whatever his father was saying to him in favor of upping the intensity of his glare. Displeasure rolled off him in waves, so thick and potent she could almost touch it.

"I'm going to assume that kiss wasn't for my benefit," Teague said wryly when Kris pulled back. "Did it work?"

On the field, the game started.

"It doesn't matter." Kris bit into her hot dog and watched the players' smooth, coordinated movements. Skylar took possession of the ball and passed it to Lacey, who dribbled it farther down the right sideline before kicking it to another teammate. "It's pure testosterone on his part. Not jealousy."

It was nice to see she could still rile him up, though.

Teague stretched, a deceptively casual move that allowed him to glance over his shoulder without making his intent obvious.

"I don't know. He looks jealous to me." Teague finished his stretch by draping an arm over Kris's shoulder. The amusement in his voice deepened. "I'd bet my new surfboard that he would tear my head off if he got the chance."

Kris smiled grimly. "You're sweet, but let's not talk about him tonight."

Nate already took up too much space in her head, her heart,

her life. Even though they were no longer together, memories of him lingered in her consciousness like a bad pop song that wouldn't go away—only worse because no amount of Spotify replays would solve the problem.

She could only rely on time and distraction.

Kris focused on the game and tried to ignore the green eyes burning a hole in her skin. She didn't look behind her again, but she *felt* him. His presence obliterated everything else around her.

Still, she tried.

The purpose of the camp's exhibition game wasn't to crown a winner. After all, the players had all attended the same summer camp and trained under the same coach. No, the game was an opportunity for them to show off their skills to the best college coaches in the country—the ones in charge of recruitment and deciding which up-and-coming talents were worth full-ride scholarships that could make some lucky girls' academic and athletic dreams come true.

Nevertheless, the audience cheered as if they were watching the World Cup finals. Kris hated sports—the idea of running around on a field in the same clothes as everyone else, sweating and passing a ball around, was her version of hell—but toward the end of the night, even she got caught up in the excitement and thrill of it all.

"Go, Skylar!" she yelled, jumping in excitement when the blond scored a goal that put her team one point ahead with two minutes to spare.

A male voice echoed her sentiment.

Kris made the mistake of looking to her right. Her gaze snagged on Nate's, and they connected for one breathless, torturous eternity before she broke the bond and retook her seat. Her heart jumped all over the place—from excitement over Skylar's goal or the brief sizzle of eye contact, she didn't know.

"So much for not liking soccer," Teague teased. He was on his fifth hot dog. The boy could eat like a horse.

"Shut up."

The buzzer signaling the end of the game sounded, and the audience erupted into a mixture of cheers and disappointed groans.

Skylar's team won 4–3. Skylar had scored the winning goal.

Sure, the game wasn't about winners and losers, but pride bloomed in Kris's chest nonetheless. She and Teague joined the crowd pushing their way onto the field, and he placed a hand on the small of her back to guide her through the crush of people. It was the comforting gesture of a friend, not the possessive one of a lover.

Kris swore she heard a growl behind her.

"You're blocking my way." The smoke-and-whiskey voice contained noticeable tendrils of irritation.

She stiffened and glared over her shoulder at Nate.

Gone was the stoic but apologetic man from Saturday night. In its place was a crackling pillar of pent-up possession and fury. Nate's expression made a thundercloud look cheerful by comparison.

"Who died and made you king? In case you can't tell, there are people blocking us too." Her cool tone belied the warning bells raising their alarms throughout her body. *Danger! Danger!*

Nate was too close. Kris could smell his coffee-and-leather scent and see the gold flecks in his eyes. She wanted to step back out of the danger zone, but that would be admitting weakness.

Instead, she reached for Teague, her fingers curling around his arm for support.

Nate tracked the movement with the intensity of a predator. Something akin to pain raked across his face before it disappeared as quickly as it came.

"Is everything okay?" Michael came up beside his son and examined Kris with mild surprise. "Hi, Kris."

"Hello, Mr. Reynolds."

Awkward silence punctuated the air.

"I'm Teague." The blond held out his hand; the other remained on Kris's waist. "Kris's friend."

Nate's eye twitched.

"Right." Michael grasped Teague's hand, seeming grateful for a normal interaction. "Nice to meet you."

"Nice to meet you too."

More awkward silence.

"I'm going to congratulate Sky before we head out." Kris last saw the younger girl in deep conversation with a woman whom, based on the familiarity with which Skylar spoke to her, she assumed was the camp coach. "She did a great job today."

Michael's head bobbed up and down. "That she did."

Nate remained silent. He hadn't said a word since his dickish proclamation that Kris and Teague were blocking his way.

He did, however, follow Kris, Teague, and Michael as they elbowed their way through the thinning crowd. A majority of players and parents had dispersed, and it didn't take them long to reach Skylar, who was still talking on the sidelines with her coach. An older man with thinning blond hair and a black tracksuit had joined them.

The coach caught sight of the foursome and said something to the man. She shook his hand, a motion Skylar repeated before the mystery man walked away.

"You came!" Skylar's face lit up when she saw her father. She tackled him in a huge hug, which he returned with a laugh.

First the MentHer gala, now the big game. Two in one week. Not bad for a man who'd been MIA on the fatherly duties front for half a decade.

Kris caught the grim set of Nate's mouth out of the corner of her eye, but he appeared less suspicious than when he'd learned Michael had shown up to the gala.

Skylar hugged Nate next, and the sight of the siblings' arms wrapped tight around each other, pride shining in Nate's eyes while his sister burrowed her face in his chest, tugged at Kris's heartstrings.

I really am going soft.

"Hey, Kris." Skylar broke away from Nate and approached Kris, stopping a few inches short. "Oops, I'm all sweaty."

Kris looked at her expensive outfit, then at Skylar's sweat-dampened jersey, and heaved a huge sigh. She opened her arms.

Skylar grinned, closing the distance between them and hugging her with the same ferocity she had her family. She was the biggest hugger Kris had ever met. "You look hot," she whispered. "I bet Nate is eating his heart out."

A smirk tugged at Kris's lips. She'd taught the girl well.

It was a good thing Skylar was fundamentally sweet, or the male Reynoldses would have had major trouble on their hands.

"Thanks for coming. You look different with your shirt on," Skylar chirped in her greeting to Teague.

Color rose on his cheeks, and Kris's smirk widened.

Who was she kidding? Skylar was already trouble.

Michael and Nate choked at the same time.

"Excuse me?" Nate's voice was all gravel and growl. "When the f—" He glanced at Skylar's coach, who was too busy scribbling on her clipboard to pay attention to the mini drama unfolding in front of her. "When did you see him with his shirt off?"

"At the beach on Monday," Skylar said, all big eyes and innocence. "That was when I ran into him and Kris and invited them to the game."

"I see." Nate's jaw flexed like he was mulling over whether

to say something else, but the coach finally looked up and introduced herself.

"I'm Coach Karsten," she said in a brisk, efficient tone. Kris appreciated her no-nonsense attitude, though the coach would look much better with a shorter haircut and a pop of lipstick. That scraggly shoulder-length thing she had going on did her no favors.

Coach Karsten ran through Skylar's performance during the game and in the camp overall. Kris was about to excuse herself—the discussion seemed more relevant to the Reynolds family than outsiders, and she didn't want to keep Teague here longer than necessary, considering he'd already given up his night for her—when the woman said something that stopped her in her tracks.

"The man we were speaking to earlier is the women's soccer coach at Stanford." No noticeable change in Coach Karsten's expression, but Kris detected a glimmer of pride beneath the words. "Skylar made a big impression on him tonight. There's a good chance he'll offer her a full cost-of-attendance sports scholarship if she plays her cards right."

Silence fell.

Skylar was bouncing with excitement, but Michael and Nate resembled statues. Kris's pulse kicked up a notch, and even Teague looked impressed.

"Holy shit!" Nate finally burst out. He swept his sister into a hug again and flashed Coach Karsten an apologetic glance. "Sorry about the language."

A hint of a smile. "I'm a soccer coach. I've heard worse."

That broke the ice. Soon everyone was laughing and hugging and jumping. Kris's heart was in her throat. She'd worked closely with Skylar on her college applications over the summer and knew how much Stanford meant to the younger girl. It wasn't just about her future; it was about her mother's legacy. Joanna

Reynolds had been a Stanford alumna who'd chosen to use her English degree to mold young minds instead of chasing Pulitzers and writing the next great American novel. Education had been important to her, and Skylar wanted to follow in her footsteps—but as a science, not English, major, because "Shakespeare is *so* boring."

The Reynoldses wouldn't be able to afford the top-tier school on their own, but a cost-of-attendance scholarship covered everything—tuition and fees, room and board, travel, even personal expenses.

"It's not set in stone yet," Coach Karsten warned. "He'll be monitoring how Skylar does during her school's regular soccer season, and the competition for full cost-of-attendance scholarships is *tough*. Stanford has already recruited most of its incoming players, and there are only one or two spots left. She has to be at the top of her game. No slacking off."

"I won't," Skylar interjected. "I won't slack off. I'm going to get that scholarship." Determination turned her words to steel.

The coach's mouth softened into a proud smile.

There was more discussion about soccer and nutrition and training tips.

Kris stifled a yawn. She was excited for Skylar, but she was also exhausted. It'd been a long day and talk of macronutrients didn't exactly fire her up.

"I'm heading out," she said during a lull. "Congratulations again, Sky. I'll see you at the workshop tomorrow?"

"Yep." Skylar glowed. "Good night. Thanks again for coming."

Kris and Teague walked off the field, with Kris making it a point *not* to look in Nate's direction. They were halfway to the parking lot when the hairs on the back of her neck prickled.

"Kris, wait."

She stopped, her heart thundering in her ears. "Go ahead," she said when Teague shot her a questioning glance. "I'll meet you at the car."

Caution lined his handsome features. "You sure?"

She nodded.

"Okay. Call me if you need anything." Her friend cast another glance over his shoulder before he disappeared into the darkness of the night.

Kris readjusted her icy mask and turned.

Nate stood a few feet away, looking like a god beneath the bright stadium lights. His hair gleamed like a halo, and the shadows sharpened the lines of his already knifelike jaw and cheekbones. His expression was inscrutable.

"What do you want?" Cool. Crisp. Clear. No hint of the painful inferno raging inside her.

"I wanted to..." He paused, a muscle working in his throat. "Thank you for everything you've done for Skylar."

"Thank-you accepted."

A hint of amusement flared in his eyes. "Most people would've said, 'You're welcome.'"

"I'm not most people."

"I know." Nate's voice lowered. Became more intimate. "Trust me. I know."

The words flowed through Kris's veins like honey until she remembered the last conversation they'd had.

I can't do this.

This has always been a short-term thing for me.

She ignored the sudden painful clench in her chest. "Was that all? Teague is waiting for me."

Turned out the other man's name was a trigger because all traces of amusement disappeared from Nate's face and a growl rumbled from his chest. "Are you two together?"

Kris couldn't believe he had the nerve to ask her that. They broke up less than a week ago. Did he think she had backup boyfriends on speed dial? Even if she did... "That's none of your damn business."

"You're Skylar's mentor, which means what you do affects her, and what affects her affects me."

That was a leap, jump, and stretch, and they both knew it.

"Fine. Maybe I am dating him," Kris snapped. "I took your advice and found someone 'more like me.' We come from the same social circle. We eat in the same restaurants and vacation in the same places. And..." Time for the knockout blow. "He's the best kisser I've ever had." Total lie, and a contradiction of what she told him the day Teague took them flying. But Nate apparently believed her because shock and dismay rippled across his features.

Nothing dented a man's pride like having his physical prowess undermined.

The sight should've elicited satisfaction, but Kris felt no pleasure. Only sadness. When had they become so cruel and vindictive toward each other? Nate had been her haven, her anchor. The one who'd understood her better than anyone else...until he tossed her aside like a pair of old shoes because they weren't "the right fit." Whatever the hell that meant.

"I should've been with him this entire time," Kris managed past the lump in her throat. "You're right. People like you and me? We'd never work. I'm meant to be with someone like Teague. So really, I should thank you for doing me a favor when you broke up with me."

Every line of Nate's body radiated tension. His emerald eyes had turned dark, almost black, and they blazed with emotion before he snuffed it.

"Good." Kris barely recognized his voice, it was so guttural and raw. "I'm glad."

Pain slashed its claws across her insides, and she knew she had five minutes tops before she lost it.

She turned and left without another word or a backward glance.

When she arrived at the car, Teague took one look at her face and backed out of the parking space with haste. Thankfully, he didn't try to talk to her; he just turned the radio on to an easy listening station and low volume to mask the sounds of Kris's soft sniffles.

She hated crying in front of other people. She hated crying, period. Yet here she was, crying over a man she'd known for, what, two months?

Pathetic.

Thankfully, by the time they reached her house, Kris had composed herself, though her nose remained red and her mascara smudged.

"Sorry tonight turned out to be such a mess." She unsnapped her seat belt and stared at the blazing lights of her house. It didn't look welcoming at all.

"What are you talking about? I had a great time." Teague ticked off the reasons on his fingers. "Soccer. Hot dogs. Hot date. Could be worse." His teasing tone indicated he meant *date* in the loosest sense of the word.

Kris snorted. "You need to up your date standards."

"Nah. Life is easier without high expectations." Teague brushed a knuckle over Kris's cheek. "Don't let the jerk get you down."

"I won't," she lied.

She kissed Teague good night on the cheek and slipped out of the car. Exhaustion settled into her bones, exacerbated by all the energy she'd spent caging her emotions in front of Nate.

Her plans to pass out in her bed ground to a screeching halt when she entered the house and found her father and Gloria waiting for her in the living room.

Weird. It was late, and her father had never been the wait-for-my-daughter-to-get-home-safely-before-I-go-to-sleep type. Most of the time, he wasn't home, period.

"What's going on?" Kris rolled her eyes at the smugness stamped all over Gloria's face, but a pinprick of dread needled at her.

Something's wrong.

"Kris Carrera." Roger unfurled himself to his full five feet eleven inches. *Shit.* He never called her by her full name, not even when she'd crashed her brand-new Porsche two days after her sixteenth birthday. "Would you care to explain what this is?"

He held up a sheet of paper.

How would she know? She didn't do documents, except—

Her blood chilled.

Her feet carried her across the room, and when she got close enough to read the black print, the chill turned to pure ice.

Roger was holding the contract she'd signed with Nate at the beginning of the summer—the one in which she described, in no uncertain terms, that she was hiring Nate to seduce Gloria in exchange for $15,000.

CHAPTER 22

SEVENTY-TWO. SEVENTY-THREE. SEVENTY-FOUR.
Seventy—

The chime of an incoming call interrupted Nate's brutal workout. He'd been at it for hours in his backyard, hoping to work off his frustration. A part of him acknowledged his punishing exercises had entered unhealthy territory, but he needed something to keep his mind off the shitstorm that was his personal life.

Sweat poured from his forehead and into his eyes, and he wiped away the perspiration before answering the call with a grunt. "Yeah?"

"Which Nate is this?" His agent and second cousin Marty sounded unimpressed by his caveman greeting. "Because I'm looking for Nate Reynolds, future movie star. Not Nate the Neanderthal."

"What do you want, Marty?"

Nate had long given up hope that Marty would come through with the Big Gig. His cousin had a dubious list of industry contacts, and his only other client was a former child actor whose last job was a B horror movie so bad it was almost good. Nate had only hired Marty because he was family, and he figured having a shitty agent was better than no agent at all.

In smaller markets, Nate could get away with self-submitting for roles, but in cities like LA and New York, talent needed professional representation if they hoped to land major studio and network projects.

Marty tsked. "I thought you'd be happier to hear from me, considering I'm about to change your life."

"Let me guess: you landed me a Marvel audition?" Nate asked wryly.

"No, but close." The other man's smugness leaked over the phone. "Lead role in a new Scott West action film. Word on the street is the studio wants to turn it into a franchise if the first movie does well. Of course, West wants an unknown for the role. You know how he is about the A-list types."

Nate sank onto the ground, stunned. "You're shitting me."

Scott West was one of the most revered directors in Hollywood, a force of nature and film, with a solid record of both box-office success and critical acclaim. However, the eccentric director only put out one or two movies a decade, if that. His last film, *Aquarius Rising*, was released twelve years ago, and he'd never done a franchise. He was also notorious for casting unknowns as leads in his movies because "stars are a goddamned pain in the ass," according to an *Entertainment Weekly* interview.

Ironically, every single then-unknown he'd cast had become A-list stars.

"I shit you not." Marty sounded more gleeful than Kurt Hummel belting out show tunes. "This is all hush-hush for now, so don't go running your mouth to anyone about this. Lucky for you, your favorite agent happened to go home with West's assistant the other night. Had no idea about her ties until after the fact. Couldn't get a script—they're passing those out on the spot. But auditions are Wednesday, so brush up on your skills and headshots, pretty boy. This could be your big break."

Nate wasn't surprised that Marty had landed news of the role of a lifetime not through professional networking but through his unofficial side gig as LA's premier Casanova. Nate had hooked up with his fair share of girls in the past, but Marty was on another, Wilt Chamberlain–esque level.

They talked business for another twenty minutes before Nate hung up. Adrenaline pumped in his veins, thick and hot. Auditions didn't mean he was guaranteed the role, not by a long shot, and competition for a Scott West lead would be fierce. Nate also had no clue what the movie was about or what type of character he was auditioning for, but he could study up on West—every film, every interview, every actor he'd cast in the past. Directors usually had a type of actor or actress they liked to work with, and Nate was going to figure out what made Scott West tick beyond the whole no-A-lister hang-up.

Casting directors oversaw auditions, but West was known to review tapes of all the auditions himself. He was a type-A micromanager to a fault.

Nate's skin buzzed with energy. For the first time since he broke up with Kris, he felt something other than soul-searing grief and pain.

Aaaaand there went the pain again. It happened every time he thought about her, or heard her name, or saw something that reminded him of their time together. Basically, all the fucking time.

The image of Kris's face when he told her he wasn't interested in anything long-term…seeing her and fucking Teague at Skylar's game…

Nate's hands involuntarily bunched into fists. God, he wanted to punch that smug blond male in the face. He'd thought Teague might be okay after their flight day, but nope. The bastard had had his hands all over Kris the other night. Yeah, he said he didn't have a thing for Kris—and Nate was the queen of England.

Loud banging on the front door sliced through Nate's possessive anger.

Michael reached the door before Nate could move. From this angle, Nate couldn't see who was making such a ruckus on a Saturday morning, but judging by how Michael widened the door and stepped aside to let the person in, it probably wasn't a Jehovah's Witness doing the whole door-to-door preaching song and dance.

Then Michael moved, giving Nate an unobstructed view of the newcomer.

His wounded heart went berserk as joy and dread suffused him in equal measure.

What was she doing here?

His father walked over and slid open the glass door separating the living room from the backyard. "Nate, you have a guest," he said quietly.

Michael's withdrawal symptoms had improved, and he no longer resembled a wax figure of himself. The symptoms should've eased a while ago, but they'd dragged on because Michael hadn't sought treatment. He wouldn't have been able to afford a proper medical detox.

Luckily, Michael's symptoms were relatively mild, given the length and history of his alcohol abuse.

"Thanks." Nate waited for his father to disappear up the stairs before he entered the living room, where Kris stood by the front door.

He closed the distance between them, battling twin urges to run in the other direction and to crush her to his chest and never let go. "Kris, what are—"

"How much?" Her eyes blazed with fury. He'd never seen her this angry—not when he broke up with her, not even when a passerby jostled her and caused her to spill her drink on her favorite top.

"I don't know what you're talking about."

Fuck, it was hot in here. He should've turned on the AC, but he'd wanted to cut down on the utility bill.

"How much, Nate?" Kris stepped forward until there was less than an inch of space between them. "How much money did my father give you to break up with me?"

A roar filled his ears.

Double fuck. She found out. She was never meant to find out.

"Kris—"

"How much?" she screamed, no trace of her usual cool, composed self in sight. She was all fire, and her anger seared through Nate's skin, scorching bone. But beneath the rage, he sensed a raw pain that twisted his gut. "How much was our relationship worth?"

"Fifty thousand dollars," he said quietly. There was no use lying anymore.

Those huge dark eyes of hers shone bright before a tear slipped down her cheek and shattered him. Before he knew it, Nate had yanked her to his chest and buried his face in her hair, wishing he could erase her pain. He could handle her fury, but he couldn't handle her hurt.

"Don't touch me." Hate infused her tone. "Don't *fucking* touch me."

Kris tried pushing him away, but he held on tight, rubbing circles on her back and whispering soothing words until she went limp in his arms.

Goddammit, how did she find out? He couldn't imagine Roger saying anything, but unless the other man told someone, he and Nate were the only ones privy to what went down in his study the other night.

Kris finally shoved him off, but her petite frame continued to tremble. She was so independent and tough that she usually appeared larger-than-life, but right now, she looked unbearably fragile, and there were dark smudges beneath her eyes, like she hadn't been sleeping well.

Agony sliced through him. Seeing Kris hurt cut him deeper than any blade could.

"I trusted you," she said. Flat. Monotone. No trace of her earlier fire.

"It's not what you think." Nate shoved a hand through his hair, his chest swimming with regret and sorrow. "Your father offered me the money. I didn't take it."

"So it's a coincidence he offered you fifty K to break up with me, and twenty-four hours later, you did just that. Next, you'll tell me you have a bridge to sell me."

God, he'd handled this all wrong. If they awarded Idiot of the Year prizes, he'd sweep the whole category.

"I didn't break up with you because of the money."

"Right. You broke up with me because we're not the 'right fit.'" She placed the words in quotation marks. "You might as well have pulled the 'It's not you, it's me' card."

"It *is* me." Nate scrubbed a hand over his face, frustrated. He wished he had more time to cobble his thoughts together in a somewhat coherent fashion, but since he didn't, the words spilled out, fast and furious. "The night of the dinner party, your father pulled me aside and made the offer. I swear on my mother's grave that I didn't accept a cent from him, but some of the things he said...made sense."

Kris crossed her arms, stony-faced. "Like?"

"Like how we're from different worlds and how we don't fit. I know," he said when she opened her mouth to argue. "You don't care about that stuff now, but our relationship is new. What happens when the honeymoon period ends? You're an heiress, you're about to graduate from a great school, and you have your entire future in front of you. I'm a college dropout barely making ends meet and in a career that's going nowhere. I have no idea what to do in fancy situations like the dinner party the other night. If we do the long-distance thing, I can't even visit you that often—not only because I can't spend that much on flights, but because I'm freakin' terrified of flying. It's gotten a little better after our flight day, yeah, but I am not at the point where I can just jump on a plane at the word *go*. You would've had to put in most of the effort, the same way you would've had to either pay for everything or give up your lifestyle to accommodate me. I can't do that to you, and I don't want us to resent each other down the line."

Nate's voice cracked. "You should be with someone who you'd be proud to be seen with. Someone who can live life with you the way you deserve and who your father approves of. I know your relationship with him isn't the greatest, but he wants the best for you, even if he shows it in a fucked-up way. You don't need me driving a bigger wedge between the two of you. And the thing is...I would've stayed by your side right up to the deadline because I couldn't bear the thought of leaving you. I thought you wanted us to stay a summer fling. Hoped you did, because even though it would've killed me, I at least knew you'd move on. But when you told me you wanted a long-distance relationship..." He swallowed hard. "I couldn't do that to you. I thought it would be easier to cut things off earlier, before..."

"Before what? Before I fell in love with you?" Kris's features hardened. "Too late."

He was making a bigger mess of things. Did what he said even—

Wait. *What?*

The color drained from Nate's face. "What did you just say?"

"I fell in love with you," she repeated. The words should've sent him over the moon with joy, but her cold, clinical tone was at odds with her words. "Or at least, the person I thought you were. Confident, no bullshit, goes after what he wants. But this?" Kris gestured at him. "All I see is someone with a boatload of excuses and insecurities he's too afraid to face. I can tell you right now that I don't give a *flying fuck* whether you have a college degree or know which fork to use at a dinner party. You know who else are college dropouts? Mark Zuckerberg. Brad Pitt. Oprah. They did pretty well for themselves. And newsflash: Etiquette can be learned. Fears can be overcome. But you didn't think of that, did you? You had a story in your head about not being good enough, rich enough, successful enough, and you twisted it to make it seem like you were doing me a favor when, in fact, you're the one who needed justification to stay in your comfort zone."

Nate was so stunned he couldn't speak. He couldn't even breathe.

"I needed you." Kris's lips trembled. "I needed someone in this godforsaken town who had my back, but you left. So screw you and your excuses. I'm done. Just like you wanted."

The door slammed shut with rattling finality behind her. A minute later, a car engine revved to life before the sound faded down the driveway.

All the while Nate stood there frozen, staring blankly at the chipped paint on their front entrance.

He didn't know how long he did his statue impression, but it was long enough for his father to clamber down the stairs and pin him with a frown.

"You're still here?" Michael's bushy brows trembled with disapproval.

"Where else would I be?" Nate mumbled. Maybe he should jump in an acid bath. Scrape off the pavement with his flesh. Throw on a red meat suit, swim out to the middle of the Pacific, and wait for sharks to do their thing.

All better options than wallowing in his self-disgust.

"Out there, chasing your girl!" Michael jabbed a finger toward their driveway. "She read you the riot act, no doubt about that—I could hear you guys from all the way upstairs—but this is your chance to prove her wrong. Instead, you're standing here like someone glued your feet to the floor. What the hell are you thinking?"

"What *I'm* thinking?" Nate's temper flared, a welcome reprieve from the chilling numbness that set in the second Kris walked out the door. "I'm thinking I'm in this damn position because I have to be the head of this household. I had to drop out of college and start making money, or we would've been out on the streets because you decided whiskey was more important than your family. For five years, I worked my ass off so you could drink your days away and shirk your responsibilities. I get that you're devastated about Mom, I really do. But guess what? *So am I.* I'm her son, and I loved her, and I didn't even get the chance to mourn her properly because I've been trying to keep us afloat from the moment we received the phone call! So don't you dare come down here and lecture me. You haven't earned that right!"

Nate's hold on his emotions had already weakened from his conversation with Kris. Now, his chest heaved with gasping breaths as half a decade's worth of frustration, resentment, and grief spilled forth, drowning him in their fury and fogging his vision.

Michael's chest deflated. His face sank into itself, his eyes and cheeks hollowing with guilt.

"You're right," he said. "I've been a horrible father these

past few years, and I haven't earned the right to give you advice or tell you how to live your life. You've acted far more like an adult than I have, and you've done such a good job at holding us together. Taking care of Sky, paying the bills, fixing what needs to be fixed." He cleared his throat, his eyes growing bright. "Your mother would be so proud of you. Me? She'd probably smack me upside the head if she were here."

Nate stared at the ground, his jaw harder than granite.

"I'm sorry it took me so long to realize how selfish I was being," Michael continued. "I loved your mother so much, and when she died, a big part of me died with her. I told myself I only needed something to get me through the initial pain and then I'd be all right. But a week turned into a month, a month turned into a year, and a year turned into...well, you know. Every time I tried to quit in the past, the pain came rushing back and I wasn't strong enough to handle it. I fell back into old habits. I know it's no excuse, but you and Sky are such good kids. I didn't have to worry about either of you getting into trouble or falling in with the wrong crowd, and I got comfortable, especially after you took over. I told myself, *Let Nate handle it. He's so much better at this than I am. So much stronger.*" His voice grew rough. "I didn't think about the toll it took on you and what it cost you to give up your life for ours. It shouldn't have taken me almost dying to realize what a fool I've been, but that night, when I lay there in the hospital half out of my mind, I saw...your mother. It was the first dream I had of her where she seemed real, so tangible I could almost reach out and touch her. And boy, was she pissed at me."

Michael chuckled sadly and shook his head. "I don't remember what she said, but I woke up feeling nauseous and sick to my stomach. Not because of the alcohol poisoning—or at least, not entirely—but because it hit me that I could've died without really knowing my children. The last time I spent any meaningful time with you and Sky was when you were still practically kids. Then I thought you two might be better off without me, and wasn't that a punch in the gut? No father wants to be a burden to their children. I should've been the one protecting and taking care of you guys, not the other way around, which is why I promised myself in that hospital bed that I'd quit drinking." A grim smile. "It hasn't been easy, as you can probably tell. But I am getting better, and I've started attending AA meetings. You have every reason not to believe me, but I mean it this time. No more alcohol. No more living in the past. It's time for me to step up—for myself and for you and Sky. You've been shouldering this burden by yourself for too long, son. Let me help you."

Sincerity and conviction backed every word.

Nate hadn't realized how long he'd waited for his father to say those words until he heard them. Once he did, the dam broke, and the tears he'd been holding back for years drenched his cheeks.

Michael clasped him to his chest, awkwardly at first, but then more tenderly.

Nate should've been embarrassed, crying like this at the ripe old age of twenty-three, but fuck it. He'd lost his mom.

His mom was dead.

The woman who read him bedtime stories and taught him how to tie his shoelaces and baked him his favorite double chocolate chunk cookies whenever he was sad...was dead.

And she was never ever coming back.

For the first time since he'd received the news that Flight 968 from Chicago to LA had crashed, no survivors onboard, Nate allowed himself to cry, and grieve, and mourn. The anger he'd held on to all these years crumbled, leaving behind a void that the emotions he should've processed after his mother's death rushed to fill.

It was gut-wrenchingly awful and freeing all at once.

The Reynoldses' dismal financial situation was the same, and their house with its leaky pipes and roof was the same. But for once, Nate felt like he didn't have to shoulder it all on his own. He'd gotten so used to the weight of his burden that he hadn't realized how much it was crushing him until the pressure eased.

"Do you mind if I give you some advice?" Michael asked once Nate had pulled himself together. "You don't have to take it—God knows I've made my share of mistakes in the past. But marrying your mother was not one of them, and after twenty years of marriage, I'd like to think I know a little something about women."

Nate released a long, shuddery sigh. "Kris."

"Kris," his father confirmed. "You're crazy about her—no, don't bother denying it. I've seen the way you look at her. It's the same way I looked at your mother from the moment I first saw her reading under an oak tree on campus." A small smile touched Michael's face. "That's the look of a soul finding its other half. If you're one of the lucky few to come across that in your lifetime, you grab on and you don't let go. Doesn't matter how much money you have, or what you look like, or where you live. You think your soul gives a crap about any of those things? All it cares about is that it's complete. Of course"—Michael's brows slashed into a deep V—"there are also the stupid few, who push the women they love away for whatever dumb reason they can think of." A pointed stare at his son. "Tell me, which category do you fall into: the lucky ones or the stupid ones?"

Doesn't matter how much money you have, or what you look like, or where you live.

It sounded so simple. Nothing in life was that easy…but what if some things were? What if love was just about two people who were willing to defy all opposing circumstances to be together because they had *that much* faith in their love? People couldn't choose who they fell for, and oftentimes, they fell for people their minds would've never picked. That was probably a good thing. Minds could be manipulated, and bodies could be tricked. Hearts and souls, though? They always knew the truth.

Nate's thoughts sharpened, crystallized—and it was all he could do not to bang his head against the wall. He'd been stupid for sure. He just hoped it wasn't too late to fix his mistake.

"Dad," he said. "Let's continue this later. I have to get the woman I love back."

CHAPTER 23

AFTER DRIVING AIMLESSLY AROUND LA FOR HOURS, Kris ended up at Marina del Rey.

As far as heartbreak havens went, it was the worst place she could've chosen. This was where she and Nate had sex for the first time. Well, where the boat where they'd had sex for the first time had departed from, anyway.

She hadn't made the conscious decision to come here, but something about the water called to her like a homing beacon.

Kris curled up on a quiet stretch of boardwalk and watched the boats bob on the waves. They resembled life-sized toys.

She wondered vaguely if Nate's friend's boat was in its slip, and—

What? She was going to take a field trip over there and reminisce about her and Nate's short-lived relationship? Play a cheesy mental montage of her favorite moments set to maudlin music like this was a 1990s Julia Roberts movie?

No thanks.

To take her mind off Nate, Kris brain-jumped to the other male-centered shitshow in her life. Apparently, she was a glutton for punishment.

"I gave you a chance." Roger's face was cold with fury. "I'd hoped you would make more of an effort with Gloria, considering she'll be your stepmother soon. Instead, you set out to destroy something you knew was important to me. How could you, Kris?"

Her contract with Nate waved in the air, flimsy but damning as hell.

Kris stared ahead in mutinous silence. Gloria's lips had curved into a smug smirk behind Roger's back, but Kris didn't bother calling her out on it.

What was the point? The proverbial shit had already hit the fan.

"Well?" An undercurrent of hurt flashed before Roger's anger swallowed it whole. "Do you have anything to say for yourself?"

She forced herself to breathe through her nose. She would not lose her cool. "I don't regret it," she said flatly. "Gloria is a gold-digging bitch. She would've cheated on you, you know. If you hadn't arrived when you did, she would've met Nate at a hotel. She'd already agreed to it."

"She's lying!" Gloria's voice rang with false indignation. "I would never cheat on you, Roger. And did you hear what she just called me—"

"Quiet," Roger thundered.

The Stepmonster shut up and glared at Kris, who ignored her—for now.

"Do you have any proof of your accusations?" her father asked in the same icy tone he used to cut down his business opponents.

Kris didn't, and they all knew it. If she had, she would've brought it to him already.

She lifted her chin in defiance. "You have your daughter's word."

Deafening silence.

"You gave me your word you would try this summer," Roger *finally said. "Instead, you got fired from your job, threw away fifteen thousand dollars hiring an actor to break up my engagement, and entered into a relationship with said actor, who used to—" He paused. "Needless to say, your word isn't worth much to me right now. From this moment forward, you're cut off. Indefinitely. No credit cards, no access to your bank accounts. I'll also be calling the lawyers tomorrow to adjust the terms of your trust fund. Clearly, you haven't learned how to control your spending—to say nothing of your scheme to frame Gloria for infidelity."*

Moisture gathered in Kris's eyes, but she would not, could not cry. Not here, in front of the gloating Stepmonster.

She didn't bother trying to convince her father that Gloria had been planning to cheat on him or how evil his fiancée was to her when he wasn't looking. He wouldn't believe her anyway.

"Fine," Kris *said, steel masking the tremble in her voice. "You caught me. I hired someone to break you and Gloria up because I hate her. You can cut me off all you want, but I will never consider her part of this family."*

Disappointment settled into every groove of Roger's face. "Then perhaps you shouldn't be part of this family at all."

Something warm and salty trickled down Kris's cheek. She swiped it away with the back of her hand.

Her blowout with her father over the contract had been bad enough. Then she found out about dear old dad's bribe. She'd snuck into his office while he and Gloria enjoyed the oh-so-harmonious sounds of the LA Philharmonic at the Hollywood Bowl last night, unsure what she was looking for but determined to find something that could bring Gloria down.

It was only fair; Gloria must've snooped around in Kris's room

246 | ANA HUANG

while Kris was out and found the contract buried in an old Jimmy Choo shoebox in the closet. Kris had already searched her father and Gloria's suite—no dice. Her father's study was the next best bet.

No one went in there except Roger, which made it the perfect hiding spot.

Unfortunately, Kris hadn't found anything of the Stepmonster's. She had, however, stumbled on—irony of all ironies—a contract her father had drawn up, stipulating Nate would receive $50,000 upon the termination of his relationship with Kris. Date of contract: the night of the dinner party, aka the night before Nate broke up with her.

Kris had been too shocked and devastated to check if Nate's signature had been on the document, but the timing had aligned perfectly. When she'd gone to his house that morning, she'd known how much her father offered him, but she'd wanted to hear him say it. Wanted him to admit how much he thought their relationship was worth.

Funny. A Carrera contract had started it all...and a Carrera contract had ended it all, or so she thought.

I swear on my mother's grave that I didn't accept a cent from him, but some of the things he said...made sense... Like how we're from different worlds and how we don't fit.

Kris squeezed her eyes shut, to no avail. Memories of Nate's voice, face, and presence consumed her, so vivid he might as well have been standing before her. She could even smell—

Her eyes popped open.

Nope, that delicious scent hadn't been her imagination. Nate was really here, his big body blocking the sun, his face cast in shadow. Then he stepped forward, and she could see his red-rimmed eyes and tense jaw.

"You're here." Relief drenched his features, brightening his otherwise weary expression.

Kris tensed. "How'd you find me?"

"Educated guess. During our night on the boat, you mentioned how much you liked being by the water and how it calmed you. I went to the slip first, but you weren't there, so I kind of just walked around until I found you."

"You walked around the entire harbor until you found me? What if I hadn't been here?" Kris asked, disbelieving.

A sheepish shrug. "Then I would've wasted a lot of time. But I had a sense you were here. And you are. Guess the soul knows what it's doing."

"What?"

"Never mind." Red stained Nate's cheeks.

She shook her head. "Whatever. I told you back at the house that—"

"You love me."

Her cheeks flushed to match his. "No, I said I was done. And I meant it."

"Yes, but you also said you love me."

Grrr. He was insufferable.

"It doesn't matter." Kris scrambled to her feet, a wave of dizziness overtaking her at the sudden movement. She paused and blinked away the wooziness before continuing, "We're already broken up, remember? We're not the 'right fit.' We're H&M and Hermès. Gap and Gucci. Forever 21 and Fendi. You made your point. Now leave me alone."

"No."

She was this close to tearing her hair out in frustration, but Kenji, her stylist in Seattle, would kill her.

"Then what the hell do you want?"

Nate looked her straight in the eye. "I want you."

He *had* to be joking.

Don't get excited, you floozy, she told her foolish,

248 | ANA HUANG

no-sense-of-self-preservation heart, which had perked up at Nate's words like a golden retriever who'd spotted its owner for the first time after months apart. *Or did you forget there are still pieces of you lying around LA, courtesy of the jerk you love so much?*

"Are you kidding me?" Kris planted her hands on her hips. "You gave your little 'different worlds' spiel just a few hours ago, and now you want me again? Make up your damn mind."

"I've always wanted you." Nate didn't back down from the force of her fury, and a tiny seed of respect sprouted in her stomach. This was the man she'd fallen in love with. The one who gave as good as he got, who was kind and understanding but wouldn't hesitate to call someone—aka her—out on their bullshit. "But I haven't been totally honest about what happened with your father."

The opening salvo of a migraine attack set in. Kris pinched her temple and reminded herself to take deep breaths.

"Tell me." It wasn't a request—and Nate's reply was a fifteen-kiloton nuclear bombshell.

He told her about his family's rash of bad luck two years ago—multiple home repairs needed, car breakdowns, a workplace injury that put Michael out of commission for two months—that sent them into particularly dire financial straits. Nate's income hadn't been enough to cover all their expenses, and he'd been desperate. So when a now ex-friend of his that he'd met through acting dropped hints about a side gig that would pay enough to take care of Nate's short-term money problems, he'd jumped at the opportunity.

Said side gig was escorting and providing Beverly Hills's rich, bored, and sexually unsatisfied with whatever they needed—dates to fancy events for those who were unattached, company and a listening ear for those who were lonely, physical pleasures for those whose husbands either neglected them or couldn't get it up without a healthy dose of Viagra.

Turned out Linda, Teague's newish stepmother, fell into the former category. She'd been dating Steven, Teague's father, but he'd been so caught up with work that she'd felt lonely and over-looked. So she'd sought other male company—specifically Nate, who got the shock of his life when he saw her at Roger's dinner party. She asked him to keep their past indiscretion a secret; Roger overheard and subsequently brought Nate into his office, where he'd made his five-figure offer.

Kris realized that given the timeline and the fact that the contract had already been drawn, Roger must have decided he wanted Nate out of Kris's life before he learned about Nate's past as an escort.

"I never had actual intercourse with Linda or any of my other clients," Nate said, his cheeks brick red. "But...we did other stuff. I tried to avoid potential clients who were married, but obviously, I didn't have a way of verifying their relationship status. It wasn't through an agency either. It was more of an inde-pendent thing, set up by my friend—ex-friend—and a couple of acquaintances of his. Anyway, that's the full story. I want you to know before you judge your father too harshly for what he did. Hell, I wouldn't want a daughter of mine dating someone like me either. There's nothing wrong with sex work, but when it's your kid..." Nate cleared his throat. "You were right. I had a shit ton of insecurities about who I am, what I did, whether I deserve you. I still do. That's why I let your dad get to me and why I ended things between us. But someone...someone gave me the kick in the ass I needed and reminded me that things like money and distance and past mistakes are nothing compared to love. So yeah. Here I am, rambling like an idiot for the past ten minutes without getting to the point, which is that I love you.

250 | ANA HUANG

Hold-a-boombox-over-my-head,   write-you-a-letter-every-day-for-years love you, and I'm sorry I've been too much of a coward to own up to it until now. I want to be with you in any way I can, and if that means living in different cities, or turning down fifty grand, or working through my fear of flying so I can see you more often, I'll do it. I'd do anything for you."

Kris stared at Nate, her mind racing a million miles a minute as it tried to keep up with all the new information thrown at her while her heart danced like a maniac at Nate's confession.

Say something. Anything.

Nothing came out.

"Unless it's too late," Nate said, his voice cracking. "Which I understand. I really fucked things up. Or if the escort thing is too much, I understand that too. But I wanted you to know before you left. See if maybe…" He trailed off.

Kris's silence hung heavy in the air, muffling the other sounds from the marina. She wanted to move and speak, but something held in her place, trapping her emotions in a glass bottle until they screamed for release.

The flare of hope in Nate's eyes dimmed the longer she stayed quiet until it snuffed out completely.

"Anyway, yeah." He took an awkward step back and avoided her eyes. "That's what I wanted to say. But I won't, uh, bother you any longer."

A pause. Then his shoulders slumped, and he walked away, his tall powerful frame cutting a dejected figure against the bustling marina.

Maybe it was the sight of Nate leaving that triggered the release valve on Kris's emotions, or maybe her brain had finally caught up with her heart. Whatever it was, she broke free of the strange paralysis that had gripped her from the moment Nate started speaking and ran after him. It was the first time she'd run in years. She was more of a yoga and Pilates person; all the perspiration that came from pounding the pavement beneath a scorching sun? No thanks.

But now, she didn't think twice of putting her Manolo Blahniks through their paces until she passed Nate and spun around, blocking him from walking any farther.

A frown marred his forehead. "What—"

He didn't get a chance to ask the rest of his question before Kris grabbed him and kissed him. If she had any doubts about whether this was the right thing to do, given everything that had happened over the past two weeks, the kiss confirmed it: it abso-freaking-lutely was.

Their mouths moved against each other, softly at first, and then with a heated passion that stole the breath from her lungs. Kris greedily drank him in, her blood pumping at the taste and feel of him—richer than any wine, headier than any drug.

It seemed love imbued embraces with a special magic because she would've floated right off the ground if Nate's strong arms hadn't anchored her to the earth.

When they finally broke apart, she couldn't help but laugh at the dazed shock on his face.

"I should've made you work harder for it after that bull you pulled the night of the MentHer gala and this morning," she said. "But you're right. We've already wasted so much time, and I don't want to waste any more playing games. Your past as an escort doesn't affect my feelings for you *in the slightest*. No, scratch that. It makes me love you more because you care about your family so much and you are so strong, and brave, and resilient. You did what you had to do, and you should not feel ashamed about it. Ever." Emotion clogged Kris's throat, and her chest pinched when she thought about everything Nate had gone through—his mother's death, his father's battle with alcoholism,

252 | ANA HUANG

the things he'd had to do to keep his family afloat. It made Kris's problems seem trivial in comparison, and she felt like a spoiled, whiny brat for complaining about her father's love life and her money "problems."

So what if Gloria was a gold digger? She wasn't the first and she wouldn't be the last. Kris had done what she could to make her father see the light, but he was a grown man. It was his life, and he had to learn his own lessons. If he and Gloria stayed married until they were both gray of hair? Great. If Gloria left him after a few years and took half of everything he owned? It wouldn't be the end of the world. Fifty percent of the Carrera fortune was still a lot, and Roger would bounce back. He hadn't climbed his way to the top of the cutthroat corporate world because he couldn't handle adversity, and Gloria was nothing compared to hostile takeover attempts and crooked business partners.

Kris was done trying to meddle in her father's life and battling with the Stepmonster, who so didn't deserve her energy. Let them do what they wanted.

As for her financial situation, she'd figure that out later.

Right now, all that mattered was her and Nate.

Nate exhaled a gust of relief at her words. "You're amazing," he said hoarsely, cupping her face with his hands. "I can't believe I was lucky enough to find you."

"It's the other way around." They were veering dangerously close to cheesy rom-com territory, but who cared? Nate was her harbor in the storm, her anchor in all the insanity, and she wanted him to know, in no uncertain terms, what he meant to her. "I love you."

Damn it, she was going to cry. In public, no less.

"I love you too. So freakin' much." Nate brushed a strand of hair out of her eye before he kissed her. Slow, sweet, tender.

Whatever remained of the walls around Kris's heart crumbled into ashes, carried away by the butterflies soaring in her chest.

In that moment, she didn't care that she only had a few thousand dollars to her name and that her father may or may not have disowned her. She had everything that mattered, and it was perfect.

"Have you broken up with Teague yet? If you haven't, I'll do it for you," Nate mumbled into hair sometime later. His hold tightened possessively around her waist. "With my fists."

She huffed out a laugh. "We never dated."

"But at Sky's game—"

"I lied. You were being such an ass, and I wanted to get to you."

Pure, unadulterated relief spread across Nate's features. "I deserved that."

"Yep," she confirmed. "Don't worry. I lied about the kissing part too." She tapped him on the mouth. "*You're* the best kisser I've ever had."

Smugness saturated Nate's resulting grin. "Damn right I am."

And he kissed her again to prove it.

Kris and Nate stayed at the marina for a while longer, watching the boats go by and discussing what would happen next. Kris had two weeks left in LA, after which they'd go long-distance. Lots of phone calls and Skype. As much flying back and forth between California and Seattle as they could manage—luckily, it was only a couple hours' flight, and tickets for that route weren't too expensive. Now that Kris didn't have access to her bank accounts or credit cards, she was also limited in how much money she could shell out on nonessentials. Plus, they agreed to be honest and tell the other up front if something wasn't working.

Communication was important for all relationships, but it was crucial for long-distance ones.

By the time they finished hashing things out, and kissed some more, and grabbed a late lunch, and kissed some more, the sun hung low in the sky and a slight evening chill rippled through the air.

"So." Nate flashed a crooked smile as they meandered down the walkway running parallel to the water. "Think it's time for another of our classic 'seal the deal' nights?"

Kris laughed. "How long have you been holding that in?"

"Only since the first time you kissed me today."

"That long, huh?" She tangled her fingers with his, enjoying the warm strength of his hand in hers. They'd agreed not to hold hands earlier in the summer because it was too cheesy, but what do you know, she had a thing for Brie and gruyere. Judging by Nate's squeeze, he did too. "I do love a good *seal the deal.*" Their night on the boat would forever remain one of her top three spank bank fantasies. "We'll have to do it at your house, though. I can't go home right now."

A wave of sadness crested over her. Kris and her father had never been that close, but he was her only parent left. While they weren't estranged, their relationship was at its lowest point in twenty-one years, and she couldn't bear to look at his face right now. It hurt too much. Even being in the same house as him these past few days had been unbearable.

Nate's mouth tightened with concern. "How are things with your dad? I don't want to be the reason you two have a falling out."

"Too late." She fiddled with her handbag strap. "We already fell out. He found out about our Gloria contract."

"Shit." Nate winced. "How'd he find out?"

"I'm guessing Gloria snooped around my room and found the contract. It doesn't matter. He knows, and he's pissed. More pissed than I've ever seen him. He didn't believe me when I told him Gloria had been ready to cheat on him with you, and he cut me off. He even froze my trust fund."

"I'll talk to him. Back up what you said about Gloria—"

"No." Kris shook her head. "I appreciate the offer, but he won't believe you either. You and Gloria only had a verbal agreement, right? She was too smart to leave a text trail and you're not exactly my father's favorite person on the planet."

"I suppose you're right," Nate said reluctantly. "But what are you going to do? About Gloria and money?"

"I'm done with Gloria. I don't want to waste my time and energy plotting against her. She's not worth it. As for money, I withdrew a couple thousand in cash before my father froze my accounts. It should last me until I return to campus, where my tuition and board are already paid for. I was going to rent a cheap Airbnb or something until I leave LA and maybe find a short-term gig so I can bulk up my finances." Kris frowned. "I'm not sure if anyone will hire me for only two weeks, but it's worth a shot. I don't want to be under the same roof as my dad and Gloria right now."

Nate was quiet for a minute. "I may have a solution to both your short-term problems," he said slowly. "I'll have to double-check, but we could use an extra hand at the café, especially since one of the regular servers sprained her ankle and is on leave until she can get back on her feet. Elijah's dad owns the café, and I know him well, so it shouldn't be an issue, but I can confirm Monday. As for the housing situation..." He rubbed the back of his neck, looking nervous. "I don't want this to be or awkward or rush things, but you can move in with me. Until you leave."

Kris's breath stuttered. "What?"

Pink tinged Nate's cheekbones. "It's not a big deal. Sky would love to have you around more, and I'm sure my dad would be chill with it once we explain the situation to him. He's, ah, the one who kicked my ass this morning for letting you go."

That was a legit shocker, but it must mean Nate's relationship with his father was improving. Although her own familial bonds were fraying, Kris was genuinely happy for Nate. He deserved peace in his home life.

"It's only for two weeks," Nate continued. "We're not signing a lease together or anything. I don't want you to feel like I'm pressuring you into something you're not ready for. I just hate the thought of you living alone in some random place in the city, especially since the cheapest apartments are in areas that aren't great for single females, and I don't want you to waste money on an Airbnb or hotel when there's room at my house."

"I appreciate that. Really," Kris said, fighting back emotion. When was the last time someone had looked out for her like this? Not because they'd been paid to do so, but because they cared? Never. "But I can't impose."

"You won't be imposing. I *want* you there." Nate rubbed his thumb over the back of her hand. "You don't have to decide now. Just think about it."

Kris wanted to say yes more than anything. Living with Nate meant more time together, and they needed every second they could get. But she didn't feel right taking advantage of the Reynoldses' hospitality, eating their food, and using their utilities when they were already struggling.

Maybe she could pay rent? Or help around the house?

Questions for another day. Kris was too exhausted to think clearly right now.

"I will." She pressed her lips against Nate's, grateful beyond measure that she had him by her side. "In the meantime...where did you park your car? I don't think I can wait until we get back to your house for our second *seal the deal*."

CHAPTER 24

"ONE LARGE NO-FOAM LATTE, HALF SKIM, HALF WHOLE milk, with split quad shots—two shots decaf, two shots regular— two packets of Splenda, and four small sprinkles of cinnamon. One avocado toast with the toast *slightly* burnt at the corners and exactly one avocado's worth of topping. No egg, extra chili flakes, and a medium sprinkling of salt. Oh, and one blueberry muffin with not too many blueberries. Or too few." The bleached blond rattled off her order in one breath without looking up from her phone.

Kris's eye twitched. In her four days as a server at Alchemy, she'd received some balls-to-the-wall orders, but this one took the cake. What was the point of putting skim *and* whole milk in your coffee? To say nothing of the other arbitrary stipulations.

How about I add three shots of spit to your ridiculous latte and you shove it up your ass?

Kris opened her mouth to say just that before she caught Nate's subtle headshake out of the corner of her eye. He knew her well enough by now to catch her before she reamed a customer out.

She took a deep breath and forced a tight smile. "You got it."

She rang up the blond's order and started working on the latte. Out of spite, she used all whole milk and left out the skim.

It was petty, but Kris never claimed to be a saint. It wasn't like the woman would taste the difference. Kris was pretty sure people came up with these ridiculous orders just to make baristas' lives miserable.

After less than a week dealing with this kind of bullshit, she had a healthy, newfound appreciation for those who worked in the service industry. The adage, "The customer is always right," was so freakin' wrong.

"I'm impressed." Nate reached across her for the vanilla syrup, his forearm brushing against her chest as he did so. Heat sizzled in her veins, and she side-eyed him, certain he'd done that on purpose. The twinkle in his eyes confirmed her suspicion. "I thought you were going to tear her a new one."

"I wanted to." Kris added the cinnamon sprinkles. "But Liza is still pissy about the time I called out that asshole for lying about his order."

The jerk had sent his burger back *three* times—claiming it was too rare, too well done, too salty, though he'd miraculously scarfed down half his food each time—before Kris lost her shit, the jerk lost his shit over her losing her shit, and the café manager lost her shit over the entire situation.

So yeah, Kris was already on thin ice. She wouldn't have cared, except Nate had recommended her for the temp position and she didn't want to get him into trouble. She may be leaving for Seattle soon, but he depended on this job.

He'd talked to Elijah's father on Monday, and she'd started work Tuesday morning. Liza, the manager, hadn't been thrilled about taking on someone with zero service experience, but Kris was decent at her job—unless the person on the other side of the counter was a jerk.

She was still learning the ropes on the whole customer service thing.

Kris plucked a blueberry muffin from the pastry case and dropped it onto a small plate. It was late Friday afternoon, and the café's earlier craziness had died down to a manageable four tables plus the occasional takeout order.

Thank God. She was looking forward to a long, hot shower followed by a longer, hotter session between the sheets.

She'd officially moved into the Reynolds house the same day she started at Alchemy. As Nate had predicted, his family welcomed her with open arms and, in Skylar's case, a hug and a squeal that they probably heard across the Atlantic. Nate had offered to sleep on the pullout couch in the living room during her stay, but she'd shut that down quick. She didn't want to displace him from his room. He wouldn't let her sleep on the couch either, so they shared his bed.

No one said anything about the sleeping arrangements. Nate and Kris were adults in a relationship, and Michael and Skylar weren't idiots. They had to know that if a couple lived under the same roof, there'd be shenanigans, even though Kris tried her best to be quiet.

She'd also convinced Nate to accept rent for housing her until she left LA. He'd refused at first but caved after she made it a nonnegotiable for her moving in. Once he did, she packed her bags, slapped a quick note on her nightstand for Risa or whoever to find, and split. She wasn't sure why she'd bothered with the note at all—her father hadn't reached out to her once since she walked out of their big cold Beverly Hills mansion.

"I'm still impressed by your restraint." Nate leaned down to whisper in her ear. "Remind me to show you just how impressed I am when we get home."

Kris almost spilled the piping-hot latte on herself.

"You're incorrigible," she said, but she was grinning.

This was the best part of the job—whenever she and Nate had the same shift, it was like an extended foreplay session. He didn't even have to touch her to turn her on.

"I try my best," Nate drawled before a new customer snagged his attention.

"You two are disgustingly couple-y." This came from Elijah—Kris had stopped calling him Blue Hair, partly because Nate had asked her to and partly because Elijah had re-dyed his hair a hot pink—who returned from his trip to the back room with a carton of oat milk to replace the empty one sitting on the counter. "This is a professional workplace."

"Please. Don't think I don't know what you do in the employee bathroom during your break." Kris kept her voice low so only Elijah could hear her.

His jaw dropped. Paired with his fuchsia hair, it made him look like a surprised anime character. "C'mon, Kris, you know I was joking," he complained. "Why you gotta call me out like that?"

"I wasn't calling you out." Kris glanced at the open window looking into the kitchen just as the cook slid an avocado toast sans egg onto the ledge. The orders from the computerized register fed straight into an electronic screen in the kitchen, eliminating the need for staff to run back and forth. "*That* would be unprofessional, and I'm such a nice coworker." She flashed a sweet smile.

Elijah stepped back. "Don't do that. You freak me out when you act all nice and innocent."

"Good. Now get out of my way. I have an order to fill."

Relief spread across the pink-haired boy's face. "That's more like it."

Kris's amusement faded when she carried the food out to the blond, who peered at her coffee and demanded to know why there wasn't more cinnamon.

"When I say four small sprinkles, I mean *four*. Not three. Not three and a half. *Four*. And the coffee's cold." The blond pushed the mug away like it was a dead rodent. "Remake it."

Really? Let's see how cold it is when I throw it all over you.

Kris drew in a deep breath. "Of course," she said through gritted teeth. Her hand trembled with rage as she took the latte back to the counter; some liquid spilled over the side and pooled on the small saucer.

"I can make it," Nate said, surmising what had happened in zero point five seconds when he saw the coffee and Kris's face. "I'll take it out to her too."

"No, I'll do it." Kris bared her teeth. "I'll add a special seasoning."

"That's what I'm afraid of." He took the mug from her and nudged her toward the register. "I got it. Seriously."

She relented, mainly because Nate was already making a new latte.

"How do you do it?" she asked, watching him pull the decaf espresso shots first. "All these terrible customers all the time."

"Not all the time. Some are great, most are neutral. They come in, pay, get out." Nate pulled the regular shots next. "There'll always be shitty people who look down on you or blame you when something goes wrong because you're the easiest target, but that's expected when you work in the service industry. You just gotta put up with it, especially since waiters depend on tips for a living."

Kris's brows drew together. She'd always known that being a service worker was no walk in the park, but there was a difference between abstract knowledge and firsthand experience. Her stomach clenched when she thought about how much shit Nate, Elijah, and the rest of the staff at Alchemy had to put up with regularly.

Even though Kris was also a waitress at the moment, she had an out. Sure, she was cut off from her funds, but her family was still rich, and her dad would eventually forgive her. She was his only daughter, and if she turned on the charm and remorse, she could get him to relent—she just didn't want to because she was pissed at *him*.

Kris had the privilege of walking away from this job whenever she wanted, but most service workers didn't. She could lash out at customers because their tips didn't mean much to her in the long run—though they helped her chip in for groceries and rent during her extended stay at the Reynoldses—but for some people, tips meant the difference between putting food on the table and starving. That meant they had to put up with even the shittiest of bullshit from the shittiest of customers.

She watched Nate take the latte to the bleached blond, who examined it with a critical eye before she deemed it worthy of drinking.

"You're a saint," Kris said when Nate returned to the counter.

A wicked smile slashed across his face. "I enjoy sinning far too much to be a saint."

"Really?" She leaned against the counter and positioned her body in a way that showed off her curves. She suppressed a smile when heat flared in Nate's eyes. "I don't believe you. You'll have to prove it."

"Oh, I will." Nate lowered his head so he could whisper right in her ear. "Starting in an hour, when the café closes and I have you bent over the table in the back room with my cock buried in your tight little pussy."

Heat bloomed in Kris's chest and spread through her limbs,

and she had to clench her thighs against the rush of moisture flooding between her legs.

Nate's filthy talk had ruined more than one good pair of underwear.

His green eyes gleamed with a mixture of heat and amusement at the flush on her cheeks and chest. "New customer," he said in a normal voice. "We'll pick this up later."

Great. Now Kris was going to be turned on and squirming for the next—she checked the clock—fifty-six minutes. More, if you counted the time it took for Elijah to vacate the premises. Thankfully, he was the only other person on shift this afternoon.

Kris's clothes already felt too tight and scratchy against her sensitized skin.

I'm going to get you back for this, she mouthed at Nate.

Nate, the sexy, infuriating bastard, merely chuckled in response.

Kris fiddled with her bracelet and tried to push the dirty images of what would happen in the back room in an hour out of her mind. The last thing she needed was to fucking moan in the middle of a coffee order.

She faced the new customer, bracing herself for another ridiculous drink order, but her shoulders relaxed when she saw who it was. "Hey, Gemma," she said. "What can I get you?"

Gemma smiled. She was the regular Kris had spotted at the café throughout the summer, and though they hadn't talked much before, they'd struck up an easy camaraderie since Kris started working at Alchemy. Sometimes, when Nate wasn't on shift and Gemma was the only person here during the slow after-lunch hours, Kris would swing by her table and chat about random things—books, movies, Gemma's cat Smokey, the abomination that was skim milk—to alleviate her boredom.

To her surprise, Kris enjoyed talking with Gemma. The other

woman was warm and friendly; coincidentally, she was also Filipino, which Kris had learned when Gemma mentioned having family in Cebu. Kris was a third-generation Filipino American— her grandparents had immigrated to America after the passage of the 1965 Immigration Act abolishing quotas based on national origin—and honestly wasn't that in tune with her heritage, even though there was a large number of Filipino Americans in Seattle. Her father didn't observe the same traditions her grandparents— both of whom had passed away when Kris was a child—had, and though he spoke Tagalog, he'd never made teaching Kris the language a priority.

The few Tagalog words Kris did know, she'd learned from Rosa...and now Gemma, who'd taken to playfully teaching her a new word or two every time they spoke.

"Hi, Kris." Gemma's eyes crinkled in a smile. "Just a small chai latte to go today."

"Sure." Kris rang her up. If only all customers were like Gemma.

"How are you?" the other woman asked as Kris started making the drink.

"Good. Hanging in there." *Other than the fact that I'm not speaking to my father, and he's going to marry the Stepmonster in a few months. Oh, and I'm broke and will have to leave the guy I love in one week. To add insult to injury, the heel on my favorite pair of Louboutins snapped the other day and I don't have enough money to fix it, much less buy a new pair.*

Kris said none of this out loud. As much as she liked Gemma, she was not in the business of spilling personal details to anyone outside her small, tight circle of trusted friends, which currently consisted of Nate, Courtney, and Kenji, her hairstylist in Seattle. Sometimes she talked to Farrah, Olivia, and Sammy, but they were still relatively new friends compared to her yearslong friendship with Courtney and Kenji. And she wasn't in love with them, which was the only way to bypass the history requirement.

Gemma's eyes darkened with concern. "Forgive me if I'm overstepping," she said softly, "but are you having issues at home?"

Kris's hand stilled. "What makes you think that?"

The older woman hesitated. "I can tell you come from a well-off background, but now you're working here... I'm sorry. It's inappropriate of me to even bring it up, but I just want to make sure everything is okay. We all go through tough times, and I want to help."

Suspicion oozed into Kris's veins. Why would someone she barely knew want to help her? She and Gemma hadn't exchanged more than a few words before this week, and while they'd clicked instantly, they weren't close by any means. Not to mention, Gemma was asking awfully personal questions.

Then again, Gemma seemed like the type of person who'd feed the homeless and adopt stray animals in her free time. If Kris remembered correctly, she'd rescued her cat, Smokey, after finding it injured and abandoned on the side of the road.

Kris, however, was no stray animal, nor was she a charity case.

She was about to tell Gemma so when the bells above the door jangled. Kris's gaze skimmed over the newcomer before his identity registered in her brain. When it did, her eyes snapped back to the man and her jaw dropped.

"Daddy?"

Roger looked uncharacteristically rumpled in jeans and a white shirt that needed a good ironing ASAP. Kris couldn't remember the last time she'd seen her father in jeans. There were circles under his eyes, and his skin appeared pale and sallow beneath his tan.

How the hell did he know where she was? Or was this just coincidence? If so, it was a hell of a coincidence.

Gemma and Nate both stiffened.

Nate's discomfort, Kris understood. But why did Gemma look like she was about to throw up?

"Kris. You're here." Relief cooled the tension lining Roger's face.

"Yeah. Question is, what are you doing here?" Her defensiveness kicked in before she could stop it. She was still smarting from the way her father had dismissed her. Sure, Kris's scheme to frame Gloria for infidelity had been shady, but she'd been *right*. Shouldn't Roger have at least trusted her enough to investigate her claims instead of immediately assuming she'd lied? Kris was related to him by blood; Gloria had appeared on the scene less than two years ago.

Nate placed a steadying hand on the small of her back, and Kris leaned into his embrace, grateful for the support.

"I need to talk to you. A lot has—" Roger stopped and stared at Gemma, who'd turned her face away and was inching toward the door like she hoped she could escape before anyone realized she was still there. Kris didn't think it was possible, but her father paled even more. "Gemma?" The name came out as a strangled whisper.

Shock slammed into Kris. Her eyes ping-ponged between her father and the woman she'd befriended over the past few days. They *knew* each other?

Gemma's shoulders slumped in resignation. "Roger," she replied.

"I can't believe it." Roger looked stunned. "You—how—"

"You know each other?" Kris was dimly aware that everyone in the café had stopped what they were doing to watch the unfolding drama, but she couldn't bring herself to care. "How?"

Gemma stared at her feet, her cheeks crimson and her knuckles white around her to-go coffee cup.

"She's your—er, she's your aunt," Roger said, his face so white he resembled a ghost. "She died twenty-two years ago."

CHAPTER 25

THIS WAS BEYOND AWKWARD.

Nate shifted in his seat, wishing he drank. He could use a bottle of vodka or three.

Nate, Kris, Roger, and Gemma sat crammed into a tiny booth at a Chinese restaurant near Alchemy. They'd driven here after the café closed because, clearly, they had a lot to discuss. Well, Kris, Roger, and Gemma did. Nate was here for moral support, even though he'd rather be in the seventh circle of hell. That would probably be less uncomfortable. Not only did Roger keep glaring at him like he was the devil himself, but Nate felt like the worst kind of intruder in an intimate family matter.

But Kris had asked him to stay, so here he was. He'd do anything for her, including subject himself to Silent Torture by Girlfriend's Father, aka the modern equivalent of getting drawn and quartered.

Nate chugged his tiny ceramic cup of oolong tea while Gemma explained why she was not, in fact, dead.

"I did get into a terrible car accident," she admitted, tracing the rim of her teacup with her finger. Her hand trembled, betraying her emotions despite her even tone. "I was pretty banged up and had to stay in the hospital for weeks. I was visiting my cousin in Quezon, and I told her—" Gemma took a deep breath. "I told her to lie and say I'd died. I used my savings and bribed the hospital staff to lie as well and to fake the paperwork—bribery is unfortunately common in the Philippines—in case anyone came asking."

"Why?" White lines of tension bracketed Roger's mouth. "Do you know how devastated your family was? Your parents, Mariana, and I—" He clenched his jaw and repeated, "Why?"

"To escape Ernesto. My husband at the time," Gemma explained. Her eyes shone with pain and regret. "He wasn't...a good husband, to say the least. He was twenty years older than me and had a temper, but I married him because he earned a decent living and my family thought he'd be able to take care of me. None of us knew what he was really like until after we married. Then, it was like a light switch flipped. He became abusive and lost it over the smallest things. My only relief was that he traveled a lot for work, so I wouldn't see him for days at a time. It was during one of those trips that I fled to my cousin's without telling him. I'd planned on running away, but I knew Ernesto was not the type to give up, especially if his pride was at stake, and he'd greased the palms of so many local officials and police, I was afraid he'd succeed at finding me. The only way to get him off my trail was to fake my death."

Gemma tucked a strand of hair behind her ear. Her hands shook harder. "It seems extreme, but I was also panicking because—" She swallowed hard. "Because Ernesto found out the truth about a secret I'd been hiding right before he left for his trip. He beat me so hard, he cracked a rib and fractured my cheekbone."

Jesus.

Roger flinched, his face white, and Nate instinctively reached for Kris's hand. She squeezed hard, tension radiating from her in waves. She hadn't moved an inch since Gemma started talking.

He didn't blame her. It was a ton to take in, in less than an hour.

"The truth about what?" Kris asked, voice strained.

Gemma answered the question but didn't take her eyes off Roger, who looked like he was about to upchuck on his side of the table. "About us."

Nate's eyes traveled from Gemma to Roger. A thick rope of tension twisted between them—the type that only existed between lovers. Or ex-lovers.

Holy shit.

"You should've told me," Roger whispered, sounding agonized. "I would've helped. I would've—"

"No." Gemma shook her head. "You were already married to Mariana. She was getting ready to move to the States. I couldn't ask her to do more for us, not when she'd already done so much."

"Dammit, Gemma, she was your sister! She loved you. I lov—" Roger drew in a shaky breath. "No wonder you never let us visit you."

"Wait." Kris's grip on Nate's hand tightened further. "You two had an affair behind my mom's back?"

Nate poured himself another cup of oolong with his free hand. Forget vodka. He would sell his left ball sack for a shitty IPA right now. Anything to take the sting out of this surreal conversation.

"Not exactly. Sort of." Roger rubbed a hand over his face. "I mean, my parents—your grandparents—were friends with your mom and Gemma's parents before they immigrated to the States. Our two families had always planned on me marrying Mariana. It wasn't an arranged marriage, per se, because nothing had been formalized, but I still felt obligated to go to Cebu and meet Mariana when the time came. I liked her, could maybe see myself starting a family with her. But when I met Gemma..." His face softened. "I fell in love."

"By that time, I was already engaged to Ernesto, even though I'd only met him twice," Gemma added, addressing Kris. "Your father and I, we didn't do more than talk and spend time with each other. I fell in love with him too, but with my engagement and our families already making plans for his and Mariana's wedding..." She sighed. "Plus, my mom was sick. Really sick. And that added to the urgency. She wanted to see both her daughters married before she passed, so we stuck to our original plans. But your father and I secretly met a few days before he officially proposed, knowing it'd be our last time alone together, and we—" Gemma sighed. "We shouldn't have done it. It was wrong. I was promised to another, and he was all but promised to my sister. But we did."

"I don't regret it," Roger said.

Gemma paled. "Roger—"

"No." Kris's father's eyes flashed. "We both know Mariana didn't love me. She married me because your family wanted her to and because she wanted to move to the States. If she'd felt anything, she wouldn't have been so cold when she learned about the pregnancy."

By now, Kris was gripping Nate's hand so tight, she cut off his circulation. He barely noticed, he was so caught up in Gemma and Roger's story.

"What pregnancy?" Kris choked out.

Gemma shook her head frantically. "Don't." Panic imbued her voice, along with a hint of defeat.

Roger's jaw hardened. "Mariana and Gemma got pregnant around the same time, soon after they married. Siblings aren't supposed to marry in the same year because it's considered bad luck in the Philippines, but with your grandmother's health fading fast, there wasn't much we could do. I'd held off on returning to the States because of Mariana's pregnancy and how sick your grandmother was. Mariana's baby was stillborn—and not mine. It belonged to the local fisherman's son, the man she'd been in love with. She was honest about that. For all her faults, she didn't want me to grieve what had never been mine—even though I still did. For her. I didn't love her, but I cared about her, and she was hurt. Gemma, meanwhile, gave birth to a baby girl."

Ice trickled down Nate's spine, along with a healthy dose of foreboding.

Next to him, Kris sat still as a statue.

"The problem," Gemma said quietly, apparently resigned to the fact that the truth was going to come out no matter what, "was Ernesto and I never consummated our marriage. He had chronic diabetes, and it affected his...performance. I hid my pregnancy the first few months, but when it reached the point where I could no longer hide it, I convinced him I had to return home to help take care of my mom, who by then was so sick she couldn't walk. Your father had hired a full-time nurse for her, but Ernesto didn't know that. He agreed, and he had no desire to care for my family, so he didn't accompany me. I didn't tell anyone about Ernesto's impotency or my pregnancy except Roger, because he deserved to know—it was his child—and Mariana, when we..." She trailed off.

"When we convinced her to take the baby girl as her own," Roger finished with a grim expression. He looked at Kris, the lines of his face both harsh and sad beneath the fluorescent lights. "The baby girl was you. Gemma is your real mom."

CHAPTER 26

NEITHER KRIS NOR NATE SPOKE DURING THE RIDE home. Roger had tried to convince Kris to return to their house in Beverly Hills, but she'd refused.

Nate didn't blame her. This entire night had been... Damn. Now he knew what it felt like to be on the set of a soap opera, except this was reality, not television.

"Do you want something to eat?" he asked, flipping on the lights when they entered his house. It was late, and judging by the silence, both his father and Skylar were already asleep. "You didn't touch your dinner."

Neither had Nate. Gemma and Roger's revelations had already been too much to swallow.

Once Roger dropped the Bombshell with a capital *B* about Gemma being Kris's real mom, the rest of the story unraveled real quick.

Mariana had agreed to raise Kris as her own because Gemma couldn't bring the baby, aka Kris, back to Ernesto. Luckily, no one had been around to witness the actual births—which came within a week of each other—except for Roger and the midwife, whom they'd paid off. They also paid someone to fix the paperwork, so it said Kris was Mariana's daughter. Mariana and Gemma's mother got to hold her granddaughter before she passed away a few weeks later, and after the funeral, Gemma returned home to Ernesto, while Roger and Mariana moved to the U.S.

Unfortunately, the midwife blabbed despite her payoff, and her husband happened to be one of the officials in Ernesto's pocket. He told Ernesto, who flipped out on Gemma, nearly killing her, and that was when she ran off to her cousin's and faked her death. She'd used the entirety of her savings to create a new identity and worked as a chambermaid in a hotel in Quezon, selling her art on the side, until she earned enough to emigrate to Canada. By then, Ernesto had died of diabetes complications, and Gemma worked up the courage to reach out to Mariana. Mariana had taken the next flight out to meet Gemma in Toronto—without telling Roger. That had been the night she'd abandoned her husband and the niece she'd promised to raise as her own daughter.

It had been an emotional reunion between the sisters, one filled with tears both happy and angry. Based on what Gemma said, Mariana gave no indication she wouldn't return to Seattle. She had, however, promised her sister she wouldn't tell Roger about seeing her—Gemma hadn't wanted to upend his and Kris's lives with her sudden "resurrection" from the dead—and that she would send Gemma frequent photos and updates about Kris.

Except Mariana hadn't returned home, and the last communication she'd sent Gemma had been a letter informing her she'd spilled the truth to Roger, that he wanted nothing to do Gemma because of her lies, and that he'd insisted Mariana cut off all contact with her sister. He'd allegedly said they already had a happy family of three, and he didn't want Gemma to ruin it.

A heartbroken Gemma had stayed away, per his wishes,

except Roger swore he'd said no such thing and that he'd had no idea Gemma was alive.

The entire story was so far-fetched, Nate actually believed it. Plus, he'd seen the look on Roger's face when he spotted Gemma at the café—no one, not even the best actor in the world, could fake that kind of shock.

"I'm not hungry," Kris said, more withdrawn than Nate had ever seen her.

Spikes of pain prickled his skin. He hated seeing her like this.

"Just a sandwich," he persuaded. "You'll be starving in the morning."

"No, I'm fine, but eat. You didn't touch your dinner either."

Nate cupped her face with his hands, forcing her to look at him. "If you eat, I eat. You don't eat, I don't eat."

Her eyes narrowed, and he saw a flash of Normal Kris. "That's emotional blackmail."

"Is it?" He thought about it. "Seems romantic to me. Or maybe I'm watching the wrong kinda romantic movies."

"Fine. Let's both not eat."

"Okay."

They made it to the third stair of the staircase before Kris huffed, turned around, and marched him into the kitchen. "One sandwich. That's it."

His mouth tipped up. "You got it."

They worked in silence—Nate arranging the focaccia bread, pesto, ham, and cheese; Kris pouring the water and setting the table with plates and napkins. He waited until she bit into her sandwich before he dug into his own.

"This is amazing," Kris murmured after a few bites.

Nate's chest puffed with pride. "Glad you think so because it's the only sandwich I know how to make besides PB&J."

"There's a big gap between PB&J and focaccia pesto."

"It's about commitment. If you're gonna go casual, you go all the way casual. If you're gonna go fancy, you go focaccia and pesto."

Kris's laugh released some of the tension bunched in Nate's chest. God, it was good to hear her laugh. It felt like an eternity since their banter this afternoon, before Roger showed up.

Only goes to prove how life can change in the blink of an eye.

They didn't speak again until they finished eating. It was a companionable, thoughtful silence, the kind that signaled one or both parties were thinking hard about something.

Nate suppressed the urge to crack jokes to get Kris smiling again and let the quiet sit. Kris needed the processing time.

"Thank you," she said, helping him clear the table. "For coming with me to dinner. I know that was a lot to take in."

"Anytime. I mean that." Nate tossed the used paper towels into the trash can and eyed Kris with concern. "How are you feeling?"

"Like my head's about to explode." She drained the rest of her water and rinsed the glass. "This day did not turn out the way I thought it would."

"No kidding."

"I have so many questions left. Like where my mom—aunt—Mariana went." Kris stumbled over the terminology. "Why she left. Why she sent that letter. And why Gemma is here now, after all these years. How'd she find me? Is it a coincidence we frequented the same café, or did she know who I was the entire time?"

"I don't want to assume anything," Nate said. "But I don't believe in coincidences."

"You don't strike me as a guy who believes in fate either."

"I didn't." A lopsided grin. "Until I met you."

Kris dropped her eyes, her hands shaking as she dried them with a dish towel. "Don't say stuff like that."

"Why not?"

"Because." She drew her bottom lip between her teeth, and it was all Nate could do not to grab her and kiss her senseless. Sometimes the hold Kris had on him and his emotions scared the shit out of him, but he wouldn't trade it for anything else in the world. "I was sure I couldn't love you more than I already did, and I don't like being proven wrong."

His chest cracked open in the best kind of way, and this time, Nate gave in to his urges. He grabbed Kris and pulled her flush against him while his mouth plundered hers, stroking and teasing until she gasped little moans that turned him harder than steel.

It was love and passion, yes, but also oblivion. He couldn't do much for her right now except be there for her and help her forget, if only for a short while.

Kris must've been on the same page because she arched against him with a desperation that wasn't entirely due to the lust thickening the air between them.

"Take me upstairs." She nipped his bottom lip, and steel turned to fucking titanium. "Make me forget, just for tonight. I can look for more answers tomorrow, but tonight…" Another nip. Another bolt of heat straight to his groin. "I need to escape."

Instead of answering, Nate lifted her, wrapped her legs around his waist, and carried her upstairs to his room, where he gave her exactly what she asked for.

It wasn't a slow, leisurely kind of night; it was fast and hard and knocked the breath out of their lungs, and he didn't stop until Kris collapsed in his arms, exhausted, and drifted asleep.

Nate kissed her forehead and closed his eyes, wishing—not for the first time—that he had the power to slay nightmares.

CHAPTER 27

KRIS STALLED FOR AS LONG AS SHE COULD.

She enticed Nate into sex again when they woke up—though it didn't take much enticing—and, unlike last night, their love-making was languid and sensual, filled with long kisses and soft caresses. By the time they got downstairs, Skylar had already left to meet her friends and Michael was mowing the lawn. Judging by the surprised look on Nate's face when he saw his father tending to the front yard, Michael hadn't operated the lawnmower in quite a while.

Kris convinced Nate to let Michael handle it—the elder Reynolds needed to prove to himself and to his children he could take care of things around the house on his own—and to allow her to make pancakes for breakfast.

Jeez, she set the pan on fire *once*, when she tried cooking an omelet, and Nate acted like she would burn down the kitchen every time she stepped within two feet of the stove.

Luckily, no pans caught on fire this time around, and Kris brandished the slightly burnt pancakes with triumph.

"The burns are your fault," she said when Nate eyed the

blackened flapjacks dubiously. "You distracted me with your kisses."

The dubious stare morphed into a slow, panty-melting smile. "I'd eat all the burnt pancakes in the world for one of your kisses." To prove his point, he sawed off the darkest portion of his breakfast with a knife and popped it into his mouth.

He even made chewing look sexy.

"You and your damn charm," she grumbled while her heart pole-vaulted in her chest. "It's not fair."

That earned her another smile.

Nate could charm the panties off a nun with that grin of his, and he knew it.

Kris set aside extra pancakes for Michael, who came into the house right as she and Nate were finishing up.

"Oh, I'll just reheat them after I freshen up," Michael said when Kris realized the food had gone cold. "No big deal."

"Did the lawnmower give you trouble?" Nate's brow furrowed. "It can get tricky, especially near the corner by the sidewalk."

"Yeah, I remember." Michael bobbed his head. "All good."

"What about the section by the fence? It's—"

"Nate, I got it," his father said gently. "Relax. Enjoy your Saturday with Kris. I'll take care of things around here."

Nate's frown deepened. "But—"

Kris caught his eye and gave a subtle shake of her head.

Nate pressed his lips together. "All right."

"We should do something about the shed in the backyard, though. It needs a good clearing out. There are tools in there that don't even work anymore." Michael paused, then added hopefully, "Maybe we could do it together. Have a father-son chore day one of these days." A nervous chuckle. "I guess it doesn't sound too fun when I put it like that."

Kris sipped her juice and stayed silent. Nate and his father were making progress toward rebuilding the trust between them, but it would take a while before things were back to the way they used to be—if that was even possible.

"Sure," Nate said. "That sounds..." He trailed off before repeating, "Sure."

Michael looked like he'd just won a record jackpot. "Great." He beamed. "We can work out the details later."

Kris couldn't suppress a smile at the elder Reynolds's joy. The man practically floated out of the room—as much as a fifty-three-year-old could float, anyway.

"I can't believe I just agreed to a day of chores with my old man," Nate said. "High school me would've been appalled."

"Don't lie. You're looking forward to it."

He pointed a fork at her. "Whose side are you on?"

"Yours, which is why I think you spending quality time with your dad is a good thing, even if said quality time involves physical labor." Kris wrinkled her nose at the thought of all the dust and sweat.

Although a sweaty Nate wasn't necessarily a bad thing...

"Yeah, yeah," Nate grumbled. He chewed and swallowed his last piece of pancake before he surveyed her with warm, sympathetic eyes. "Speaking of dads, are you ready to see yours?"

A heavy block of dread dropped into the pit of her stomach. "No, but I'd rather get it over with." Kris fiddled with her bracelet. "Just like ripping off a Band-Aid, right?"

"Right," Nate confirmed. "And if you need me, I'm a phone call away."

She nodded.

She was not looking forward to her first conversation with her father postbombshell, but it had to be done. She couldn't stall forever.

Forty minutes later, Kris found herself staring at her family's Beverly Hills home. Her father—and Gloria—were inside those walls.

The block of dread multiplied while she sat frozen in Nate's car, tempted to call the whole thing off and hit the beach instead.

Avoidance: the answer to life's problems.

Kris had avoided thinking about the implications of yesterday's revelations so far, and she'd like that to continue, thank you very much. Sorting through her emotions regarding her real mother, her parents' twisted history, and her aunt/fake mom's out-of-the-blue betrayal required more time and therapy than she cared to commit to.

She'd grown up her entire life thinking her mom had abandoned her...and she had in a way. But she'd been so hung up on the abandonment, she'd never given much thought to what would happen if her mother reappeared in her life—and she'd certainly never thought about what she might do if she found out her real mother wasn't who she thought she was.

"Come inside with me." Kris gripped Nate's hand, letting his warm strength ease her nerves.

He didn't argue. He simply nodded and followed her to the front door.

Kris rang the doorbell, already regretting her breakfast decision. The pancakes and butter and maple syrup churned in her stomach, and she might hurl into that flowerpot—

The door flew open. Risa, the housekeeper Roger had hired to keep the mansion in acceptable shape throughout the year, didn't remark on her boss's daughter's one-week absence from the household, but her relief was apparent.

She ushered them in and lured Nate to the kitchen with promises of homemade banana bread while Kris headed for her father's office. It didn't matter the house or location—you could almost always find Roger in his office.

"Call me if you need anything." Nate pressed a quick kiss to her lips before they parted ways.

God, she loved that man.

Having Nate nearby provided Kris with the strength she needed to put one foot in front of the other without upchucking into the nearest antique vase. By the time she arrived in front of her father's study, the block of dread had shrunk...by about two millimeters.

The door was ajar, but she knocked anyway and waited for her father's "Come in" before she entered.

Roger stood in front of the floor-to-ceiling windows overlooking the back of the estate, a glass of pale brown liquid in hand. He wore a charcoal sweater and jeans, and tufts of dark hair stuck out like he'd just rolled out of bed. Stress and exhaustion carved deep grooves in his face.

"Kris." His low voice rumbled over her, and for some inane reason, she wanted to cry.

"Daddy."

They stared at each other, the air between them heavy with broken promises, unearthed truths, and remaining secrets.

They had a lot to talk about.

———

After one hour, twenty-three minutes, and thirty-nine seconds of Nate doing nothing except staring, pacing, and hoovering Risa's delicious banana bread, four things happened in rapid succession:

1. Nate ran out of bread to eat.
2. Gemma showed up looking for bread, Roger, and Kris (not necessarily in that order).
3. Kris and Roger showed up. The former nearly fell

over when she saw Gemma, while the latter asked for—aka demanded—a "chat" with Nate.

4. Nate received three back-to-back phone calls from Marty, which he ignored because he had enough drama in his life right now without arguing with his cousin/agent over whether to audition for some shitty straight-to-DVD movie that would probably do Nate's career more harm than good.

"Sorry, there's no more bread." Nate stared woefully at the empty loaf pan on the kitchen island. "I ate it all."

"Jesus," Roger said. "*All* of it?"

"That's okay," Gemma assured Nate. "I didn't really want the bread. I just wanted something to calm my nerves." She darted a glance in Kris's direction.

Kris crossed her arms over her chest. Red rimmed her eyes and tipped her nose, like she'd been crying.

A wave of fierce protectiveness swept over Nate. He wanted to tug her into his arms and shield her from anything that might make her cry—her mom(s), her dad, Gloria, that ugly green sweater that made her recoil when she saw it at the outdoor flea market he took her and Skylar to the other day.

Since Kris was standing next to her father, who frowned at Nate like Nate had just announced he'd tested positive for STDs and was intent on spreading it to the older man's daughter, he stayed where he was. That didn't stop his heart from aching. This whole situation was so fucked up.

Nate's phone buzzed with another call.

Dammit, Marty.

Roger's frown deepened, and an irritated Nate silenced his phone. A second later, his screen lit up with a text message.

Marty: CALL ME! IT'S URGENT!!!

All caps, three exclamation marks. Nate would've been concerned, except the last time he'd received a similar message from his cousin, Marty had needed a double-date partner for the blond twins he'd met at the Grove.

Needless to say, Nate didn't take Marty's all-caps-three-exclamation-marks messages all that seriously.

"What are you doing here?" Kris asked Gemma. Her voice, while not unfriendly, oozed wariness.

Gemma fiddled with her bracelet, and Nate realized Kris had the same tic when she was nervous or distressed.

"I asked her to come." Roger cleared his throat. "We have a lot of unanswered questions from last night and I thought we should wrap those up after we had time to sleep on...everything."

"Kris, do you mind if I speak with you? Alone?" Gemma asked softly.

Kris's shoulders visibly tightened. Her eyes darted from her father to Gemma to Nate, who gave her what he hoped was a reassuring smile. Gemma seemed like a decent person, but if she hurt Kris, he was going to have it out with her.

He was sick to death of shitty parents.

"Okay." Kris nodded in response to Gemma's question.

Relief spread across the other woman's face. "Okay," she repeated.

Nate forced himself not to follow as Kris and her biological mother disappeared into another part of the house, leaving him and Roger alone.

Shit.

Nate wished he hadn't eaten all the banana bread. A slice of that heavenly goodness would've gone a long way toward easing the scowl on the Carrera patriarch's face...or not. There was a strong possibility Roger's features had frozen into a perpetual disapproving grimace.

"I don't like you," Roger said.

Damn. Talk about cutting to the chase.

"Yes, you made that plenty clear when you tried to bribe me into breaking up with your daughter," Nate said, equally blunt. No point in trying to kiss ass. It wouldn't get him anywhere anyway.

"Let me finish," Roger growled. "I don't like you, *but* I... appreciate how you've looked after Kris these past few days." He choked out each word like it was a shard of glass slicing his throat open on its way out. "I know about the café and her living at your house," he added when he saw Nate's surprise. "I put someone on her tail when I found her note saying she was moving out for the rest of the summer. She's my daughter, and I won't let anything happen to her. That being said, I still think you two aren't well suited. You're too different, and that's not even taking into account your past...activities. But I can tell you genuinely care for her, and Kris cares for you too." More grimacing. "So I'm willing to step aside and allow you two to stay together for however long this thing between you lasts."

Nate's emotions fluctuated from shock to irritation to amusement in the two minutes it took Roger to give his little speech.

Trust Kris's father to deliver the world's most tepid stamp of approval. You almost had to admire the guy.

"Thank you," Nate said. "But with all due respect, there are a few things I want to clear up. One, Kris doesn't need anyone 'looking after' her. I supported her and cared for her because I love her, but she would've done just fine on her own. Two, we may be from different worlds, but judging from what I heard yesterday, I'm not the only one in this room who's learned firsthand that love doesn't give a rat's ass—excuse my language—about where you live or how much money you have or whether you *think* someone is well suited. Plus, it'd be boring as shit—again, excuse my language—to be with someone who's exactly like you. Finally, while I appreciate and am humbled by your quasi-approval of our relationship, please believe me when I say there isn't jack shit you could do, say, or offer me that would keep me away from Kris. You're not 'allowing' us to do anything. It's our decision whether we want to be together—hers and mine. I will *always* stand by her side, so unless she tires of me one day, I'm here to stay." Nate shrugged. "I'd say sorry, but I promised myself I wouldn't lie anymore."

A stunned silence filled the kitchen.

Nate was sure the other man would clock him in the face, but then Roger did something that shocked him even more than a sucker punch in the eye—he laughed. Loud and hard, like it was the first time he'd laughed in years.

"You've got balls, kid," Roger said when his amusement died down. "Which is good, because Carreras don't respect people without balls. But let me be clear—this is a one-time occurrence. Speak to me like that again and I'll have my guy fix that pretty face of yours."

Roger sounded more like a mafia don than a respected businessman, but Nate supposed there wasn't a huge difference between corporate bosses and mob bosses in the dog-eat-dog world of capitalism.

He one hundred percent believed Roger had a "guy" and that said guy ran all manner of unsavory errands for his employer.

"Understood."

Nate wasn't a pushover, but he wasn't an idiot either.

His phone lit up with yet another call from Marty. He'd put it on silent, but the flashing screen was almost as annoying as Smash Mouth's "All Star"—the ringtone his cousin/agent had programmed for just his calls—played on repeat.

"Are you going to get that?" Roger raised his eyebrows. "Your phone has been going off nonstop since I stepped into the kitchen."

Even though Nate didn't have the energy to deal with Marty, he took Roger's advice. It was best to get the call over with so he could go back to worrying about how Kris's conversation with Gemma was going.

"Thank God!" Marty yelled when Nate picked up. "Where the hell have you been? I've been *calling* and *calling* and *calling*—"

"Sorry." Nate interrupted the other man's litany of *calling*s. "I was busy."

He shifted his weight from one foot to the other, hyperaware of Roger's presence a mere five feet away, though Kris's father appeared engrossed in his own phone. He was frowning and tapping on that thing like it could predict stock prices for the next fifty years with one hundred percent accuracy.

"Doing what?" Marty demanded. "Never mind. It's not important. What is important is what I'm about to tell you. Are you ready? Are you sitting down? Are you—"

Nate released a weary sigh. "Just tell me."

"Fine." A dramatic pause, during which Nate could feel his patience stretching thin. *"You're on the short list for the Scott West film!"*

Nate's eardrums rang from the volume of his agent's—because Marty was acting as his agent right now, not his cousin—excited yell. It was so loud, it bled into the air surrounding Nate and caused Roger to look up.

"Did you hear me?" Marty sounded breathless. "You are on the motherfuckin' short list for a motherfuckin' Scott West film. You and three other guys. All relative unknowns, because this is West we're talking about. I've seen the other guys' reels—they ain't that good. You're much better, and I'm not just saying that because you're my cousin. You have a real shot at getting this, and then it's fucking A-list, no-more-auditions-needed, cover-of-*Vanity Fair* time, baby! Your callback is in one week, and..."

While Marty rambled on, alternating between logistics and wild dreams of the future, Nate struggled to catch his breath. He felt like he'd paddled out to sea on a calm day, only to get swept up in an unexpected tidal wave.

He'd auditioned for the Scott West film a few days ago, but he hadn't expected much. He definitely hadn't expected to be short-listed this quickly—or at all.

Holy fucking shit.

The import of the situation sank in. Nate's chances of starring in a Scott West film had gone from one in a million to one in four. He had a twenty-five percent chance of getting everything he'd ever wanted. Career-wise, at least.

After a lifetime of looking up at the stars, he was finally close enough to almost touch them.

Almost wasn't the same as *certainly,* but it was a helluva lot better than anything Nate had achieved so far.

He was vaguely aware that Roger had disappeared in the past ten minutes, but Nate didn't question where the other man went. He didn't do much except stand in dumbfounded silence, his heart racing, his palms sweating, and his mind whirling with a million thoughts and ideas and to-do items.

Kris.

Of all the people in the world, Nate wanted to share the news with her first, but she had enough going on right now.

Nate paced in a small circle while Marty doled out dubious advice with a few gems mixed in. "...West himself will be there. Wear gray—it's his favorite color. I don't know why, because gray is so depressing, but any bit helps..."

He'd thought this summer would be like any other. Boy, had he been wrong.

First, he'd met Kris, and now this. His possible big break, which he learned about in the kitchen of the man who'd tried to pay him $50,000 to break up with his daughter. The same daughter who'd just found out her mother wasn't really her mother and that her *real* mother was her aunt—long presumed dead—who'd had an affair with her father.

A laugh broke out of Nate's chest at the absurdity of it all.

Somehow, when he wasn't looking, his life had turned into a movie.

CHAPTER 28

KRIS HAD NEVER NOTICED HOW LOUD CLOCKS WERE.

Ticktock. Ticktock. Ticktock.

She fisted her hands, resisting the urge to punch the library's stately grandfather clock in its noisy, ticking face. If she did that, the only sound left would be silence—heavy, oppressive silence, the kind filled with secrets and things best left unspoken.

Too bad Kris had never cared much for the way things should be left, best or not. She'd lived a lie her entire life, and she wanted the truth—the entire truth—right now.

"How did you find me?" Her sharp question severed the thick wordlessness between herself and Gemma. She frowned before shaking her head and clarifying her question. "At Alchemy. You were always there. Was it a coincidence, or did you know I'd be there?"

Gemma twisted her hands in her lap, looking like a nervous schoolgirl. There were echoes of Kris in her features—the eyes, the slant of her cheekbones, the shape of her nose. Now that Kris knew they were biologically mother and daughter, she couldn't believe she'd never noticed the resemblance before.

Inanely, she realized her father hadn't lied when he'd told her growing up that he and her mother had been a love match, except said mother wasn't the woman Kris thought she was. Literally.

"I knew." It came out as a whisper. Gemma coughed and said in a clearer voice, "After I received Mariana's letter, I heeded her wishes and left you and your father alone. I wanted to keep an eye on you from afar, just to see how you were doing and...and feel like I was part of your life, in a way...but I resisted. I was afraid if I saw you, I would give in to the temptation to talk to you. I was selfish, running away from my family like that and putting them through the grief of thinking I was dead, even if I thought it was justified, and I considered not knowing you my penance. You already had a mother, I thought. You didn't need me. Until..."

Kris's pulse thrummed in warning. "Until what?"

"Mariana came to see me," Gemma said. "Three years ago."

The blood rushed to Kris's face. *Three years ago.* Her mother, or the woman she'd thought was her mother, had been alive all this time and, apparently, well enough to seek out her sister. Even if Mariana wasn't Kris's biological mom, she was family. She'd promised to look after Kris and had raised her for the first two years of her life—until she'd abandoned her. Not only that, she'd warned Gemma to stay away, ensuring Kris would grow up without a mother figure.

Kris hated a lot of things—waiting in line, cheap knock-offs, assholes who cut her off on the freeway, serial killers, and rapists—but in that moment, she'd never hated anyone as much as she hated Mariana.

"What did she say?" Kris sounded wooden to her own ears.

"She was sick. Cancer. When she sought me out, she was on borrowed time and she wanted to make amends." Gemma's gaze dropped, her eyes suspiciously watery. "Kris, your mother—your aunt—Mariana—" She stumbled over the phrasing, apparently unsure how to refer to Kris's relationship with Mariana now that the truth was out. She wasn't the only one. "You have to understand, she wasn't a bad person. She was my sister, and I loved her. But she could be...selfish. Entitled. She was the greatest beauty in our town, and everyone did whatever she asked because she was so beautiful and smart and charming. The only time she didn't get what she wanted was when it came to love. She was in love with Antonio, the local fisherman's son, but she couldn't be with him because she was promised to Roger. It was her one unselfish act, giving up the love of her life to be with your father for our mother's sake. She knew Roger didn't love her either, and that made things worse. It stung her pride. The one thing Mariana held in higher esteem than anything else was her pride. When she lost her baby—the one thing she had left that was hers and Antonio's—and found out her husband had a baby with her sister...well, she was furious."

Gemma's face twisted with grief, regret, and sorrow. "I don't blame her for her anger. I never did. She was right to be upset, and I was so grateful she agreed to raise you as her own. You deserved a healthy, whole family, and I thought that was what you were getting. But Mariana..." She hesitated. "She never got over the fact that you weren't really her baby. When she came to see me years ago, she admitted that every time she looked at you, she was reminded of Roger's and my affair. But for all her anger, she was loyal to me. She thought I was dead, and she pushed aside her hurt out of respect for my memory. Once I contacted her, though, all that anger came rushing back. I saw hints of it even during our first reunion. She was *furious*. With the situation and especially with me, for living life on my terms, free of cares and responsibilities. It wasn't true, but that was what she thought, and she resented me for it. She wanted me to pay, which was why she sent me that letter, alleging Roger wanted nothing to do with me. She also couldn't stay. She said she couldn't bear pretending to be in a happy family any longer, not when every day with you and your father reminded her of what she'd lost. So she left. It was a punishment for those she'd felt had wronged her."

"Including me." Kris curled her hands into fists until her nails dug into her palms. She couldn't breathe, her brain spinning with a velocity that stole the oxygen from her lungs. *It was too much.* A lifetime's worth of secrets and revelations dumped on her in the space of forty-eight hours—and that wasn't counting her conversation with her father earlier, when he'd explained why he had gone looking for her at Alchemy and why Gloria wasn't around.

"No. Not you." Gemma looked horrified. "Me and Roger. We were the ones who'd wronged her. You were just a baby."

"One she couldn't stand." Kris set her jaw. "But you and Daddy weren't the only ones in the wrong. She'd cheated too. She had a baby with another man."

"We couldn't blame her for that," Gemma said, her eyes heavy with guilt. With penance. "The three of us, we all wronged each other in our own ways, but ultimately, we loved people we shouldn't have loved."

"She didn't do what she did out of love. She did it out of spite." Kris hadn't known Mariana, not really. She'd built the woman up in her mind all these years because she figured there had to be a good reason why she'd abandoned her family. Perhaps Mariana had been kidnapped or suffered an accident that caused amnesia. The timing didn't quite make sense, but a daughter would grasp on to anything that painted her mother in a good light.

"She did," Gemma said honestly. "I won't lie and say what she did—abandoning you and Roger like that without a word—wasn't selfish and hurtful beyond measure. She ran away instead of dealing with her issues, and she took her anger out on an innocent child. She created a new life for herself in New Orleans, under a new name, with no thought to the lives she'd left behind. But this wasn't so different from what I did, and when she asked for my forgiveness, I gave it to her."

Kris noticed Gemma spoke of her sister in the past tense. She knew the answer, but she asked anyway. "Did she beat the cancer?"

The grief deepened and etched itself into the contours of Gemma's face. "No. She died six months after we saw each other again. She'd planned on visiting you and Roger too, but I think she thought what she did was beyond redemption. Plus, her condition deteriorated rapidly, and she became too sick to travel."

"So you knew the truth for years and you didn't say a word." Bright, piercing hurt flared in Kris's chest. "If you hadn't run into my dad at the café, I would've never found out the truth. I'm your *daughter*. Your biological daughter." She blinked back the moisture gathering in her eyes. "How could you stay away for so long?" *Didn't you know how much I needed a mom?*

Kris had thought she'd outgrown the need for a mother after she turned eighteen, but in reality, no one ever outgrew their need for a mother.

"Oh, honey." Tears welled up in Gemma's eyes and she rushed to embrace Kris, who instinctively turned away, torn between twin desires to throw herself into her mother's arms and to make her suffer the way she'd suffered the past twenty-one years.

Gemma fell back, but the tears tracked down her face without abandon. "You're right. I'm sorry. To tell you the truth, I was terrified of showing up after so long. I wasn't sure how you or your father would react, and a part of me wanted to hold on to fantasies of what *could* be instead of deal with the reality of what *would* be. That was on me, and I am so sorry. But I did hire a private investigator to check up on you." She bit her lip. "That sounds creepy, but I wanted to make sure you were okay. I found out your father started dating a woman named Gloria, that you'd gone abroad to Shanghai for a year, and that you would be in LA for the summer. He told me you stopped in Alchemy a lot, so I started showing up, hoping to run into you. Trying to figure out what I'd say once I did, especially with your father getting married soon."

Gemma drew in a deep breath. "I was going to tell you, I swear. But your father showed up and, well." A helpless shrug. "It wasn't how I wanted to break it to you, but I'm not sorry you know. Like you said, I should've reached out a long time ago."

Kris stared at the grandfather clock, taking in its elaborately carved, reeded columns and polished-brass pendulum while she debated where to go from here. She was furious at everyone—at Mariana, for being so selfish and vindictive; at her father, for lying all these years about her real mother; at Gemma, for not reaching out sooner—but they'd already wasted decades. Did she want to waste more time being upset over the past?

If this had happened at the beginning of the summer, she would've thrown a tantrum and given her father and Gemma the cold shoulder for weeks, if not months. But now, after everything that had happened—after meeting Nate and realizing the importance of every second spent together—she couldn't bring herself to lash out.

It would take her time to digest everything, and she wasn't ready to call Gemma "Mom" yet, but she was willing to give her a chance. See where it went.

"My dad isn't getting married to Gloria," Kris said. "Ever."

Gemma's brows lowered. "But I thought—this November—"

"He ended it the day he came to the café." Satisfaction blossomed in Kris's stomach, as beautiful and long-awaited as a night-blooming flower. The sudden death of her father's relationship with Gloria was the one unequivocally bright spot in this tangled mess. "He found out she was cheating on him."

Kris thought Gloria was smart enough *not* to carry on an affair right under Roger's nose, especially before she'd sealed the matrimonial deal. Apparently, she'd overestimated the Stepmonster's intelligence.

According to Roger, he'd found a burner phone filled with explicit texts and pictures between Gloria and her personal trainer. The Stepmonster had denied it, but the proof was in the pudding: she'd been cheating on Roger for at least a month.

Roger, who'd already been suspicious after Kris's claims and who had not appreciated Gloria's lack of concern over her soon-to-be stepdaughter's welfare over the past few days, had dumped her on the spot. He'd gotten Kris's whereabouts from Teague and shown up at Alchemy to apologize, only to run into Gemma.

The rest was history.

"Oh." Gemma sucked in a breath. *"Oh."*

"Didn't your PI tell you?"

"I—no," the other woman said, looking dazed. "I ended our contract after I came to LA and saw you for the first time. I wanted to get to know you myself, not get the information secondhand."

Kris swallowed the lump in her throat. "Maybe," she said slowly, "we could have a real coffee date next week and...start the whole getting-to-each-other process?"

It would take time to heal the wounds of the past, but Kris was going to focus on the present and future instead of bygones. There was no use dwelling on things she couldn't change.

Gemma's eyes shimmered as her mouth curved up into a hopeful smile. "I'd like that. I'd like that a lot."

CHAPTER 29

One Week Later

"THAT WAS ONLY SEVENTY PERCENT AWKWARD, WHICH was better than I expected," Nate mused. "I think in a few years, we can knock it down to fifty."

Kris rolled her eyes and bumped her hip against his. "Don't be a smart-ass."

"C'mon. You're telling me you weren't expecting another bombshell or three to drop during dinner?"

He had a point. They'd just finished dinner with Roger and Gemma in Koreatown—LA had some of the best Korean food in the country—and Kris *had* been waiting for yet another box of secrets to spill for the entire meal. Luckily, nothing unusual happened, except when one of the other patrons recognized Nate from his three-episode guest arc on a popular crime show a few years ago. The woman, clearly a tourist, had asked for a picture and an autograph, which Nate delighted in giving. It'd been his first-ever autograph.

"Fine. You're right—this time," Kris conceded. They entered the boba shop near their dinner spot. She was stuffed from Korean BBQ, but she could always make room for bubble tea. "Did I tell you Gemma's moving to Seattle? She's an artist, so she can work anywhere. She won't be living with us, but she'll be close by, and my dad already told his assistant to halve his travel days going forward."

Kris flashed back to her and her father's conversation in his office last week.

"I didn't think about how my absence affected you, and I'm sorry," Roger said, weariness and regret evident on his strong, proud features. "You've always been so independent, and I never expected business to take off the way it did after you were born. It's no excuse, but I honestly thought working long hours and providing for you was the right thing to do."

"I am independent." Kris rubbed her thumb over a tiny chip on one of her nails. She'd have to get that fixed later. "But it'd be nice to feel like I'm part of a family. A real one. Like, we don't have to eat dinner together every night, but maybe once a month? Or something."

That seemed like a fair compromise. Up to this point, Kris and her father had shared maybe three, four meals together in a calendar year. She didn't count events or dinners with her father's friends and business associates, which were basically work gatherings disguised as social get-togethers.

"Counteroffer," Roger said.

Kris sighed, recognizing her father's negotiation voice. "Proceed."

His mouth quirked up in a small smile before he grew serious again. "Dinner once a week when we're both in the city. Flexible days, to account for our unpredictable schedules. And..." He paused. "I'll cut back my business travel to one hundred and eighty days each year, max."

Kris's mouth parted in shock. Roger's terms were the equivalent of her willingly giving up her Porsche convertible in Seattle and her favorite limited-edition, hand-painted Dior handbag.

From dinner once a quarter to once a week? That was a lot.

But as she gazed at the man with whom she'd lived all her life but whom she didn't really know, she surmised once a week might be perfect after all. Daily would be too much; biweekly or monthly too little.

Trust Roger to strike the ideal balance on his first try.

"Deal," she said. "As long as neither of us has to cook."

"That's great." Nate squeezed Kris's hand. "You deserve to get to know your parents—especially your mom—better."

"It'll be a long time before I call her Mom. It's too strange. But one day...maybe."

Kris still needed to work through her feelings about Mariana. Even though the woman wasn't her biological mother and had been a part of her life for only two years, she'd lived in Kris's heart and imagination for far longer than that. Roger, too, needed to work through his grief. Kris imagined that, while he hadn't loved Mariana the way he'd loved Gemma, his complicated feelings toward his ex-wife mirrored her own. Gemma had told him about Mariana's death and why she'd left all those years ago, and his reaction had been a similar mix of shock, anger, and sadness, peppered with guilt. It would take time for the Carreras to heal from their past, but they'd get there.

Meanwhile, Kris and Gemma took tentative steps toward building a relationship and crammed in a coffee date, a shopping date, and a spa day together in one week. Kris was pleased to discover that Gemma had excellent taste in footwear, agreed that deep tissue massages were better than Swedish massages, and harbored an everlasting love for teen movies from the 2000s, including the iconic *Mean Girls* (all hail Regina George) and

Bring It On (despite the irritating perkiness of Kirsten Dunst's character).

"How are things with your dad?" Kris asked after they placed their boba tea orders.

"Same." Nate raked a hand through his hair. "I mean, in the sense that we're working through our issues and taking it day by day. It's getting easier, though, and Sky's happy."

"Good. I'll miss her," Kris admitted.

"Really? Who else will you miss?"

She picked up their boba from the counter and handed Nate his drink while shooting him a sardonic look. "You are the world's most obvious fisher."

"I don't know what you mean. It was just a question." His mouth curved with mischief.

Kris smirked, but a tangle of dread knotted itself in her throat. It was Saturday night. Her flight left for Seattle Monday morning, and classes started Tuesday.

They had a little over twenty-four hours left together.

Thanks to the whole Gemma drama, it had been easy to push thoughts of her and Nate's imminent goodbye to the side, but there was no denying it: their time together was running out, and Kris, who'd never been the sentimental sort, was devastated.

Her father had reinstated her access to her cards and bank accounts, but she'd kept her job at Alchemy until Nate's coworker with the sprained ankle returned to work on Thursday. She had, however, moved back into her family's house after Roger kicked Gloria to the curb. Nate, Skylar, and even Michael had insisted she was welcome to stay through the end of the summer; while Kris would've loved the extra time with Nate, she didn't want to impose any further, even if she had been paying rent.

Besides, she and Nate spent every night together anyway—she either slept over at his place or he slept over at hers. Usually hers, given she had her own wing of the house and they could make as much noise as they wanted without worrying about someone hearing them.

"That's not a conversation for tonight," she said as they stepped back out into the muggy evening. "Later."

Like in the next century.

Kris didn't want to say goodbye to Nate. Ever.

His face softened. "Kris—"

"You bitch."

Kris's straw froze halfway to her mouth. She narrowed her eyes at the speaker and wiped the surprise from her face when she saw it was Gloria.

What the hell was she doing here?

The ex-Stepmonster flaunted head-to-toe designer, but her red hair was messier than usual and dark circles shadowed her eyes. She stood on the edge of the sidewalk, glaring at Kris and Nate, her hand strangling the strap of her handbag.

It was sort of sad.

"I'm sorry, do I know you?" Kris asked. "You kind of look like someone who tried to weasel her way past a prenup and into my father's millions but was dumb enough to cheat on him with her personal trainer, of all people. Talk about cliché." She took a loud, purposeful slurp of her taro bubble tea. "Anyway, you can't be her because while she was a total bitch, she had the decency not to wear Louboutins from three seasons ago."

Gloria's lips flattened into a thin line. "You think you're so smart. Once your father finds out what you did—and he *will* find out—he'll never forgive you."

"It seems your memory has degraded as much as your fashion sense," Kris said coolly. "My father already knows about the contract with Nate."

"I'm not talking about that," Gloria hissed. "I'm talking

about the bogus phone with the texts and pictures. I don't know how you got your hands on those photos, but your efforts to frame me are pathetic."

Kris's brows drew together. Call her crazy, but Gloria sounded like she was telling the truth about the phone. Either that, or she was a world-class actress. Kris wouldn't put it past the other woman.

"It's not my fault you weren't more careful," she said, watching Gloria's reaction closely. "Plus, considering the wedding is off and my father wants nothing to do with you, I'd say my *alleged* 'efforts' aren't so pathetic."

Gloria's cheeks flushed until their color matched her hair.

Part of Kris was tempted to taunt the ex-Stepmonster further, but honestly, she was over it. The woman was out of her and her father's lives, and she had little desire to waste more of her precious remaining time in LA battling a defeated opponent.

"Since you're still here in LA, I assume you've either been shacking up with your trainer or staying at a hotel in hopes of getting my father alone and making him change his mind. Friendly tip: he won't, so stop wasting your money. I also assume, given your appearance here tonight, that you've been following him or me. Again, stop wasting your money and time and move on. We have." Kris smiled. "Have a nice life."

She tugged Nate down the street, leaving a speechless, sputtering Gloria behind.

"Perhaps we should walk faster in case she snaps and tries to Mace us," Nate whispered.

"Good idea."

Kris waited until they rounded the corner before she broke into a run and a laugh, with Nate close on her heels.

She'd stewed in resentment and hate for so long, she hadn't realized how much they weighed her down until she was freed of them.

She was still laughing when they reached his car, and she replayed Gloria's stunned expression in her mind.

There was, however, one thing she wanted to confirm.

"Nate?"

"Hmm?" He pulled out of their parking space and onto the main road.

"You know anything about the allegedly 'bogus phone'?" She'd been focused on Gloria during the confrontation, but she'd noticed Nate's mouth quirk up at that line.

"Nope." There went that mouth quirk again. "Why would I?"

Kris tapped her perfectly manicured nails on the car door armrest. "Too bad. I had a fun reward in mind if you had." She shrugged. "Oh well."

"What kind of reward?" Suspicion tempered Nate's tone, like he was sure he was walking into a trap but couldn't help himself.

She smiled sweetly. "Did I ever tell you I have basically no gag reflex?"

She'd given him BJs before, of course, but she'd been saving that fun little tidbit for a special occasion.

The car swerved to the right before Nate corrected it. "No," he wheezed.

"Well, I don't." Kris feigned a yawn. "I used to experiment with all sorts of things to see if they'd trigger the reflex—bananas, cucumbers, carrots. But nope. I can take them all."

Nate's grip tightened on the steering wheel until his knuckles turned white. "Are you *trying* to get us killed?" he growled.

"No." Kris upped the saccharine in her smile. "I'm trying to get to the bottom of this 'bogus phone' deal."

"You don't play fair."

"Fairness is for losers."

Nate huffed out a laugh. "Fine." He glanced at her quickly before refocusing on the road. "I planted the phone with Risa's help. Turns out she's not a big fan of Gloria—said something about Gloria insulting her roasted chicken and making off-color comments? Plus, she likes me and felt bad about what happened between you and your father. Anyway, she caught Gloria and her trainer arguing one day when Roger was out of the house. From what she could tell, they really *had* been hooking up, but Gloria broke things off after Roger arrived and the trainer was pissed. She'd been ignoring his calls, so he showed up at the house and Gloria freaked. Risa didn't catch any of this on camera, but she called me—"

"Wait." Kris held up her hand. "Why does she have your number, and why did she call you instead of me?"

"We bonded over her banana bread, and she knew you were already in trouble for our, er, earlier scheme so she didn't want to drag you into another mess."

"You exchanged numbers because of...banana bread?"

Nate shot her a slightly affronted look. "Yes, it's very good banana bread, but that's not the point. The point is, she called and told me. We didn't try to wait for evidence again because we didn't have time, so I asked Teague for help. Apparently, he's an amateur hacker—the guy has way too many hobbies—and he doctored the messages and included a few photos that were on Gloria's real phone's camera roll. Not naked photos. Just, uh, suggestive ones that go with the fake messages, because we couldn't find any actual messages between her and her trainer."

Kris was speechless. It was happening more and more frequently, and she wasn't sure she liked it. But *this*... "That is so underhanded and evil. I love it." Then she frowned. "Wait. *Teague* helped you? When did you speak with Teague?"

A sheepish expression took over Nate's face. "I may have looked up his contact info and paid him a visit to talk."

"To talk."

"Yes."

"About what?"

"About him never touching you again unless he wanted me to break his fingers," Nate said casually.

"Nate Reynolds!"

The guilt morphed into a smirk. "He got the message. He's not so bad—as long as he's not touching you."

Kris groaned. "You're insufferable. He's my *friend*."

"He can be your friend without pawing you like he did at Sky's soccer game."

"We'll discuss this later. The conversation is not over." But there was a more pressing issue at hand. "Why would you, Risa, and Teague do that? Help me with Gloria, I mean."

Nate, she understood, but Teague had no dog in the fight, and while she and Risa were on good terms, they weren't friends or anything. Plus, if Risa got caught, she'd be out of a job.

To think they'd gone to all this trouble to get rid of Gloria for her...it was unfathomable.

"Because we love you," Nate said. "Okay, I think Risa did it out of hate for Gloria—proving you should never, ever insult a woman's food or, you know, make racist jokes—but Teague is your friend and I'm your boyfriend. Who loves you most," he added. "Just so you know. I'm up here and everyone else is down here." He punctuated his explanation with the appropriate hand gestures. "Gloria was right when she said the phone and messages were bogus, but she really had been cheating on your dad. You'd been on the right track with your plan, but since it fell through, I figured I'd pick up where you left off. I just didn't tell you since I wanted you to have plausible deniability if it blew up in our faces."

Kris's stomach fluttered in a way that was possibly unhealthy. Some girls swooned over roses, some girls swooned over jewelry, but Kris? She swooned over guys who hatched diabolical plans to get rid of evil stepmothers-to-be.

"Pull over," she said.

Nate looked alarmed. "We're on the freeway."

"Take the nearest exit and pull into the first empty parking lot or side street you find."

Something in her voice must have gotten to him because he did as she asked with no further protest. Fifteen minutes later, they parked in the lot of a closed shopping mall.

"Are you okay?" Nate asked, concern etched on his face. "Do you—holy fuck." He hissed out a breath when Kris made quick work of his belt and zipper and freed his hardening cock. "What are you doing?" His voice had dropped several decibels and was strained beyond belief.

She flashed a mischievous smile. "I'm giving you your reward."

Then she showed him exactly what a girl with no gag reflex could do.

CHAPTER 30

NATE DISCOVERED THERE WAS A DOWNSIDE TO GET-
ting the best blow job of his life in his car: he could no longer
drive without getting hard. Every time he got behind the wheel,
he pictured Kris's head bobbing up and down on his cock and
bam! Instant hard-on.

"You've ruined me," he said, feeding her another strawberry
and watching with interest as a trickle of juice slid down her chin.
"I'm going to have to constantly take care of myself in my car now.
If I get pulled over by the cops for lewd behavior, it's your fault."

Kris swallowed the fruit and laughed. "I'm sorry. I'll make it
up to you."

"How?"

"Lots of phone and cybersex?"

Nate thought about it. "That works." He leaned forward and
slowly licked the juice off her chin before he moved his mouth up
and grazed his teeth over her bottom lip.

He'd borrowed his friend Will's boat again for their last night
together in LA. It only seemed fitting, considering this was where
their official romance began.

Hell, at this point, the vessel held so much sentimentality for Nate, he'd have bought it from Will if he had the money.

"I'm going to miss how you taste," he murmured. "I should eat my fill tonight. Enough to last me for another month." After that, it was going to be him, his hand, and Kris's voice, if he was lucky.

Depressing as hell, but better than nothing. He'd take Kris any way he could get her. If that meant long stretches of lonely nights until the next time he could see her, then so be it.

"Only if I get to feast too," Kris said, her voice hoarser than usual.

"You drive a hard bargain." Nate traced circles on her inner thigh with his thumb. "Okay. Unlimited feasting tonight for both of us, phone sex every hour, cybersex every day, *and* one of us visits the other at least once every three months."

Once every three months wasn't nearly enough, not when he wanted to be with her every second of every day, but it made sense given their schedules.

"Nate!" Amusement twinkled in her eyes, and he ate that shit up like candy. He loved seeing Kris like this—unguarded, her joy and zest for life shining through the walls she'd erected around herself. He knew very few people had the privilege of witnessing this side of her, and he wasn't taking it for granted. "If we had phone sex every hour, we would do nothing else."

"I fail to see the problem. Also, might I remind you, you promised me—and I quote—'*lots* of phone and cybersex'?"

Kris's mouth twitched. "Fine. Phone sex twice a week and cybersex once a week."

"What? That's not a lot," Nate grumbled. "I feel cheated. Gypped. Robbed."

She rolled her eyes, but her laughter sparkled in the night air. "We don't want it to lose its magic. If we had cybersex every day, don't you think we'd get bored?"

"Not at all." He heaved a deep sigh. "But fine, I agree to your terms." He swept his palm down the length of her thigh and gently squeezed her knee. "Honestly, I'd take anything. Phone and cybersex or no. I'm just happy to be with you, even if we're not together physically."

God, that was sappy, but Nate meant every word. Yes, he loved having sex with Kris, but if he had to choose between sex with her for a short while and no sex but a lifetime by her side, he'd choose the lifetime option. No question.

Kris's eyes, mouth, and body softened all at once until she was melting into him—her curves pressed against his, her gaze locked on his own. "We're really doing this, huh?"

"Yeah." Nate's mouth tipped up. "A long-distance relationship. We're going to kick its ass."

He'd never been one to turn down a challenge. He was a fighter; so was Kris. They were going to make this LA-Seattle thing work, come hell or high water.

Besides, Kris only had one year of school left. After that, who knew?

They hadn't discussed her postgraduation plans yet, but Nate hoped she'd return to LA for good. That, however, was a conversation for another time.

Tonight, he just wanted to enjoy the last hours of their summer together.

Speaking of which...

"I also have some news." Nate cleared his throat, an uncharacteristic ripple of nerves cresting in his stomach. "It's been in the works, but I didn't want to say anything until I was sure."

Kris's brow arched a fraction of an inch. "Okay..."

"I got the lead in the new Scott West movie. I found out this morning."

The wind whistled by, ruffling Nate's hair and filling his

nostrils with the salty scent of the sea. Fuck, it felt weird to say those words out loud. Surreal, like he was a dream version of himself.

He'd been floating around in a strange bubble of *this can't really be happening* since he received the call from Marty.

As Marty had predicted, Scott West himself had been present for the callback auditions. He didn't speak or move the entire time, but Nate had had a gut feeling that the director liked him. Or maybe he'd liked Nate's gray shirt, because yeah, gray *was* Scott's favorite color.

Did that help seal the deal?

Who knew? Who cared?

Nate was going to star in a motherfucking Scott West film.

It'd killed him to keep the auditions a secret from Kris, but he hadn't wanted to jinx anything. Now that his new role was confirmed? He wanted to scream it from the rooftops.

Kris's eyes grew round. "Scott West, the Oscar-winning director? The one who makes a movie, like, once a decade?"

He chuckled. "Something like that."

"Holy shit, congratulations!"

Before he knew it, they were tangled together—Kris's arms and legs wrapped around his neck and waist, her lips firm and insistent on his, her scent enveloping him like the world's best-smelling blanket.

Heat raced through Nate's veins, and he hissed when she ground her hips against his. He responded in sync, cupping her ass with his hands and exploring her mouth with urgent, pent-up need.

"If I'd known this was how you were going to react, I would've told you sooner," he rasped when they broke for air.

"You should've." Kris nuzzled his neck. "This is incredible news. It's your big break, and you deserve it."

Another, larger ripple of nerves.

It was funny. Nate had spent his entire life dreaming of stardom, but now that it was close enough for him to touch, it was terrifying. Exciting too, yeah, but what if he messed things up?

There was nothing more nerve-wracking than having your dreams come true and not knowing how to handle it.

"We don't know that," he said. "The movie could be a flop."

Scott West hadn't directed a single flop in his life. The man had the Midas touch when it came to critically acclaimed blockbusters. But there was a first time for everything, and Nate didn't want to get his hopes up.

"No, it won't," Kris said firmly. "The movie's going to break records. It's going to be one of those legendary franchises that everyone lines up to see in theaters on opening day, and you're going to be the newest, hottest addition to the A-list."

He grinned at her confidence. "You have a lot of faith in Scott West."

"No, I have a lot of faith in *you*. You got this." Kris paused. "I swear to God, if you ditch me for some up-and-coming starlet while I'm in Seattle, I'll fly back here and pin your balls to the wall."

"As you should." Nate pulled her into his chest. "Don't worry. You'll forever be my red-carpet date."

"Excellent. I love dressing up in designer gowns and strutting down red carpets with arm candy."

His grin widened. "I love you, Kris Carrera."

Kris ran her fingers through his hair, her eyes pools of liquid chocolate in the moonlight. "And I love you, Nate Reynolds."

Their lips met in another kiss. It started soft and sweet but soon escalated to a heat level that sent all of Nate's blood rushing south.

He slipped his hand beneath Kris's thong and found her wet, warm, and ready.

His cock pulsed, screaming at him to get a move on already, but he didn't want to rush this. They had hours before sunrise, and he was going to make good use of every second.

Nate laid Kris on her back and tugged her underwear down her legs while she watched him with hot, hooded eyes. She was so beautiful, it made his heart ache, and when she orgasmed around him, her head tilting back and her mouth falling open with pleasure, he knew without a doubt that his heart would never belong to him again.

It was hers. Always.

CHAPTER 31

Four months later

"KRIS, YOU HAVE TO STOP MAKING OUR SISTERS CRY."
Courtney took off her knit beanie and fluffed her thick brown
curls with one hand as she sent a pointed glance in Kris's direction.

"Blair's a pledge. She's not officially a sister until next semester, and all I said was her haircut looks like shit." Kris slipped out
of her Saint Laurent boots and flexed her feet against the plush
carpet of her off-campus apartment. *Finally*. She'd been running
around all day, doing stupid sorority shit, when all she wanted
was to drink a glass of wine and finish designing the invites for
MentHer's holiday fundraiser. "I was being honest. It's not my
fault she's so sensitive."

"She spent three hundred dollars on that haircut."

"Again, not my fault."

Courtney folded her arms over her chest. "You've been crank-
ier than usual."

"You know Christmas cheer irritates me." Kris liked the

presents and her family's annual trip to St. Barts, but the cheesy holiday movies, ugly sweaters, and those godforsaken Christmas songs playing incessantly no matter where you went? Gag her with a spoon.

And okay, fine, she was also a teensy bit cranky because she hadn't spoken to Nate in two weeks. He was filming in the middle of the Nevada desert, and between the spotty cell service and his crazy workdays—as well as her own packed schedule—they hadn't so much as texted since Thanksgiving.

"Does this mean you're not going to the Sigma party tonight?"

Kris grimaced. "I would rather dye my hair with drugstore box color."

Her friend and sorority sister laughed. "I guess that's a no. But let's grab brunch tomorrow, okay? All my finals are papers, so I'm leaving Thursday. Have to prepare for the big Christmas shindig at my house."

Courtney lived with her aunt, uncle, and *five* cousins. They were like a big smiley Brady Bunch come to life, and they took their holidays seriously. Courtney owned a handmade sweater for everything from Valentine's Day to Fourth of July to fucking National Pancake Day, courtesy of her aunt.

Kris was convinced Courtney's aunt was a serial killer.

"Sure. I leave in a few days too." Kris grabbed the arts-and-crafts kit Courtney had lent her from her room and returned it to her friend. She'd only rushed Theta her sophomore year because Courtney, whom she'd met and befriended at freshman orientation, had already been a member and begged her to join. She hadn't expected it to involve *so much glitter*. "We're staying Stateside this year."

Surprise flitted across Courtney's face. "No St. Barts?"

"No. My dad said I should have a *normal* Christmas at home, whatever that means." Kris frowned. "Plus Gemma has to stay in town for an art exhibition, and he wants us all to have dinner together."

Courtney's mouth curved into a small smile. "That sounds nice."

"I guess." It did sound nice, but Kris would never admit it.

Roger had kept his word and traveled minimally in the months since they left LA. He and Kris ate dinner together once a week, sometimes more—the Carreras' mansion in Broadmoor was a short drive from campus, so it wasn't difficult. Gemma occasionally joined them. She'd rented a modest apartment not too far from Broadmoor and had converted the spare bedroom into her art studio.

Kris had visited it once with Courtney, who'd freaked when she found out Kris's real mother was none other than Gemma Cruz. Apparently, Gemma was a rising star in the art world. Kris had never cared much for paintings, but she had to admit Gemma's hyperrealistic renderings were out of this world.

They'd gotten to know each other much better these past few months, but theirs wasn't a mother-daughter relationship—yet. Roger and Gemma, though...

Kris smirked when she remembered how flustered they'd looked when she'd arrived early to dinner one night and found them in the living room with their heads bent *very* close to each other.

Clearly, their flame had rekindled after all these years.

"I'll see you tomorrow." Courtney smacked a kiss on Kris's cheek. "Hal's Diner?"

"Of course."

Hal's served the greasiest bacon and thickest milkshakes in the city. It was fantastic.

Once Courtney left, Kris drew a bath and put on soothing music. She sank into the bubbles, mentally going through her to-do list for the MentHer fundraiser. Even though she was in Seattle, she'd volunteered to help with their marketing and design needs in her free time. MentHer didn't have the budget for a dedicated marketing person, the work could be done remotely, and Kris missed Susan and the girls, especially Skylar.

Shit. Thinking of Skylar made her think of Nate, which in turn made her depressed.

Kris couldn't believe she'd turned into one of those girls who moped about when she couldn't talk to her boyfriend for a few weeks. It wasn't like Nate was ignoring her; he had a job to do. So did her vibrator, which she was going to—

An incoming call interrupted the calming melody playing from her "Chill Out" Spotify playlist. Kris dried her hands with a nearby towel before reaching for her phone so she could decline the call. She did not appreciate interruptions during bath time— until she saw the name on the screen.

Her heart rate went from five to five hundred in zero point one second. Anticipation and pleasure kicked in, followed by a strange rush of nerves.

"Hey." She didn't sound like herself. Too breathless, too excited.

But she couldn't bring herself to care.

"Hey." Nate's whiskey voice had all her lady parts standing at attention. Her nipples puckered into diamond points, and moisture that had nothing to do with her bath slicked her core. Yes, she was *that* sexually frustrated. "What are you up to?"

Kris leaned back, not bothering to suppress the giant smile spreading across her face. "I'm taking a bath."

There was a pause. "Really." It wasn't a question, and Nate's voice had gone from whiskey to gravel.

"Mmhmm." It came out as a purr. Kris placed him on speaker, set the phone on the porcelain rim, and leaned her head back until it rested on the waterproof cushion she'd fixed to the head of the tub. "Ask me what else I'm doing."

"What else are you doing?"

A pleasurable ripple of goose bumps erupted all over her flesh following Nate's low growl.

"I'm thinking of you and me, fucking in the tub." Kris closed her eyes and slipped one hand between her thighs while the other played with her aching nipples.

Usually, they didn't jump straight into the phone sex. They'd catch each other up first—on Kris's classes, on Nate's shoot progress. They'd share funny stories, lingering doubts and nightmares, and little things that had irritated them or made them smile since they spoke last, like Kris being forced to dance and dress up as a Spice Girl for one of her sorority events—damn Courtney; at least Kris had snagged the Posh Spice role—and Nate nailing one of his scenes in one take.

But it had been two weeks, and Kris was too impatient and frustrated to wait. Her vibrator wasn't the same without Nate's voice as an oh-so-sexy complement.

He didn't speak now, but his heavy, quickened breathing told her he was hanging on to every word she said.

"I'm sitting with my back against your chest, riding you." Kris could picture the scene in her head, as clear as day. Heat pooled in her belly, and she tilted her pelvis, wishing Nate was actually inside her, filling her up.

"Yeah? Do you like how that feels?" he murmured, his question black silk over crushed ice, rife with lust and an edge of something even more primal. "Having my cock buried deep in your pussy?"

Absence made the heart grow fonder—and the sex talk filthier, which Kris didn't mind. At all.

She gasped, her fingers slick with a mix of water and her juices

318 | ANA HUANG

as she rubbed furious circles on her clit. Her cheeks flushed, and her skin stretched hot and tight in arousal. "Yes," she moaned. "God, yes."

"I know you do. I bet you like it even more when I reach around and play with your clit and pretty nipples…"

As Nate detailed exactly what he'd like to do her body, Kris arched up, her breath coming out in short pants. The bathwater had turned lukewarm, but she might as well be sitting in lava, she was so hot. Her skin burned, and heat sizzled down her spine, chasing release. *So close. So, so—*

"Don't come," Nate ordered. "Not yet."

Kris whimpered in protest. "But—"

The sound of the doorbell broke through her fog of lust. Who the fuck was visiting her at this time of the night?

"Is someone at the door?" Nate asked, still in that gravelly voice.

"Yes, but they'll go away."

"Answer it." A pause. "Put some clothes on first."

Kris had never taken well to orders, but she couldn't deny the flutters in her stomach at Nate's territorial growl.

The doorbell rang again, and she groaned.

"I'll be right back," she said, irritated and frustrated by both her delayed orgasm and the unwanted interruption.

"I'll be here," Nate drawled.

Kris splashed out of the tub and wrapped herself in a fluffy thousand-thread-count Egyptian cotton robe before padding into the living room. She opened the door, ready to give whoever was on the other side a piece of her mind.

Instead, her jaw dropped, and her mind blanked.

Nate grinned, looking sexier than ever. He'd bulked up for the movie, and his tan had deepened from all the hours spent shooting in the desert. His eyes glittered like cut emeralds against his bronzed skin, and they zeroed in on Kris with the heat and intensity of a nuclear missile.

"What—how—"

"Figured we should finish our conversation in person," he explained with a slow, sexy smile. "As much as I love our dirty-talk sessions, I like the feel of you coming around my cock even more."

Kris's knees weakened.

There'd be time for questions and answers later. Right now, she needed him inside her. ASAP.

"Come here." She grabbed a fistful of his shirt and yanked him toward her.

Their mouths and bodies clashed with an urgency that could only exist between lovers who'd been deprived of each other's company for too long.

Her robe dropped to the floor. His shirt flew off and landed on a nearby lamp. His jeans followed.

"Want to make it to the bathroom to finish the fantasy, but don't think I can wait that long," Nate mumbled, his stubble rasping against her skin as he trailed kisses down her throat.

"We'll do the bathroom later. In the meantime—" Kris backed up until her thighs hit the couch. "This is fine."

More than fine.

In fact, when Nate thrust into her at the same time his mouth reclaimed hers, it was perfect.

———

Kris and Nate made up for lost time in every room of the house before they ended their marathon in her bedroom, panting and boneless from multiple orgasms.

"Hey." Nate smiled down at her, rubbing a lock of silky multi-toned hair between his fingers. Every time they saw each other, they fucked like it had been years and talked like no time had passed. The days apart were hell, but the reunions were glorious.

"Hey." Kris stretched and let out a lazy yawn before snuggling up to him again. "Now are you going to tell me what the hell you're doing here?"

He laughed and pressed a kiss to the top of her head. "We wrapped up the desert shoot early. Production will pick back up in LA after the holidays, but I thought I'd surprise you before I headed home."

Nate had missed her with every fiber of his being. Sure, he was enjoying the hell out of his first shoot as the lead—despite the hellish desert heat, the sixteen-hour days, and the eccentricities of Scott West, he loved acting and everything that went along with it. He'd had to quit his job at the café because, as accommodating as Elijah's dad was, you couldn't disappear for months at a time and expect to keep your gig.

Nate had been surprisingly bummed—he'd liked his coworkers at Alchemy—but the rush and adrenaline once he arrived on set helped. There was nothing like stepping into the role of someone else, of being so immersed in a character who lived lives you'd never had. He hoped the audience would connect with the story as much as he did when the movie screened in theaters. Being able to escape into a fantasy world—one where the good guy wins, the bad guy gets what he deserves, and the romantic interests live happily ever after—was a refreshing break from reality.

Except, for once, Nate's reality was better than fantasy.

Drowsy from exertion and pleasure, with Kris in his arms and her amber scent filling his senses—this was perfection.

Too bad perfection had a time limit.

"How long are you staying?" Kris asked, tracing her fingers over his abs.

Nate's stomach muscles contracted in response, and his sex stirred, eager for round five or six or ten. He'd lost count.

"For the weekend." He flashed a languorous smile. "I hope you don't have plans because I have a lot of...fun activities for us in mind."

A majority of which involved them naked and horizontal. Or vertical, diagonal, whatever. He wasn't picky.

Kris's eyes glittered with sensual heat. "Let me guess. Brunch and yoga?"

"Sure. Yoga is you doing downward dog with me behind you, and brunch is me eating your pussy." Nate chuckled at the faint pink tinge on her cheeks.

"When did you become so filthy?"

"I've always been this filthy. I just didn't show it when I was chasing you, but now that I've caught you, I'm revealing my true nature."

She slanted him an arch stare. "Caught me, huh?"

"Yep." He was all smiles and smug male satisfaction. "Same as you caught me. We're two fish in a net, tangled together for—" He caught himself before he said *forever*. "For a long, long time."

Kris dissolved into laughter. "That is the *worst* metaphor I've ever heard."

"Perhaps we should do less talking and more doing, then?"

"Smooth," she drawled. She propped herself up on her elbow, her expression turning serious. "But first, I have something to tell you. Well, two things. One, I have brunch—*real* brunch—scheduled with Courtney tomorrow, so don't think about tying me up in bed all morning."

Nate actually pouted. "Goddammit."

"Two." Kris hesitated, and wariness prickled the back of his neck. "I spoke with Susan last week."

"Okay..."

Nate knew Kris was still volunteering with MentHer, albeit remotely. She had a gift for marketing, event planning, and fundraising—probably because she'd attended so many fundraisers herself. She knew exactly how to reach out to donors and squeeze the green from their wallets.

"The organization is growing, and grants aren't enough to sustain all its operating costs. They need to step up their fundraising efforts, and they've created a new role—director of fundraising and development." A pause. "She offered me the job."

Surprise, excitement, and pride bloomed in Nate's chest. "That's incredible!"

Kris had always talked about how dissatisfied she was with standard public relations—for Hollywood, for corporate, even for fashion. But she loved MentHer, and this was the perfect role for her.

Plus, MentHer was in Los Angeles.

His heart skipped at the thought. It was almost too much to hope for, but... "Did you accept?"

Kris's lips curved into a smile. "I did. I'll continue to volunteer next semester, but my official start date as a paid employee is in June. Enough time for me to graduate and move."

"To LA."

"To LA," she confirmed, her smile now a full-blown grin.

Nate wanted to say something along the lines of *holyshit areyoukiddingmethisisawesome!* but he was afraid it would come out a jumbled mess, so he did the next best thing: he kissed Kris silly. After that, he alternated between fucking and making love to her until they were both so exhausted, they couldn't move.

He'd been willing to do the long-distance thing with her for however long it took. He hadn't taken it for granted that she would move to LA after graduation—her family was in Seattle, and what if she found her dream job elsewhere?

It was hell not seeing her every day, but she was worth the frustration and lonely nights.

However, Nate hadn't known how much their physical separation weighed on him until Kris confirmed she was moving to Los Angeles.

"I love you," he said, tangling his fingers in that thick gorgeous mane of brown and caramel and mahogany that he adored so much.

Kris's huge brown eyes blinked up at him, as tender as he'd ever seen them. "I love you too."

They sealed their words with a searing kiss that warmed Nate to the bones.

Yes, they had another six months of long distance left, but six months was nothing compared to forever.

CHAPTER 32

Four and a half years later

"I'M GOING TO TEAR HIS HEAD OFF," NATE DECIDED. "That's the right thing to do."

Kris rolled her eyes, a mixture of amusement and exasperation stamped on her face. "I don't think your sister would appreciate you murdering her boyfriend on her graduation day."

"Sisters never appreciate the things their brothers do for them. It's a law of siblinghood."

Nate glowered at Teague, who was chatting with Michael like he had every right to be there.

The fucker was four years older than Skylar and annoying as ever with his blond hair and Ralph Lauren polo. Nate had thought the blond was all right after he helped with the Gloria thing all those years ago, but that was before Teague started dating Skylar.

Nate didn't care that Skylar was twenty-two years old and, as of today, a Stanford grad with a biology degree. She was his baby sister, and it was his job to protect her from privileged little shits.

He was still suspicious of how Skylar and Teague allegedly ran into each other "by accident" at the Grove when she came home for winter break a couple of months ago.

Judging by how quickly they jumped into a full-blown relationship, he was convinced they'd been talking before then.

"Stop. Breathe. Calm down," Kris ordered. "Your sister's coming."

Sure enough, Skylar appeared in the crush of laughing, crying graduates and proud parents, her golden hair streaming behind her and her rolled-up diploma clutched in one hand. She wore the standard black graduation robes and cap, a red stole with the university seal, and a huge grin.

Some of the tension eased from Nate's shoulders. It was hard to be upset when she looked so happy.

"You made it!" She tackled Nate first, as bubbly as ever.

He laughed, squeezing her so hard, he lifted her off the ground. "Wouldn't miss this for the world."

He was so damn proud of her. Keeping up with her classes, internships, and soccer at a school like Stanford was tough, and it wasn't like he—a college dropout—could coach her through it. But Skylar had handled it all with poise, aside from the occasional lapse in judgment—like that time she'd inhaled two pot brownies at a frat party and called Nate at two in the morning, rambling about Aristotle and Taco Bell.

Kris had helped too, guiding Skylar through the pitfalls of college and early adulthood not because Skylar had been her mentee but because the two had developed a true sisterly bond. Sometimes, it was *too* sisterly—if Nate had a dime for every time they'd ganged up on him, he wouldn't need to work another day in his life.

Skylar greeted their father next, followed by Kris.

Nate was gratified to see Teague was last in the receiving line, though the gratification morphed into disgruntlement when the little shit kissed Skylar on the lips.

"Come on." There was laughter in Kris's voice when she spotted the scowl on his face. "Let's take some pictures."

Nate grunted his agreement. His fist could meet Teague's face later.

They shuffled around until Skylar had posed with everyone in various groupings.

"Family pic last." Kris held up her phone and gestured for Nate to join Michael and Skylar beneath an oak tree.

Once the photo shoot was over, they huddled around her and scrolled through the pictures, laughing at the ones where Skylar pulled a funny face or Nate made bunny ears above her head.

"Very mature," Skylar said, playfully punching his arm. "I thought you outgrew that prank in middle school."

"Old habits die hard," he quipped, but he fell silent when the last photo came up.

It was a normal photo—just him, his sister, and his father standing together, beaming at the camera.

But it was its ordinariness that made it special. The Reynoldses looked like your average functional American family—and, miracle of miracles, the appearance matched reality. Michael was strong and healthy, going on five years sober. He thrived as a construction site manager and lived in their old house in North Hollywood, which Nate had bought outright after the check from his first film cleared. He'd offered to upgrade his old man's digs, but Michael refused, saying he didn't need a big old house when he lived by himself. He spent his weekends fishing and watching sports with friends or working on home improvement projects. He said it kept him busy, though Nate heard through the grapevine—aka Skylar—that Michael had started dating again. She claimed she'd seen their father on an online dating site over the holidays and that she'd overhead his whispered conversations with a woman named Diana.

Clearly, Michael wasn't comfortable telling his children he was dating again, and Nate wasn't going to push him. He and Skylar were on the same page when it came to their father's love life—no details needed, thank you—but Michael deserved to find happiness again. No one could ever replace their mom, but Joanna Reynolds had died almost a decade ago, and she would've wanted them to move on.

Skylar, meanwhile, was enjoying life as much as a twenty-two-year could. She'd graduated magna cum laude, and she was leaving for Thailand in a few weeks for a gap year in Southeast Asia before putting her biology degree to good use as an environmental scientist. Teague was joining her for the first half of her trip, which ground Nate's gears, but he'd long given up on trying to tell Skylar what to do. For all her smiles and bubbliness, she could be stubborn as a mule.

Kris said the stubbornness proved Skylar and Nate were related, given they looked so different. Nate, in retaliation, had pinned Kris beneath him and had his way with her, keeping her on edge for an hour until she'd apologized and begged for release.

That had been a fun night...

"Excuse me." The shy voice tore Nate from his stroll down X-rated memory lane.

The speaker, a brunette clad in the same graduation paraphernalia as Skylar, stared at him with starry eyes and pink cheeks... "I'm sorry to interrupt, but are you Nate Reynolds?"

Nate shifted gears and flashed the smile he reserved for fans: friendly but professional, charming but not flirtatious. "Yep."

The girl squealed in excitement, the stars in her eyes multiplying. "Do you mind if I get a picture? I'm sorry—I know this isn't the best time, but I am your *biggest* fan! I watched *Triple Vendetta* in the theater three times!"

"Sure," Nate said easily, earning himself another squeal.

The girl shoved her phone into what had to be her mother's hand—they had the same hair color and similar features—and grinned so hard he was surprised her face didn't crack.

After that, the floodgates opened, and everyone in the vicinity wanted a picture, an autograph, a handshake. Nate indulged most of them, but after the thirteenth or fourteenth meet-and-greet, he politely excused himself, saying he needed to return to his family.

As his impromptu fan circle dissipated, Nate found Kris, Teague, and his family staring at him with varying degrees of grins and smirks.

"My brother, the big action star," Skylar said dramatically. "I should sell embarrassing baby photos of you on eBay for extra cash."

"Do it and I'm impounding your car," Nate threatened. He'd bought Skylar a BMW as a belated graduation/congrats-on-getting-into-Stanford present with the proceeds from his first movie.

She gasped. "You wouldn't."

"Try me."

"Fine." She pouted. "No baby pics for sale, but the BMW better still be here when I come back from Asia."

"Only if you check in at least twice a week and bring back one of those lanterns from Vietnam. They look cool as fuck. Sorry," Nate added when his father frowned at the f-bomb.

Michael shook his head and sighed.

"How do you put up with him?" Skylar asked Kris.

Kris laughed. "I have my ways."

The youngest Reynolds wrinkled her nose. "I don't want to know."

They hung around on campus for a while longer—Skylar seemed to have separation anxiety and stared at every building, tree, and shrub with sad, nostalgic eyes—before heading out for lunch.

Nate fell into step with Teague while Kris, Skylar, and Michael debated where to eat.

"Break her heart and I'll break your face—to start," Nate said without preamble. His smile came off more threatening than friendly. "Got it?"

Teague appeared amused. "Understood. You don't have to worry—I'd rather die than hurt Sky."

"Good, because that's what's going to happen if she so much as sheds a tear over you."

The other man chuckled, and Nate debated the merits of punching him in the face even though he technically hadn't done anything wrong except breathe and exist.

Oh, and date Nate's sister.

"You and Kris seem to be in a good place," Teague said. "I haven't seen her this happy in…well, ever."

Nate's "smile" widened until he was all but baring his teeth. "We are, so don't get any ideas."

"I'm not." Teague's own smile was wry. "I really like Skylar, and Kris and I have always just been friends."

"Really." It wasn't a question.

"Trust me, I don't feel for her that way, and it's mutual. I remember telling you the same thing during that summer I took you guys up in my plane."

"I didn't believe you then, and I only half believe you now. Anyway, I'm not worried about Kris." Kris, Nate trusted one hundred percent. Teague? Not so much, whether it was with his sister or the love of his life.

"I know. But the way you feel about Kris? That's how I feel

about Sky," Teague said. "So with all due respect, you can snap at me all you want, but nothing you say or do is going to drive me away. I understand you want to protect your sister, but she's a grown woman capable of making her own decisions. I also want you and me to be on good terms—both for Sky's sake and because you seem like a decent guy when you're not snapping at me. If I hurt her for any reason—and I swear, I'd never willingly do so—you can come at me with all you got, but for now, let's shelve the overprotective-brother routine, yeah?"

Nate could count on one hand the number of times he'd been this surprised. He was torn between two reactions: 1) break Teague's face, as he'd said he would do earlier, or 2)...

A laugh rumbled out of his chest, quietly at first and then loud enough that the trio walking ahead of them glanced back with curiosity.

A grin split Skylar's face when she saw what was happening, and Kris's eyes twinkled before she said something that diverted the other woman's attention.

"You're okay," Nate said, clapping Teague on the back. He still didn't like the guy, but at least his sister's boyfriend had balls. That deserved some respect.

Plus, it didn't escape Nate's attention that Teague's words sounded quite familiar. He had given Kris's father his version of the same speech four years ago.

By the time he and Kris returned to their hotel that night, Nate had forgotten all about Teague. They'd spent the day with Skylar—first lunch, then a spontaneous mini-golf excursion, followed by dinner and drinks.

Kris had grimaced at the mini-golf idea but followed through with it like a champ. The sight of her handling a putter had been hot as hell.

"I recommend you take up mini-golf as a hobby," Nate said,

watching Kris undress with hooded eyes. "Preferably in one of those short golf skirts."

"In your dreams," Kris teased. Her ring flashed beneath the lights as she unhooked her bra and the scrap of black lace drifted to the ground.

Nate hardened immediately, both at the sight of her breasts and the ring on her finger. It was a five-carat pear-shaped Harry Winston diamond—Kris's dream ring, according to both her mother and Courtney.

After years of making up for lost time, Gemma and Kris had developed a true mother-daughter bond, and Courtney was one of Kris's oldest friends. As a result, Nate trusted their intel implicitly.

Good thing Scott West's *Triple Vendetta*, featuring none other than Nate Reynolds, had been such a blockbuster hit. Enough that it'd gotten the franchise green light, and Nate had signed a four-movie contract with enough zeroes to make his eyes water. That, plus the endorsement deals that flooded in after Nate was branded Hollywood's hottest new star, made purchasing the five-carat diamond a drop in the bucket.

He'd popped the question in Italy, after he and Kris snuck off to the Amalfi Coast when the principal production for the *Triple Vendetta* sequel in Rome wrapped. After years of exposure therapy, Nate had gotten over his fear of flying. He got nervous whenever there was turbulence, and his stomach hitched with each ascent, but that was nothing compared to his earlier aerophobia.

Nate still remembered every detail of the proposal—the dress Kris wore, her expression when he'd dropped to one knee, the sound of the waves lapping against the shore in the distance when she said yes and tackled him with a kiss.

It'd been the best night of his life.

Kris climbed into bed and snuggled into his arms.

"If you're really nice to me, *maybe* I'll wear a short golf skirt during our honeymoon," Kris murmured. "As long as we don't actually play golf."

Nate chuckled and stroked her soft skin, her scent burrowing into his nose and shooting straight down to his cock. "Trust me, golf is nowhere on my honeymoon itinerary."

Their wedding wouldn't happen for at least another two or three years. They'd both agreed to a long engagement for multiple reasons, including Nate's crazy filming schedule and Kris's equally busy calendar juggling her roles as director of fundraising for MentHer and board president for the Joanna Reynolds Scholarship Foundation for low-income high school students.

Kris and Nate had established the foundation last year. He'd contributed some money, but the bulk of its funding came from Kris's trust fund, which had paid out when she turned twenty-three—despite his threats, her father had never changed the terms after he found out about Kris's scheme to frame Gloria for infidelity. While they'd both had a hand in shaping the foundation's goals, hiring its staff, and building out the logistics, Kris was the one who kept it running like a well-oiled machine. In fact, she'd been the one who'd suggested starting a scholarship fund for high schoolers whose families couldn't afford college in memory of his mother. That was the night Nate knew, deep within his gut, that this woman was his forever.

He'd known it for a while, but that was the first time it struck him to his core. So much so, he almost shed a tear when he'd gruffly agreed the foundation was a good idea.

Nate had called Gemma and Courtney the next day and bought the engagement ring the day after that.

"How are you feeling about your parents' wedding?" he asked, sinking deeper into the pillows and tightening his grip around Kris's shoulder.

That was another reason they were delaying their wedding. Gemma and Roger were getting married first, and Nate wasn't stupid enough to put Kris through Wedding Mania twice in a short period of time. He liked his balls attached to his body, thank you.

"Good." Kris hitched a nonchalant shoulder, but he could tell she was getting choked up. "We knew it was coming."

Indeed. Roger and Gemma had danced around their relationship for a frustrating two years before they bit the bullet and officially started dating. They had progressed at warp speed since then, and their wedding was in two months.

Nate, in an ill-advised slip of the tongue, had joked to Roger that he'd gotten the whole thing backwards. You were supposed to date and get married *before* having a child, not after.

To be fair, Nate had been jet-lagged and delirious from seventy-two hours of no sleep, but Roger's menacing scowl reminded him once again why he was an action-movie guy and not a comedian.

"It's nice to see my parents together, though," Kris murmured. "Two decades is a long time to go without your other half."

Ain't that the truth. Nate went crazy at the thought of two days without Kris, much less two decades. His out-of-town shoots were the worst. Luckily, they'd perfected the art of long distance, and sometimes Kris found the time to sneak away and surprise him on set.

"It's funny," Kris said. "My study abroad friends always say our year in Shanghai changed their lives, but not me. I met some great people in China, yeah, but it was the summer after that that was the game changer. Meeting you. Meeting Mom. It was almost like fate."

"Not almost." Nate brought her hand up to his mouth and kissed her knuckles. "It *was* fate."

EPILOGUE

Three Years Later

NATE AND KRIS REYNOLDS'S WEDDING WAS DUBBED the Wedding of the Century by the press, bloggers, and gossip rags who followed every detail with breathless anticipation in the months leading up to the big event.

> *Five hundred of Hollywood's biggest stars at a castle in Italy! A custom-made Sarah Burton for Alexander McQueen wedding dress! A live performance by one of the world's top music superstars!*

Kris read about the wedding so much she was sick of it, and she hadn't thought that was possible. It got to where Nate had threatened to cut off her access to the internet if she didn't stop grousing over everything the idiot outlets got wrong.

First of all, her wedding dress cost $85,000, not $70,000. Second of all, Riley K. was definitely *not* on the guest list, despite Bobbi Rayden's protests.

In a strange twist of fate, Bobbi was now Nate's publicist, and she seemed to have forgotten about Kris's ill-fated summer assistantship. Either that or she overlooked it because Kris was engaged and soon to be married to one of the most famous actors in the world.

Knowing Bobbi, it was the latter.

Kris didn't begrudge the other woman. She was the one who messed up with the Sabrina Winters shoot, and Bobbi was a shark at her job. When Nate told her about his past as an escort, she'd created five different rock-solid crisis management plans depending on how the news leaked and who the source was.

Thankfully, they hadn't had to use any of the plans yet, and after seven years, the statute of limitations for prostitution in California had long run out, so they didn't have to worry about legal ramifications should information about Nate's past ever leak.

"You look beautiful." Gemma surveyed her daughter with misty eyes as she cupped Kris's cheek with her hand. "Absolutely beautiful."

All thoughts of Bobbi, trashy pop stars, and crisis management flew out of Kris's head as a lump rose in her throat. "Thanks, Mom."

The mist in Gemma's eyes thickened.

It had taken a long time for their relationship to reach the point it was at now. Kris didn't call Gemma "Mom" until thirteen months after she found out the truth. She'd been happy to have her mother back in her life, but when said mother was not who you thought she was and it was your first time speaking and meeting her in over twenty years...well, they'd had a lot of shit to work out.

Which they had. And now, for the first time in her life, Kris felt like she was part of a complete family.

Her parents had gotten married two years ago in a simple ceremony in the Philippines, where they'd first met. Neither set of Kris's grandparents was alive, so besides the minister, Kris had been the sole witness, and dammit, she'd cried—tears of joy but still. It'd been embarrassing.

Now, it appeared she might repeat her imitation of a fountain—she could already feel the pressure building behind her eyes.

"No one cry," Olivia said on cue. "It'll mess up your makeup and we don't have time to retouch it before the ceremony starts."

Thank God for Olivia Tang.

The pressure receded, and Kris straightened, her heart pounding for a whole different reason. In less than an hour, she'd officially be Mrs. Kris Reynolds, and she was both excited and nauseated. Excited because, hello, she'd hit the jackpot with a husband like Nate, and she loved him so much, she wanted to scream it from the rooftops (not that she would—how uncouth). Nauseated because she was getting *married*, and after all these years, all the planning, it seemed surreal that she would be someone's wife.

Kris flashed back to the summer after her junior year of college and wondered where the time had gone. She'd been so young, so brash and confident that she didn't want or need the opposite sex. That love wasn't for her and that men were bores, chores, man whores, you named it.

Look at her now, about to walk down the aisle and profess, "Till death do us part," in front of five hundred people.

Nerves shot through Kris's veins and rendered her immobile.

"Are you okay?" Gemma asked in Tagalog.

Thanks to lessons from her mother, Kris was proficient if not fluent in the language. She didn't learn Tagalog for practical purposes—most Filipinos spoke English, even in the Philippines, where English was an official language—but to...connect with her culture, she guessed. Kris had grown up in a wholly Americanized household, and though it'd never bothered her before, she craved a deeper connection with her cultural roots the older she got. Not just the language, but the history, the music, the customs and superstitions—though Kris could've done without that last one.

Now, she was paranoid about the number of stairs in any of her houses being divisible by three, which was considered bad luck. She'd had to redo the entire staircase in her and Nate's new Beverly Hills pad because it'd had twenty-one steps.

"I'm fine," Kris replied, also in Tagalog. She smoothed a shaky hand over the front of her wedding dress. "Just a little nervous."

The last part she said in English.

"That's normal," Farrah Lin said gently. Like the rest of Kris's bridesmaids, she wore a buttercup-yellow Lela Rose dress in a cut that best suited her body shape. "Before I walked down the aisle, I was so nauseous I thought I would throw up, but when I saw Blake standing there..." A dreamy look overtook her face. "All the nerves disappear, and you only see him."

"I hope not because I'm not marrying Blake," Kris quipped. "Polygamy is not my thing."

Laughter ripped throughout the suite, and Farrah scrunched her nose with a smile. "Very funny. You know what I mean."

"I know." This time, Kris was the one who squeezed Farrah's arm. "Thank you for being here. All of you." She gazed around at the other women in the room—her mom; Courtney, her maid of honor; Olivia and Farrah, whom she'd met in Shanghai a lifetime ago and who had, against all odds, stayed two of her closest friends despite time and distance; and Skylar, her soon-to-be sister-in-law, who gazed back at her with a ginormous smile and shimmering eyes.

"Of course we're here. Like we would miss this." Courtney's

dark blue eyes lit up with a mixture of love and mischief. "Besides, after your bachelorette party—"

A chorus of groans interrupted her.

"Oh God. Don't remind me." Olivia covered her eyes. "I'll never be able to look at a lollipop the same way."

Kris's wild bachelorette getaway at an adults-only resort in Jamaica was unforgettable for sure—except for all the moments they *had* forgotten after blacking out from too much alcohol.

Then there were the moments Kris *wished* she'd forgotten, like the Beach Incident. And the Lollipop Incident. And the—

"I was going to say, after your bachelorette party, we, uh, want to make sure your wedding goes off without a hitch." Courtney cleared her throat. "Anyway, we love you and wish you all the happiness and great sex in the world, minus the lollipops."

Gemma coughed delicately.

"Sorry, Mrs. C," Courtney added.

"Do I want to know about the—"

"No," Kris and her bridesmaids replied at the same time.

Gemma shook her head. "That's probably for the best."

"Trust me," Kris said. "It is."

After a few more minutes of shooting the breeze and fussing with their hair and makeup, Courtney announced it was time to head down.

This is it.

Kris's hand trembled as she picked up her wedding bouquet. Her nerves increased twofold, zinging through her body like out-of-control Ping-Pong balls.

They stayed with her as she, her mom, and her bridesmaids made their way to the castle's grand hall, where the ceremony was being held. Her father, the ring bearer (Nate's cousin), the flower girl (Kris's cousin on her father's side), and Janet, the wedding planner, were already waiting by the closed doors leading into the hall.

Gemma gave her husband a quick kiss and Kris another loving squeeze before she slipped into the hall so she could take her seat in the first row as the mother of the bride.

"Look at you." Roger clasped Kris's hands while Janet shuffled them into the order of procession. "My daughter, getting married. I can't believe it."

"Don't cry, Daddy," Kris warned, her throat tight. "I can't take that chance. My mascara isn't waterproof."

He laughed, though the sound came out more watery than usual. "Understood." He kissed her cheek. "I love you."

The tightness increased. "I love you too."

Then someone flung the doors open, the chords of the wedding march soared in the great hall, and the wedding party filed out one by one until it was Kris's turn.

She took a deep breath and stepped into the hall, grateful for her father's strength by her side. Five hundred pairs of eyes locked onto her as she walked down the long white-carpeted aisle, but Kris ignored them, her gaze drawn to the only man who mattered.

Nate stood at the altar next to Elijah, his best man. Nate's golden-brown hair gleamed beneath the lights, and he filled out his black Tom Ford tuxedo so well it should be illegal. His eyes blazed with so much love and adoration, Kris couldn't breathe.

Just like that, her nerves disappeared.

Farrah was right. Kris could only see the man she loved—and she couldn't believe she'd ever been nervous about marrying him.

When she reached the altar, he flashed that slow, sexy smile of his—the one reserved just for her—and Kris's bones turned liquid.

And after they said their vows, and the minister proclaimed them husband and wife, and Nate kissed her senseless to a resounding chorus of claps and catcalls, Kris knew, deep within her bones, that everything had turned out exactly the way it was meant to.

They held the wedding reception on the castle's enormous grounds, where a mini-city of tents, lights, and tables reigned. A good number of guests were fellow Hollywood people, but everyone Nate and Kris cared about was there too: their families, including Marty, who had stopped dicking around after Nate hit it big and was now one of the most sought-after agents in the biz; Kris's study abroad friends from Shanghai; MentHer staff with whom Kris had particularly bonded over the years; Risa, the Carreras' retired LA housekeeper, who ran a thriving banana bread business after Nate shouted her out on social. At age sixty-eight, she was the internet's favorite baking grandma. Nate's closest pre-Hollywood friends were in attendance as well, including his best man, Elijah, and groomsman, Will, who'd lent Nate his boat all those summers ago. The boat now belonged to Nate and Kris—Nate had bought it from Will as a five-year dating anniversary present for Kris. He could've bought any number of bigger, newer boats, but none of them held the same sentimental value.

Nate also spotted Teague and his family, with whom he'd spent quite a few holidays by now, given how serious Teague and Skylar were. He wouldn't be surprised if Teague popped the question soon; though Nate would never admit it out loud, he could have a worse brother-in-law than a wave-surfing, plane-flying, computer-hacking film animator.

He'd still break Teague's face if he hurt Skylar, though.

Teague's father and Linda had split up two years ago, citing "irreconcilable differences." Nate wasn't sure if Sam Collins ever found out about Linda's indiscretion while they were dating, as neither he nor Roger had clued him in (no one wanted to open that can of worms), but Sam looked so happy with his new girlfriend, it didn't matter.

The reception ran into the early hours of the morning. It was a wild, exultant affair, filled with the expected (Courtney leading a conga line; Kris's friend Luke Peterson from Shanghai, whom she always complained about for being so "uncouth," burping out the alphabet to the fascination and disgust of other guests) and the unexpected (Scott West dancing with Susan, the MentHer director; Nate's father and his girlfriend, Diana, getting down to the latest Cardi B hit with surprising skill), but nothing shocked Nate more than the scene he stumbled on when he tried to sneak a private moment with his wife.

Wife.

The word sent all sorts of emotions swirling through his body. When he'd seen Kris walk down that aisle, resplendent and beaming and—dare he say it—teary-eyed, he'd been afraid he would break down himself.

Luckily, he'd spared himself the embarrassment and kept it together throughout the ceremony, the receiving line, the best man and maid of honor toasts, the cake cutting...

Jesus, weddings were *long.*

As much as Nate appreciated his friends' and family's well-wishes, he wanted to be alone with his wife. Not to spoil their wedding night, because he wasn't an asshole, but because he needed a breather from all the people and a moment to connect with Kris.

Ironic how it was their wedding day and yet they'd had less than five minutes alone together so far.

"Where are we going?" Kris laughed as he tugged her closer to the castle, where there were plenty of shrubberies and marble statues to get lost in.

He'd have opted for a room in the castle itself, except there were a zillion stairs leading to the back entrance and the building was a maze.

No one had time for that.

"Wherever Janet can't find us," Nate said, naming their highly organized, highly scary wedding planner.

He spotted the pursed-lipped woman out of the corner of his eye and quickened his pace, pulling Kris around the corner just before Janet's eyes homed in on them.

Kris landed against his chest, and he tightened his arms around her. She glowed in the moonlight, her silk reception dress pouring over her curves like cream, and Nate marveled for the millionth time how lucky he was to have her by his side.

"Hey there, Mrs. Reynolds," he said, his mouth curling up into a satisfied grin.

She smirked, no doubt spotting the devilish glint in his eyes. "Mr. Reynolds, are you trying to seduce me at our wedding reception? Next to"—she glanced at the statue towering next to them—"a statue of Cupid? Well played."

He hadn't noticed Cupid hovering there like a creeper until now, but whaddaya know, even the gods and castle grounds' layout were on his side.

"Of course not." Nate feigned innocence. "I—"

A sound to their left interrupted him.

Nate's eyebrows shot up to the sky when Olivia and Sammy tumbled out from the shrubbery on the other side of Cupid, clothes rumpled, hair mussed, and—was that a hickey on Sammy's neck?

Damn. Go, Sammy.

Nate didn't know too much about the pair's backstory, but he did know that they used to date in Shanghai, that they'd broken up the summer after returning to the States, and that they'd hated each other ever since. Nate had witnessed their animosity first-hand several times.

Animosity and sexual tension, he amended.

Though judging by the state of their clothing and their

deer-in-headlights expressions when they saw Nate and Kris, that tension had just found a release valve.

"Hello," Kris said, her voice suspiciously bland. "Nice night for a stroll."

It was fascinating, watching Olivia and Sammy turn the color of a fire hydrant at the same time.

"Y-yeah." Olivia took a tiny step away from her ex(?)-boyfriend. "Um, I'm going to rejoin the party. See if...anyone needs help."

She ran off like a bat out of hell.

Sammy watched her leave, his face grim and hard.

"Everything good?" Nate asked. The other man looked like he couldn't decide whether he wanted to chase Olivia down for a repeat of whatever they'd been doing or drink himself into a stupor.

"All good." Sammy flashed a tight smile. "Congrats again, guys. The wedding was beautiful, and the reception is kick-ass, but I'm beat so I'm gonna call it a night." He paused. "If you could, uh, keep this—"

"Don't worry," Kris said. "We won't tell anyone."

Sammy responded with a quick nod and left for the castle, which doubled as a hotel and where several guests had opted to stay for the wedding weekend.

"Talk about surprises," Nate said once the other man was out of earshot. "Sammy and Olivia, huh?"

"Part deux in the works." Kris shook her head. "They're worse than Blake and Farrah. At least they got over their shit and worked it out. But Liv and Sam have been doing this dance for years, and it's exhausting. Not that it's any of my business."

"Really?" Nate sized up his wife with a suspicious glare. "So you're going to be hands-off their relationship or whatever they have going on?"

"Until I get bored. Though Liv, ironically, is the biggest meddler out of all of us," Kris mused, tapping a finger on her chin.

"Says the woman who once paid someone fifteen thousand dollars to get rid of her father's fiancée." Technically $7,500, since Nate hadn't completed the contract terms, but who was counting?

She gasped. "I can't believe you're bringing that up. First of all, that wasn't meddling—that was protecting my father's heart and money. Second of all, I happen to know that scheme worked out well for all parties involved." A short pause. "Except for a certain redhead."

"Gloria," Nate remembered. He hadn't thought of her in years. "Wonder what happened to her."

Kris hitched a shoulder. "Don't know. Don't care. She's in the past."

"How enlightened of you," he teased. He stroked her cheek with the back of his hand, thinking of the day they'd met in the parking lot outside Alchemy. She, icy and guarded. He, wary and defensive. Both with chips the size of glaciers on their shoulders.

How much life had changed since then.

"That deal was the best I ever made," Nate said. More than any multimillion-dollar movie contract or endorsement for sure, because it'd brought Kris into his life.

"You think so?" She looped her arms around his neck. "Because I think I got the better end of the deal. A couple thousand dollars and you're mine for the rest of our lives."

"Damn right." Nate lowered his head until his forehead rested against hers. "And you're mine."

"Always."

But as they kissed beneath the stars of the Italian countryside, they knew the price of their love wasn't measured by money but by their hearts.

One's heart in exchange for the other's, forever.

It was a helluva deal.

Two exes, one house. What could go wrong?

Find out now in *If We Were Perfect*, a steamy second-chance romance featuring Olivia and Sammy.

BONUS: Read about the Lollipop Incident from Kris's honeymoon! Type this link into your browser: BookHip.com/ZRGMZH

Continue on for a sneak peek at the next If Love installment

if we were perfect

"HE TRIED TO GIVE ME A LAP DANCE, FARRAH. IN THE middle of a four-star restaurant." Olivia Tang paced the length of Ishikawa's black-marbled bathroom, her heels clicking against the tile floors in agitation. "I like this place. The sushi is great, and it scores at least an eight out of ten on everything else I require from my favorite dine-out places—service, ambiance, decor, location, clean bathrooms. I refuse to be banned for my momentary lapse in judgment in agreeing to dinner with a guy named Wesley."

Her best friend, Farrah Lin-Ryan, laughed, the silvery sound tinkling over their transcontinental call in a wash of familiarity. Olivia hadn't heard that laugh in person in months—not since she, Farrah, and their other friends, Courtney Taylor and Kris Carrera (soon-to-be Kris Reynolds), flew to Miami for a girls' trip in February. She missed having her best friend in the same city, but a phone call was better than nothing, especially when she was on yet *another* disaster of a date.

"Say you have an emergency and cut the date short," Farrah suggested. "I'll call you in a few and pretend I'm a close family member that got rushed to the hospital."

"I would, but I want to try the dessert." Olivia ran a hand through her sleek just-below-shoulder-length black hair and examined her reflection. She'd been optimistic about tonight and had run out of the office so she had enough time to get ready. Two hours later, her hair was perfect, her makeup accentuated her bright dark eyes and rosebud lips, and her elegantly provocative black dress clung to her slender frame. Comfy but sexy heels added an extra three inches to her five-foot-five frame.

What a waste.

All that time, energy, and makeup for nothing.

"They're famous for their dessert," Olivia added, oddly compelled to explain why she was staying. "Caramelized apple and kuromoji ice cream served with muesli."

There were few things she wouldn't do for good food. Maybe it was because she couldn't cook to save her life, so she relied on other people's cooking skills for culinary satisfaction. Whatever it was, Olivia's food obsession had taken her to sometimes sketchy, always delicious places since she was old enough to distinguish between a hand roll and a maki roll.

"Sounds yummy. Well, you're in the middle of the main course, right? You're almost there. Just make sure Wesley doesn't, um, pull another Magic Mike." Farrah sounded like she was trying not to laugh again.

"Yeah, yeah, make fun of me, you happily married newlywed," Olivia grumbled. "You're not the one slogging through the swamps of single life in modern America."

"Newlywed or not, I still love you."

"I know." Olivia sighed. "I better get back out there before Wesley thinks I fell in the toilet or something. I swear, this dessert better be worth it."

"I'm sure it will be. Call me later and let me know how it goes? Love ya."

"Love you too."

Olivia hung up.

The date had been a colossal waste of time, but it would be less of a waste if she stayed for dessert. She'd weighed the pros and cons already: sacrifice an extra half hour for dessert and leave with greater satisfaction, or escape early with no satisfaction at all (beyond the delicious sushi she'd already consumed). The past hour and a half were a sunk cost; she couldn't get it back.

She concluded that greater satisfaction outweighed thirty minutes of her time. Olivia had an obligation to herself to ensure her night wasn't a *total* waste, and she'd been dying to try Ishikawa's signature dessert since she read about it in *Mode de Vie*'s "Food Features" section.

She exited the bathroom and tried not to grimace when she saw Wesley polishing off another sake at their table. According to his dating app profile, he was a real estate agent who liked vintage wine and travel—just like Olivia—and he *was*. What it'd failed to mention—and what he'd announced ten minutes into their dinner—was that he also moonlighted as a stripper at the Cock Pit.

Yes, that was the name of Wesley's nighttime employer, and yes, according to her chatty date, all the non-stage-performer employees had to dress up as flight attendants.

Olivia had nothing against strippers. She loved *Magic Mike XXL*. A shirtless Channing Tatum, Joe Manganiello, and Matt Bomer all in the same movie? Yes, please. But there was a time and place for them, and tonight was neither the time nor place for Wesley to "show off his moves," as he'd announced he would do half an hour ago.

To be fair, he was also unabashedly drunk. For a six-foot-two, 190-pound specimen, he couldn't hold his alcohol *at all*. He had, however, managed to climb onto a speechless Olivia's lap before she shoved him off and excused herself to go to the restroom.

"You're back!" Wesley exclaimed, like she'd just returned from a trip to Italy and not the toilet. "How was the bathroom?"

"Fine." She pasted on a smile and flagged down a server. "Can we order dessert, please? Two caramelized apple and kuromoji ice creams. Thank you."

She wasn't sharing, and if Wesley didn't like her dessert choice, too bad.

Olivia had put up with an unwilling near-lap-dance; he could put up with ice cream.

"Dessert already? You didn't finish your food yet." Wesley stared at the remaining sushi on Olivia's side of the table.

"I will by the time they bring it out."

He laughed. "No way—" He stopped when Olivia dug into her remaining food with the gusto of a starving thirteen-year-old boy who'd just come home from sports practice. Translation: she demolished the rest of her meal in two minutes flat. "Whoa. You eat faster than I do. That's hot."

Wesley got out of his chair.

Oh no.

This was what she got for meeting up with a rando from a dating app. It wasn't Olivia's first time meeting with an online match, but it was her first time agreeing to dinner with someone whom she hadn't properly screened. Usually, it took more than a day of messaging back and forth before she took things to the next level, but she'd needed to blow off steam after a grueling first year in her MBA program and an equally grueling summer dealing with her jerk-face colleagues.

Okay, fine, her last final had been five days ago, and she'd only worked with said jerk-faces for two days, but still. Olivia deserved hazard pay for dealing with their immature, sexist asses.

People thought Wall Street in New York was bad? They never met the San Francisco branch of Pine Hill Capital, the prestigious private equity (PE) firm Olivia had worked for since she jumped ship from investment banking five years ago.

"Wesley, sit," Olivia ordered, unconsciously using the same tone she used on dogs.

"I never finished showing you my moves earlier."

"I don't want to see your moves." Olivia flashed a tight smile of thanks at the server, who returned with their ice cream and shot a strange look in Wesley's direction but didn't say anything.

The top two buttons of Wesley's shirt were unbuttoned, revealing a sliver of muscled chest and spray-tanned skin. He wasn't bad-looking, but if he didn't sit down in the next two minutes, she couldn't be held accountable for where she might lodge her shoe.

Olivia scooted her chair closer to the table so he couldn't climb into her lap again. She spooned some ice cream into her mouth and—*Oh. My. God.*

All thoughts of sticking her heel where the sun didn't shine flew out of her head as she focused on the cold, creamy mound of heaven in her bowl. It was *amazing*. Definitely worth thirty minutes of her life, but once she finished dessert, she was hightailing it out of here—Wesley could take care of the bill—and she'd never have to see him again.

Olivia wondered if she could eat Wesley's portion of dessert too. The poor ice cream was melting, and he didn't seem like he would stop "showing off his moves" anytime soon. Saving that perfectly flavored scoop from dying a useless death was practically a moral imperative.

"Olivia, look," Wesley said, sounding suspiciously whiny for a twenty-nine-year-old. "You're not looking. This is my booty pop. Women love it."

Someone kill me now.

At least they were in the back corner of the restaurant, away from the kitchen and most other guests. The nearest diners—a handsome couple in their midforties—shot Olivia and Wesley the same strange look their server had earlier, but Wesley hadn't done anything *too* egregious yet, like take his shirt off. The couple soon got distracted by their food, while Wesley booty-popped to his heart's content.

"Sit. Down," Olivia repeated.

He didn't.

Fuck it. She finished her ice cream and swapped her empty bowl with Wesley's full one. He didn't deserve dessert.

"I can't believe you don't like my moves," Wesley slurred, sounding offended. He sidled closer, and she realized he'd unbuttoned several more buttons until half his chest was showing. If a restaurant staff member saw him, he'd be thrown out for public indecency. "I'm the star of the Cock Pit. Women *specifically* request me for their bachelorette parties. I make over a thousand dollars a night. I can squeeze a penny with my—"

Olivia never found out what he could squeeze a penny with—thank God—because she chose that moment to turn her head to the left. Just a few inches, really, until she could see over Wesley's shoulder. In the grand scheme of things, the small movement was nothing.

Or it *would've* been nothing had her gaze not collided with a pair of familiar onyx eyes that sucked her in like a black hole. Nothing escaped—not light, not sound, not the painful beats of her heart. Just like that, everything disappeared except for the man her younger, naive self had thought held her universe in the palms of his hands. Even Wesley ceased to exist, and he was practically on top of her.

Olivia's breath rushed out in a shaky gust of exhilaration, embarrassment, and loathing.

"Olivia?" Her name fell off Sammy Yu's perfect lips like a long-forgotten love song, evoking memories of golden days and beautiful nights.

Those dark eyes darted from her spoonful of ice cream—frozen halfway to her mouth—to Wesley's bared chest before finally resting on her face. She spotted glints of confusion and amusement, and it was the latter that fueled her with the strength to level a glare at Wesley so menacing, he immediately backed off.

"I'm going to the restroom," Wesley announced, indignation oozing from every pore. "It's clear my booty pops are not appreciated here."

He stalked off, his half-open shirt flapping in the breeze. He didn't spare Sammy a glance.

Sammy's mouth twitched. "I wasn't aware booty pops were on the menu."

"Funny. We—*I* was just leaving," Olivia said with as much dignity as she could muster. She set her spoon down. The ice cream had melted anyway, and she could bolt right now while Wesley was in the restroom.

Usually, Olivia would never do something so rude, but she was fed up with this day. It kept going from bad to worse—and running into your ex-boyfriend while on a terrible date definitely counted as "worse."

"You mean you don't want to go home with that fine, booty-popping specimen?" Sammy feigned shock. "Say it ain't so."

She glared at him. "Sarcasm doesn't suit you."

The Sammy she knew wasn't sarcastic unless it was in a fun, playful way, but the man standing before her *wasn't* the Sammy she knew.

He was still tall and handsome—so handsome the mere sight of him sent a pleasurable shiver through her body. Same eyes, same high cheekbones and strong jaw, same dark hair—though he wore it shorter now than in college. But his lean frame had filled out with more hard-hewn muscles, his eyes sparked with more cynicism, and he possessed a self-assurance one only gained with age.

With his camel coat, black dress shirt, and hard expression, Sammy couldn't have looked more different from the good-natured, math-pun-loving, lived-in-a-T-shirt college boy she once knew. He was all man now, and not one that had any love lost for her.

"What are you doing here?" Olivia demanded. He hadn't responded to her sarcasm dig, and the silence was bugging her. She almost wished Wesley were here so she'd have a buffer. What was taking him so long, anyway? Did he fall in the toilet?

Then again, Olivia had holed herself in the restroom for a good twenty minutes talking to Farrah, so she couldn't throw stones.

Sammy's eyebrows rose a fraction of an inch. "This is a restaurant. I'm here for dinner, same as the rest of the patrons. What are *you* doing here?"

"Uh, you answered your own question. Dinner." The *duh* was implied.

"You don't live in San Francisco."

"I do this summer. I'm working at the SF branch of my company instead of going back to New York." Olivia wasn't sure why she was telling him all this. They weren't friends anymore. Unfortunately, they had tons of mutual friends from their college study-abroad program, and they were constantly forced into the same space thanks to said friends. Farrah's wedding, Kris's upcoming nuptials, group trips, and reunions...things Olivia couldn't back out of because of either loyalty or a strong sense of FOMO (fear of missing out). Sammy's thoughts must've run along the same lines because he showed up at almost every event too.

As a result, they'd settled into an uneasy, somewhat civil truce that consisted of them ignoring each other and parking themselves on opposite sides of whatever room or table they found themselves in.

"Hmm." Sammy appeared displeased by the revelation that she would be in San Francisco for the summer. Thanks to Farrah, he knew she was working on her MBA at Stanford—Olivia had almost killed her for letting that piece of info slip, to which Farrah merely responded, "Why? Are you afraid he'll show up on campus and you'll have hot, sweaty makeup sex?"

Ha! As if. Eight years was a little too late for makeup sex.

As for Sammy's displeasure, too bad. He didn't own the city. She could *move* here if she wanted (she didn't, but she *could*).

"Olivia? Is that you?"

Olivia stiffened when a familiar blond sidled up next to Sammy. Golden hair that fell past her shoulders in shiny waves, red lipstick that matched her Ted Baker sheath dress perfectly, a face that would make a supermodel weep.

Jessica.

"It is you!" Sammy's girlfriend grinned. "Sam didn't tell me you were in San Francisco."

She called him Sam? *No one* called him Sam.

But Sammy didn't so much as blink an eye at the moniker.

"I'm here for the summer." Olivia forced a smile and repeated her explanation. "I just finished my first year of business school at Stanford, and I'm working at my company's SF branch until classes start again."

"I didn't know she was in the city until we ran into each other here." Sammy slid an arm around Jessica's waist, and Olivia fought the urge to upchuck. She'd only met Jessica twice before— once at Sammy's Fourth of July barbecue in New York three summers ago and once at Farrah and Blake's wedding. Funnily enough, she'd wanted to upchuck both those times too. "She was just leaving. She has to go before her date comes back." A tiny smirk tugged at the corners of his mouth.

Olivia glared at him; he stared back with one infuriatingly arched brow.

Jessica, to her credit, didn't press on why Olivia was leaving her date high and dry. Instead, her smile widened. "We should all have dinner sometime. There's a bunch of great restaurants in the city I'm sure you'll love."

Ugh. Why did she have to be so *nice?* It would be easier to hate her if she were a total witch. Not that Olivia had a reason to hate her ex's current girlfriend or anything. She didn't even like Sammy anymore.

"I'm sure Olivia's busy." Sammy's voice contained a note of warning.

"Too busy for dinner?" Jessica shot her boyfriend a look Olivia couldn't decipher.

"Thanks for the invite. And yeah, let's grab dinner sometime." Olivia would rather roll around in a puddle of sewer water than eat dinner with Jessica and Sammy, but this was the twenty-first century. People made vague plans with no follow-up all the time. "Listen, I have to go. There's an emergency at my apartment."

She needed to get out of here. Wesley was going to be back any minute, Sammy was sucking all the oxygen out of the room, and Jessica...well, Jessica was making her stomach churn.

Not because the blond was mean or had said anything wrong, but because she was there. With him. Olivia hated seeing them together, and she hated herself for hating it.

Jessica's brows dipped. "Everything okay?"

"Yes. I just have to go check on...stuff."

"You have Sam's number, right? If you need help, give him a call and we'll be there."

"Thanks." It was weird that a woman she barely knew was acting like they were best friends and even weirder that said woman seemed intent on throwing her boyfriend back with his ex, but that wasn't Olivia's problem.

Sammy remained silent, his expression unreadable.

Olivia mumbled a goodbye, paid for her dinner against her earlier plans—she didn't trust Wesley to cover their tab or tip appropriately—and hailed a cab home.

While the taxi wound its way through San Francisco's hilly streets, she tipped her head back and closed her eyes, exhaustion sinking into her bones.

God, what a night. First her ridiculous date, then running into Sammy and Jessica.

She hadn't reached out to Sammy when she'd moved to California last year, even though he'd been the only person she knew in the area. Stanford was a forty-five-minute drive from San Francisco, and she'd been swamped with schoolwork. Plus, while they were no longer on hostile terms, they weren't exactly friendly either.

"Get it together, Olivia," she muttered under breath.

Dwelling on the past was a waste of time, and if there was one thing Olivia hated, it was wasting time. The average life expectancy for a female in the U.S. born in Olivia's birth year was seventy-nine years. That was 28,835 days, 41,522,400 minutes. She had an ever-present clock in her mind, ticking down those days and minutes until they reached her inevitable, if unknown, death date. Some might find that morbid, but she found it reassuring. Olivia thrived on structure, and life had a beginning, middle, and end, as all things should.

The mental clock had the added benefit of reminding her how precious her time was. If she wasn't productive, happy, or relaxed, it was time wasted.

Tonight? A colossal waste, and she wouldn't drag it out by wondering, for the millionth time, if there could've been a different ending for her and Sammy. If she'd stood up to her mother, if she hadn't lied, if Sammy hadn't said the things he'd said...

Olivia shook her head, shoving thoughts of the past back in her mental "Do Not Open" drawer where they belonged. To distract herself, she pulled out her phone and tapped out notes for Monday's meeting until the taxi rolled to a stop in front of her apartment building.

San Francisco rent was even more ridiculous than New York—and that was a high bar—but she'd gotten lucky with the studio apartment she'd sublet from a friend's friend. She was still paying a ridiculous amount of money each month for something the size of a shoebox, but it could've been worse.

Olivia unlocked the door, eager for a hot shower and sleep. She couldn't wait—*what the hell?*

A thick, musty smell slammed into her nose before her brain registered the scene in front of her: the floors of her apartment glistened beneath two inches of water.

"You've got to be kidding me."

Her high, shocked voice echoed off the walls and absorbed into the puddles destroying her belongings. Her mattress, which she'd placed on the floor since her bed frame hadn't arrived yet? Donezo. Her beautiful wool area rug? Unrecognizable. The cardboard boxes she'd yet to unpack because she'd been so busy at work? Half-disintegrated.

There's an emergency at the apartment.

Olivia's earlier excuse came back to her, and she wanted to throw up. She wasn't the superstitious sort, but a tiny part of her wondered whether she'd manifested this nightmare. She'd only been gone for a few hours. How the *hell* had this happened?

She pressed her palm to her temple and tried to deepen her shallow breaths.

It was nine at night, she was exhausted, half her belongings were ruined, she had no clue where to *start* cleaning this mess up, and she had no friends in the city. No one to help her.

A wild sound emerged from her throat, and it took her a few seconds before she realized she was laughing. Hysterically.

For once in her well-planned life, Olivia Tang had no clue what to do.

Acknowledgments

A big thank-you to everyone who helped bring *If Love Had a Price* into this world! I'd originally envisioned the story as a novella, but once I started writing, Kris and Nate grabbed ahold of me and refused to let go until I told their story in full (which is very typical of them). Ironically, *If Love Had a Price* is now the longest book in the If Love series, but when you're a writer, you expect these things to happen. :)

Thank you to all those who made this book possible and handled the tight deadlines with such grace—I'm in awe of you!

To my beta readers, Aishah, Leslie, and Jen, for your feedback and encouragement and for helping me tell the story in a way that does Kris and Nate justice.

To my editor, Shelby Perkins, and proofreader, Krista Burdine, as always, for whipping the manuscript into shape. You're the best!

To reviewers and bloggers for taking the time to read and share this book. Your support means the world to me.

And, of course, to my readers for trusting me with your time and for going on this journey with me. I wouldn't be where I am today without you, and I am forever grateful.

Sending you all my love.

xo, Ana

Keep in Touch with

Ana Huang

Reader Group: facebook.com/groups/anastwistedsquad
Website: anahuang.com
BookBub: bookbub.com/profile/ana-huang
Instagram: instagram.com/authoranahuang
TikTok: tiktok.com/@authoranahuang
Goodreads: goodreads.com/authoranahuang

About the Author

Ana Huang is a *New York Times*, *USA Today*, *Publishers Weekly*, *Globe and Mail*, and #1 Amazon bestselling author. She writes new adult and contemporary romance with deliciously alpha heroes, strong heroines, and plenty of steam, angst, and swoon sprinkled in.

A self-professed travel enthusiast, she loves incorporating beautiful destinations into her stories and will never say no to a good chai latte.

When she's not reading or writing, Ana is busy daydreaming, binge-watching Netflix, and scouring Yelp for her next favorite restaurant.

Also by Ana Huang

KINGS OF SIN SERIES
A SERIES OF INTERCONNECTED STANDALONES
King of Wrath

King of Pride

King of Greed

King of Sloth

TWISTED SERIES
A SERIES OF INTERCONNECTED STANDALONES
Twisted Love

Twisted Games

Twisted Hate

Twisted Lies

IF LOVE SERIES
If We Ever Meet Again **(DUET BOOK 1)**

If the Sun Never Sets **(DUET BOOK 2)**

If Love Had a Price **(STANDALONE)**

If We Were Perfect **(STANDALONE)**